Love Palace

A Novel

By Meredith Sue Willis

Irene Weinberger Books

An imprint of Hamilton Stone Editions
Maplewood, New Jersey

Library of Congress Cataloging-in-Publication Data

Willis, Meredith Sue.
Love Palace / by Meredith Sue Willis.
pages cm
ISBN 978-0-9836668-5-1 (alk. paper)
1. Self-realization in women--Fiction. 2. Social settlements-
-Fiction. I. Title.
PS3573.I45655L68 2014
813'.54--dc23

2014004749

Irene Weinberger Books
Maplewood, New Jersey

See more Irene Weinberger Books and
Hamilton Stone Editions books at
hamiltonstone.org and ireneweinbergerbooks.com

E-book editions available from
Amazon.com and Smashwords.com

Cover by WSM Technical Services

This book is dedicated to Andy,
again and always.

Also by Meredith Sue Willis

For Adults and Young Adults

A Space Apart
Higher Ground
Only Great Changes
Trespassers
Quilt Pieces (with Jane Wilson Joyce)
In the Mountains of America
Oradell at Sea
Dwight's House and Other Stories
The City Built of Starships
Out of the Mountains
Re-Visions
Meli's Way
Their Houses
Soledad in the Desert
Saving Tyler Hake

For Children

The Secret Super Powers of Marco
Marco's Monster
Billie of Fish House Lane

About Writing

Personal Fiction Writing
Blazing Pencils
Deep Revision
Ten Strategies to Write Your Novel

Love Palace

Meredith Sue Willis

Part I

Part I

I had a meltdown after my birthday. I had managed to slip past forty and forty-one in a fog, ditto forty-two, which was when I was breaking up with my longtime live-in boyfriend. But birthday number forty-three hit me with the fact that I wasn't in my fourth decade but my fifth, and I needed a job

It was a transitional time not just for me. It was a year before the false hopes of the Obama election. You had a constitutional right to abortion, but not to get married if you were gay. We still looked at classified ads in paper newspapers, and the iPhone had been introduced but not widely adopted. Which is to say that phones were mobile but not smart. I took a step back and saw myself: alone, chronically underemployed, and barely managing payments on my ill-kept apartment across the river from New York City. My boss was having cash flow problems and hadn't paid me in six weeks, and I hadn't paid my therapist in six months.

During the years of the longtime boyfriend, who I call Rotter the Third (Rotter Two being my divorced husband and Rotter One being my father), I had taken myself out of the job market at a time when I might have been rising toward some reasonably lucrative glass ceiling. Rotter the Third was a bond salesman, and we had a nifty apartment in the city. He did better and better, until he was doing so well, thank you, that he could afford to marry someone half my age. On his tab, when I was out of the job market, I got a leisurely Masters in English and also security for the downscale rental on the Jersey side of the river.

I considered my assets: men, if I wanted them. Men like to look at skinny women, but in bed they enjoy flesh. I'm good in bed, too, by which I don't mean particularly skilled, just happy. I have always felt good when I'm naked in bed with someone.

After that, I ran out of assets and drank a bottle of merlot all by myself and called my boss's answering machine and quit my job. I told him what I thought of his high minded ideology and personal boorishness. I told him I was sick of his grungy office and his cash flow problems, and I quit.

I spent the rest of that weekend and most of the next week in my apartment watching TV I ordered in pizza and buffalo wings, and when I ran out of cash and couldn't face going to the ATM machine, I ate spaghetti. When the jars of red sauce ran out, I ate it with margarine and garlic salt.

There is something really satisfying about sinking to the bottom like this. I had the image of myself as a girl in a swimming pool, sunny day, shallow end, water warm. As an experiment, I go under and let my breath out slowly. I sink till I am sitting on the bottom in the silence. If I don't go up soon, I'll be dead.

Low self-esteem is a way of life with me and my mother and my sister, although baby sister masks it well, what with being a hot shot lawyer with a fancy condo, also in Jersey, with a spectacular view. Mom works at even lower-level jobs than I do, and some of her men have been true bottom-feeders, Dad being Exhibit A. I used to look up words for the kind of man he was, and my favorites were all Britishisms: blackguard, knave, miscreant, reprobate, and, of course, rotter. It's because the Rotter left us, I believe, that my sister and I have body image difficulties and an impressive laundry list of other problems.

On the other hand, it was Rotter's mother, our Nana, who took care of us. Good old dumpy Nana, our stability while Mom moved around looking for a better job and/or a better man. Nana was our stability even when we were adults. I stayed with her for six months when my marriage broke up, and I somehow always expected I'd go back to her again, but then she had her stroke and went to a nursing home where I almost never visit.

For a long time after Nana's stroke, my therapist Madame Landowska took care of me, until the cash flow tough love crisis, when I couldn't pay. Madame said I could not have an appointment until I paid something on my debt.

"How can I do that?" I wailed. "I don't have a job!"

"I am afraid you are not serious about getting well," she said. "You chose to leave your job. I think you are taking advantage of me."

"I'm desperate!" I howled.

"You are a very intelligent lady," she said. "You are intelligent enough to know it is necessary to be employed in this country."

"I'm not a lady, I'm a deeply neurotic woman."

"Ah," she said, "but you are not sufficiently serious about getting well, Mar-ta." Marta, she calls me, not quite able to do the "th" in the middle of "Martha."

I don't owe her that much anyhow. A number in the medium high four digits. Eight years of devotion, and she throws me out.

To prove my desperation, I stayed in the apartment way beyond finishing the red sauce. I stayed until I got totally bored with watching cooking shows on TV, so I washed my hair, got in my car, which started after only six tries, went to the cash machine and then to Pietro's for the Any Day is Sunday Brunch. I ate at the bar, with a neatly folded copy of the Want Ads in front of me, circling possible job openings with a green pen.

Long before Robby came in, I had begun to circle ads in the social services section. I don't know why, maybe because I had the feeling that the helping professions might help me too. I'd never been a do-gooder– my generation came of age under the regime of Ronald Reagan!– but I needed a change, and I was steering clear of office manager, editorial assistant, and anything too much like what I'd been doing since Rotter Three decided that, unlike his hedge funds, I was not increasing in value.

Then Robby walked in. Everyone noticed him. I didn't know his name yet, of course, but I couldn't keep my eyes off him. He sat at the bar too, and even in the greenish pink Pietro's light, he had magnificent, smooth, young skin. There was one empty stool between him and me. I was drinking Mimosas and eating Pietro's special Eggs Benedictine with Canadian bacon, Hollandaise sauce, and a splash of liqueur.

I couldn't decide if he was a boy or a man. Dark blonde, an all-American jaw, liquid brown eyes, broad shoulders and a long narrow waist. He was dressed for spring in short sleeves and light colors, even though it was a raw cold day. I decided that he was so good looking he had to be gay. He ordered a Coke and ate pretzels from the basket, staring straight ahead at the bottles and mirror.

I felt a familiar rising tide, the beginning of something. An adventure. A lovely self-destructive adventure.

Bi-sexual, I decided, not gay.

Up through my shoulders, in my lungs. Just one more one-night stand. I've done everything else, eaten badly, gotten my therapist mad at me, rent due. I'll take one more step down before I go job hunting. Pick up a baby stranger! Feel totally shitty! Adelante! Yes!

I began talking about eggs and Canadian bacon and Pietro's little flourish with the Benedictine. "It's better than you'd think," I said.

He turned to me and smiled pleasantly and said in a light baritone that he had stopped eating meat when he was a child. He used to get nauseated by anything richer than ginger snaps. No cookies with raisins, chips, or creme. As he got older, he could tolerate nuts in small quantities, chopped fine in the cookies.

"A baby neurotic," I said fondly. His nails had been chewed.

Each finger tip had the tiniest lozenge of nail surrounded by flesh.

"My mother eats broiled fish and runs three miles in the morning," he said. "My dad eats what he wants, but he has a workout room at his office."

"I only eat high cholesterol foods with extra salt," I said. Not very witty, but I didn't care. If I slept with him, it would be a lark. I felt like my biggest problem was if I should stick with Mimosas or switch to Screwdrivers. Robby had an innocence, as if he'd been privately educated in a monastery.

We exchanged names. I told Robby I was just coming out of an agoraphobic period. "I'm the star neurotic of Dr. Landowska's string. I have dysfunctions most people have never dreamed of."

Actually, I wasn't feeling particularly neurotic, except for the rush of self-destructiveness, but maybe it was just sexual energy, fuel for an upswing. I told Robby about my therapist and how I had quit my last job and was looking for a new one. Robby ate pretzels. His eyes were big with listening. "I've had my troubles," I said. "The First Rotter– that's my father– deserted us, and our mother was gone a lot too. We usually lived with Nana, the Rotter's parent, source of our Jewish genes. I have my reasons for being miserable, although my therapist doesn't find them as convincing as she should."

Yes? Madame always says. Yes? I am sorry for your family problems. But your mother always came back.

To which I reply, She chased the Rotter and caught up with him long enough to get pregnant! She came back to dump the baby on me and Nana! And she was emotionally absent even when she lived with us for six months or a year now and again.

But your grandmother, says Madame, who raised you and your sister. She was a fine woman. And you too, you are an intelligent lady with many assets.

I'm not talking about intelligence! I scream. I'm talking about feelings!

So, she says. Yes. You feel very bad?

Damn straight I feel bad. And I'm not a lady. I'm promiscuous whenever possible.

Robby had pale bare ankles and docksiders with no socks. He turned his stool to face me and said with unexpected firmness, "You're ready for a change, aren't you?"

"You got that right."

"I mean, you're looking for a job." He pointed at the want ads beside my Eggs Benedictine.

"Yeah, I'm starting tomorrow. To get serious about job hunting, I mean."

He said, "I might know about a job."

"Seriously?"

But it was clear he was a serious person. He looked at me for a long time. Looked at my forehead, at my chin, at my chest, looked at me the way a little kid on the train stares over the seat at you.

He said, "Today is my twenty-first birthday."

"Well, Happy Birthday, baby. That makes me almost twice your age."

"The same as my mother."

I said, "So what are you doing here all alone on your twenty-first birthday?"

"Oh, I'm not alone." He smiled a dazzling smile and began to talk about someone very important to him. I kept having this feeling he was building up to telling me he was gay.

It has always been one of my fantasies, to do what I had let Robby do to me, to observe a person as long as you want. I have an early memory of standing next to the Rotter's easy chair–I would have been under four, of course, if he was still living with us. In my memory, I am watching him nap. I recall giant nose hairs and a field of bristles on his cheek.

I got my turn to examine Robby while he talked about his big shot friend. Robby was pale around the eyes. Institution, I thought, inspired. A woman in my group therapy group who is cousin to a really famous family that we are all pledged (what a waste of good gossip) not to reveal, said you can always tell people who've been In by a certain kind of paleness. Even if they've been in good places where you get to spend time out of doors, they still have spiritual paleness.

Robby was talking about this important person who had done a lot for him. This person who could do things for me. Help me make my change, anything I wanted. Did he mention a job again? Or maybe only that This Person could do anything for anyone.

"This is Fairy Godmother talk, darling," I said, but Robby kept going. I was having a smooth sliding-board-into-warm water buzz. A shaft of sunlight had come in one of the back windows, remarkable in itself at Pietro's. I used to come in here when I first moved into the area, scoping it out immediately as the Right Place to pick up the Wrong Men.

There was a pretty up-front competition in my therapy group over who was most self-destructive. Dr. L. considered that my debt burden made me an excellent candidate for first place. Money grubbing bitch, I thought, missing her sorely. One of my main reasons for starting to look in the want ads so soon was in order to go back and complain to Dr. Landowska.

Robby was still talking about this powerful friend of his. And then, he suddenly looked at me directly and said, "I'd very much like to introduce you to him."

And he extended his arm down the bar. Naturally, I looked to see who I was going to meet. There was nobody else at the bar. A couple in a booth, out of the line of his gesture. A group of guys at a table watching something on television with lots of green grass, golf, or maybe polo. But no one in the immediate vicinity.

"Him," said Robby softly. "Jesus. He's standing right here, next to me, now and always, and he wants to be standing next to you too."

I let out air. Crazy as a bedbug, although at least crazy with a tradition. At one period in my life I tried out churches. The Rotter and Nana don't practice Judaism, and Mom, Baptist trailer trash, only goes to church when she visits her people in West Virginia. So I used to go with friends, a Pentecostal church for a while, and then to a Born-again Megachurch. Nana was a free love atheist old Leftist, which was all the more reason for me playing Born Again to make her mad. She didn't mind when I tried a Church of Holiness so much because they were black. She forgave black people their addiction to religion because of their status as oppressed, and she had a certain respect for the former priest Berrigan brothers, but she didn't like most white churches.

Robby leaned forward. "John says he'll touch your heart and ease the ache."

"I'm having trouble with your pronoun antecedents," I said. "I thought we were talking about Jesus."

"John is our spiritual advisor, and he gave me a new way of understanding Jesus. Jesus doesn't judge you, he lifts up your spirits and makes you free to walk in His path."

I crunched on some ice and wondered if I should have another drink.

"He wants to get to know you," said Robby. "He sent me to find you. Once you have Him in your life, you can have all you ever dreamed of."

"Who are we talking about now?"

"Jesus," he said, closing his eyes. "Jesus sent me, but John gives me direction."

I looked at myself in the mirror behind the bar. My face was framed by José Cuervo and the tequila with the worm in the bottle. I looked alert and receptive. I didn't believe for a second that Jesus had sent the crazy little bedbug, but I did wonder what had attracted him to an old lady like me. Was it my perky smile or my shiny hair? Not my skin, not compared to someone really young like him. Maybe my legs. Had I been stretching a leg when he came in? I have long legs for my height.

I said, "Well, you probably shouldn't waste your time, Robby. I'm half-Jewish, you know, wrong half, but my Jewish grandmother raised me. Although her real religion is Socialism. She's in a nursing home now, not doing so well, congestive heart failure on top of a stroke, but when she first went there she rolled around in her wheelchair bothering all the old ladies with her petitions."

It seemed hard for him to come back from what he was saying, which was practiced, possibly even memorized. He cleared his throat. "That's another wonderful coincidence."

"What is?"

"Jesus was Jewish too."

My God he's dumb, I thought. Unless it was thorazine. "Listen, Robby. You're a very nice young person, and I hope you have a happy birthday, but I don't want to mislead you. Religion is the last thing I'm interested in right now. Food, a job, maybe sex, but not religion. I have a deep debt to my once and future therapist and I've pretty much maxed out my Visa and MasterCards. Does He do financial planning?"

"All of those things. He can cure you. He cured me."

"Of what? I mean, excuse me, but what did you ever have that needed curing?"

"I've always been. Different."

"Who hasn't?"

"And also–I've been–away."

It was true then; he'd been hospitalized. I was proud of my perspicacity. I said, "What did you need to be cured of? You can tell me. I'm old enough to be your mother." I waited for him to deny it, but he didn't, the candid little bastard. I said, "Go ahead and tell me what you needed to be cured of."

"I was attracted to other men."

"Ahh. Or, as my grandmother would say, nu? Lots of people are attracted to the same sex, you should go and live happy. Properly protected for sexually transmitted diseases, of course."

He shook his head. "My family isn't like that. We don't believe in it."

"Oh please. Sexuality isn't a belief system."

"I hid from it. It was a great burden on my heart. I was in despair, and I– and I–"

"Tried to kill yourself?"

He looked up. "How did you guess?"

"Because I've been around the block. You tried to kill yourself only not very hard–"

He extended his wrists which had bands of thin white scars.

"Poor baby," I said. "And you had a breakdown, and you've been away somewhere–"

"Almost a year. It's a very beautiful place, and they have music in the summers. I prayed for Him to take it away, and He did, and now I'm free. It sounds simplistic, but that's the beauty of it."

A little ditty formed in my mind: The Lord He say, Don't be gay, just kneel and pray, Go free today. Best poem I'd written in years, compliments of this cute, sexually confused little proselytizer. "So now you've switched to women?"

"I've been celibate.

"Sublimination works for some people," I said. I could feel my neuroses clearing away like a stuffed nose shot up with Afrin. I could feel the breezes. I'd take a poetry workshop. I'd get a job counseling teenagers. "Did you ever do it? With men?"

"He was protecting me, even before I knew Him."

"Let me get this straight, so to speak. Are you saying that you, a twenty-one year old American male in the twenty-first century, have never had sex?" I had a wonderful rush of energy and lovely bad thoughts. "That's fairly remarkable, but it doesn't prove you don't love men. It only proves you've repressed your sex drive. Don't you think you should sleep with a woman, just to prove you've really changed? This is only if you really want to be changed, of course. I know you trust him. But look what he's thrown in your way." I was suddenly a force, a devil bubbling with persuasive powers. "Here you have before you a woman who has ceased to believe she can be loved– "

"He loves you– "

"But I don't believe it. I don't know him. I only know you. I need to be convinced that I'm lovable. Me, without a job, slightly overweight– "

"And getting older," he added for me.

"You're not supposed to agree with me that I'm unlovable,

Robby. You're supposed to come home and love me."

Robby closed his eyes: "He loves you! He loves all of us, right through the blemishes and the sickness at heart. I know because I've been there!"

"Have you? Well, you may have been there, but you haven't been to my apartment." I was feeling unreasonable joy. I was going to expose my apartment to this boy–a far more difficult thing than to undress and have sex. My actual body, as opposed to my body image, is the least of my problems. I've never looked especially good in clothes because of the big breasts, both sides of my family, Jewish and hillbilly, have way too much bazooms for fashion, even including my size two baby sister. Naked, however, I am ample and graceful. And I have great faith in the power of men's libido to overcome their socialization. In this area, I have experience.

I decided that if I could get Robby to come home with me, my luck would change. I would make the phone calls. I would have a job within the week. A good job, enough money to go back to Madame. Get rid of the five pounds I'd picked up, and be so self-confident and svelte that I could bid farewell to Madame and the group forever by August when Madame went to her house on Long Beach Island.

Dr. Landowska says there are worse reasons to have sex than in order to feel beautiful, but there are also better ones. And much better ways to feel worthwhile. It was like a lot of what Dr. Landowska says: practical, true, and way beyond my ability to put into effect.

One of the best things about therapy is that I have interesting dreams as Dr. Landowska likes to hear about them. I said, "There's a place that recurs in my dreams. I call it Ramshackle Street. It has lots of jerry-built, jury-rigged tenements like the city, but it's really in that stupidhead industrial hell hole of a town in New Jersey where I lived when I was a kid."

"Yes?" said Dr. Landowska.

"There are frame houses with wooden porches, balconies, fire escapes, twisted hallways, deep stair wells. The sky is like a little channel overhead, deep greenish black if it's night in the dream and yellow if it's day. A depressed street. Nothing growing, no plants, some pathetic four-legged animals of indeterminate species. Lighting so poor you have to peer and squint. Nothing is ever clear except the buildings."

"Ah," said Dr. Landowska.

"Ah yourself, Dr. L. I'm trying to create an atmosphere. So in my dream, we–you and I–are in one of those buildings trying to find a room where we can have our session. And every room is occupied. In some of them, people are sleeping or having meals on boards laid between twin beds. Middle aged men are smoking cigars in their underwear. I get anxious because I'm afraid we're using up my time looking for a room. The last door opens onto the street, where, under an extremely Freudian lamppost, lies this little small dog with its entrails spilling out onto the cobblestones. I say, 'Someone should put it out of its misery.' You give me a disapproving look and, then, with your knees carefully aligned, because you have on a tight skirt, you lower yourself to crouch beside the dog. You are wearing this suit with big shoulders, like a career woman in an old movie, you know, what's her name. Joan Crawford."

Dr. Landowska said, "I never liked big shoulder pads."

"Well, it looked like they had made this suit just for you. You squatted down and cooed and babytalked the dog, and then pulled a nickel-plated gun out of your hand bag and shot it between the eyes."

"I am so cruel!" said Dr. Landowska.

"The dream isn't over. I made this dramatic gesture, stood back and pointed at you–*j'accuse*, you know. 'You!' I shouted. 'You shot it!' But the dog wasn't really dead. It had a small red hole in its forehead and it couldn't get up, but it kept panting and wagging its tail."

I stopped and pressed my lips closed. Dr. L. steepled her fingertips, a ring on just about every finger. She said, "And you think?"

"I think the dog is me. Foolishly, I keep coming back to you for more. The end was that you stood up and looked at me. I was noticing everything about you, you were monumental in this suit, wearing gold around your wrists–and don't tell me you don't like gold, I know you like gold jewelry."

"I do," said Dr. Landowska, "I do like gold."

"Well, in this dream, it was on your arms and in your ears, and around your neck, and you had a big gold tooth."

"Like a pirate."

"Yes, and your hair was all waved and blonde, raised over your temples by decorative combs, gold of course. Czarina of all the Russias, Valkyrie of the West."

"You know nothing of European history or geography, either, Martha."

"Queen of Poland, then, and probably Hungary and Yugoslavia too."

"And all the time the poor little dog lies there bleeding," she said. "You must be very angry at me."

"I think I am always spilling my guts. Like the dog."

"Ah. Yes. You would find this painful?"

"What do you think, Dr. L.? Must you be so obvious? I'm the disgusting little doggy with its guts hanging out and no one loves me, and you come and shoot me down."

"Tell me how you feel about the waved blonde hair."

"Your vanity astounds me. You don't even pretend to hide it! Sometimes it's like you're from another dimension."

"Start wherever you want. "

"How about the cigars? How about the lamp post?"

"You may start with lamp posts and cigars if you prefer," said Dr. Landowska serenely.

I do a lot less hooking up with strangers these days, thanks to Dr. L. and the general slowing down of my metabolism with advanced age. I have less tolerance for drinking and the noise in pick-up bars, too. Mostly in the last year or two I have held off till Rachman is in town on business, which isn't very often because Rachman's travel to the U.S. has been sharply curtailed since the World Trade Center. Also, he has become more religious, he tells me. He has a very Muslim family life back home in Egypt, although he refuses to tell me how many kids he has. He still likes to wine me and dine me, but he is more conflicted about it. He does not drink back home. What I like about Rachman is that I know exactly where I stand.

I thought I knew where I stood with Robby that night too. Enjoying something fresh and new. Recalled to life. Robby seemed to consider me therapy, or maybe visible proof of the Power of Jesus. He was sweet and sort of breathless, so proud of himself, and fell asleep immediately afterward, on top of my green satin comforter that still isn't paid for. I doubled the other half of the comforter over him and took a shower. I was so energized by having sex for the first time in six weeks that I wiped the hairs out of the sink and gave the toilet a quick swabbing. Then I straightened the apartment. I had already kicked a pizza box under the bed when we first arrived. Now I made a laundry pile and gathered up two black plastic bags of garbage and stacked newspapers.

I was doing all this naked, and I jumped when Robby spoke: I had almost forgotten he was there. He said, "You have a soft body." He was all wrapped up, just his face showing, very cute.

I said, "Do you want some tea or coffee? I don't have any food, but I have tea and coffee, and I think maybe some packets of instant hot chocolate."

He chose the hot chocolate, of course.

While I was boiling water and washing out a cup, I said, "You were really a virgin, weren't you?"

"I don't know."

"What do you mean, don't know?"

"I don't know what counts."

"You mean, like, does there have to be penetration or whatever? So, what have you done?"

He murmured, "Touch."

"Touch what? Yourself? You can answer yes or no. You and someone else? You touched each other. You and another boy. You and another boy touched each other?"

He nodded. I stirred the powder into the hot water and brought it to him. He had to get out of the covers, bare torso, a little silky brown hair in the middle of his chest.

"And you felt bad about it? I hope you don't feel bad about today."

"Jesus sent me to you."

"Did he, honey? That's nice." I always love a good rationalization, and confessions. Confessions have a dramatic quality that intensifies everything else. "I could make some confessions too," I said.

He sipped hot chocolate and said, "Tell me."

"When I was in high school, this football player liked me, or pretended to. Anyhow, I accepted his invitation to go to his house even though I knew his parents were away, well, actually I invited myself. And his friends came over."

I have told this so many times, in so many variations. In group therapy they used to roll their eyes: Oh please, not Martha and the Randall Football Team again. It wasn't the entire team anyhow, just three boys total. The only one who never got tired of the story was our middle-aged business owner, some kind of paper product imports, I think. He loved to hear about sex.

"Go on," said Robby. "Tell Him."

"I'm telling you."

"He's listening, let it out, doesn't it feel good to tell it?"

"It turns you on, doesn't it?" They're all voyeurs, I thought. Robby and the old guy in group and maybe Jesus too. I ran a finger down the little diamond of silky brown hair on his chest, and he closed his eyes and smiled. I said, "I wasn't sorry, either, until afterward, when they passed the word around to everyone. Good old Randall. Ring-Around-the-Blue-Collar hellhole Randall. For a while, those three or four months, I did it all–I got laid, went all the way, came across, went down, went under. You name it. I think I wanted to make them notice: Nana, my MIA father, my mother. My sister the little academic star."

Robby sipped hot chocolate.

I said, "Nana was oblivious. She didn't notice, and she was committed to free love anyhow. And my mother never even found out. I ran out of steam, and stopped doing that. I found myself a couple of friends, and calmed down by smoking marijuana at lunch

25

hour." I waited. Finally, I said, "Your turn, Robby. You have to tell about what was good and what embarrassed you."

"This guy. I thought I loved this guy, the one I told you about."

"Yes, you touched each other and you don't know if that counted. You were just kids."

"We were in the youth group together at church."

"I love sex that starts in church. It's so transgressive."

"We prayed together. We knew we were doing something bad, so we prayed in church. And– "

"Started feeling each other? In church?" My group would have liked this a lot, well the importer guy would have, anyhow. "Where in the church?"

"In a pew, we were just sitting there, praying. In the dark. After youth group. We made a date to pray again, but really pray. Only the next time, he didn't come, his father did. His father was the head pastor."

"Omigod."

"I was expecting to meet the boy, and instead, his father–he had told his father–his father went up to the pulpit and threw on the lights, and started preaching a sermon just for me–"

Robby's face crumpled, and tears ran out of his eyes. "Oh Robby," I said, "poor Robby. There's nothing like expecting something nice and getting something bad. It's like biting into a piece of candy and breaking your tooth."

"He told me that it's bad enough, to do that, to be that–but the ones who seduce others into it, they're the worst–"

"You were just two kids experimenting!"

"But if I hadn't wanted it– it wouldn't have happened. What I went through– it was from my own sinfulness."

"Poor baby."

"I like you so much," he said.

And this time, after he'd carefully set his cup on the floor, he was the one who leaned over and kissed me first.

Later, I said, "This is a gift, you see, for both us of us. It's what we need."

There was a crooked little smile on his face.

"You just like doing it, don't you?" I said. "You don't care who you do it with, you just like It. Am I right?"

His skin was so smooth and damp. I could feel the springiness of muscle and the tremor of life under his skin. I had a flash, just a passing hunch. that he really did like boys best. It was not his–how do you call it–performance. That was just fine. Couldn't

26

have been better. But there was something about the way he spoke about that preacher's son, and John, and Jesus.

He said, "We could get married."

That got my attention. "You and I?"

"Listen, come and have supper at the Love Palace."

"I forgot," I said. "I forgot you were supposed to be converting me."

"Just come, I want you to meet people. It's not a church, it's sort of a community center. We help people."

Why not, I thought. Get out, meet some nice Christian boys. "Okay. Should I wear anything in particular?"

"He doesn't care. And we can give you a job, too, you know. Jesus is arranging all this. I know you're looking for a job." He pointed at my newspaper I brought home with me. "We advertised. That was how I knew in the bar that you were what I was looking for. We've had an advertisement in the paper for a couple of weeks. Jesus made you circle it."

"I circled the job at your place?"

He picked up the paper and studied it. His face fell. "No, you didn't circle it. But it's in the same section where you did circle things."

He handed the paper to me and pointed. I remembered the ad. I skipped over it because even though it was in the social services section, it was for an Administrative Assistant/Executive Director, which has sounded to me like they had no idea what they wanted. "If you've been advertising for weeks, how come the job is still open?"

"Because Jesus has been holding it for you. He's been holding you for me and the job for you."

Okay, he was a nut case. But I liked his smell and his smile. I put on fresh underwear, fresh jeans, my nice denim shirt and my denim jacket. Robby helped me carry out the garbage.

"Don't you have a coat, Robby? It's the middle of March."

"I always go inside," he said. Then, "Martha, I know you don't believe it yet, but He brought us together for a purpose. You aren't married, are you?"

I controlled my impulse to tell him how cute he was "I'm divorced. I'm just coming to have supper and see what kind of place produces you, Robby. I don't want to get married, but thanks for asking. I have a lot on my mind."

"He'll take care of it," said Robby.

4

I drove Robby back to Pietro's in Guzzler-the-Heap, my car like they don't make anymore, thank the Goddess. An engine that will still turn over after nuclear war if you can find enough gas. "What do you think of my car?" I asked him. "It was owned by an old lady who didn't use it for the last ten years of her life. She never had a garage and it sat in her driveway, which explains the condition of the body." The color had originally been bronze, I was told, but the right front fender was white, a result of the lady's last drive, after which she got the car repaired but not repainted, then never drove it again. The inside was in pretty good condition, except for an unexplained slash on the passenger portion of the split front bench which I kept covered with a fake Indian blanket.

"Cool," said Robby.

"1977 Oldsmobile Cutlass Supreme Brougham."

He laid a hand on the blanket. "That's a decade older than I am."

Oh Lord, I thought, oh Lord. Why am I going to dinner with a bi-sexual baby religious fanatic?

But I thought I knew why. Back when we were small enough to be companions, my sister Mari and I used to do things we called adventures– a walk to the corner store, a picnic of pb & j sandwiches on the swings in the park. All it took was to say, We're having an adventure, and it became one. All I ever really wanted, I thought, was for every day to be an adventure. I had climbed out of my hole, at least for this one gorgeous afternoon as blue and gold as a high school marching band in October. Of course, it was March, and I had hated all the patriotic school spirit nonsense, but I was on an upswing.

Robby pointed at the tape deck. "Is that a cassette player?"

"It's more than a cassette player, baby. It's an Eight Track tape deck. Didn't you ever see one of those?"

He actually leaned forward for a better look. "An eight track? Does it work?"

"It still works as far as I know. There was just one tape in the car, Jim Nabors, who played this TV. doofus, Gomer Pyle? Not that you'd remember. I played a it a few times, and then one day the tape all unreeled. So now I have no tapes, but I listen to the fine am radio to get the weather."

"I'd like to hear an eight track," said Robby dreamily. Then, "There's my car," pointing at a red Miata.

"That? That's your car? I thought you were a poor little

missionary."

"It's really my mom's car. Ever since I had the break-down—well, before too—she gives me stuff. It's got a big scratch on the fender, but you can't see it from here."

He wanted me to ride in the Miata with him, so I left the Guzzler at Pietro's. We were compatible drivers, anyhow, clinging to the right-hand lane.

Robby said, "You'll have to meet my mother and father."

"No thanks."

"They're on the Board of Directors of Love Palace. Them and John and other people from our church. I bet they're going crazy wondering where I am. Eleanor and Warren, I mean, my parents. I was supposed to go to Pinnacle for my birthday."

"Pinnacle," I said. "Now that's a snowy white Anglo Saxon protestant town, is it not? And your mother and dad: Long and slim and blonde?"

"Mom's very nice," said Robby. "She won't give you a hard time. She'll like you."

"Am I right, though? Is she slim and elegant?"

He hesitated. He always seemed to be trying to tell the truth, like a character in a Russian novel. This had potential for being tiresome. "I don't have enough perspective on her to, you know, notice her figure."

"You know if she's fat or thin!"

"When I close my eyes, I see her face. I see her face on a level with mine, and I know she always looks nice, and anxious about me."

"Never mind, Martha knows. Your mother is slim and elegant and she would make me feel like a— like an ox."

"The important one is John," he said. "Eleanor and Warren don't matter."

We turned off the elevated highway at a sign that said "Hudson Blvd.-Waterfront District." They had been promising to redevelop this area for years, the way they had already redone the next neighborhood, the Warehouse District where my sister lived. The Waterfront was supposed to be the next big thing, old wharfs to become bistros and boutiques.

Hudson Boulevard was boulevard-like only in being wide, and its name changed to Water Street as it curved down the hill around the Bishop Stebbins Senior Houses, a big nineteen-sixties project of enormous high rises set in fields of rubble with a few basketball courts and some people sitting in a bus stop looking like they had been there a long time. The project wasn't for senior citizens, if I recalled correctly, it was "Senior" to distinguish the Bishop Stebbins it was named after from the present Councilman Bishop Stebbins Junior, a preacher and politician like his father. The buildings were well-known in the news for drugs and crime.

After the projects came a succession of rubbled-over empty lots, most of them fenced with razor wire. "Yeah, this is depressing," I said, already wishing I had brought my own car for a quick getaway, but at the same time, since I consider myself able to get out of tight situations, I made a mental note about where you could theoretically catch a bus.

After the rubble came an old-fashioned skid row of empty lots and tenements, some occupied, some not; a bar called the Blue Lagoon with some multi-cultural derelicts in front; then a second hand shop with bedsteads chained to window gates even though the store looked open.

Robby said, "The kids call it Water Rat Street instead of Water Street. The good buildings are at the other end."

I squinted, and saw a short block of attached houses that might be the good buildings he was talking about, or maybe he meant the glass skinned high rise just beyond, eighteen or twenty stories, changing colors as the cloud cover shifted. "I know that high rise," I said. "You can see that from everywhere around. You see it from my sister's condo, which is not that far as the crow flies. Not that I have any idea how the crow flies."

"Yeah, Riversedge Renaissance. The contrast is really sharp, don't you think? The projects at one end, Riversedge Renaissance at the other."

"Sort of like department store anchors at a mall."

As usual, and I could see this would be a problem if I spent much more time with Robby, he didn't get my humor. "Yeah, you're right," he said. "It captures something about America.."

A bus came up Water Street. It would be a long time till the next bus, should I decide to bail out. Well, I could always borrow a few dollars and call a cab.

He pulled over in front of the lone building across from the little row of attached houses. The building had a fresh coat of bright blue paint, or rather, a fresh coat of paint about halfway up. "This is it," he said. "This is Love Palace. We meant to call it Love Place, but everyone started calling it Love Palace."

"Robby, tell me the truth. What goes on here?"

"It's like an old fashioned settlement house? Except not old fashioned?"

"A post modern settlement house. Okay. And you park your car here?"

"Nobody pays any attention to the alternate side parking. They don't do much street cleaning."

"Don't be dumb! I mean, do you park your fancy schmancy Miata on the street? This would be old home week for the Guzzler, but a convertible?"

"Usually, I don't have a car with me," he said. "I was supposed to go out to Pinnacle today, that's why I had the car. But nobody bothers our cars."

I didn't believe it. We breathed in chilly, garbage-scented air. The tenement across the way was boarded up, but a group of boys stood around under a fire escape with a boom box, doing business or hanging out or both. I said, "This has all the earmarks of a really a crummy neighborhood."

"Yeah, it does, doesn't it?" He looked around. "I was thinking the Good News Crew would be out here."

"That would be?"

"Our music group. Gil does keyboard and synthesizer. He's the real musician. The girls sing okay, but Gil is really talented. It's rock 'n' roll with a message. Christian rock."

A hamburger wrapper came flitting across the street and wrapped itself around my ankle. I kicked it off. "I'm thinking I won't stay," I said. "I've got a lot to do—"

A skinny man wearing a suit jacket and an Afro was walking toward us.

"Here comes Ace," said Robby. "You have to meet Ace. He was a Black Panther in the sixties, and now he's a tenant organizer."

"A real Black Panther? Like Kill Whitey Kill Kill Kill? Or is that a Comedy Central skit?"

"No, it wasn't like that at all," said Robby. "He'll tell you. They gave milk to the babies. Hi, Ace," he extended his hand eagerly and insisted on some kind of complicated shake.

Ace said, "You have to work on that handshake, Robby."

Robby's cheeks took on a little flush of what appeared to be pleasure, and he introduced me.

"Martha," said Ace, perfectly bland and polite. "Pleased to meet you." He had a little gray in his wiry beard and an energetic way of moving. He changed directions to walk with us, on my left side, Robby on my right.

I said, "Robby tells me you were a Black Panther."

He gave a nice baritone grunt. "Robby tells everything that isn't nailed down. Yeah, I was a Panther."

"Cool," I said. Should I tell him that my grandma had been a Communist in the forties? "So what are you now?"

"A college professor!" said Robby. "Tell her, Ace! He teaches mathematics to the young brothers and sisters who got fucked over by the education machine!"

Ace looked pained. "I'm an adjunct at County Community. Basic math."

I was liking Ace. He had a nice controlled energy and a way of looking at Robby with wry tolerance.

We were in front of the blue building now. Robby said, "I'm taking Martha to meet John."

"Well, John's the man to meet around here all right," said Ace.

I had a moment of panic, afraid to go in. I said to Ace, "Aren't you coming in?"

"Not me," he said, giving the building a look I couldn't read, so I gave the building a good look too. Someone had plastered over its bricks and a lot of its architectural features so that its one bay window on the second floor popped out like a hernia. A long crack ran from the top all the way through the new paint to the tacked-on stoop roof. High up on the old paint was the faded image of martini glasses and vertical lettering that spelled out "LOVE P LACE." There was a big swath of white paint over what must be another A.

"So it really was Love Palace," I said. "Was it a whore house?"

Ace burst out laughing. I love it when people laugh at my wit. "You got it," said Ace. "This was once Big Bill's Topless Bar and Commercial Sex Scene."

"And now–and now what exactly goes on here?" I was still clinging to Ace as the most normal person in sight.

Robby seemed eager to go in. "Service. We look for what people need."

Ace said, "They give the people Jesus songs in one-two time."

"We serve meals, we help Ace rehab apartments in other buildings. We help the homeless."

"Like me?" I said. "I'm about to be thrown out of my apartment."

Ace got serious. "Thrown out of your apartment? What for?"

"Oh, I haven't been paying the rent— it's not a big deal—"

"Haven't been paying your rent for what? Lack of services?"

"No, more like lack of job. I just got behind. I've been moving a lot of my stuff to my sister's. I paid my therapist instead of the rent."

Ace shook his head. "You can't withhold rent unless you have a reason and an organization. When you get evicted for cause, nobody much can help you. I'm on my way somewhere, but I can talk to you later about that rent business." He left us, after Robby had insisted on practicing the handshake one more time. I wanted to go with Ace.

Robby said, "Don't worry, Martha. He will find you a place to stay."

"Ace?"

"He will," said Robby, pointing up. Were his brains fried? He stepped up and gestured toward the door, cocked his pretty head.

I kept my feet planted. Robby said, "Come on in. I'll introduce you to the Good News Crew too. We started the band after Gil found some amplifiers really cheap at the pawnshop." He lowered his voice. "It took me a long time to sing with them. It reminded me of when I used to be in the choir, you know, with the boy I was telling you about."

"The one you loved."

Robby said, "I never wanted to sing again, but He helped me."

We were still standing on the stoop. "Listen, Robby–I'm having second thoughts–I'm really not very inspired by religion in general. I mean, I'm not a potential convert, you know? For a while I experimented with various belief systems, and I don't have anything against people using what works for them, but it's not for me."

Robby nodded. "The kids aren't very religious either, really. They're like runaways and drop-outs. The religious connection has gotten unfortunately thin. Gil doubts everything, except music. Kristen and Cara are just here because John saved them. He got in touch with their families and cut a deal, and the families aren't supposed to bother Kristen and Cara till they're ready to talk. They're staying at least through the summer, that's what he negotiated with their parents. He's really good with things like that. He has a lot of other duties. He's here now, though, there's his car."

I caught a glimpse of an Oldsmobile of about the same vintage as the Guzzler, then something heavy and silvery, a Benz or a Lexus. That will be the reverend's car, I thought, the big shiny one.

I gave up and went in. What the Hay, you know? Love Palace was dim, the main floor probably more or less what it had been when Big Bill had his topless girls here, except it was set up as a lounge now. There was a staircase on one side and a swinging door and metal pass-through and counter at the far end. Also down at that end was a rather grand conference table, but most of the floor space was filled with randomly arranged vinyl couches and easy chairs. There were people in a lot of them, too: one man sleeping under newspapers.

"Some of our clients," said Robby proudly, from the foot of the stairs. "Waiting for dinner."

On the wall under the staircase was a large painting of what I took to be Jesus, dressed in more or less the same style as the derelicts only his sweat shirt was purple. He was carrying a scrunch-faced little brown person on his shoulder, a midget possibly meant to be a child. Representationally speaking, the painting was pretty bad, but the colors were creative.

"Cara did the mural," said Robby.

"Nice concept," I said. "Homeless Jesus." I was beginning to feel cheerful. Maybe it would be nice to be brainwashed. All the proselytizing groups you run into, including the ones I'd flirted with— they always had these slick world views, everything tied up so blessedly neatly. This one seemed like it might be low-key and funky, more like my own natural view of the world.

Dr. Landowska would say, Martha, always you are looking for the easy way in.

I said, "So it's like a settlement house, and your Reverend John oversees it. And there's a bunch of former runaway kids who live here, and you have a band."

At the top of the steps were two doors, one to another flight of stairs and one to an office. Robby went into the office, but I stopped in the doorway.

It was tiny with no windows, a computer crammed onto a table on one wall, a vinyl couch like the ones downstairs, a desk, a phone/fax askew on a stack of paper reams. A man leaning his backside on the front edge of the desk, touching nothing else, beautifully dressed in gray draped slacks and open-throated shirt, jacket tossed over his shoulder with European aplomb. Fabrics with a good hand (a phrase from Nana, who had done time in the garment industry). A truly fine-looking man, my age or a little older, wavy dark hair, going gray at the temples in the most dignified way, springing back from his high forehead that you would never mistake for balding.

He had this quality: like, he was the vacuum cleaner, and I was a piece of fuzz on the carpet.

Robby did names and said John was at the church in Pinnacle as well as the founder of Love Palace. I was doing eyes: I don't trust light eyes, and would never have stayed with Madame the Polish Valkyrie had she not had nice normal brown eyes in the middle of the blondeness. Robby has brown eyes, and Nana and Mari and even Mom— but my dad and I have blue eyes, and I don't trust either one of us.

When I finally let myself look at John's, I still wasn't sure what color they were. Intense, but no color. I focused on his right cheekbone and the tiny vertical line between his eyebrows. He extended his hand. "Welcome to Love Palace, Martha. It's a pleasure to meet a friend of Robby's. Robby, your mother has been calling. She has a cake."

Robby looked petulant. "I never said I'd go out there. I want this birthday to be— what I want it to be, not what my parents want it to be. And so far, it has been. John, I need to talk with you. I've been with Martha today."

"I'm just on my way out," said John.

"Don't want to miss the curtain?" I said, not wanting him to try any tricks, intimating he was off to save the world when he was really on his way to Broadway. He had an absolutely stunning smile, and teeth that looked freshly refinished.

"Seventeenth and eighteenth century court music at the Performing Arts Center," he said, "with original instruments."

"We won't take long," said Robby. "Something happened—"

"Oh, I think you should go ahead," I interrupted. "Don't miss your music. Robby just wanted to get permission for me to have supper here."

"You don't need permission. Everyone is welcome. That's what we're about here, welcoming."

Yes, I thought, really enjoying his smile. Just suck me up, Big Vacuum, I'm ready and waiting.

"No," cried Robby. "Don't go yet. Martha and I—we've—begun a relationship. I mean— " he paused significantly, "a real relationship."

This caused a nice round silence.

I said, "Well, okay, I think, on second thought, I'll pass on supper, Robby. I'm in the mood for a nice slice of pizza— "

His face was exalted, totally focused on John. "But there's much more. I know I was supposed to find her. She's looking for a job and she's being evicted from her apartment— "

"I'll find a job, Robby. Honest. I totally exaggerate my circumstances. I'm going to stay at my sister's, most of my important stuff is already there. It's just a little wiggle in the lifeline—"

"So I thought she could take Rhonda's job, and she and I may want to get married."

"No, we don't want to get married. I don't!"

John said, "I see. Let's sit down, then and talk for a few minutes." He resettled himself on the desk, and Robby grabbed my hand and pulled me down beside him on the couch, where a stack of magazines promptly fell into my lap.

Robby and John both hopped into action and Robby moved half of them back to the arm of the couch and John put the other half on the floor. "Listen," I said, "I don't know where Robby is going with this. He didn't consult me about his announcement. This is like, you know, a goof for me."

John resettled himself on the desk edge and made a spire with his fingers, just like Madame, except that her spire is Russian Orthodox or maybe Catholic, I never got the Central European church affiliations straight. John's had the solid, clean-lined look of a university bell tower.

I said, "I'm just a garden variety recidivist neurotic with intermittent agoraphobia and low self-esteem. I went out today for the first time in a few days and ran into Robby in a bar, and we picked each other up and he came home with me, and he was very sweet, and I appreciate his offer, but I'm not really a candidate for—whatever it is that's going on here. Besides, I'm half Jewish."

"Half Jewish?" said John.

I knew he'd do it, the therapeutic repeat-the-phrase. But I forgave him because he had such a wonderful serenity even as the moments were ticking away. "Robby invited me for supper. I thought I owed it to him to listen to the pitch."

"Let's not talk about what we owe people," said John, stroking his chin with his impeccably clean nails. "Or about pitches. I've never really found that productive. Let's talk about what we want. That's my idea about Love Palace. The real issue is what people want, which is sometimes but not always the same as what they need. Robby, what do you want?"

Robby gazed into John's face adoringly. You, I thought. He wants you. And I will too, if I stick around. Robby said, "Martha made me feel like a man. Jesus killed my old devil, and Martha— is an angel from Him. I discovered I could have feelings for a woman. For Martha."

"Making love is a good thing," said John.

"What I want is, I want to marry her."

"You want to marry her?"

"I want to marry her, and bring her to Jesus. I know, I know. You can't make someone. She has to do it herself, but I wanted you to talk to her."

John gazed unhurriedly at Robby, then unhurriedly turned to me. "And you, Martha, what do you want?"

"Meaning in my life." It just popped out. I was trying so hard not to say You that I let this other thing slip out. "I want meaning, but I need a job. I need the money and a reason to get up in the morning."

"We all need that," said John. "We all need a reason for getting up in the morning."

And, I thought, to pay off Madame so I can go back into therapy and tell her about you and Robby and my adventure at the Love Palace. I said, "Robby did a good deed today. I'm going to have dinner with you guys and go home and try to get a job. I feel really jump-started. There are lots of things I need, love and companionship and all the usual, but right now, it's practical arrangements I need."

"What kind of work do you do?"

"I have a master's in literature, but I've been doing copy editing and office management."

"Desk top publishing? Computer skills?"

"Oh, sure."

"Excellent," he smiled.

"You see?" said Robby. "I told you, she'd be perfect for Rhonda's job."

"Who's Rhonda?"

"She was our executive director," said Robby. "This was her office."

John was watching Robby and watching me. "Yes," he said. "She did a lot of good work for us. She got us to incorporate; she got some grants that have since run out. Do you do grant writing, Martha?"

"Nope," I said. "I guess I'm not your girl."

John nodded. "I'm sure you could learn. We've also been struggling to start a little newsletter. We need an editor for the newsletter, also someone to oversee some of the daily operations here. Are you interested?"

I said, "Is the salary fifteen dollars a week, or twenty?"

"Give me a figure," he said. "We could include a room here. Possibly even an apartment," he said.

It was how he said things, with an almost Southern accent, but that isn't right, it was just a smoothness, not slow, but you felt like there was plenty of time. And also, just faintly, I could feel this vibrato in his voice.

"This is great," said Robby. "We really need a responsible person. I don't mean responsible like old, just responsible."

John said, "You could have your meals here, of course. Depending on what you like to do, what you're good at doing. Rhonda was good at grant writing; she set up the Board of Directors. I'll tell you what. Make up a budget, bring it back in the morning and we'll fix on a salary." John glanced at his watch. "How does that sound?"

I said, "Why did Rhonda leave?"

"She got a better job."

And then this imp-Martha that sometimes comes out and dances on my shoulder and tells lies said, "It's an interesting officer, but sadly, it's too late. They're going to evict me tomorrow."

"Then get your things tonight. Robby will set you up in a room upstairs."

Martha-the-imp widened her eyes and put her hand on her hip. "I'd need cash up-front."

"How much?"

"A couple of hundred to, you know, rent a van to bring some stuff to my sister's since I'd be moving from an apartment into a room." I pretended I was just letting the imp have an airing, but at the same time, part of me was aware of a door opening. It was as vivid as one of my best therapy dreams: I was wide awake, I would say to Madame L., I was talking to these people, and there was this white metal door that kind of glowed as if the metal were hot, but it wasn't hot, it was cool, and it was opening into a bright landscape, and I was stepping through. If I kept my stuff at my sister's, I could bail out anytime I wanted.

John said, "Could you stay around till I get back this evening? I know it would be late, but I have to go out now, and I don't have the cash on me. I'll bring you the money, if you can wait, and we'll strike a deal."

"What about getting married?" said Robby.

John offered him the smile. "A job I can provide unilaterally, but marriage, Robby, requires two people."

I said, "It was charming of you to ask, Robby, but we only met this afternoon."

"Sometimes that's all it takes!" he said. He was squeezing my hand, over and over in an annoying way. "Isn't that right, John? Sometimes your heart knows immediately? Doesn't His hand reach right in through the flesh of your chest and grab your heart all at once, suddenly?"

John got up. He began uttering a little sermon as he moved toward the door, no hurry, but you didn't doubt he was leaving now. "Robby," he said, "the Spirit comes in many, many ways. Sometimes it prompts you to act, and sometimes it urges you to be still. You told me what you wanted. Now I'm going to tell you what you need. When you told me what you wanted, I heard 'Quick Fix.' I heard, 'Silver bullet–answer to all my problems.' But what you need, Robby, is to think of Martha. Let's think of Martha's needs. Can you be satisfied that Martha is here with you tonight? She's going to have supper here and stay for the evening. Can you enjoy Martha right now? Then we'll see if she wants to come and be with us tomorrow too."

Robby finally let go of me and covered his face with his hands. "I'm such a punk," said Robby. "I'm such a piece of shit."

I had this urge to confess. I lied about being evicted tomorrow. That was a fabrication. I'm behind on the rent, but not that far behind. But I got hold of myself and said, "Let's think of John's needs too. He's going to be late if he doesn't get moving."

"Robby," John smiled, "set up a meeting tonight. I want to talk to the Crew when I come back tonight. I have some things on my mind."

He was leaving, he was gone. I put an arm around Robby. We listened to John's descending footsteps.

"He's right," said Robby into my left bosom. "I'm so selfish I never think of anything but my own needs. It's all rotten–whatever I do. I could be handing out food to the hungry and my mind goes–rotten."

"Don't be so hard on yourself. If you want to hear about inappropriate wandering minds, let me tell you about mine."

"I've been so selfish," he sobbed. "You're so good to me. Stay, Martha, don't leave me."

I pulled his head farther over onto my ever ample bosom. Too bouncy for most weight-bearing aerobic exercise, and the boobs attract male attention even when you've got the flu and just want to go to sleep. Robby felt nice there, though. Very warm. Maybe

I still had time to have children, I thought. Do I have it in me to nurture? Rotters II and III would say no, but they were assholes. I patted Robby's back and looked around the office. I could straighten this up, I thought. I'm not a bad office manager. This clutter was just supplies plus people dumping things here since Rhonda. Before I signed on any dotted lines, though, I intended to find out why she really left.

After a while, I noticed a framed cover of *Time* magazine. I had to twist my neck to see it, because it was behind the couch where we were sitting. It was familiar, from a few years back. A picture of a good looking dark-haired white man holding what appeared to be a dead or dying black man. It was a famous photo, and the nickname suddenly came to me: Prison Pietà, the media used to call it.

"That picture on the wall, Robby. Is that John? I knew I knew his face. It was that prison riot. John's the guy holding the guy who got shot?"

Robby sat up. "That's John."

"What was he, the chaplain?"

"I think so. He doesn't talk about it, but he's famous. It's like having Jesus in the room with you."

He doesn't talk about it, but the picture is here, I thought. Yes, John has charisma, and Robby is a sweetheart, and this is a nut house, and I am out of here, very soon. But I was still in adventure mode, and also I was curious if John would actually come back with the cash. And, of course, I wanted to see John again.

5

Robby and I went downstairs where a handful of men were fooling with the old but large television. There was a disturbance at the door, and some young people came in arguing and clunking instruments and amplifiers against doors and walls. This would be the Good News Crew. They were grumpy and unspiritual, and I felt right at home. Robby grabbed my wrist as if I were another amplifier and dragged me over for introductions. The other boy, as tall as Robby, was Gil, and his dyed red hair was shaved close over his ears but long and curly on top. Auburn eyes and a light tan skin that made my socially conditioned brain wonder about his ethnic background. The slim girl, very good-looking, perhaps even hot, was named Kristen, and she was putting her hands all over Gil, patting him, soothing his fevered brow.

He shrugged her off. "If those punks don't stop playing their boom box while we're trying to perform, I'm not going out again."

The second girl was Cara, chubby and sullen-looking. I thought she was prettier than Kristen, but I'm prejudiced in favor of non-skinny people. She was glaring at Kristen and Gil.

I said, "Cara. You're the muralist. I like your work." This wasn't really a lie, I rarely lie because there are so many pieces of truth. I liked the fact she had done the mural, and I liked Jesus's purple sweatshirt. I liked it that she had the perseverance to finish the ugly thing.

She stared at me. "I have to redo the little kid," she said.

"Yeah, he doesn't look quite like a child."

"She," said Cara, flopping onto a couch and glaring at me now. "It's a girl. And I write music too. I'm very expressive."

And ill-tempered, I thought, and smiled pleasantly at her.

Robby helped Kristen and Gil put things in the closet, and Gil went on and on about the boom boxes and rowdy teenagers and no one listening to their music. They ignored me. It was like going back twenty-five years to high school.

Gil dropped onto the couch too, and Cara ostentatiously scooted away from him. "I've had it with this place," said Gil. "I'm getting out of here. I don't have to stay here."

"No one has to stay," said Cara.

Kristen dropped down on the other side of Gil and put her arm behind his neck, played with his ear on that side. His cheek twitched. Cara gazed at the ceiling.

Robby put an arm around me. That got their attention. "John is hiring Martha," said Robby.

"To do what?" said Cara.

"Rhonda's job."

"Nothing's definite yet," I said, "just an idea being floated. "

Robby said, "We need some management."

"We need something," said Kristen into Gil's ear. "This place is a disaster. Gil isn't really going to leave, though. Are you?"

"Watch me."

"We need some people to improve their attitude," said Cara. "Those boys with the boom box, it's their street, you know. We're the ones who came down here and invaded them. They didn't ask for our help."

"Gimme a break," said Gil. "They're like everyone else, get what you can, fuck the rest."

Cara had a nice doggedness along with her expressive personality and 15 extra pounds. "They were just living their lives and we came in and started trying to convert everyone."

Kristen stroked Gil's cheek.

"Listen," said Robby. "Everyone be nice. We don't want Martha to think we sit around quarreling all the time."

"But we do," said Kristen.

"Martha and I are thinking about getting married," said Robby.

Gil let out a sort of whinny. "Oh my God. Oh Christ! Robby!"

"It's true," said Robby.

"Not it's not," I said.

"Robby, you little jerk." Gil tossed his head and turned to Kristen. He kissed her full in the mouth, and she arched her back and groaned. From the men around the televison set came a sound of suppressed hooting.

Cara watched them kiss. "It's somebody's turn to set the table."

Kristen came out of the kiss, tossed her lovely hair, and leaned her lovely head back on the couch. "I'm sick," she said. "I feel like a wet dishrag."

"I'm having my period too," said Cara, "and I'm not whining about it. Whose turn is it to set the table for dinner?"

"Mickey Mouse shit," said Gil. "I did breakfast."

"You did not," said Cara. "You were supposed to do breakfast, but you were the last one up and everyone did their own."

"I was ready to do it. Everybody was already gone, it wasn't my fault."

"Oh forget it," said Kristen. "I'll set the table."

Cara said, "Does that mean you're taking Gil's turn or are you trying to change the schedule?"

I said, "I'd be glad to pitch in."

Gil said, "Why don't the bums ever do it?"

"Clients!" said Cara. "They're our guests!"

"We'll help," said Robby. "We're all helping." When the girls got up, Gil lay down on the couch and threw a long leg over the back pillows. The two girls, Robby, and I moved to the back of the room where there was a badly balanced break-front with a coffee pot next to that enormous Board of Directors table and a lot of metal folding chairs. Behind the table were the swinging door and metal pass-through, presumably to the kitchen.

I said to Kristen, "So the clients don't help?"

"Some of them do, cleaning up, what not. But we usually set the table." She turned to Cara. "Where are the napkins?"

"They're supposed to be with the paper plates. I'm not in charge of supplies this week."

I had this funny sensation of being with a comfortably bad-tempered family. There had usually been three of us, me and my sister Mari and Nana. We sniped and snarled for a dozen, though, while Nana creamed root vegetables and pretended she couldn't hear. Mom would be off looking for work or living with some guy, but it was still crowded in that little apartment over a florist shop in Randall, New Jersey. Nana let us fight it out; she probably thought squabbling with your sibling toughened you up for the Final Conflict. Or maybe she had always been around contentious families. Or maybe her hearing really was that bad.

Nobody could find the napkins. They looked under the table and on the sideboard and in the breakfront and on the shelves next to a lot of dusty hymnals.

Robby said, "We shouldn't be using paper anyhow."

Kristen said, "You don't think the energy it takes to run washing machines and dishwashers is bad for the environment?"

"The dishwasher is broken," said Cara. "The choice is between paper and hand washing. That stupid dishwasher never worked, not for one minute!"

I decided to look in the kitchen. I pushed through the swinging door, and was immediately stunned by the glitter of stainless steel. It was a fully equipped industrial strength kitchen. Everything else I had seen till now was second hand, but this kitchen was another world: copper-bottomed pots and pans hanging from the ceiling, a back wall of refrigerator units with clasp locks, a work table in the center, half stainless steel and half butcher block, sinks with high pressure spray tubes hooked out of the way, an eight-burner stove, and a huge automatic dishwasher standing open, with a puddle of water on the tiled floor in front of it. Next to it stood a bristly little individual wrapped in an apron, with a cigarette stuck to his lip.

The cigarette stayed in place as he said, "No ladies in the kitchen!"

That night, nothing fazed me. "It is one fine kitchen, too."

"I don't like women in my kitchen." He pulled a pint bottle from the waist of his apron and took a pull, still without removing the cigarette, then fixed it safely back in the waist of the apron. "They call me Danny Boy," he said. "I have a name, but damned if I'm going to waste time remembering it."

"I'm Martha," I said. "I came in looking for napkins. Are you the cook?"

"I've been a cook since before you were born. I cooked for some of the biggest restaurants in New York before I was a bum. I'm a bum now, but I'm the cook for this place, and I make a damn good stew."

I said, "I'm looking forward to it. Did you happen to see the napkins?"

"I don't do set-ups and I don't bus tables. I'm the chief cook of this loony bin!"

"How come the dishwasher is broken in a brand-new kitchen like this?"

"Goddam poor quality construction is why," said Danny Boy.

I saw a bundle of pre-folded napkins on top of boxes of other paper goods, near the garbage cans and the back door. I picked them up, and said, "Well, here they are. And you really do have a great kitchen."

"I've worked in better!" he called after me. "Don't think I haven't. I'm a bum now, but I worked in the best!"

They hadn't put out the plates yet. They were still discussing the environmental impact of dish washing. I set the napkins on the table. "So how many do you expect for dinner?"

Cara said, "Where did you find them?"

"In the kitchen with Danny Boy."

"Oh, you met Danny Boy."

Robby began to lay out plates. Cara began to put out the napkins, and I followed with the silver-ware, real, not plastic. It looked like the five of us plus four guests. There was room for at least twice as many. They put half the places at one end and half at the other.

44

Robby said, "We found Danny Boy in front of the Blue Lagoon. He's come a long way."

"We saved him," said Cara.

"Well," said Robby, "Strictly speaking, we didn't save him–"

"Stuff it, Robby," called Gil from the couch.

Cara said, "He was so totally drinking himself to death."

"I hate to disappoint anyone, but he's sucking on a pint bottle in there now."

"He still drinks a little," said Robby.

"But he's functioning," said Cara. "That's the difference. He gets dinner out for us every night."

"If you don't mind stew and biscuits and biscuits and stew," called Gil.

The homeless guys had queued up next to the pass-through, first a grungy white guy who looked like a younger, taller Danny Boy, then a grungy black guy, then two more of an indeterminate color who might have been Hispanic or else jaundiced white guys. The white guy in the front said, "I don't mind stew and biscuits. I wouldn't mind some stew and biscuits right now!"

As he spoke, the metal gate crashed up, and Danny Boy's scrawny arms shoved a bowl across the counter. "Come and get it, bums!" he yelled. The stew stopped just short of the edge of the counter. Pitchers came next, also slid to the very edge.

"Does it ever spill?"

Robby looked pleased. "Nope. It's one of Danny Boy's talents. It always stops right at the edge. Since he got his drinking under control, anyhow. When he first came here, he couldn't have cooked a meal, let alone scooted that stuff across and have it stop at the edge."

I'm positive that the plate of biscuits would not have stopped in time, but the second man in line snagged it. Most of us sat down, but one guest waited for the butter and a bowl of beans. They put all the food at their end of the table except for a second platter of biscuits that Cara had grabbed. Everyone started serving themselves, but Robby called, "Hey guys, let's do Grace!" and pressed his hands together, shoved the point of his fingers into his forehead. The girls lowered their heads, as did Gil. The men at the end of the table froze with their hands on the platters and serving utensils suspended in mid-air. "Dear Jesus Lord in Heaven!" cried Robby. "Forgive us for our greediness and our involvement in what is not your work but only ours!"

I picked a little crumb off the nearest biscuit. Fresh out of the oven, light and crumbly.

"But of course, Dear Lord Jesus," said Robby, "if you look at it one way, everything is Your Work."

"Amen," said Gil.

"Amen," said Kristen.

"Forgive us our many, many trespasses," Robby said, and finally sat down. "Amen."

The men emptied the stew bowl, and Robby took it back to the kitchen and brought out more stew and more biscuits. The biscuits were as good as they looked, and the stew was tasty too, the meat a little fatty but cut in small pieces and flavorful. "He's a good cook," I said. "I'm impressed."

Cara said, "If you like stew for dinner every night of the week."

Gil said, "Damn, I think there's a new vegetable in it tonight! What do you think? Is that just undercooked potato or is it some kind of weird tropical thing?"

Robby said, "We're having a meeting tonight, late."

"We had a meeting last night," said Cara.

"John called this one. He has some things he wants to share with us." That shut them up. "Personally," said Robby, "I hope he wants to talk about a certain lightness of attitude here."

"Do me a favor," said Gil, "and save it, okay? John will talk about what he wants to."

At that moment there was a crashing through the swinging doors, and here came Danny Boy, bearing a metal baking sheet of jam tarts, each one a circlet of glazed gold with a deep red center. The tarts must have come right out of the oven, because he was holding them with a cloth. He planted both feet, extended the tray toward the table, tipped just enough that we could see the tarts, and began to sing in a quavering tenor:

"Oh Danny Boy, the pipes, the pipes are calling!
From glen to glen, and down the mountainside.
The Summer's gone and all the roses falling
It's you, it's you must go and I must bide."

His voice seemed to pick up strength as he attacked the high notes in the chorus.

"But come ye back when summer's in the meadow,
Or when the valley's hushed and white with snow,
It's I'll be there in sunshine or in shadow,
Oh! Danny Boy, Oh, Danny Boy, I love you so!"

It was so sharp and keen, that sentimental old Irish potato of a song! I don't know what did it to me– the surprise mixed with my feeling of being in some kind of family maybe– but all of a sudden, I had tears in my eyes.

"But when ye've gone, and all the flow'rs are dying,
If I am dead, as dead I well may be
Ye'll come and find the place where I am lying,
And kneel and say an Ave there for me."

I was seeing poor Nana in the nursing home. She wasn't dead yet, just warehoused at Miriam Sisters. Nothing Irish about Nana, and less religious than Irish, but old Danny Boy got to me. Poor dear Nana, the good times all gone– brewed tea sweetened Russian style with jam, gray-pink scuffies and swollen ankles, her boyfriend Irv who used to make coins come in and out of our ears. Irv already dead, Nana would be soon. Dead dead, everybody dead. Come and say an Ave here for me. I joined in on the last chorus, all of us, even Gil. But we fell back to let Danny Boy go falsetto on the last bar:

"But come ye back when summer's in the meadow,
Or when the valley's hushed and white with snow,
It's I'll be there in sunshine or in shadow,
Oh! Danny Boy, Oh, Danny Boy, I love you so!"

At the end of the final verse, he sank to one knee and extended the tray of tarts. We all clapped and cheered, and the homeless guys stomped and whistled.

"You see what I mean?" said Robby.

Danny Boy himself was suddenly almost sweet. "Thankee," he said, "Oh thankee, my dear friends."

The jam tarts were top-notch. I especially admired the glaze on the pastry. The light came on in the coffee pot at just the right moment, and the coffee was strong and black and I was introduced to White Frank and Black Frank and the other guests and clients, and suddenly Gil and Kristen and Cara and Robby were all smiling and charming and I felt privileged to be in this fine palace of love.

6

While we were cleaning up after dinner, I pieced together some facts: Love Palace was a sort of array of social services with classes and playgroups for kids– or at least that was the idea. Everything supported financially by the church where Robby's parents went and John King was– something. Maybe assistant minister. The church people had bought the building, put in the fancy kitchen, and staffed it with interns or runaways or whatever the Good News Crew was. Cara thought it was only about a year old, but Robby said it was at least three years old. They all agreed John would know.

"And what do you do day-to-day?" I asked.

"Whatever needs doing," said Robby. "Dinner for people who need it–"

"The bums," said Gil.

"Alcoholics Anonymous on Thursday nights."

"I think they moved to Wednesday," said Kristen.

"No, they moved to another site," said Cara.

This led to a debate about whether or not AA was still meeting at Love Palace, and the one thing everyone agreed on was that if Rhonda was still here, she would know.

Robby went on. "Another thing is the Tenants' Council from the building across the street. They meet here, Ace runs that. And there's an Enrichment play group for little kids."

"We did have the teenagers too," said Cara, "but there were some problems."

"Theft," said Kristen.

"It wasn't helping the teenagers to just have them steal stuff," said Cara.

Gil snorted. "How were they supposed to tell regular stuff from Free Market stuff? The Free Market is the high point of the month. That's when the Pinnacle church ladies show off what big hearts they have." The Free Market, they told me, was like a tag sale, only free: tables and tables of stuff, and all you had to do was line up on the right day and come in and take what you wanted.

Robby said, "Ace says people drive in their vans from miles around to come to this– but my mother, well, she and her friends like doing it." The kids rolled their eyes. Robby looked defensive. "My mother has put a lot into this place. She worked things out with the church. Without her, we wouldn't have as much of John's time as we do."

Just as we were putting away the brooms, Danny Boy

announced that we were out of milk and he didn't do groceries. Cara and Kristen volunteered to go, because they needed what they called Personal Items too. Robby gave them the key to the Miata, and Gil made jokes about the Tampax run.

Robby and Gil dropped onto the couches and started to argue about music, whole musical worlds I'd never heard of. Back in high school, I had hung out with a sub-group of drug users who made a point of ignoring Bon Jovi and Guns 'N Roses and pledging allegiance to the Grateful Dead. We kept making plans to follow their tour and be Rainbow people, but we were always either too timid or too drugged out. I had also liked Born in the USA and the Police. Robby was a particular fan of some Christian Rock group called Jars of Clay and The Listeners or was it The Listening. Gil preferred Techno to Christian rock, or maybe it was Techno-folk or Christian techno-folk? I zoned out. It was like listening to people talking with very heavy accents who broke into their native tongue occasionally.

It all gave me a kind of nostalgia for college life. I'd lived in a dorm only for about a year, but I'd liked the lounge and smoking and drinking and discussing. I'd flunked a lot of classes, though, and finished late as a commuter. I was much more focused while I was getting my Masters with the support of Rotter the Third. It may not be obvious when I'm in one of my funks, but I'm a hard worker, all my family works hard. Even my old man the original Rotter used to work hard picking ponies, or so my mother says.

Robby was complaining that all Gil cared about was synthesizers. If all you cared about was synthesizers, what difference did it make if it was a Christian Rock group or some other religion or no religion?

"That's my point!" said Gil, flashing with reddish energy. "Your Christian rock isn't about music at all. It's bubblegum with a cross on the cover. Christian Rock encourages crap because it insists music isn't the main point!"

For me and my little group, music wasn't the point either. It was identity. For me personally, I had just been happy to have friends. Otherwise, I would have been stuck in the four little rooms over the florist's shop, an overweight teenager with too many piercings, wearing black, watching my sister study, listening to Nana and Irv slurp tea and talk about the good old days when unions had class consciousness. I had this flash that everyone was a misfit if you looked at them from a certain angle: these two good-looking tall boys, Nana and Irv, even Madame Landowska, if someone dropped into her private rooms early some morning when she was, say, peroxiding the hair on her upper lip or eating her breakfast of cottage cheese (she told me once that's what she has for breakfast).

The girls came back with milk, and they also bought two pints of Cherry Garcia ice cream. We ate with paper bowls and plastic spoons. No one offered any to the guys named Frank or to Danny Boy who'd gone out to watch televison with them. After the ice cream, we all curled up on couches and chairs. After a while, the Franks and the other guys except for Danny Boy left.

And then there was a little something, a splash of ozone in the air, a metaphorical bell tinkling, and John materialized among us. Had I fallen asleep? He was standing between a couch and a chair, smiling, resplendent in his monochromatic clothes, the touch of silver waved at his temples. He stood at parade rest, hands clasped in front of him, an athlete during the national anthem.

Everyone sat up straight, the sleepy ones stretched. Robby said, "John!" with such an exhalation of delight that I wondered who he really wanted to marry. Danny Boy turned off the television and approached us with his hands folded as if for prayer.

Maybe the thing that surprised me most was that Kristen and Cara unfolded themselves from the couch and hugged John, without squabbling, just both of them arms around John's torso, he was tall enough that his extended arms gathered them close. They seemed as happy as puppies to be close to him.

I said, "How was the concert?"

John turned his face to me. "Excellent. The music had a kind of crystalline clarity that cleared my thinking, and suddenly, I knew what I wanted to say to you." I had this feeling he meant Me, Martha. I was pretty sure he meant all of us, but the way he said "you" was so totally personal. "It was harpsichord music," he added.

"I'd love to get my hands on a harpsichord," said Gil.

John released the girls, his face glowing with the confidence of someone who'd just got laid. I looked for ruffled hair or lipstick on his shirt, but he seemed as fresh as he'd been four hours ago. Maybe it was the two teenagers cuddling up to him. He said, "If you want access to a harpsichord, we can do a little research."

"Would you really?" said Gil, all his irony and sneers gone.

There was a glow in the circle. The girls sat down again, but John remained standing. "Shall we begin with a short evening reflection?"

Danny Boy crossed himself.

John said, "Let's speak of taking stock of our experiences." It wasn't clear if he was addressing a Higher Power. The operative factor, I thought, was his midnight-blue voice. The voice wrapped around us. I thought: My brain is going delta wave. He's a hypnotist. I exaggerated, of course, in my effort not to be pulled under by him, but I do believe these things fall along a continuum, and what John was doing was in the same line as hypnotism and meditation and altered states.

There was some content to what he said: he was in favor of life review, he expressed a positive view of harmony; he murmured that life isn't easy for anyone, not for saints and altruists but not for thieves and murderers either. Hard for the poor and oppressed but hard for the others too, and we should respect ourselves for the struggle.

I liked the idea of respecting ourselves for the struggle.

He also said that he, or maybe it was Jesus, would always be there for us, for each and every one. He wanted to be sure we all had his cell phone number, so I suppose it was John, not Jesus. Then he didn't say anything for a while. I looked up, refreshed as if I'd had a short nap; it seemed to be over, although it had been very short. Cara looked sleepy. Gil stretched, as if he was ready to go to bed, or out for a smoke. Danny Boy crossed himself again, said, "Thankee," shook John's hand and went to the kitchen.

John waited till he was gone, then sat down and said, "I wanted to talk a little longer with the rest of you, just a few minutes more."

"About Martha?" said Robby.

"I'm going to have a conference with Martha before I go," said John, "but this is for all of you. Something– related–but different. I want to talk about a very special and crucial moment in our lives. I believe that many of us– Robby and Martha, and myself, but all of us– we're at a very special moment. We're at a liminal stage. We're in the Limina."

No one said anything, and I decided not to expose my ignorance of the word, although it sounded vaguely familiar, maybe something from an anthropology class.

But after raising everyone's anxiety level a little, he explained: "Limina," said John, "is that place between. It is a place between places, a moment between time. A threshold. And we here at Love Palace are at a threshold. What we thought we knew has become cloudy. What was sharp has slipped out of focus. We are in a place of– I won't say doubt, I want to say, a place of

Unknowing. Of the certainty of unknowing. It is an exciting, creative moment. We need to treasure and embrace it, to bathe ourselves in the light of the Limina."

Cara said, "I think I'd rather be in a safe place."

Robby said, "You will be, if you know Jesus."

And to my surprise, John said, "No, Robby, Jesus is not about safety. Jesus is not the end of doubt, but the beginning. Jesus is Himself the plunge into unknowing. He is Lord of the Limina."

There was a kind of intake of breath around the circle. Beside me, Robby went perfectly still. John said, "Jesus is about doing things you never imagined were possible."

Robby said, "We have to trust Jesus."

John said, "Jesus is about questioning– everything– including Himself. We have to break ourselves loose from the strings and ties that hold us from taking the steps forward. We need to go into the delightful terror of unknowing."

"Let me get this straight," said Gil. "There are no answers?"

John opened up his arms as for a big hug. "Join me in the Limina, my friends. There is nothing more certain than that."

Gil repeated, "You're taking it all back?"

"I'm inviting you to the next stage, where all is permissible."

Dostoyevsky, I thought. That's from The Grand Inquisitor speech.

Gil said, "No, really, are you saying, like, anything is okay?"

"No," Robby was frowning. "You aren't saying that, are you, John?"

"Ivan Karamazov," I said. The kids stared at me blankly. "Everything is permitted. Ivan Karamazov said it in *The Brothers Karamazov*. It's a quotation from a book." John nodded, but I couldn't tell if he had read it. The kids certainly hadn't

Robby said, "Tell us what you mean."

John laid his exquisite long hands on his knees and fixed his deep eyes on Robby. "Robby, did you think nothing would ever change?"

"I need stability, John! You know I need stability! I mean, it's like the replacement for my meds."

"Change can be viewed as a kind of stability."

"Why are you doing this? Why are you changing everything?"

"I'm changing nothing. I'm pulling back a curtain."

I felt genuinely concerned for Robby. I didn't quite get it: the rest of them seemed if not happy, at least willing to go along with the revelation, except for Robby. John leaned even farther forward. "You're on the threshold of something– you're on the threshold of something with Martha, aren't you?"

"Jesus told me to," he whispered.

"Did he?" said John, smiling, so handsomely smiling. "Did he tell you, Robby, or did you make that decision yourself?"

Robby looked like he was about to break into tears. "Are you saying everything we know is wrong?"

"I'm saying, let yourself feel how you're balanced on the threshold. Delight in this moment."

Gil said, "This is really interesting. John's saying that the real message is change, right?"

"What about Jesus?" said Robby.

They were all so restless. They got up, one by one, all except me. Robby on his feet, shifting his weight, like someone about to run away. Cara and Kristen bouncing a little, Gil locking eyes with John.

Who suddenly turned at me. "And you, Martha?" he said. "What do you think of all this?"

I wasn't going to be sucked in. I said, "This is daily life for an old lady like me. I thought everybody lived in the Limina."

John clapped his hands together and laughed. "There! Do you know, this insight came to me through Martha? Do you know that?"

Robby grabbed at my shoulders. "Martha, you'll stay with us, won't you, Martha?"

I said, "I don't know. I haven't had my meeting with John yet."

"Then let's go talk," he said.

"Wait," said Robby. "I don't understand about Jesus and the Limina."

"Jesus is the Limina," said Gil. "That's so cool."

John's eyes were amused, flickering, flashing: he was still and calm, and his eyes were all over us. He said, "You'll be in this place for a long time, Robby. Relax." Then he nodded to me and stepped over to the big table where we'd eaten. The others watched from the couches. He reached in the breast pocket of his jacket, then looked distracted, tried his pants pocket, finally found a money machine envelope in the side pocket of the jacket. He handed it to me, and it felt fat in my hand.

He said, "You'd better count it," he said. "Precision with money is not my strong suit."

"But money's fungible," I said, feeling smart. "It substitutes for other things. It moves around. That's the most liminal thing of all, isn't it?"

John laughed and touched my arm, just a pat, just a tingle, the briefest possible. He touches everyone, I thought. It's part of what he does.

I counted my money. "Twenty fifty-dollar bills. That's a thousand dollars. That's a shit-load of money to hand over to a stranger, Reverend."

"Half a month," he said. "I know it isn't much, but we don't know yet if it's full-time, or part-time, or short-term. It's a trial on all sides. And of course you also get room and board."

My hands began to sweat from holding all those fifties. I'm not used to having money in my hands. I realized, of course, that I had already decided. "And if I take the job, what if I write some grants and actually bring in money. Does the salary go up?"

"I don't see why not."

"I have to finish getting out of my apartment, arrange a truck, take some of my stuff to my sister's. But, okay, I'll give it a try."

"Excellent." He raised his voice. "Robby, is the van back from the shop? Why don't you and Gil take it to Martha's tomorrow and help her move." Robby leaped to his feet, but John gestured him to wait. "When you're ready, Martha, you'll start work. We'll trust you to know when. That's our specialty here. We want people to come in their own time. Get moved, settle in, be ready. We trust you."

Something in me wanted to cry out, I trust you too! But I controlled myself. "I'll organize the office. Probably day after tomorrow. Then I'll do your newsletter. How's that?"

"It's up to you, Martha."

Robby drove me to Pietro's where I'd left the Guzzler. He was very quiet. I made a couple of overtures, but he would only answer Yes or No.

Finally I said, "Does John drop these big philosophical bombshells often?"

Robby drove me to Pietro's where I'd left the Guzzler. He was very quiet. I made a couple of overtures, but he would only answer Yes or No.

Finally I said, "Does John drop these big philosophical bombshells often?"

"He tries to challenge us."

I kissed him, and he was still quiet and troubled. "Are you okay?"

"I don't know," he said. "I want everything to hold still. I know

John is stirring us up for a good reason, he always does it for a good reason."

"Well, I don't know about that, but I know he's right about change. He's got his own special word for it, but it's all about change."

"What is," said Robby, "is. Change is."

"Are you going Zen Buddhist on me, Robby?"

He grabbed my face and kissed me this time, deep, deep. That's better, I thought. I like kissing, at least with a young person with sweet breath.

He pulled away. "He likes you. I mean, he likes everybody, but he respects you."

"Robby, do you think about John all the time?"

"I think about what he says."

"Well, I think he's a little scary. I've got this urge to take his money and never come back."

Robby laughed as if I'd made a joke. He laid his hands on the sides of my breasts, seemed to be weighing them. I was ready for some heavy petting at least, but he sighed and laid his cheek on them, just rested there. "He chose you," he said dreamily. "It will be okay in the end."

7

My things were still in boxes, half in my sister's basement and half in my new room at the Love Palace, but before I unpacked, I called Dr. Landowska. She agreed to an appointment if I brought a payment on my debt and paid cash for all new sessions until we were square. She had a cancellation that afternoon, so after finding the phone books in the Love Palace office and calling a plumber for a stuffed toilet and returning Kristen's wallet which was closed up in one of the phone books, I went to my session with half my fifty dollar bills in an envelope, handed them to her, and lay down on the couch.

Madame's couch, by the way, is not one of your Freud-in-Vienna leather benches but rather a soft-pillowed, green-on-green jacquard sofa, protected by paper doilies for the patients' greasy heads and dusty feet. Her walls display gilt-framed impasto paintings of roses and peonies and Breton coastlines. I have wasted a lot of money telling her my feelings about her overstuffed bourgeois style.

She said, "Now, Martha, tell me about the leader of your new cult."

"Oh. My. God, Dr. Landowska," I said. "Cult! I belonged to a few organizations in my youth– Jews for Jesus for about a week, the Pentecostal churches in high school and Church of Holiness. This is not a cult. This place is run by a mainline church in Pinnacle, New Jersey."

"But your desire to give over all your problems to someone else, this is how cults happen."

"I get a new job with perks and cash up front and you're already insulting it? And of all the things I told you about, the agoraphobia, having sex with this kid Robby, why do you want to talk about the assistant minister of the church?"

She didn't say a word. Of course I didn't have to talk about John. She waited. There was the faintest shush of impatience from her stockinged thighs.

"He's very good-looking," I said, "John, the one you called the cult leader. All of the kids seem to worship him. He talks about something he calls the Limina, which means everything is constantly about to change, and there's nothing stable."

There was no thigh shushing this time. Madame is interested in religious experience. Once she took our therapy group for a weekend to her favorite Zen retreat–she arranged it, but of course we paid for it– for sleeping on the floor and eating oatmeal. It was a disaster, too: one group member left therapy and became a Buddhist; the old guy who likes to hear about people's sex lives got a back spasm during the second sitting and had to be evacuated by ambulance; and as for me, I had a fit of rebellion and refused to do the weed pulling meditation and sneaked off down the hill to town with my least favorite group member with whom I went drinking. We ended up fucking in someone's garden shed. And that episode really cost me a lot of money talking about what I'd done.

I said, "This interests you, right? His New Age sermon?"

"Yes," she said, "but I am not so sure this is what is interesting you."

"It's a job that interests me," I said. "I'm there for the job. They're hiring me to figure out who is using the building on which night. It's a place with teenage runaways and alcoholics trying to dry out. It's a new start for me, if I like it. I've put my stuff at my sister's except for a few things in this little dorm room at Love Palace where I'm going to organize their office and write a newsletter. If it doesn't work out, I'm gone. That's all."

She grunted. For someone who has a closet full of very expensive shoes, she makes a lot of animal noises.

"That's it," I said. "Honest. I had sex with the boy, but that was like social work. I'm going to save money to pay you off and finish my therapy don't you dare laugh, and then I'll buy a condo and become a solid citizen. A solid senior citizen by then, but still. That's what you want for me, right?"

She said, "You have not yet told me how much you want to make love with this cult leader."

That's Madame for you. Cut to the chase. I almost sputtered Oh. My. God, again, but the louder you sputter, the more she doesn't believe you. "He's very attractive," I said. "I'm being careful about being sucked in by John," I said. "I'm going to avoid sleeping with him."

"This is an excellent intention," said Madame. "Your record is not so good on this."

"And what if I did sleep with him? I'm over forty, Madame, what's wrong if I get lucky?"

"It is lucky to be promiscuous?"

"I only sleep around when I'm on a downswing," I said. "It's my drug of choice, you know that."

"I think you sleep with people when you are on the upswing

too."

I let that pass. "Robby wants to marry me."

"The young teenage boy?"

"He's not a teenager, he turned twenty-one. Yes, I know he's half my age. Yes, yes, this is another wrong man. I know, Madame, I know it is all wrong men for me, it's my pattern and my addiction."

"I would not go so far as to say addiction."

"You used to."

Her thighs shushed. "I think you have more self-awareness. In any event, you've been very busy, have you not? A great deal has been happening in your life."

It was near the end of the session. I said, "John, my boss, is sort of a celebrity, too. Do you remember that famous Time magazine cover from ten or twelve years ago? The prison riot out in the Midwest or somewhere, I forget? And this chaplain in a white shirt is holding this guy who's been shot?"

"No."

"It was all over TV, in all the papers– one of the major news photos of the decade!"

"I don't watch the news."

It amazes me sometimes how oblivious she is to her adopted country. "Well, he was the chaplain, I think. He was involved in the negotiations between the prisoners and the authorities, and maybe they took him hostage for a while– he was very brave, interviewed all over the place, famous for his full fifteen minutes, maybe more." I waited for a reaction, but of course she never heard of Andy Warhol either. "It's just a job, Madame L. Even my mother, Mrs. Show-Me-the-Price-Tag, will think it's a good deal, a salary and room and board. What's the big deal? And also I'm part of something interesting, and maybe even useful."

"Yes?"

"Yes! Don't you think I might have a faint desire to do something in the world for someone besides myself? And also, they make me feel like the soul of sanity. No joke, Dr. Landowska, it's the snake pit, you know? Oh never mind, more pop Culture. I thought was maybe your era, too, the shoulder-pad actresses. Didn't you have showings of American movies back in Transylvania? Snake Pit is an old black-and-white movie with Olivia de Havilland? She also played Melanie in *Gone with the Wind*. Unless it was her sister, the blonde one. Anyhow, they put this woman in a loony bin and it cures her craziness. Like shock therapy."

"You consider this job shock therapy."

"Maybe."

"It is a job below your skills."

"No. And if I learn to write grants, I can upgrade my job. Besides, when have I ever had a job you thought was good enough for me? You think I get crap jobs because I think I'm crap."

"Remember the little dog in your dream? Always a victim."

"Dr. Landowska, you're missing something. At the Love Palace, I haven't even started, but I already feel good, competent. I go diving in the piles of papers for a phone book and find a wallet that belongs to one of the girls. They think I'm a genius. I'm going to shape this place up. I feel like I'm on the verge of a change. Maybe it really is Him, meaning Jesus, as Robby always whispers, did you ever think of that?"

"Or him meaning this man you have a crush on. What I am hearing at this point, Martha, is that you want very much to be connected in."

"Yes! Yes, I do. Is that so bad?"

"Only that you want to do it so quickly, like an instant dinner with no cooking."

"Why can't you just encourage me for once!"

"Ah," she said in one of her deep wise tones. "Poor Martha." She hesitated. I had a feeling something profound was coming, one of her cool slices into my steaming innards. She said, "Time is up for today, Martha."

"What were you going to say?"

"I was looking at the clock. We can continue next time, Martha," she said.

"If I pay cash!"

"Yes, Martha," she said. "You must participate in your therapy as an adult, not as a needy child."

8

My first love was a little boy who lived across the street and had puppies. I don't know if it was the boy or the puppies, but I yearned to be with him or maybe have him or be him. It's hard to say what love means when you're four, even though you feel it as powerfully as at any other age. One hot day in the apartment, and I think I was being punished, or maybe not punished, I've always had a tendency to feel I'm being punished when things aren't going my way. I was definitely inside and wanted to be out. Maybe I was too small to be out on my own. I don't even know if we had Mari yet, but if we did, I was probably being punished for something I'd done to the baby.

Across the street there was a building with a driveway beside it. Usually this driveway had its gate closed and was filled with trucks and cars, but this day, it was open, and my little boy was squatting there with two white and black puppies. He squatted and held them. I hadn't loved this little boy on other days when I watched him play with his brothers or eat a popsicle. But I loved him this day with his puppies.

So I went over to be with him.

I let myself out, went down the steps, out the door. The florist was standing outside in the sun, and he looked at me in a strange way. I remember being looked at and I remember thinking that this was important, what I was doing all by myself, that I was crossing the street alone for love and the florist was seeing me. It wasn't the world's busiest street, but it was certainly a commercial street, and I don't know if I looked both ways or just went. Because the next part of the memory is simply me squatting with the little boy and the two puppies, and I remember that I loved the way we all smelled. The puppies smelled and the boy smelled, and it was like I had done magic: I had been up in the window and I had transported myself down here and now what I had imagined was real. I hugged the puppies and the boy. I was squatting there with my arms around him and the puppies when Nana came striding furious across the street to grab me and take me back upstairs.

When I looked out the window the next time, I was definitely being punished.

But I didn't learn my lesson: I only learned that you have to grab things and smell them and get as much as you can before they take you back upstairs.

I plunged into my job at the Love Palace, not expecting it to last. I was feeling strong and healthy compared to the rest of them, especially my little Robby, who moped around for two days, shocked over the Lord-of-the-Limina business, and also because I had told him I wasn't sure we should keep having sex. Madame hadn't made me promise, but I was doing it to prove something to her, knowing that she considered celibacy, at least in my case, a good discipline. Robby moped some more and talked about the importance of reinforcing his heterosexuality. John wasn't around at all. I didn't fully unpack my suitcases, which turned out a good thing. More about that later.

Madame had a cancellation, and I had another catch-up session and boasted of how organizing Love Palace helped me organize myself. I told her about my first love when I was four, and she said again that perhaps what I wanted was to be a part of something. I said, Duh, and she grunted. You never know with her, what's going to turn out to be constructive and what she'll call avoidance.

The day after the session, I got the dishwasher fixed. I opened a drawer in the kitchen, picked up the dishwasher manual, and called the 800 number printed in large type on the first page. It turned out we had the Platinum-level service contract, and they sent a guy over the same day. Why, I wondered, did they need me to do this?

But clearly they did. I could do a dozen things before Robby and the others even got up in the morning. I felt a glow of competence and superiority. I moved empty boxes out of the office into the hall to be carried down later. I installed software. Everything was top of the line. I thought of John's soft pleated pants, and while I was thinking of him, he called.

My heart jumped like a high school sophomore. He was calling to find out how I was doing, about me. I told him about the dishwasher. He poured on praise. "I knew you were what we needed, Martha," he said. "I follow my instincts on these things. I have faith in your good influence."

I wanted to know where he lived. I wanted to know if he was married. I wanted to see him.

But it was a short conversation; he made no promises, he told me nothing personal. It left me glowing– the delta wave voice, his modest celebrity. John had taken time out to call and see if I was settled in.

Then Robby came down the hall from his room to the office, drowsy and affectionate with his teeth freshly cleaned, I let him kiss me, and I kissed him back, and I thought I had proved what I needed to prove to Madame, so I took him back down the hall to my little bedroom and he laughed with a kind of gurgling enthusiasm and his energy seemed to transfer to me, to hell with Madame, I could do everything, all at once, it was like I was starving, I was all over him, none of this nonsense about the male entering the female, it was me enveloping him, on the single bed with all my boxes piled along the walls I tried to consume him, his skin fine and taut and he smelled like a little boy, like my little boy with the puppies, but no Nana was going to interrupt me now, and he laughed with delight, and when we were finished, I had him move all the cardboard boxes of supplies and software to the recycle bin.

Lucky for me, Madame was out of town for a week, and by the time I saw her again, I was having sex with Robby every day. No commitment, I told her, it was all part of the whole. He needs me to prove he's a man, I just need it. I'm getting old, Madame, I told her. I deserve this.

But I think what was more important to me than having sex with Robby, and maybe the reason in the end that Madame didn't object was that I really liked working at the Love Palace. She had said she thought I wanted to be part of something, and I think she was right. On the one hand, it was a bizarre set-up, but on the other hand, it was fun. Part of the fun was teasing out more information about what was going on there. It wasn't that anything was a secret, only that nobody seemed to have a sense of the Big Picture. John was central to the operations, but no one knew exactly what his role was. Robby thought that John and his parents, the Petersons, were on the Board. What about John's family? I asked. His wife. Robby looked puzzled. I don't think he's married, he said. He's pretty private about his personal life. How often does he come around? Robby said it varied.

I told myself I didn't care, but of course I did. The Good News Crew including Robby had no idea if the church in Pinnacle owned, rented, or leased the building. Why had the Pinnacle Church had taken on the project in the first place? As best I could tell, it was to give their teenagers a taste of Social Service. Was it someone's idea of a way to round out their college applications? Maybe some of the kids were on probation for a drug bust and needed community service hours? The original kids were gone, anyhow, except for Robby. Robby had gone to the hospital instead of to college and was now back, a little older than the rest of the Good News Crew. Gil and Kristen and Cara turned out to have come only a couple of months before me, and there was a bargain with their families that John was supervising them. Gil and Cara's families kept the bargain, but Kristen's family kept trying to get in touch with her, and she threatened to run, and John negotiated, and generally kept the crisis under control. At least once, I took the phone call from the anxious father and mother who wanted to know who I was and what was going on there. The father in particular was pretty aggressive, and I finally told them I was the new Executive Director and John would get back to them at his leisure

I eventually found a file with information on the incorporation of the Love Palace, which did indeed have a Board, and it did include the Petersons and John. I thought of calling Rhonda, but no one knew her contact information. When Ace the ex-Black Panther college math teacher stopped by to use the copy machine, I asked him what he knew, and he gave me a lecture on political demographics. Pinnacle, said Ace, is twenty-five miles west of the decrepit and redeveloping waterfront neighborhoods like Water Street and the Warehouse District where my sister had her condo. What was left in the immediate environs of Love Palace I could see for myself: a couple of dumpy apartment buildings, a Single Room Occupancy hotel, the Blue Lagoon bar, a used furniture store which (Ace informed me) was primarily a place for fencing stolen goods, and, of course, Love Palace itself. Beyond us to the north were the great blocks of the Bishop Stebbins housing project; to the south was the looming blue glass skin of Riversedge Renaissance, with my sister's Warehouse district beyond.

And the meaning of redevelopment, the meaning of the Warehouse district and Riversedge Renaissance, said Ace, is that they are cleansing the streets of the poor, the working class, and the ethnics—

Who is they? I demanded.

The ones who live in Pinnacle, said Ace with the gimlet eye. The poor and the working class will be moved to soften up the next neighborhood for eventual maximization of profits by the Ruling Class.

I always glaze over when someone says Ruling Class. It makes my stomach growl, as if Nana were about to serve dinner.

Ace had to go teach, but he said he'd give me the rest of the lecture at the Tenants' Council meeting the next morning which he wanted me to cover for the newsletter I was supposed to be writing.

That night, as he had begun to do, Robby slipped into my room. I didn't sleep well with someone else in bed with me. I'd been sleeping solo for a while, but I liked so much having him there, curled on his side, waiting for me to begin. His next lesson. I smelled the soapy clean of him, not that I would have minded healthy young sweat either, but he always showered for me. He didn't seem to have any idea of the effect of his loveliness on other people.

I said, "Robby, did your mom and dad really set up this whole deal just for you?"

"What whole deal?"

"Love Palace."

"Not for me. For everyone. For the people here, too. That's the main thing, to help the people."

"But there's nobody left but the boys at the Blue Lagoon! The really poor people are either in the Bishop Stebbins apartments or gone."

"There are still people in the buildings across the street."

"Yeah, yeah, I know. Ace's tenant council and the playgroups. I'm not complaining, I just don't get it. Why did they choose here? I mean, Danny Boy and the Franks are the least likely to change their habits of anybody."

"Wait till Free Market day. You'll be amazed how many people show up."

In the end, because of being in the moment, I decided I wouldn't care about original intentions and numbers of clients served. In the end, it was soapy clean Robby who mostly kissed if he'd been kissed first, but whose returns were enthusiastic, and increasingly skillful.

He whispered, lying back, pleased with his performance and his pleasure, "We'll get married and then everything will be fine."

"Let's stay in the limina, Robby," I said.

The next morning, the morning of the Tenants' Council meeting, Robby and the Good News Crew slept late, as they usually did. I got up and went to the office where White Frank was waiting to tell me the rice had come.

"Rice?" I said.

"It's just some rice in a truck. You have to sign for it."

Five hundred pounds of just some rice, an occasional donation from a supermarket chain. 25 huge bags of rice. The truck driver said, "Where's the lady that used to be here?"

"Rhonda?" I said. "Rhonda moved on."

He lifted half a lip, Elvis style. "I can see why." He handed me a manifold to sign, and told me he used to live around here. "It was a nice family neighborhood then," he said, staring at White Frank as if he were personally responsible for changing it. "People didn't have much, but they worked."

"Yeah," I said, "well, I guess there were jobs back then too."

He said, "How long do you figure you'll last?"

Before I could give him a snippy answer back, Black Frank joined White Frank to carry the rice into the store room next to the kitchen. After they'd done that, I had them tie up the newspapers in the lounge for recycling.

I thought I'd better start the newsletter, which was the only official duty anyone had given me. John had promised an editorial, and I made up a masthead, but after a while, I got restless and went back downstairs to go through the walk-in closet next to the main room. I kept finding projects that the famous Rhonda had apparently started and never finished: a scrapbook with one page of photos, Good News Crew kids who weren't here anymore. A notebook with ideas for a PowerPoint presentation for possible funders. No photos of old Rhonda herself. I had the feeling she had left in a hurry, and I theorized total disgust with the lack of discipline– the Good News Crew, for example, was still asleep. Or maybe there had been some kind of irreconcilable differences, a big blow up with John or maybe Robby's mother who I wondered if I could avoid meeting but probably couldn't.

I had just discovered what appeared to be a brand-new Hoover vacuum cleaner all the way in the back of the closet when Ace arrived with some women and children and a box of donuts. They met at the big conference/dining table on the main floor.

Ace was very businesslike, wearing glasses and carrying a clipboard and a briefcase stuffed with file folders. He introduced me to the women, the Executive Committee of the Tenants' Council of 317 Water Street. The youngest woman, Malika, had lots of metal in her hair and on her wrists and ears and big boobs in a scoop-necked yellow tee shirt, beautiful skin, and stretch jeans. She looked me over and didn't smile in response to my smile.

The other two appeared much less prosperous, especially the woman with the children, short and soft, wearing an old fashioned or possibly even home-made skirt. Her name was Esta Brown, and, as if to balance Malika's glare, she smiled all the time. The third woman was white. Her name was Chickie, and she smelled of cigarette smoke. She reminded me of my mother, partly because of her bleached hair and partly because of her cigarette smoker's rasp. She complained about not being able to smoke anywhere anymore. In the old days, said Chickie, setting out the doughnuts, watched closely by Esta's little kids, in the old days you could smoke where and when you wanted. Whatever happened to freedom? Was this America or what?

Esta said to me, "Are you who cleaned it all up so nice?"

"I'm working on it. With help."

Ace said, "Her main job is a newsletter. Martha, you are invited to cover this meeting. We need media coverage. Feel free to take notes."

"Write an article about Smokers' Rights," said Chickie.

I said, "You could write an op-ed article about it. I'd be glad to publish it."

Chickie snorted. "Me write an article. Yeah, right."

Esta said, "She has to take care of her mother. Her mother has Alzheimer's Disease, you know."

Malika sat down next to Ace and leaned toward him, not quite touching, and gave me a look. Relax, honey, I thought. I've got one of my own, younger than that, too.

Ace spread out his files; the other women sat down. He handed me a legal pad and pen. He had been prepared for this. He said, "The Tenants' Council."

"We call it the T.C.," said Esta. "It's 317 plus there's still one family living in 315."

"They left," said Malika.

Ace frowned. "That means they've emptied out all the other buildings. This is where it's happening on this block. This is where the people are being shafted. Talk to these people, Martha, not the teeny-boppers. Write it down."

Not to be pushed around by Ace, I said, "Let me get a couple of factual things first. Could you give me your whole names–"

"Why?" said Chickie.

"That's the official way," said Esta, who was giving a doughnut to her toddler. He managed to lean in her lap and eat at the same time, strewing powdered sugar all over her skirt.

Malika glowered. "Just tell the truth, don't bother with the last names."

Esta said, "Martha didn't get any coffee yet. Martha, you get some coffee before you work." So I did, a plain donut and a coffee with a lot of milk. I liked Esta. Nice people are nice.

Malika still glared at me. "I'm glad somebody likes those old doughnuts with no sugar."

Esta said, "Martha, you can have my cream doughnut, my kids eat any kind."

I said, "I like plain best. Really."

Ace looked impatient while we did donuts, flipping through papers, glancing over the tops of his glasses to see if we were ready yet. Finally, Chickie started in complaining about water bugs, and mice, which seemed to be the signal that the meeting had started. She had enough trouble taking care of her mother, and now there were water bugs and mice.

"Mice!" said Malika. "Listen, I'm not talking about little mice, I've got rats. I've got big rats."

Ace nodded. "What do you know about tenants' rights, Martha? You ought to, given what you told me. We're debating whether or not to withhold rent because of the rats—"

"Just do it," said Malika.

Rats, I wrote, trying to look investigative. Withhold rent.

Ace said, "Do you know the law about legally withholding rent?"

"No, but I wish I did, because of what happened at my old apartment."

Malika said, "Nobody has to get evicted. What did your T.O. do?"

"I don't think we had one," I said. "This was more my fault than theirs. I'd been like sick–"

"They can't evict you if you're' sick!" said Esta. "Oh, Ace we ought to do something for her–"

"It's really okay," I said, "and now I have a room here, so I'm fine."

Esta took on an uplifted expression. "Reverend John gave you a room, didn't he?"

"Well, yes, but I do have a sister who lives over a couple of blocks away–"

"In Bishop Stebbins?"

"No," I whispered, "in the Warehouse District."

"The condos," said Malika darkly.

"YuppieWorld," said Ace. "That's another place they threw out the working class people."

I decided to sacrifice my sister for an appearance of solidarity. "Yeah, my sister is Yuppie to the core. But I don't think her building displaced any people, it had been a factory that they closed forty years ago or something—"

Chickie said, "My uncle used to work there. This was a nice neighborhood back then."

Just what the man with the rice had said.

"Well it ain't no more," said Malika. "And I'm out of here as soon as I pay off my credit cards."

"This is not about any one person," said Ace. "It's about economic forces. The main thing to keep in mind, what this situation is teaching us, is about the way the capitalist system works. The capitalist system could care less if your uncle had a job, if this was once a thriving working class neighborhood. If the working class was all thriving, that's a negative to the capitalism system. The capitalist system wants every little person busy scrambling around to find enough to eat so they never notice how they're being oppressed. They chase the poor people out of this place, and they go to some other neighborhood where the landlords and blockbusters use them to soften up the housing market and get things turning over, and then another neighborhood gets redeveloped with big profits for the capitalists."

Now I remembered: Ace had wanted to finish giving me the lecture.

Malika sucked her teeth. "I just want a decent place to live. I don't give a damn if Capitalism or Communism or the Nation of Islam gives it to me."

Ace said, "We're going to start by fighting the landlords. We're going to organize."

"That's right!" said Esta.

I was on Malika's side: who cares who pays as long as you get a place to live and get to go see Madame.

"The problem is," said Ace, "that we can't put pressure on the landlord if we don't know who he is. The leases say what to pay your rent to, but not who."

"Why do you care who?"

"I know the answer to that one," said Chickie. "We want to shame the jerk."

"I'm going to take him one of my rats in a little cage," said Malika, "with a ribbon on it and a card that says Have a Nice Day, MoFo."

They all laughed, Chickie choking on her coffee.

Ace said, "We haven't been able to find out who owns the building. We know they plan to demolish the houses to put up another Riversedge Renaissance, but we don't know who they are."

"Isn't it public information?"

"Yes and no. There's a whole set of holding companies between the people who pay the rent and the people who really own the company. Now," said Ace, leaning forward, "here you can be a big help to us, Martha. We want to get to this landlord, whoever he is. They make it hard, slow, and expensive to find out."

"But we're going to find out," said Esta, "aren't we? We're going to find out and go talk to that man about the rats? I found my little boy playing with one of the things and I keep my house clean! I put the garbage out two times a day–"

"They're emptying out the houses all around," said Malika, "so the rats move over into our house."

The rats got me, of course. The idea of rats and baby flesh. I mean, my sister ended up with a nice apartment that had a view of the Hudson River and New York harbor, but how did that balance round-faced Esta Brown in her homemade skirt finding her baby playing with a rat?

In the end, they all gave me their full names and the names of all their children. Esta had four altogether, and Malika had one, a daughter that she worked extra shifts to send to Catholic school, which they all agreed was better than the neighborhood public school. The neighborhood school, they told me, had rats too. Chickie was on disability for chronic breathing problems, living with her mother who liked to take off her clothes when someone came to visit, but not to put that in the newspaper. Ace made me take notes on his theory of population displacement and profit, and Malika gave me a gruesome description of how nasty naked tails are. They cause fires, contamination, and disease, she said, and we call them Norwegian but they really came from China.

Just as I was scribbling down about the rats, and Esta and Chickie had begun to clean up the doughnuts, John came in. He was wearing understated browns today, his face broad with the smile of someone who expects to be welcomed. Esta ran to him and grabbed his right hand in both of hers, and Chickie struck a flirtatious pose with one hand on her hip. Malika pouted, but didn't sneer, and when John came to the table, he asked her something I couldn't hear that made her smile. Ace concentrated on methodically putting his papers into his briefcase.

Without disengaging from Esta, John moved close to Ace, who said he had to be on his way, he had a class.

John turned to me last. "How is it working out, Martha?" he said. "Is it still going well? I'm sorry I haven't been around yet, but it's given you an opportunity to settle in, yes?"

Esta said, "She's writing an article about us!"

"About the rats," said Malika.

Esta wanted John to eat something, and I noticed that he took a donut but only ate maybe a quarter of it. He sat down, and they gathered close. Ace zipped his bag and strode to the door, where he waved me over.

He jerked his chin back toward the little group about John. "A little bit of preacher man and they forget everything they ever knew about class struggle."

"You don't like John very well."

"I don't like to see people buying what they're selling."

Esta called, "Come over for prayer circle!"

"Fuck that shit," murmured Ace. "Listen, I usually get reimbursed for the donuts and coffee. Will you take the receipts?"

Esta was coming to get us. Ace thrust some crumpled papers at me and escaped.

Esta was disappointed, but at least she got me. I sat between her and Chickie, and she started the prayer, with a firm voice, praying for the tenants' group and for Chickie's mother and for Malika to find a new apartment and for Martha to write a good newspaper, and then she sort of introduced John as the next speaker, and he took over with a low-voiced, really very simple prayer, asking for us all to be open to the best in ourselves and each other. He did not use the God word, I noticed. On the other hand, he didn't use the Limina word either

I liked the hand-holding: Chickie's grip surprisingly tight, Esta's hand hot and damp.

Afterward, Malika had to go get dressed for work, and Chickie had already left her mom too long, she said. The last time they had a Tenants' Council meeting her mother had turned all the burners on the stove on high. Esta said she wanted to talk to John about something private. He glanced at me. "Martha, do you need anything?"

"No," I said, "I'm good. I'm going to lock myself up in the office for a couple of hours and write the newsletter."

He said he'd come up after he met with Esta.

I went upstairs, pausing for a minute on the mezzanine. Esta's kids came over, the little one sat on John's lap, the bigger one leaned close and showed something to him while Esta talked and talked. He seemed to have all the time in the world.

I sat down at the computer in the office with my notes, but I could feel him still in the building. This, I told myself, isn't sex. This is just the charisma thing.

I stared at the screen and waited.

And soon heard some laughter downstairs, a creak on the stairs, then silence, and I pretended I was busy, and waited, and it was still silent, and finally I couldn't stand it, and rolled around just as he walked in the office, as if I'd been sitting there waiting for him all along, as indeed I had.

He smiled and sat down on the newly cleared couch directly under the framed *Time* magazine cover. It was definitely one of those images that molds the perceptions of people of a certain age. My age cohort didn't have any real wars, just Old-Shit-for-Brains Reagan's little incursions into whichever Caribbean country he didn't like that week. We were already grown-ups for Bush versus Saddam Round I, let alone the rest of it. I think what we missed out on was feeling that we had any personal connection let alone influence on history. We certainly weren't prepared for everything that would hit the fan after the turn of the century. Still, we had our media moments, our meaningful images, and Prison Pietà was one. And John was the Prison Pietà guy.

And he was sitting there underneath his picture with his arms up and back behind his head. "Everything looks wonderful," he said. "You've pulled the office together in an amazing way."

"It really wasn't in such bad order. It was mostly just supplies that never got put away. Rhonda left the files fine."

He smiled, again that sense that he had as much time as you needed, and I was aware of John's fragrance. I had always noticed it, but it seemed especially strong this day, from across the office. Was it a personal redolence or an extremely expensive cologne?

I said, "Why did Rhonda leave?"

He pulled his arms down, looked more serious. "Personal problems," he said. "She was a fine, creative person. But she–" He stopped, nodded. Privileged information, I thought. Did preachers have the same restrictions and responsibilities as therapists?

So I nodded back. He's a couple of years older than I am, I thought, but not much. In the photo, I think he had a little more hair and no silvering. In the photo, he gazes just slightly above and to the left of the photographer with an expression at once accusing and serene. Neutral clothing, not too different from the clothes of the man felled by bullets that he is embracing, who is turned away so that you don't see his face. It is a black and white photograph, so you also don't realize at first that the dark color on the prisoner's jumpsuit and John's hands is blood. Until you notice the blood, the most striking thing by far is John's face.

I said, "It's you, isn't it? Prison Pietà?"

He seemed to know I had been looking at it. Maybe celebrities have to be ready for questions like that. "A long time ago," he said.

"The picture's crooked."

"Rhonda put it up," he said. "Take it down if you want."

"Why? Robby and the others are inspired by it. You'll have to tell me about it. I mean, if you talk about it."

He smiled and got up. No hurry, but I could see he was about to leave.

I said, "Do you wear cologne?"

"What is it you want, Martha?"

That fragrance, I thought. I want to be close to it. Buddha and Mohammed were supposed to have trailed it behind them. Jesus too, no doubt–but not Moses. I would bet that Moses was always a sweaty, smelly, cantankerous old sumbitch, especially during the forty years in the wilderness.

I said, "I want you to give me the piece you promised for the newsletter. An op-ed personal perspective sort of thing. I was thinking you might tell your personal story."

He said, "I'm going out of town. I'm sorry. How can we handle this?"

"You could email it over."

He shook his head. "I'm an oaf when it comes to technology. I barely know how to use a computer. What if I gave you some verbal bullet points, and you– I hate to ask you– could you just put it into sentences for me?"

What was I going to say? I poised my fingers over the key board, and he took a few steps in one direction, then the other. "Let's talk about the Limina," he said.

"Not your background?"

"Another time," he said. And went off on what was essentially a short version of his talk from the other night. We're all in the moment, the moment is always changing, Jesus is the Lord of the Limina.

I said, "Since we're nonsectarian according to our bylaws, should you really talk about Jesus?"

"Yes, perhaps. Let's say, 'The present is on the threshold, social action and religion alike call us to step over the threshold, to embrace the change.'"

I felt him behind me, reading the computer screen over my head. He leaned in closer, and I was a little dizzy with his fragrance. I could feel the heat of his body, too, and then, as natural as anything, he braced himself on my shoulders, left hand on my left shoulder, right on right. There was his weight, and then, slowly, more weight, pressure, pressing me down. Shit, I thought. Is this where we're going?

We heard footsteps, and John pulled back. It was Cara and Kristen with the little preschool kids. They filled the doorway, and John picked up two children and created another little scene with him and the kids and the girls all cooing together on the couch. So I got out the camera I had found brand new in its unopened box under a stack of file folders and snapped the corny tableau.

Then, when they had gone, I made John sit down in front of the computer and read what we'd written. I stayed across the room. "It looks fine," he said. "You'll just check the grammar, make sure it makes sense?"

Robby burst in. "John!" he cried, his face as open and happy as a little kid. "Martha!"

Robby embraced him, a quick move, forehead to John's, then he reached over and embraced me too. "I'm in the Limina, John," he said. " Martha and I are in the Limina."

I took more snapshots: John with Robby, John under the Prison Pietà. Then Robby insisted on taking a picture of me, and John took one of me and Robby, and then Robby took one of me and John, with John's arm around me, burning. John finally left and Robby went to get breakfast and I stayed in the office and worked on John's article, full of a sense that something big was coming.

9

During the next few days, we got the newsletter copied and collated and distributed. The Good News Crew carried it up and down the street and to the Bishop Stebbins houses. Robby and Gil took copies out to Pinnacle to the church, and the word was that the Board of Directors (a.k.a. Robby's mom and dad) were favorably impressed. John asked me to send copies to the parents of the Good News Crew, as he was going out of town for a couple of weeks.

Meanwhile, I did double sessions with Madame, saying how I liked the job, the feeling of competence, but also how I was attracted to both Robby and John, which she thought was a sign of a healthy interest in life, but that I would be even more powerful if I exercised impulse control and didn't have sex for a while.

I talked it over with Robby, who was supportive if not thrilled, and I actually managed celibacy for two full weeks that unusually hot June, keeping the door to my room locked. John wasn't around anyhow, and the Good News Crew made it feel like summer camp running up and down the hall in their underwear, everyone sharing a filthy bathroom. Of course one of the main characteristics of summer camp– which I had never attended as a camper but once as a disgruntled counselor– is that it doesn't last.

I had definitely begun to yearn for my own bathroom.

Every evening Robby held my hand and led me into a corner of the lounge and asked respectfully if the celibacy experiment was over. May I come in tonight? he would ask, and I would say, Not tonight, baby.

I also started working on the finances. Balancing the checkbook at Love Palace turned out to be a lot harder than the newsletter. I complained to everyone. Then, one afternoon at the end of the two weeks when I thought everyone was out with the little kids, I sat down for another go at the checkbook. After a little while, I heard a sound in the doorway, lifted my head expecting to see Robby back for a hug and a talk about resuming our sex life, but it was John instead. He smiled, but didn't come directly in.

"You're back," I said. "Did you have a good trip?"

"Yes, very good. Are you busy?"

It surprised me that he would wait for an invitation. "I'm balancing the checkbook," I said, "or trying to. Come on in."

He sat in his usual place on the couch. He was wearing a short sleeved white shirt like a Southern preacher. "Martha," he said,

"I haven't really had a chance to tell you how excellent the newsletter was."

"Yes, you did."

"The phone is not the same. Nothing is a substitute for being in the same physical space with someone. Touching. I am a great believer in human touch, the laying on of hands."

"Cool," I said. And where was he going with this?

He said, "How soon do you think we can get out another issue? It is going to help us keep the church in Pinnacle supporting us. It gives us a tool for outreach."

"As soon as I get the checkbook balanced."

"Excellent. I have some ideas for articles, and this time I promise to do the writing myself."

His forearms had a particular color of hair that I like, dark but with golden highlights. I said, "It looks like you've been at the beach."

"No, no beach." And then there was some silence, and I tried to be serene and still, the kind of person who touches because it is a good thing. But I was starting to itch under his gaze. He said, "Martha, you have an ability to make order where there was disorder. Martha, Martha, Martha."

And my name in his mouth gave me a whole new vision of myself– a Martha with zaftig shoulders and bosom and stunning décolletage. Martha with a vast clean, practical intelligence and organizational capabilities. Martha on the verge of infinite possibilities.

I was feeling the sucking, into a big hot tub where you could stretch out and luxuriate. I said, "The checkbook is a disaster. Also, I can't figure out who gets reimbursed. Do we subsidize the 317 Tenants' Council meetings?"

"Within reason," said John.

"Okay, fine. But then there are these withdrawals from ATM machines, all over the state and in New York too. Two hundred dollars here, three hundred there, big fees because it's not our branch. How many people have bank cards? I mean, I'm sure it's is all totally legitimate."

"It could be Eleanor or Warren. I have a card, Rhonda had a card."

"Nobody got it back when she left?"

"I would think we did, but I don't know. I believe Robby has a card."

"I'll ask Robby."

"And maybe a couple other of the young people."

"A couple of other? Which ones? Doesn't anybody know?"

He was quiet for a couple of seconds. Very seriously, he said, "Martha, this proves my point, you see. This is the first time in months that anyone has tried to deal with these things. Eleanor and Warren Peterson and the church have a lot of other interests to say the least, and Love Palace has always been a little ad hoc. Rhonda tried to regularize things–"

"Unless she's the one withdrawing from the account."

"I think I remember getting back the card. Maybe."

"Well, okay, let's assume it's just sloppiness and nobody is stealing. And if it is a thief, I hope they don't know how much is in the account. Because that's the other thing. Even with all the withdrawals, there's almost twenty thousand dollars in that account, according to the latest bank statement, which came this week."

"That much?" Again, he was silent, and I thought he was going to make a financial suggestion of some kind, like hire an accountant, but instead, he said, "Have you looked at the apartment yet?"

"Does this have something to do with the bank account?"

"No, just something else I forgot to do. I'm very bad on details, Martha. I wanted you to think of using the apartment. The one down the hall from the bedrooms."

"I never saw an apartment."

"There's a door there, between two of the bedrooms, a short hall and then the apartment. I meant for you to use it. Let's go take a look."

"I can't afford an apartment."

"If it's included in your salary you can. I meant it from the beginning, but I forgot. More evidence of my poor grasp of details." He stood up and opened his hand toward the door. "Let me show it to you, to see if it suits you."

I said, "John, I'm not even sure I'm staying here. I don't have a great track record on commitment. You can't just keep giving me things–"

"Why not? I'm a Sermon-on-the-Mount absolutist. Jesus said, 'The lilies of the field, they neither toil nor spin yet Solomon in all this glory was not arrayed like one of these.' In other words, when the goodness of this world comes rolling like a mighty wave, Martha, let it wash over you. The things, the love. You deserve all the riches the world has to offer."

I suppose if John had offered me eternal salvation or even if he'd quoted Jesus on something other than how the lilies of the field get a free ride, I don't think I would have gone out the door with him, but I went, feeling the thrill– an adventure with John. He insisted on a broad courteous gesture of having me go out first, so I had to pass close enough to feel the warmth of his body, and he touched my back, lightly, casually. He's a toucher, I reminded myself. Besides, hadn't he said I deserved everything the world has to offer?

John had a key to that door I had thought was a closet, and it opened into a little hallway with another door at the end. He used the same key there. "Just look it over, Martha, and if you like it, it's yours."

The kitchen was on the right. Thick green enamel paint on the cabinets and a door into the bathroom, also old but not filthy. The orange mineral deposits in the tub. The bathroom had a door to a small bedroom, and the bedroom also had a second door, to the living room. Everything seemed to have doors to everywhere.

John was waiting in the living room which turned out to have the bump-out bay window that looked so strange from the street. The light showed the dinginess of the paint, but there was a dry cleanliness to the place that seemed to be waiting for something.

The only furniture was an open futon with a summer-weight comforter in a tie-dye print.

John said, "What do you think?"

"It's quiet," I said. I looked out the window across at the apartment buildings, then down on the stoop roof of our entrance, where a lot of trash had collected, including the extended wing of a dead pigeon.

Then, across the street, a sliver of cityscape, not enough to get a person all excited, but it did give you a mild awareness of the greater world. In the mid-distance, on the other side of Water Street, a direct view into one of the top-floor apartments in 317. Where someone was staring back at me. I saw long hair first, then naked breasts, and I thought it was a young blonde, then realized the breasts were too long, the hair white not blond, and I guessed it was Chickie's demented mother. I waited for this to strike me as a bad omen, as a reason to avoid this apartment, this building, but instead, Mama Godiva waved at me, and I waved back.

"That must be Chickie's mom," I said.

John came up behind me and I felt him there, and he put his hands on my shoulders the way he had the day we wrote his piece for the newsletter. The weight of his hands, deeper and deeper into my shoulders.

He's making a pass, I thought, using that odd old-fashioned phrase in my mind.

"What do you think?" he said again, continuing to do the wonderful thing with his hands on my shoulders. "There's extra furniture in the basement."

"I have furniture," I said, and I stepped out of his touch, just to prove to us both that I could do it. I turned around to face him.

He seemed hesitant, almost unsure of himself. He stepped back too, as if to deny any intentions.

What was most seductive to me, I think, was how closely he was paying attention to me. John with his hair pushed back off his forehead, the little vertical line between his brows, studying me, reading me for signs. Maybe because he wanted to get me onto the futon, but it was still giving his full attention for this moment, to me.

Well, I thought, here we are in the Limina.

"You'll take it?" His white shirt glowed in the dim room. The collar was open and his chest showed. He looked slighter than usual to me, more boyish, immensely appealing. Offering things to me like some kind of courting bird with colored stones.

I said, "Okay, yes, I'll try it." And then I went nearer. I stood in front of him, and he was as passive as Robby. I touched him just on his jawline, both sides. "How much of this did you plan?" I said, putting my other hand on the other side of his face and using those jaws to pull myself forward.

He wrapped his arms around me. We started with an embrace. There was not a kiss but a matching up of limbs and torso, pressing my chest to his, legs to legs, arms outstretched.

"Seriously," I said, "Did you plan this?"

He was silent. He assumed a waltz position and backed me toward the futon. I let him do it, tingling at each point we touched. He wasn't talking, and that was okay, I wanted to see what this felt like, and it was one of the freshest, simplest love makings I've ever had. It was fluid and equitable. I had been afraid of him, but he was like a girl, I thought, not that I had much experience in that line. No, I realized, like a boy. I pulled my head back at one point and said, "I've got condoms in my room–"

But he had one with him. Which was the one thing that broke the spell momentarily, that he had indeed come prepared. But didn't I know this? Wasn't I glad he was prepared?

It passed quickly, the little flat note. We were like puppies, as if he were my little boy across the street. I thought once before I let myself go under, Of course he planned it, but wasn't that a sign of his attentiveness to me too?

Later, when we were lying quietly, I looked at him lying on his back, eyes closed, cheeks slack, and I thought maybe he was older than I'd guessed. I said, "Is this one of the perks of Love Palace? Is this how you hold everything together?"

He kept his eyes closed and seemed slightly sad. I didn't think he really wanted to talk, but I did. I said, "I don't want to hurt Robby."

He nodded. "Robby needs you."

"And you." He put one hand on my breast. I said, "We're not playing in a modern version of Wings of the Dove. That's a Henry James novel about a triangle. The two lovers make a plot so the man can marry a rich sick girl who will die and let them be together."

He stopped stroking me and propped himself up on one elbow and only now opened his eyes. Then he began to dress himself and me. He didn't hurry, and he continued to be extremely attentive, handing me my underwear. Reaching for my jeans before he put on his own. God, he had a flat stomach. Even Robby was softer around the middle than John. A naturally lean and hungry body.

"Do you work out?" I asked. "You don't tell anyone anything about yourself."

He smiled. "Martha, Martha, Martha," he said.

For all of his apparent leisureliness, he seemed to have other things to do today.

"For a preacher, you don't talk much," I said. "And you seem to be in a hurry."

I expected an argument, an explanation. Instead, he pulled me to my feet and stroked the hair back from my face. "You are a beautiful human being, Martha," he said. "You have no idea of your potential."

Then he kissed me on the lips, for the first time. And then he smoothed the futon, neatly wrapped the used condom in a tissue and dropped it in his pocket. He went out, leaving no trace of our having been there, except the apartment key on the futon.

I walked around the second floor for a while. I had accepted the key, so that meant I was taking the apartment, didn't it? But what did taking the apartment mean? One thing I was sure it meant was that I had to be through with Robby. That this whole relationship with Robby was a mistake.

I waited for a reaction. I told myself I had had sex with John just for a lark. I didn't believe it. I had a session scheduled with Madame for the next morning. I would straighten it out then. I should be relieved that the nonsense with Robby was over.

Back in the office staring at the bank statement again, I thought I would be a fool to take the apartment. That I was a fool even to think of staying here. That I should pack up now and go to my sister's. Or get in the Guzzler and drive west.

But what about Nana? Not that I had been visiting her. That I did feel guilty about. I had a brief thought of taking the apartment and bringing her to live with me. I'd give up men, do the job here and take care of Nana. But I hadn't been to see Nana in so long, I had no idea if she could even sit up anymore. They probably didn't have my name on the visitors' list. Did your name have to be on the list? It wasn't prison, was it?

My eyes were still out of focus over the bank statement. Would John call me and say it had been great? Or to say, Let's not do this again. No, I thought, he would go on to his next appointment. I sat for a long time. I had never heard the building so quiet. Where were the kids? Where were the clients?

The phone rang, and I grabbed it, expecting John, but it was Robby calling from Pinnacle. His parents wanted him to stay over, and they wanted me to come out for dinner. They were eager to meet me.

I immediately lied: "Oh, sorry, Robby, I have plans with my sister. Besides, I thought I was going to meet your mother anyhow on Wednesday at the Free Market. You stay, though, and make your mother happy." Stay, I thought, so I don't have to face you until after my session tomorrow.

I could hear a female voice in the background, more femme than I'd expected. How about this weekend, she was saying when it was clear I wasn't coming tonight. The Free Market is too busy for a real visit. Robby sounded disappointed, but passed on the invitation for Saturday.

"Saturday's fine," I said. Saturday was far away. If I broke it off permanently with Robby, he could go out and be comforted in the bosom of his family. Foolishly, I added, "I'm thinking about moving into the apartment that I didn't even know existed."

He sounded thrilled. "Did John show it to you? If you're thinking about the apartment, that means you're thinking about staying."

"I haven't decided. I'm thinking about it."

"You'll stay. You'll take the apartment and you'll stay."

I was annoyed. Robby was a darling, and Robby had suffered in his little life, but he was also a boy who was accustomed to getting what he wanted. I said, "I'm talking to Madame L. first thing tomorrow. Then I'll decide. About the apartment. Just about the apartment."

"You're going to take it," he said with a little more bass in his voice tone than I was used to. Then he seemed to pull the phone very close to his mouth and whisper. "And then we'll get married."

"No," I said. "That is really not going to happen. Sorry, Robby."

"Yes, it is."

Didn't he pick up in my voice that he and I were almost definitely over now, totally impossible? "Shut up, Robby," I said.

"But you know what I'm thinking."

Then he told me to say hi to my sister for him, and for a second, I didn't know what he was talking about, then remembered I'd said I had plans.

Something about talking to Robby changed the tone of the day for me: he always cheered me up, even when he was sad. Of course it was over between him, and me, but I still cared for him.

I called Mari, figuring that my lie would be less bad if I at least talked to her. I caught her walking down the street somewhere. I said, "I don't suppose you're available for dinner tonight?" She was silent. I thought for a second the connection had broken. "Mari?"

Then she said, "To what do I owe this honor? And no, I'm working late tonight."

"Okay," I said. "I thought you might want to see my new apartment. Or maybe, help me decide if I want it. I may be taking this new apartment. They're including it as one of the perks of my job. Do you want to come over and see it tomorrow?"

She had to finish up something important, she said, but maybe Wednesday.

"Well, I haven't completely decided to take it. I may not stay here at all. I'm still thinking about moving to California. Or Oregon."

"Then why do you want me to see the apartment?"

"It's complicated. I probably will take it. I mean, it's free and it's got a private bathroom."

"Do you want me to come or not?"

"Yes, come, please."

I was about to hang up, but she said, "I went to see Nana yesterday."

"Oh God. Look Mari," I said. "I know I don't go. I know you go every two weeks."

"Sometimes every week."

"I'll go with you. Soon."

"She's not going to last long, you know."

Yes, Mari, yes, I repeated in my head as the conversation ended. I'm the bad sister, you're the good sister. I've always been very bad.

10

Madame, of course, when I told her everything, ticked her tongue against her teeth and said Martha, Martha, Martha just like John. "What will we do with you Martha?" she said. "First you have sex with the young boy and then you promise yourself not to have sex and now you are having sex with the cult leader."

There was so much wrong with what she said, that I just stretched my legs on the couch, and focused on the nearest of her crowd of oil paintings: a small brownish oil of a tidal scene– hill, sand, some foam and rocks. The little seascape had a frame three times as big as it was. She also had a bust of herself done in orangish stone by a grateful patient. I thought it was an appalling act of hubris to have that sitting in her treatment room. When I complained, she always asked me what the bust meant to me.

She said in that same long-suffering tone, "Martha, Martha, Martha, what will we do with you for accepting the advances of any handsome man who comes your way? What will we do with you? This is dangerous for your health as well as for your psyche."

"I'm living in the moment, Madame," I said. "I'm living in the moment and also using condoms. I came to sort this stuff out, not to be condescended to by you."

"You confuse sexual desire and needing to belong. You are becoming promiscuous again."

"That's not true! It was a one-time thing. It just happened. And it makes me feel beautiful, okay? Did you notice? I've lost five pounds."

She was silent for a moment. I could hear her changing directions slightly. "I noticed that you had a glow. I see now the glow is from sexual indulgence."

"You are such a bourgeois prude," I said. "I mean it. It had been six long months since I had sex at all, not counting one quick overnight with Rachman when he was in town. Then Robby, and now this. It was merely companionable–"

"It is the most intimate act between a man and a woman–"

"Says you, Madame. It's an important part of a relationship, but it certainly doesn't have to be, and it's certainly not the main thing. I will be perfectly happy if John and I never do it again. In fact, I think it's likely that we won't. It was just a thing– we got carried away."

"Carried away?"

I had already told her the whole thing, at least in outline. But when she repeated my words and then closed her mouth to let me think it over, unresolved details came bubbling up like flotsam after the Titanic. "I didn't do anything wrong," I said. "I mean, okay, it probably would have been better not to do it, but it was just like the kids say, hooking up. I'm free and he's free, as far as I know."

"And what about your young friend Robby?"

"What about him? Robby is what you said, my young friend."

"Who wants to marry you."

"I don't want to marry Robby. The whole point of this is that I'm living on the edge, in the Limina as John says. It's true that I'd been– what should I say– admiring him. I was interested. I guess I am interested. He's got charisma, Madame, he really does. And a lovely natural fragrance or else an expensive cologne. He's even famous, a little. Do you remember I told you about the prison riots and how he was a chaplain and saved lives?"

"Are you then one of these grouper girls?"

Once again, I was appalled that I could understand exactly what she meant. "A grouper is a kind of fish. And no, I'm not a groupie. That not my style at all. What I am, I think, is in a state where I could do anything. I feel like everything is mine, and I am tasting what the world has to offer."

"This is an addict's high, Martha. Always you have looked for this dangerous high. This is like the Sports Teams in your old town–"

"Don't start Madame. It was three guys on one team."

"With Robby, you have had a kind of relationship."

"And you decide what's a relationship and what's not? I sleep with Robby. It's a very limited relationship. It's not getting married, which would be crazy. It's also true that he's fragile and very attached to me and to John. So maybe by some lights, this thing with John was a mistake. But I have no commitments to anyone, so if I don't do it again, I'm okay? Yes? I mean, I didn't promise Robby I'd be faithful."

She drummed her fingers. "I cannot explain this religious leader," she said. "Why would he fall into this? What is his motivation?"

"My charms?" I said.

"He is perhaps a sexual addict too," she said.

"Oh God, Madame," I said. "He's not on the couch, isn't that what you say when I start analyzing other people? And besides, isn't that what all religious leaders do? They want to merge with their flocks? Through sexual connections with their flocks? Not that I intend to be part of his flock."

She shushed her nylons, a sign that the clock was approaching the end of my hour. "And for you, of course," she said, "this is once again your father."

"I thought it was the whole Randall football team."

"You may make jokes, but you are in a crisis. Always you set yourself up with men who are distant from you, established and older men—"

"Unless they're fragile younger men."

"Men who will leave you as the father left you. Seriously, Martha, I think I want you to swear away from this man, from having sexual relations with him, until we have completed our analysis of this."

"I already said I wasn't going to do it with him again."

She said, "You do these things to thumb your nose at your lost father. To show him you don't need him. You set yourself up for failure with the mature man or you do things to shock and displease the father. You do not have such a good a record with men at the track. I ask myself with each new man: has Martha now given up her habit of promiscuity? How is this man different from the sad defiant business with the baseball team?"

"It wasn't baseball! I wish just once you'd bother to get something straight about American culture. It's disrespectful not to get the details right about someone's culture. It was football, American football, not British. And it wasn't the team, it was three boys. You never miss an opportunity to bring up the Randall Football Team."

"It is, I believe, central to your psychological narrative. You bring it up often yourself."

"It's different when I bring it up. When you bring it up, it's prurient. It was only three boys, and we were all high."

"Ah," she said, and I could feel her serene smile, her pale hair flipped under, her high cheekbones and half-closed eyes, slanted, a genetic legacy from the Golden Horde. "We will talk more next time about your father and the team and your old and young lovers."

She was right, of course, about the meaning of the Randall Football Team incident. I blame it squarely on my father. I also blame Mom, who only came to see us after another man had treated her badly. You see the connection, of course: bad treatment from men equaled an opportunity for me to be with my mother. Or something along those lines, the thing about psychotherapy is that meanings shift as needed.

The football team incident was at the beginning of high school. Mom had just blown in once again with her urban doxy/ rhinestone cowgirl vibe. Even though Nana was the mother of the Rotter, she and Mom got along very well, and Mom was always welcome. Mari and I were thrilled when she came and devastated when she left. She always promised she was going to get married and make a home for us, and there were a couple of failed efforts, once for half a year down near her relatives in West Virginia in a godawful little mildewed house that we hated. It had spiders and orange water and weeds, and we hated the kids at the school. I was already beginning to go a little Goth at the time, and it was before I experimented with religion, so I was a really bad fit. I took the bus back to Nana, and as soon as the school year ended, Mom brought Mari back too. By the beginning of high school, I couldn't look at Mom without critiquing her boots, her hair, everything about her. She crowded us. She filled our four rooms with her suitcase and make-up kit. She laid into my orange hair and didn't understand that you were supposed to know it was dyed. Nana always stepped aside when Mom arrived, because, after all, Mom was the mother. Nana just made a pot of something gray for dinner and went out to a political meeting. I think she and Irv were making a popular front with the anti-nuke people in those days. Mom went on and on about how she was going to get this terrific job in a ski resort, and as soon as she was settled she was going to buy a beautiful condo on the slopes and send for me and Mari.

This time I stared her in the face and said I didn't believe her and I was never leaving again. It certainly wasn't that I loved old Randall High, although, in retrospect, I guess I really did love Nana and our overheated four rooms over the florist.

Mom took it personally, and screamed that I didn't appreciate what she'd been through for us goddam it to hell. Mari had been hiding out in the bedroom, and she appeared and said she had to go to the library, but I stuck around and cursed out Mom, and then Mom floundered around packing her stuff, and finally left it half packed and went out to a bar or somewhere. Who knew, who cared. I was the last one left standing, as it were.

I had started having sex earlier that year (reconstruction of time sequence here thanks to Madame Landowska), right after Mom's previous visit. I don't know how much I liked the boy, but I liked sex very well. I wasn't orgasmic yet, but I definitely liked the touching inside and out. So that night I called my boyfriend, but he was at his fast food job and I was alone in the little apartment where the heat had come on and I was sweating already, and no boyfriend, so I called this other boy who I had begun to be interested in anyhow, a guy in my math class I talked to sometimes, the second string center on the football team. Even though he was a jock, we hit it off and enjoyed each other in a dumbass way. In fact, if things had gone differently, we might have actually gone out in the end as I was getting tired of the first boyfriend.

But what happened instead was, I called him, and he was home alone, and he invited me over and we went downstairs to his family room and started to make out. We did some grass, which he didn't have much of, and drank some beer, and then we fooled around some more, and then he said, Hey, let me call my friend, he's got some great grass, we'll have a party.

Fine by me, all I wanted was not to go home and see Mom or Mari or Nana, and the friend came over with another friend, with the grass and some beer and a slasher movie, and I don't know if the rest was planned or opportunistic, probably opportunistic, but it doesn't matter because how it played out was no surprise to me, and I was a full participant. After a few joints and with music on and the sound on the movie off, and some more beer, my friend started showing off, kissing me and touching, while the other two pretended to watch the video. I could have walked out at any point. I mean, I was hardly high, and we aren't talking rapists here, we're talking off-season j.v. football players on a week night. More to the point, we're talking mixed-up, low self-esteem Martha, who thinks, Fuck it fuck it fuck me.

So after a while, the other guys start snuggling up too, and then old Martha dances for a while, all by herself, and then she strips down to her underpants and dances some more with her breasts bobbling– okay, Madame, I stripped down to my underpants– I, Martha, and I had one of my times when I really felt the beat of the music and that was all that mattered and I felt like my body was actually good for something and pretty soon I was on the couch with the second boy and then the third one.

And the other funny part is, whatever tales the three of them told next week about banging and fucking and such a ho'– in spite of how my first boyfriend was crushed and full of rage and started even worse stories about me out of revenge– in spite of how I regretted and suffered, I want to say that I was not surprised. I knew when we started drinking and smoking that I was going to regret it, and it was as if regret was something solid and dependable in the world. I wouldn't say that I knew exactly how much I was going to regret it, but I knew I would be sorry. And I said fuck it. Fuck it Mom, fuck it Daddy.

But I also want to say that, the thing itself, the party, was not bad at all: nothing rough, just getting naked with three boys and fooling around, and they said the nicest things about how soft I was, and how beautiful I was–and I still believe that for that moment, we really were having fun, and I was in charge because I was beautiful, and they wanted me.

They thought they were in pig heaven and invited me over on Saturday night to one of the other boys' houses, and it was probably how I said No that sparked the retribution. This would no doubt have happened at some point, anyhow– the rumor of photos, the story that I had done the whole team. All the delighted innuendos and exaggerations. For six weeks I wore mask-thick amounts of white make-up and the same oversized black sweater tunic with big shoulder pads every day. I felt the backside of me–neck to buttocks and upper thighs– burning in the eyes of my fellow students. It was as if the back of the clothes had been cut away and my rear end was exposed, and I had to walk down the hall of Randall High past the cheerleaders' lockers and the student council office and the girls' bathroom with everyone pointing at my mandrill butt.

The guy called me again, and didn't exactly apologize, but I had the feeling he would have apologized or he would have arranged another party, depending on what I wanted. I told him I never partied with the same gang of losers twice. I was pretty dry-eyed and hard-shelled about the whole thing, and did not cry on my pillow, but no matter how hard I had tried to bake my protective enamel, nothing really hid the burning butt. It took the rest of the school year for the fun to die down.

Mari had to have heard about it, since the junior high was on the same campus as the high school. She stopped speaking to me for a while, and even Nana must have picked up something, because toward the end of the six weeks, I came in from school one day at a time she would ordinarily have been at work, and found her sitting on a kitchen chair facing the front door. She had on her black beret and her big black leather handbag, and she told me she had an appointment at the doctor for me. The doctor turned out to be an expensive gynecologist a couple of towns over. Nana paid cash out of the black leather bag, and I was surly, but disease free and not pregnant. I got fitted for a diaphragm.

The funny thing was that I had been celibate for the entire six burning weeks, and the trip to the gynecologist sealed my determination in some vague way. Maybe it was merely that Nana had let me know she was paying attention and taking care of me. The only thing she ever said was, "Love is a good thing, but you shouldn't let the *momzers* take advantage."

Once I had my own diaphragm and had finished my quick and brutal personal ride through the wages of sex, I began a major switchover. First I accepted an invitation to church from a girl who was such a fat loser that she may never have even known about the Randall football team. I hated her dumb church, but it gave me the idea to start my desultory survey of the varieties of religious experience in industrial New Jersey– more than you'd think, actually, including a colorful congregation of Charismatic Greek Orthodox, Jehovah's Witnesses, some Gaia Goddess Unitarians, and of course the Pentecostals and the Church of Holiness and Jews for Jesus. I had high hopes for the JFJ people for a while, but their story was as irrational as the rest and their singing sucked.

Meanwhile, along with the churches, I was using my reputation to get in with the little group of Goths and Deadhead wannabes, so few that they had to hang together in Randall. They called themselves the Skids, and with them, and, indeed, with the churches, the sex rumors added to your value. The church people were always making over me for conversion purposes, and with the Skids, I let the story grow and added what were supposed to sound like sarcastic exaggerations but might be taken either way. Oh yeah, I'd say, I have a thing for offensive linemen. Defensive backs are too dumb even for me, etc. etc. I never corrected the numbers, and I intimated that I knew where to find S&M clubs in the City if anyone every wanted to go. It didn't matter whether, if, or who believed me: the Skids were all of us into fantasy in one way or another: the boys did Dungeons and Dragons or planned bands that never got organized and Rainbow people summers that never happened. We sat in diners and ate Italian hot dogs while we discussed how to make the world safe for vegetarianism.

I actually enjoyed the rest of high school, at least off and on. The thing with the football players made me get serious about finding a niche for myself.

11

When I got in from my appointment, Cara met me in the office. She dropped onto the couch, round and pouty. She was dressed, too, her lovely full belly pooched over her tight and low shorts. She would be beautiful naked or even under some gauzy silky fabric but looked fat in pants designed for someone skinny. Like Kristen. Or my sister.

She said, "I'm looking for Gil."

"In the morning? In the office? When did Gil ever do office work? Doesn't it ever occur to you to play hard to get?"

She scrunched up her nose. "You act like it's still the nineties," she said. "When it was all feminist or whatever to hide your feelings. People are much more open now."

I said, "Well, it looks to me like Gil gets to do the picking and choosing."

She scrunched her nose again, trying for a superior sniff, but her face crumpled and she started to cry.

I had this feeling I was supposed to go over and embrace her or pat her shoulder at least, but it's not my style. I did manage to offer her the tissue box.

She sat up and blew her nose, and I sat on the couch too, so I wouldn't have to look at Prison Pietà. "I don't care about Gil," she said. "I mean, I care about Gil, but mainly it's just so depressing that everyone has someone except me. Robby has you and Kristen has Gil, and I just want somebody of my own. So I'm not alone anymore. Not that things are so great with Kristen and Gil. He went to the city last night without her and he isn't back yet."

"He stayed out all night?"

She almost smiled. "Gil doesn't believe anyone will ever look out for him except himself. Did you notice? His parents never respond to anything. They're glad he's off their hands. Gil doesn't trust anyone except himself. John says we have to be kind to one another while we're learning to trust."

"Is this from one of John's little sermons?"

She said, "John isn't like exactly a twenty-first century kind of person, but I think he's hooked into something timeless?" With a question mark at the end of her sentence. And then I wondered exactly how close John was to the kids.

I said, "Does he do one-on-one counseling with you?"

She blew her nose. "He would if we asked, I guess. But he

isn't here all that much. Gil isn't here much either. He's just hanging around till he figures out something better. Kristen's family is always offering her things? They aren't supposed to call, but they do. That was the agreement, but they call her all the time. My parents are between Kristen's and Gil's. Mostly, they leave me alone." She didn't look as if this exactly made her happy either.

I said, "Why don't you give them a surprise and call them first."

"Being away from them is the whole point! You don't think I want to talk to them, do you?"

"Honey, I haven't the faintest notion what you want."

"I want some money."

"Don't we all."

"No, I mean for the play group. We want to take the play group on a field trip today."

"What kind of field trip?"

"The movies. It's so hot."

I had a lot of thoughts, like What movies and How many kids? And no wonder the money seems to flow out of the accounts here like a busted water main. But instead I gave her fifty dollars cash. When she was gone, I felt more cheerful. Cara reminded me of me at that age, except for the crying, and I kept wanting to say, Things will get better! Or at least, you'll get used to how bad things are.

What the heck, I thought, I like it here, at least part of the time.

To make it official, I called Mari at the office. I love talking to the secretary and being put through. Oh, good afternoon, Ms. Miller, the secretary says. I'll put you right through to Ms. Miller.

Mari was not with a client or out for lunch. She picked up, and I said, "Hi, Ms. Miller, it's me, Ms. Miller."

"Oh," said Mari. "It's you."

"Did you know I've never had a job where they called me Ms. Miller? I've always been Martha, even when I was an adjunct professor they called me Martha."

"If you actually cared, you could have had people call you Professor."

"But I never cared. And here, at this place, it's like *de rigueur* that everything is informal. The place is run by an absentee charismatic religious leader and a bunch of teeny-boppers."

"Are you're taking the apartment?"

"Yeah, I think I will. I wanted to come and get some of the stuff out of your storage today. My television, some dishes. You know. Do you think you could call the super and tell him I'm coming?"

"Okay."

"I bet you thought it was going to be in your basement for the next twenty years. I bet you thought I'd never take it away."

"No, Martha, I always thought you could do anything you wanted to do."

"Be nice."

"Why are they giving you this apartment?"

"Because they have one. It's in the same building, and it's totally funky, but in a cool way, like something from a nineteen forties movie or an Edward Hopper painting. Not in the class of your condo, of course."

"You never did like my condo." She sounded bitter. I wondered if this was the first day of her period. "You're probably going to sit around your retro palace and feel superior."

You have to love your sister for assuming you've got the better deal just because you're the big sister.

She would call her super, she said, how was I going to move, who was helping me, and she'd take off Wednesday and come over see it and help me clean or something. I was touched.

Downstairs, the girls had decided not to take the kids to the movies after all. Gil had just got back with a bag of McDonald's for everyone. This was how they functioned, drifting from a plan for the movies to McDonald's. Even whether it was a "big kids" or "little kids" play group seemed to change depending on who needed babysitting, most often Esta Brown, so most often little kids. Still, it was cute, the Good News Crew and the kids. I went upstairs for the camera, and when I got back, Robby had come back too, wanting hugs and kisses.

"So guys," I said, "Do you think you can help me move some stuff this afternoon? In the van?"

Cara said, "If you need the van, you're going to have to put gas in it because Gil took it to the city."

I stared. "Do you mean to say you were in the city all night with our van?"

Gil looked strung out. He shrugged. "I'll pay for the gas."

Robby looked at me and then at Gil. "You should have asked, Gil. Seriously."

"Seriously, Robby, I don't have my mother forcing me to use her sports car all the time."

"Be nice," said Cara, apparently feeling better since everyone was back and squabbling.

I bit my tongue: what if Gil not only treated our van like his personal property, but also our money?

Cara said, "I was thinking we could still go to the movies, but if we can't use the van, Robby will have to take us in the car."

I said, "I think I need Robby and the van both to help me move my stuff."

"Into the apartment," said Robby. "She's moving into the apartment."

They all stared at me. "Wow," said Kristen. "The apartment!"

Cara frowned. "Who told you could have the apartment?"

"John." I had a feeling that I was saying his name in a strange way, that it stuck in my lips.

Cara said, "He never offered the apartment to any of us. Robby, why is John giving the apartment to Martha?"

"It was supposed to be for some homeless family," said Kristen.

"Or," said Robby, "for some married couple."

I said, "I was hoping someone would help me move a few things over here from my sister's."

"We have the play group," said Kristen.

Esta Brown's biggest boy had finished his Big Mac. "We're going to the movies," he said.

"No," said Cara. "We had McDonald's instead."

The kids started whining and Robby offered his car, but there weren't enough seat belts, and this whole thing of taking kids around in private cars seemed pretty sketchy to me anyhow, so in the end, the girls agreed to take the kids on the bus, and I took Robby and Gil and the van, and I drove. Down Water Street past the empty lots, past the looming post-modern presence of Riversedge Renaissance. Then came several blocks under renovation, and finally the Warehouse District and Mari's fancy apartment in the former factory.

Moving my stuff took longer than I expected, but we worked well together, Gil and Robby lifting. The two of them were just the same height, with similar builds, Gil a little rangier in the shoulder department, slightly longer leg to torso ratio, Robby dark blond, Gil with that exotic stiff red-brown hair and tawny skin and eyes. I had a passing fantasy of keeping them both with me like a brace of Irish setters. Okay, I imagined a little more, one on either side of me in bed, the blond and the bay, me wrapped in their lean limbs. Madame would no doubt say this was further evidence of my sexual addiction. Then she'd convince me that I would be much happier with some celibate treat like a soak in the tub with perfumed candles on the toilet seat or maybe a nice plate of cheese pirogi.

We worked up a major sweat in the heat, and by the time we got back and dumped the stuff in the main room of the apartment, the sun was turning all the buildings a deep saturated red. Gil said he'd had it, and he was going to bed. The girls weren't back yet, so we told Danny Boy he should maybe do cold cuts instead of stew for dinner, and Robby and I went out.

We were the last couple in a Chinese restaurant that Mari had recommended. We had to go back toward the Warehouse District, but just a couple of blocks. It had been the China Tea Cup for about a million years, and then when the area began to come up, they remodeled and started cooking their actual original native cuisine, which they remarkably remembered how to cook after all the years of chop suey. Or else smuggled over some native cooks.

It was really good, and Robby started saying how the only thing that would allow him to accept the instability of life in the Limina would be for me to marry him.

"Stop that nonsense, Robby," I said. "It really won't work. You're a darling, but I can't marry you."

I was feeling calm and relaxed, even hopeful. What had happened between me and John? Nothing real, that was for certain.

Robby tipped his head sideways over the sautéed dried string beans and said, "Please pretty please marry me Martha."

"You need a haircut, Robby."

"You can give me all my haircuts once we're married."

"You can't expect to do something as grown up as get married when you expect other people to make all the decisions— where we're going to eat, what movie if we go to the movies—"

He reached over the table to take my hand. His wrist passed too close to the rice and had sticky grains on his wrist bone. "I have something for you," he said, and I had this awful cringe that it was going to be a ring, but no, out of the canvas newsboy bag he'd been carrying, he pulled a white box stamped with a fancy gift shop name in Pinnacle.

I opened it, pushed aside the crumpled paper, and found an utterly simple utterly beautiful crystal pear.

"It's a paperweight," he said, "but it seemed clean and strong, like you."

I held it in both hands, a perfect pear, a lovely pear, heavy-bottomed like me, a pear resting in my hands, the stem incised lightly in the top, a hint of abstraction against the fullness of the fruit.

"Martha," he said, cupping his hands around my hands around the crystal pear, "you have made such a difference in my life. They all say so, Gil, John, my mother. I know you only love me in a certain way. But love is love, whatever kind it is, when there's so little time."

"So little time for what, Robby? Who said there's so little time?"

"I don't know. I didn't mean that." His eyes were raking over my face, very wide, wetness in them making him glitter. "There's so little time because it all changes so fast."

"You don't have to take John so literally. You're just a kid. I'm twenty years older than you, Robby. You and Gil joke around like little kids–"

"What's that got to do with anything? I don't want to marry Gil," he said. "I want to marry you. I want you in my life. Every day."

"I'm already in your life."

"I had been doing all this rule-following. And John is making it clear that Jesus isn't about rules, that Jesus is about freedom. That we can be free." Is that it, I thought vaguely, to do whatever you want? Which is certainly what John appears to do.

I said, "I think you want me to take care of you, Robby."

"I want us to take care of each other," he said. "And I'm much less needy than I was. I'm full of hope." He straightened his back suddenly, seemed to have hit on what he viewed as a real winner of an argument. "Besides, Martha, I'll take care of you! My parents– they're on board with this. We can buy things, if you need anything. I've already told them I want to marry you and they're thrilled. "

"You have to stop telling people."

He grabbed my hands and closed them around the pear. He kissed them. "Please please please," he said, kissing up my knuckles and onto my wrist. "Please, please–"

He told me he had never been so happy. Every time I told him no I wouldn't marry him, he said he just knew this was going to work out. I drove back to Love Palace, and Robby fell asleep. He laid his head back the same way he did in bed– tipped back with a slight smile on his lips, throat extended and exposed, arms relaxed in his lap. I loved to run my hands over his smooth shoulders, to lift his legs at the calf, feel the weight, hold parts of his body. Maybe a third of him, chest, legs, covered with a soft, brownish gold hair. He often went a day or two without shaving, and little prickles came out on the front of his chin and along his jaw. They were golden too.

I tried to remember what it had been like with John, and I remembered it had been fresh and childish, somehow having more to do with Robby than with John. How could I marry Robby? I'd be able to get senior tickets to the movies when Robby was my age now. He'd be just filled out and mature when I was beginning to shrink into old age. Of course, it would never last that long. I was far better at bad relationships than at good.

I drove slowly, wondering. If I married him, what about John? Would I still see Rachman when he was in town? Would I try to have a baby? Would I get tired of running my hands over Robby's beautiful straight limbs and watching the tiny smile play over his lips? Would he not, sooner or later, begin to become less passive and grateful in sex and begin to seek out what pleased his eyes, which I couldn't believe was my body with its pear-shaped bottom. Models are used up by the time they're twenty-five, and movie stars my age are playing the mothers of men they went to high school with.

On the other hand, there was the medical insurance. I was definitely getting too old for no insurance. Probably dental too. And it was flattering, that he liked being with me. We had fun. We had things in common.

Like John.

That was disturbing. John was always disturbing.

I drove the long way around while I thought. Up the hill, past a little row of shops, Jo-Jo's Caribbean Cuisine greasy spoon, the massive Bishop Stebbins apartments, some as blank as tombstones in the night and others with lights, knots of men clustered under the street lights.

"Wake up, Robby!" I said as we came down the home stretch past the Blue Lagoon. He released a couple of little sobbing breaths, and then turned his face toward me and yawned. "You're amazing. You just drift off in the middle of a conversation."

"I'm still in recovery," he said. "Did you say yes you'd get married while I was asleep?"

For a moment, everything about him annoyed me. Especially his hospitalizations in better places than I ever had a vacation in. "Give me a break, Robby. Get a life. Go back to college."

"I never started college."

"Oh, don't take everything so literally. It makes me nervous."

"Brides are always nervous. Eleanor is so looking forward to meeting you."

"What's she planning to talk to me about?"

"About how supportive they'll be if you say yes."

I parked in front of Love Palace.

"Really, Martha," said Robby. "When will you decide?"

"It's a no, Robby. It's almost definitely a no. It has to be no. It's too ridiculous to be anything but no."

He grabbed my hands and made me do an awkward galumphing dance to the door. "You're going to say yes," he said. "Eventually. I can wait. We're going to have a wedding. My mom will make us a wedding."

If I did decide to marry him, I thought, there would certainly be no wedding. The experiment with celibacy, on the other hand, was over.

12

On Free Market day I woke up and remembered that not only would I be meeting Robby's mother and seeing John, it was also the day Mari was coming to help me set up my apartment. I was alone, as Robby had spent another night in Pinnacle to help his mother. I started down to the lounge to see if Danny Boy had made coffee, but I was stopped on the mezzanine by a movement in the office. Ace, wearing a blue blazer, was using the copy machine.

He looked at me over the top of his glasses. "I'm making copies for my class."

"Don't they let professors make copies at the college?"

"Yes, but I'm running late, and you have to line up for the adjuncts' machine. It's a class system there too: a copy machine that only works part time for the untenured. Do you have a problem?"

"I don't know." He continued making copies. I added, "It does seem like a lot of people use this place for their own business."

He looked at me over his wire rims. "The Love Palace corporation is supposed to be here for the people. I don't do this all the time. If you want me to stop, speak up now because I'm almost finished."

I sat down on the couch so I wouldn't see the Prison Pietà, but I could feel its presence over my head anyhow. "I ought to put out a jar and people could at least make a donation when they make copies."

To my surprise, Ace said, "That's not a bad idea. This joint is like some giant giveaway most of the time. Especially today when your people come to enjoy the spectacle of everyone scrambling for the freebies."

"My people?"

"The Lady Bountiful Church Ladies."

"I'm not a Church Lady. And besides, I thought you said the problem was that nobody but antique dealers came to the Free Market. That it wasn't really for poor people at all."

"That too."

"I'm having trouble getting my brain around some aspects of this place. Somebody is stealing money."

Ace shouldered his bag. "I hear Father John gave you the apartment upstairs."

"And it's a rumor mill."

Ace said, "There'll be families needing that apartment soon, the way things are going. Housing is what people need, not used Cuisinarts. We should all be working for universal health care and affordable housing and a redistribution of wealth."

I followed him out and down the stairs. "Sometimes you sound like some kind of old time communist."

"I am."

"Nobody's a communist anymore."

"I'll tell you about the Party one of these days."

"Are you serious? The Communist Party?"

"Not the CP," he said. "Progressive Labor. The real communists."

"You're a college professor and a Communist?" I said. All I could think of was how much I would have enjoyed telling Nana, if I ever visited her. Or if she had been *compos mentis*. They had especially valued black communists back in the day.

Ace said, "Someday people will look back and be amazed that we lived without guaranteed housing and universal health care."

"What kind of health insurance do Communists have?"

"It depends on their day job. Me, none. They don't do insurance for adjunct professors. Besides, it's an act of solidarity with my uninsured brothers and sisters," said Ace.

"Oh bull," I said. "That's such a load of bull! Don't you know that the Iron Curtain dropped? Capitalism has prevailed, Ace! Ideology is so over!" I was suddenly yelling like a crazy lady. I was hanging onto the mezzanine banister like a bad actress doing *Streetcar Named Desire*.

Ace made a grand gesture with his free arm, and bellowed back, "That's ideology too! That's the ideology of the Bosses! That's the ideology that will convince you to let everything go on just like it is. And you're right about it being old. It's the way it's been for centuries!"

He stomped out, and the guys under the newspapers started to wake up.

My outrage dissipated. After all, I thought, he and Nana and Irv were probably right, but so what? It was too late for all that.

Danny Boy was sleeping in and hadn't made coffee at all, so I put the big urn on and asked the Franks to stack newspapers and clean out the toilet on the main floor. I was annoyed at myself for caring, but I wanted the white behinds of the Pinnacle Church Ladies to be able to rest on the seats if they so chose. Black Frank said they were supposed to push back the couches too, and I got out the Hoover so they could vacuum where the couches had been. Meanwhile, I was thinking about health insurance, and Ace not having any, and not me either since my old boss decided to cut back on extraneous expenses and demoted me to part time. If I married Robby, I could have insurance and investments and durable goods. Even if the marriage didn't last very long. I could redistribute a little wealth in my own direction. Robby wasn't asking me to say I loved him, just to marry him. What would be the harm? I'd go see my gynecologist, get my teeth straightened. This morning I had a bump on the inside of my gum that might be a stuck peanut skin or might be cancer.

Cigarette butts, newspapers, wastebaskets overflowing with doughnut boxes and coffee containers. The big table was cluttered with McDonald's wrappers and an ugly sticky brown spill. I got wet paper towels from the kitchen for that, reaching over Danny Boy's cot where he was sleeping and smelling not so great.

I was going to go upstairs to find something better to wear when a woman came in, and for a terrible second I thought the Church ladies had arrived early– but then I realized it was Mari. Her clothes always astonish me– I like clothes well enough, although for me it's always figuring out where to put the boobs. I tend to buy on sale, colors I like and then later decide if what I bought flatters me. Mari on the other hand, spends a good per centage of her salary on clothes. She was wearing the kind of casual tee shirt that you can pay a hundred dollars for easy. She didn't notice me immediately, just coming in, taking off her sunglasses, scanning the space with her special determination. She gives me an arpeggio of emotions: pleasure, identification, jealousy. Something I'm supposed to do and haven't yet. When she was an infant, my job was to entertain her, and I used to dance and tell stories and make puppets out of toothpicks and napkins, always watching her serious little face for a response.

"Yo Mari!" I shouted, and hurried toward her. We hugged, rather formally.

"Who's that?" she nodded toward the Franks moving furniture.

They were looking particularly moldy today, especially White Frank with his pale blond brushover and scrapes on his cheek.

"Clients," I said. "We've got everything here. We have a communist organizer and drop-out preppies and former mental patients. And these guys. Do you want a cup of coffee? What does it feel like to be off work?"

In person, she always surprises me. I think this goes back, too, to my first impressions of her as a baby. Then, it seemed like every time I noticed her, she had a new trick: she could walk, she was reading books; she had a cast on her forearm; she was getting breasts. I had done all those things before her, except for the cast. I had my period first, went to high school first, had sex first, got my driver's license. But that was about the only way I won the competition: Mari had never, not for five minutes, not during the monthly bloat, had a weight problem. She never got a D, she never was a scandal for her sexual misconduct. Was always presentable, always correct, even this early in the morning, coming to help me wearing that outrageously expensive tee shirt.

As we sat down with our coffee at the big table, I said, "What color is your tee shirt?"

Her chin made a tiny move to the left. "I don't know. What color is *your* tee shirt?"

"Mine is blue. Lenny's Fish House was giving them out free the last time I was there. But that's the point, my kind of tee shirt comes in blue, red, or yellow. Your kind of tee shirt has some thick rich edible name. Lemon Mousse? Butterfat?"

She folded her hands in her lap. "I'll leave now, Martha, if you're going to be passive-aggressive. I came over here to help you out with your new apartment, but I'm not going to stay if you're going to do that."

I had to chew on the insides of my cheeks, because part of me wanted to do exactly that, the teasing, attacking, putting down. Maybe it was her hair, layered so that it never fell in her eyes and she didn't even have to wear a headband.

On the other hand, she had made this concrete offer to come over for the day, and you don't get that so often from your sister, or maybe you do, but I don't.

"I am in a mood," I said, trying for humility, "but I really want you to stay. I'm sorry. I've got who knows how many church ladies coming to do this tag sale thing, which is not my direct responsibility, but I have to be around. Also, I'm going to meet Robby's mother. That's the boy I've been telling you about."

"The one who has a crush on you?"

"Yeah, something like that. I'll tell you all about it later. All these women are going to descend from Pinnacle and Do Good. I'm hoping to stay upstairs and work on the apartment."

She said, "Is the tag sale thing why all those people are lined up outside?"

I hadn't known they were out there. Mari had things in her car, so when we went out, I was astounded and appalled by the line of people reaching from the door of Love Palace to the Blue Lagoon. At the front of the line were two short heavy women wearing silver bracelets and tight pants. They had two rolling suitcases each. Behind them was the second-hand shop guy and his weird son, and behind them, a woman wearing operating-room greens followed by old men and little girls and every age and gender in between. There were station wagons and vans parked on both sides of the streets. I didn't see a single person I knew except for the second-hand guy. They had folding chairs, thermoses and bags of donuts. It was a real multi-racial, multi-cultural crowd too: the rumor of free loot apparently floats everybody's boat.

Mari had little spots of color on her cheeks as she pulled Nordstrom shopping bags out of her trunk. She was unperturbed by the crowd, probably because she had no preconceived notions about what went on at Love Palace. Also, one of her great advantages in life over me has always been her ability to focus. She's near-sighted (contact lenses of course) which I theorize helps her blank out everything she isn't interested in at the moment. She used to do her homework at the kitchen table with me carrying on loud arguments with Nana about whether I could go to a concert while Nana's boyfriend Irv ranted about some item in the news that proved once again the moral bankruptcy of the capitalist system.

Whereas I seemed to be unable not to see everything at once, all the terrible possibilities for all the years of the future. Robby and his mother and John and Mari in the same space at the same time. Cancer of the ovaries and terrorist attacks in Jersey.

We went back in, and I gave Mari a tour of Love Palace. I felt unexpected pride in the stainless steel industrial-strength kitchen (even with Danny Boy sleeping there) and the office I had organized myself. She liked my crystal pear from Robby.

"You could use a secretary," she said. "You shouldn't have to do all the typing and inputting data yourself."

"Send me yours," I said, "while I'm waiting for the upgrade here."

She took it seriously. "I would, if you had, say, a half-day project. It would have to be for something concrete, though, like one set of data or organizing some file cabinets."

I said I'd think about it. We went upstairs, and I told her about the Good News Crew; about John's Reflections; Robby's worship of John or was it Jesus. I thought I did a good job of saying John's name in a normal tone. I also slipped in that Robby had rich parents. I didn't say he wanted to marry me yet. She's a good listener, interested in everything, reserving judgment. I expect that makes a good lawyer, always getting more information than you give. I told her about the rats and Ace and how we were going to find out who owned their building and then go picket him or something.

She said, "It shouldn't be that big a deal to find the owner, unless someone's making an effort to hide."

"Would you help us?"

She shrugged. "Maybe, but they're wasting their time. This whole area– I mean everything between my condo and the waterfront– it's all slated for renewal. It's way too late to save one little building."

"But aren't they required to leave some places for people to live in?"

"Required by who? What's in it for the developers?"

"Good press? A kinder, gentler, more compassionate greed? I don't know. But it's really unfair, you know."

"You sound like Nana."

"God, Mari, it had to rub off on us, you know, all that stuff she spewed."

"Well, it looks like it did on you, I don't know about me."

I felt oddly proud. Mari and I agreed that I really had to go visit what was left of Nana in the nursing home.

I showed Mari my old room, still with some of my clothes waiting for the closets in the apartment to get cleaned. The door to Robby's room was open, and there was no visible floor, only jeans, tee shirts, pages of music. I said, "It's remarkable to me how someone so beautiful and physically clean– he even shaves neatly– can live like this." I was beginning to creep up on telling her about the marriage proposal. "He's out at Pinnacle with his mom, helping load up for the Free Market. He thinks he's going to move in with me."

"Ah," she said.

"And I haven't said no yet. He's so pretty, Mari. Wait till you see him." We stared at his dirty socks for moment longer. Softly I said, "He wants to marry me."

Kristen spoiled the moment by coming out of her bedroom in what appeared to be a nightgown, although I suppose it may have been a dress. I introduced her. Kristen gave Mari a limply polite little handshake, and I led Mari down the hall to the new apartment.

It was its musty, orange-lit spacious self. She put down her bags, walked to each corner of the living room. "Lots of light," she said.

"I like it, although we're looking at decades of dust. I don't seem to have a natural affinity for new things. I was going to have one of the Franks bring up the vacuum cleaner."

"I like it, though," said Mari. She put her hands on her thin little hips and looked around. "Really, it's like you said, but it could be very nice. I'm going to work on the bathroom, if that's okay."

I said, "Did you hear what I said about Robby?"

She was still surveying the place. "You mean he wants to marry you? I wasn't sure if I was supposed to take it seriously or not."

"Of course not," I said. "I mean, I'm not taking it seriously. I mean, there might be reasons to do it, but he's much too young."

She said, "If you married him, you'd have to pick up after him all the time. I had a relationship once with this guy who trailed stuff behind him, you know, socks, wallets."

"Did I know him?"

"I don't think so. It was over before I got around to introducing him to family. He was the wittiest guy I ever went with, handsome, a lot of fun–"

"A good lover?"

"Yes, but I couldn't stand the mess."

"You broke up with him because he was messy?"

"It was more than messy, I think he was disorganized in some morbid way."

"Well, in Robby's case, I think he's just typical of his age." And then was sorry I'd mentioned age again so soon. I added, "They have a lot of money, Mari, so I'd get taken care of too. I don't have any savings."

"God you sound practical. So–Jane Austen."

We were silent for a second, and I was still waiting for the big question, did I love him? She shrugged. "I'm glad I'm going to meet him. But if you decide to do it, let me take a look at your pre-nups. Especially if he has assets."

She had her own agenda: she wanted to give me my gifts and clean my bathroom. She had actually bought bathroom cleaning supplies that her cleaning woman recommended plus a rug and toilet lid cover– Egyptian cotton, thick and textured. She pulled this stuff out of the bags saying she hoped I liked it, she had picked the natural color because it would go with anything. Since my bathroom had orange tiles and fixtures stained by to match, we agreed natural would be just fine. She had also brought me a ceramic soap dish, toothbrush holder, and tissue box cover in nice earthy colors. She was raring to go.

I was a little disappointed, of course. I hadn't meant to tell her about Robby at all, and now I was disappointed that she didn't want to discuss my love life. I might even have gone on to get her opinion on the lapse with John. But she tied on a little yellow head scarf and sprinkled abrasive powder in the tub. Her cleaner had told her to work from inside out, she said. I told her I was going to go down to see if the Church Ladies had arrived.

As I left, she said, "Mom would love a wedding."

"Well, that's enough to stop me for sure."

I changed clothes to meet Robby's mother, put on my rayon blend lavender camp shirt and jeans. Then I went down to the mezzanine to look over the action.

Which had definitely begun. Gil and the Franks were opening up the last of four long folding tables in the form of a big square. Well-dressed ladies were coming in like a fire brigade, passing shopping bags with even fancier names than Nordstrom to Cara and Kristen. Other women were laying out stuff on the tables: dishes, baby clothes, small appliances. Drapes and tablecloths, flowered linens, bed-in-a-bag sets that looked unopened. Gift boxes of soaps and candles and jars of honey and jam and tins of tea. Robby was rolling in a rack of what appeared to be silk shirts. I spotted John, surrounded by a flurry of women, just like at Tenants' Council. But one woman on the far side of the tables had not run with the others to cluster around him. That would be, I was sure, Eleanor.

She was tall like Robby with straight posture and medium-length hair, blonde of course, low-cut jeans to show off her flat stomach. Her butt was flat too. The butt made me suspect she was more like fifty than forty, and maybe even over fifty. She too was surveying the room, observing the disturbance around John, looking at the tables, and then she and I zero'd in on each other, and there was one frozen second, then she started waving and striding around the square of tables with the same easy lope as Robby. She intersected with Robby, grabbed him by the arm, and brought him toward me.

We met at the foot of the stairs. Robby was smiling at me, and she was frowning intensely. She didn't wait to be introduced, but exclaimed, "You're Martha!" She extended her hand before I could extend mine. "I'm Eleanor Peterson," she said, "and I have been so eager to meet you."

We shook hands. "Me too," I said, "I'm very glad." I was mostly glad to have it done and done quickly, to butcher Shakespeare once again.

She had excellent make up, but it didn't hide the laugh lines: she was definitely older than me, one of my fears had been that we'd be the same age. But it doesn't matter, I reminded myself. This is over with me and Robby.

She said, "Warren asked me to tell you he's sorry he can't be here today. He's looking forward to meeting you Saturday, although there's a chance he's going to be out of town, in which case he wants to take you to lunch very soon. But I expect him Saturday night!"

Robby said, "He knows better than to miss one of her dinner parties."

"Robby won't stop talking about you— This is probably the wrong moment to say it, but I think it's important to have one thing clear: I want you to know that we totally and unreservedly support you and Robby. Totally. No, don't say anything, sweetie–" (this to Robby, but she kept her eye on me) "and Warren can't get over your newsletter. All of us adore the newsletter! I don't mind telling you that we've been having a hard time with the Board— What are those kids doing with all that money? And then, like an answer to our prayers, documentation! Articles! And whatever Warren says, don't let him tease you– we loved the article about the Renters' Club!"

"Tenants' Council," I murmured.

"Warren knows that landlords don't always do the right thing, and as I said to him, it's a learning experience for those women, like job training."

Out of the corner of my eye, I could see John still with the Pinnacle women, but a couple of them had now detached and were coming toward us.

"Well," I said, "I'm finding it all extremely challenging, but–"

The women were waving at Eleanor. "I'm sorry," she said. "I don't want to interrupt, but they need me. We'll talk later–I have to know–with all that's going on–all you're doing–how are you finding the apartment?"

I don't know if I had expected her not to know about the apartment. I think I had a vague mental image of John being in charge and the Petersons and the Board off at some distance, benignly dispensing financial support and praise, but apparently Mrs. P. was on top of everything.

"Fine, it's great. My sister's here today, cleaning. She'll be down later. She's a lawyer in real life." This sounded stupid, didn't it?

"How wonderful. I can hardly wait to meet your sister." She separated herself from Robby, leaned back to me, touched my arm just briefly. "I want to say again, and it's last thing I'm going to say on the subject, I'm going to say it once more, we're so very grateful Robby has you in his life."

She pulled back, gave Robby a peck on the cheek and headed back for the action. For John. Who seemed to be watching us even as he was talking to the Pinnacle ladies. Watching us and approving.

Robby said, "She likes you."

Almost immediately Eleanor darted back. "Martha!" she said, "I want you to meet my friends–" And she introduced me in quick succession to what seemed to be about fifteen identical blond skinny women, all imitations of her, a little younger, a little older. Sorority sisters. Robby stuck with me, bless his heart, seeming in this social situation amazingly mature. He repeated their names for me. Then the Pinnacle ladies withdrew inside the square of tables like pioneers in circled wagons. I had meant to get the vacuum and go upstairs, but I thought I'd better stay to see a little of this, and also to exchange some word with John, to get that over with too.

Eleanor said, "Open up, Robby!" and Robby pulled open the doors, and the hordes burst in. It was pretty breathtaking, really. Out of self-preservation, I moved back toward the stairs, and found that John had joined me. "What do you think?"

Inadvertently I shivered. These were the first words he had said to me since– the incident. The sex incident. "About the Free Market? Or what?"

He smiled. There was as far as I could tell absolutely no change in his demeanor toward me.

I said, "It's the way sale days used to be at the big department stores, before malls. Like in the cartoons. And Eleanor was very nice to me."

He said, "We all are delighted with how you're pulling things together at Love Palace."

As if there were absolutely nothing between us. What did I want? A passionate whisper? When can I see you? I think I was looking for an opportunity to say Never again!

Instead, he was already moving away from me. Eleanor was

gesturing to him, Robby was approaching. John was going.

Well that was a letdown, I thought.

Robby was back, put his arm around me, asked me what I thought.

"Funny, that's just what John asked me. You mother is lovely, and the Free Market is a zoo. Seriously, Robby, who is this helping?"

I had a whiff of that healthy Robby flesh. "My mother," he said.

My eyes drifted across the room. The two heavy-set women with rolling suitcases were already leaving, their suitcases stuffed. John held the door for them.

Gil had a wallet. "Look it," he said. "It's real leather. I'm taking it. All I have is this old nylon sports wallet that's falling apart."

I said, "I thought you were supposed to make a donation if you took something."

"Oh yeah," he said. "Sure, like it would make a difference if I put in fifty cents." There had always been something a little underhanded about Gil in my opinion. He started putting bills from his old wallet into the new ones, crisp twenties.

The kind you get out of an ATM machine.

Robby leaned over and nuzzled my neck. Was Robby kissing my neck for his mom to see? Did John care? Did Gil have a Love Palace bank card? I don't have much natural talent for intrigue, neither the kind of game John was playing nor spying on potential thieves. I either understand something all at once, or I get to it so gradually I don't realize I'm working on it at all. Or else I never get it. I tried to glean something from Gil's face, his stiff reddish hair, his strange light brown eyes. He had freckles across his nose, on his smooth forearms.

I'll be watching you, Gil.

Gil was looking at someone over my shoulder, and I turned, and it was Mari coming down the stairs with her hair tied up fetchingly in the yellow bandana.

Everyone was delighted to meet her, Eleanor explained the way the Free Market worked and John held her hand and washed her in his light, and I was briefly, wildly jealous: he does that to everyone, I thought. That's how he makes you feel special. At least I'd never have to explain to Mari about Love Palace again. You had to know Mari to recognize this look, because she didn't smile, she didn't lean forward, but suddenly, she was no longer masked, she was totally present. John made sense of it all for her.

13

By the time the highway began its slow climb to Pinnacle, I was sorry that I had let Robby drive. I like to feel my exits are totally my own business. What if it turned out that I wanted to escape Robby?

"I shouldn't be coming," I said. "This is going to look like I'm making a commitment which I most emphatically am not making. Robby, are you listening?"

He smiled.

"Who's going to be there? I mean, your parents I know. But exactly who else? The church ladies from the Free Market?"

"I know you're anxious, Martha—"

"Just tell me who, don't try to calm me down."

"My parents and John and Olivia—"

"Olivia? Who is Olivia?"

He hesitated, then said softly, "My mother's cook-housekeeper."

"Oh my god, they have a staff? They have a staff? They have servants, Robby?"

"Olivia is the only one who's full-time. I've known her my whole life. She's like a member of the family."

"Oh please. Did you really say that? Does Ace know you have a servant? They're rich, aren't they? Your family is really really rich. Complete with a faithful family retainer— the only retainer my family had was my sister's dental appliance, and we were so poor I didn't even get orthodontics—"

"Olivia was the stable part of my life when everything was happening."

"Poor little rich boy. No, this isn't helping, Robby. Another time we can talk about your relationship with Olivia, what's bothering me now is the very existence of Olivia. I think you'd better take me home. This isn't working, Robby, it really isn't."

"Martha—"

"Rich people make me extremely nervous, Robby. People who have old family retainers and mansions and their own personal chaplains the way your mother has John—"

Robby pulled the car into the breakdown lane. He was already in the right-hand lane driving slowly, so it was done very calmly and deliberately. He pulled on the emergency brake and turned toward me. The night was coming on already, things would be cooling down. The passing cars rocked us.

"There's no reason for me to go to Pinnacle," I said. "I'm sorry, but our relationship has no future, Robby."

"Martha," he said, "my family has a lot of money. It's a fact."

"Right. My point precisely."

"It has nothing to do with us."

"Wrong."

"Most of the money is from my mother's family. But they're just people. They have problems like anyone else."

"I believe they have problems," I said, "but I don't believe they're like everyone else." I was astounded by how he was ignoring my insistence that there was no future to our relationship. When had he become so self-confident that he could tell me I was wrong?

He reached over with both hands, out of the dim light, and pulled me toward him. I closed my eyes. There was a silence except for the deep whizz of cars passing us and the tremble of the little car in their wind. I felt calmness seep into my head and down my shoulders. I opened my eyes, and Robby was still there, a mature, thoughtful, other-oriented Robby.

I pulled his hands away from me, but held them, and he in turn closed his eyes. "You're different," I said. "You've gotten older. Why do I feel like you're years older than I am instead of vice versa? When did you stop stumping for Jesus?"

He said, "I'm living for what's here now. You've helped me, John has helped me. I don't have to go out in public places and yell Jesus because the Jesus factor is working on me and in me and through me every day."

"The Jesus factor?"

"It's a quality, a state of being, Christians call it a state of grace, or getting religion, it doesn't matter. John's point is that the thing itself is what matters, not what you call it."

John, I thought. John John John. I sighed and released his hands. "Okay, Robby, I'm ready. I'm glad you're feeling better. I'm ready to go have dinner, but no commitment, and please don't make any wild statements about what can't possibly happen."

He laughed and took his time getting back on the highway.

I said, "This is at least partly me, I know. I confess I have a prejudice or a fear or maybe both about rich people."

"Me too," said Robby. "I won't say this at the house, but I do believe you're going to marry me, Martha. I love you not just because you make me better but because I want to take care of you too."

"If you do say this in front of your mother, I'll walk out, you know. If you try to pressure me with some kind of bizarre announcement in front of your family. I am not going to be pressured, and I'm not going to marry you. So don't even say the M word? Okay?"

He laughed. "Okay, okay. I already said I wouldn't."

I had been to the downtown of Pinnacle at some point in my life, although I wasn't sure when: shopping? To a movie? It had nifty shops and an old fashioned department store and fine churches and a landmark train station, but I'd never been to the residential areas. Which began with big Victorians and Queen Annes, expensive, but nothing I couldn't imagine myself having dinner in, but then we passed through a park, and on the far side, up another hill to the Estates, which were at the pinnacle of Pinnacle, as it were. many of them hidden by stone walls and gates and deep wooded properties.

The Petersons' house didn't have columns or pillars. It had a broad lawn, a low wall and a gate that might or might not have some security devices hidden in the structure, then a driveway among droopy fir trees and the house built low to the hillside.

"It's got great views from inside," said Robby, driving around the back. "It was designed for this site, my mother can tell you the architect. It's supposed to fit in seamlessly."

"Harmonizing with the land," I said. "The most expensive luxury of all."

The back side of the hill had garages and a parking area and probably some landscaping, but it was getting too dark to see the details. John's Lexus was there plus something small and nondescript. Robby parked, and started up stone steps. I paused to adjust my clothes. I'd worn my brown linen pants suit and a low cut camisole, but of course the linen had long since wrinkled. This is stage fright, I thought, as Robby opened the side door. Existential embarrassment.

We slipped into the climate control zone, a few more steps up into an enormous kitchen with terra cotta tiles on the floor and Italian tile splash guards, a skylight with hanging plants, a woman in a black dress at the stove– and then through the swinging doors Eleanor in white, "Robby, you brought her in the back way! Oh that is so Robby, Martha, we can do much better with a welcome here–you look lovely!" Then Eleanor up close with the quick kiss, her perfume and in the ambiance a fruity olive oil and garlic. Robby dragging me to the woman in the black dress.

"This is Olivia," he said, putting his arm around her shoulder the way he did mine sometimes in a kind of pride of possession, and she reached out for a shake: a tall, serious-faced dark-skinned woman, taller than Eleanor, not as tall as Robby, broad-shouldered. Hand strong and damp. I didn't quite get if the black knit dress was a uniform or not.

Olivia and I said we were pleased to meet each other, but I had the distinct feeling that in her mind the jury was still out, or perhaps the jury was already in and I was not what she had hoped for.

Eleanor kept the words swirling around us. Warren, unfortunately, at the last minute after all, was terribly disappointed, Baltimore, but he was going to take me to lunch as soon as he was back in town. This was going to be the four of us: her, me, Robby and John.

Oh no, I thought.

"And Olivia," said Robby. Olivia shook her head and went back to the prep table where she was assembling something with garlic and shrimp. "I insist," said Robby. "Olivia has to sit with us—"

"Of course," said Eleanor. "Olivia is family. She knows she's invited."

"Not a chance," said Olivia, with the smallest hint of the Islands in her voice. "I set the table for four already, and I have a meeting later."

"Church?" said Robby. "Is it prayer meeting or choir rehearsal? If it's prayer meeting, we have John, and we can have prayer just the same as your church."

Eleanor said, "You wouldn't want Olivia to have to reset the table if she doesn't want to, Robby."

Olivia looked him in the eye. "Not this time, Robby, baby."

He sighed. "The next time, Olivia. Or maybe better, you'll come to—" he glanced at me. "To any special celebrations, if we have any special celebrations, Olivia."

Olivia grunted, and Eleanor went off on a silvery peal of laughter and led us into an enormous living space with vast windows overlooking a deck and the view I had glimpsed from the parking area. On the far side of a dense mahogany-colored carpet was a wall unit with a bar and John mixing drinks. John in a pale leaf patterned Hawaiian style shirt tucked into slacks, looking as if he'd had a hair cut since the Free Market.

There was going to be contact. John was embracing Robby then turning his wide open smile to me, a smell of aftershave, no connection to who he had been when he were together. As if not even the same person. Was he never going to give any indication that something had happened between him and me? Did I want him to?

Of course I wanted him to. And immediately, it rose up in my mind, a little goal, the kind of short-term objective that makes me a decent organizer when I put my mind to it. I would speak to him alone tonight, if only for thirty seconds.

I was glad after all that I didn't have Robby's dad to deal with as well.

John passed out martinis.

"Oh Robby," said Eleanor when Robby took one. "Not that I mind you having a martini, heaven knows."

"I'm off the meds, Mom."

"Are you? That's good, I know, of course it's good that you're off the meds, but–"

John said, with a little more familiarity than I expected, and maybe even the tiniest hint of exasperation, "Leave him be, Eleanor."

It was such an old-fashioned locution, Leave him be, like something my mother's West Virginia relatives would say. Eleanor responded by relaxing, everyone quieter and calmer in John's presence, even me.

I said, "It's a lovely living room–"

Robby said, "This is the family room, the living room is up there," and waved vaguely at a second level, toward the front of the house.

"This is where we do everything, though," said Eleanor. "That space up there, it's been almost a total waste, once or twice we've had something formal there."

She didn't offer me a tour of the house. It occurred to me that tours were something lower middle class people did, like my mother, who assumed when she got a new apartment or townhouse or bedroom suite or whatever that the main business of your first visit was to see the new stuff. Take note, I said to myself: my mother is just as white and Anglo-Saxon protestant as Eleanor, but my mom's butt is still in the double-wide.

I would have adored a tour.

Eleanor going on about how she was always thinking of getting something smaller. Robby drinking one big defiant gulp of his martini, then setting it down. Eleanor directing her remarks to me, and John an observer as much as Robby, sitting on the arm of an easy chair.

Eleanor was the obvious mistress of small talk. I tried to chime in, feeling a little sorry for her having the full responsibility with two silent men and me, but everything I thought to say sounded wrong.

I was also starving. Olivia finally came in with a little plate of home-made croutons, each with a shrimp and a tiny heap of pepper, garlic and tomato. It smelled great, but there seemed to be so few. Robby didn't take any and Eleanor only took one. John ate a few, and I tried to hold myself to no more than twice the number John ate, but meanwhile my stomach growled and I was beginning to feel grumpy. If you were going to have hors d'oeuvres, it was my opinion that there ought to be a lot of them. And a platter of cheese in case anyone was really hungry.

I knew my attitude was not classy. So what. I was hungry.

Eleanor switched the subject to what Robby used to do when he was small, how long Olivia had been with them, and finally, Olivia appeared in the doorway again, and it was time for dinner. To my horror, there were still four shrimp things on the plate, uneaten. I was going to grab at least another one, but John appeared to be moving to touch my elbow, so I dodged into the dining area without eating any more.

Eleanor had said there were too few of us to use the big dining room, so we were eating in the dining nook which had a chandelier that hung from an extra-high ceiling with sky lights. We were bumped out into the night where the land fell away. In the distance were the lights of the airport and one of the distant suspension bridges.

I said, "It's like coming in for a landing, isn't it?"

"It's an inspiring view in all seasons," John said.

Eleanor put me on a banquette with the most views, John in the chair to my right. Robby slipped in on the banquette beside me. It wasn't going to be an easy getaway, and the martini without cheese and bread hit me suddenly. Olivia stayed with us, standing between Robby and Eleanor. She reached for Eleanor's and Robby's hands. Robby picked up mine and Eleanor took John's. For a moment, I didn't get it: what strange rite of the wealthy was this? A five-way mind meld?

But of course it was saying grace.

John said, "Let's close the circle, Martha, and bless our meal."

John's hand proved to be less alive and demanding than Robby's, but it was still John's hand, and I bowed my head but kept my eyes open just for safety's sake while John said one of his not-quite prayers, this one about the flourishing of our bodies because of the blessings of food and the flourishing of our spirits because of the blessings of fellowship. I didn't think he used the G word, but I was pretty sure he had blessed something. I was definitely feeling the martini and also feeling that I was surveying the entire East Coast.

Robby insisted on going into the kitchen to help Olivia, and they came back with cold cherry soup and little slices of nut bread, more like dessert than dinner in my opinion, but delicious of course.

"My mother made the soup," said Robby, and Eleanor pish-pished.

"That's about all I can cook, frivolous things."

"It's wonderful," I said, realizing I was almost finished, far ahead of the others. And had an insight that it wasn't the hunger that made you lower class, it was the need to grab the last chicken leg for fear Nana would give it to your little sister or Irv would inhale it between paragraphs on the coming collapse of capitalism.

"Would you like more?" said Eleanor.

"No thanks, no–"

"Take mine," said Robby.

"Absolutely not! Please! It was just so delicious that I got carried away. Like William Carlos Williams."

They stared at me, waiting for the punch line.

"It's a poem. A famous modernist poem? 'This Is Just to Say'– that's the title, it's a poem in the form of a note you'd leave on the kitchen table: 'I have eaten all the plums that were in the icebox?'" Shut up, Martha, I told myself, this group doesn't do poetry. You're talking too much. "I guess it doesn't sound so modern, does it, with an ice box instead of a refrigerator? Well, anyhow, Eleanor's soup was delicious. So sweet. And so cold."

What's the point of a degree in English these days anyhow, nobody gets the references.

"Delicious soup indeed," said John. "Sweet and cold, just as Martha said."

What the hell, I thought. I eat when I'm hungry, and I can quote poetry even if nobody gets it. I admit it made me feel a little lonely and sad, maybe even maudlin under the influence of the martini, and John was opening a bottle of wine now too. Too late, I thought, too late to be skinny and high class.

Olivia brought in beautifully grilled baby lamb chops with a clutch of tiny new potatoes and string beans on each plate. I noticed that John and I got three lamb chops each, Robby two, and

Eleanor one. Olivia said, "There's more in the kitchen. I just don't want to waste good food on these picky eaters."

John cut into it immediately and said, "Olivia, all I can say is that it is up to your standard, which is the highest there is."

She seemed to be waiting for me, so I cut in and took a bite too, and it was outrageously, splendidly, absolutely the best lamb I ever tasted. "That is amazing," I told her, "truly amazing." She nodded briskly and went back to the kitchen.

Eleanor bent her head and polished hers off with such speed that I began to doubt her upperclassness after all. "Robby, you're not going to push it aside, are you? You're so skinny!"

Robby said, "I'm not going to eat it. Someone can have mine, but I have to have the bones back so Olivia won't feel bad."

"Oh Robby!" Eleanor had this downright pathetic look that annoyed me. As if Robby held the key to her happiness. "Please eat!"

"I'm a vegetarian, you know that."

She turned to me with the pathetic puppy look. "I worry about him all the time– he had an eating disorder, you know–"

"Vegetarianism is not an eating disorder," said Robby.

"I don't mean now, I mean when you were a teenager. We didn't recognize it for a long time, we thought it was something only girls get–"

Robby tossed his head and snorted, filled his mouth with all the potatoes at once. "I was fucked up," he said. "Okay?"

It occurred to me that I'd never heard this side of Robby before, the boy trying to fend off his mother. That she made him as nutty as my mother did me. I don't mean she caused his mental illness, but just that she clearly drove him everyday crazy.

Robby went on. "I was totally fucked up, we all know that, but it doesn't meant that the factory meat farms and slaughter houses aren't fucked up too. Do you think if Jesus were with us today he wouldn't be out on a picket line outside the meat factories?"

John wiped his mouth. "Eleanor, didn't you tell me this was organic lamb, from a farm where we know the animals are treated humanely?"

"Yes!" said Eleanor. "Of course it is. I never serve Robby anything else. You know that, Robby."

He was looking at John. "I still can't eat it."

"I'll tell you what," I said, "I'll trade you half my potatoes and a bone for one chop, and you can trade the other one to John. My sister was a vegetarian for five years, and she still says it was the healthiest period of her life."

Robby did as I suggested, and John too extended his plate and took a chop. Eleanor looked ready to cry, but knocked back her wine instead. John refilled everyone's glass. Robby ate a tremendous quantity of potatoes and salad and beans.

I was finally no longer starving and only moderately drunk, so I decided it was time to direct the conversation in a way with some value to me. I asked some of my questions about Love Palace and the development of Water Street.

"Oh dear," said Eleanor. She had started gnawing with her front teeth only on her bone, holding it delicately between neutral-to-pink-nailed fingers. "I'm not sure of the details, " she said. "John? Do you know about the renewal plans around there?"

John shook his head, still eating.

I said, "It's the church, isn't it, that actually owns Love Palace?"

John nodded through a mouthful, and Eleanor said, "The mortgage or the title papers. I'm not sure. I guess the church holds the paper? The Board of Directors of Love Palace is certainly people from the church."

John smiled benignly at us other three. "You know me," he said. "I'm not a detail man. I'm interested in the heart of the enterprise."

"You are the heart of the enterprise!" cried Robby.

Oh please.

And suddenly I had the firm if somewhat boozy insight that I was not going to stand in line for John's attention. And that I wasn't leaving tonight without getting some recognition from him of what had passed between us, and letting him know it was over.

John said, "At any rate, the building doesn't matter, what's going on with those kids matters."

"And the other people on the street," I said. "Ace and his Tenants' Council."

"The women's group," said Eleanor. "Your article in the newsletter."

"They're afraid they're going to lose their homes," I said.

"Oh no," said Robby. "Definitely not. We'll make sure of that, right, John?"

Eleanor said, "I think you ought to do an article on how we're expanding the Love Palace work. About John's new campaign. Don't be shy, John, we're going to have a speaking tour, give the message in different venues."

Robby, who seemed to know all about it, said, "John's going

to speak to the world. But, John, don't forget, we still need you at Love Palace."

"I'm there," said John. "One way or another, I am always with you."

Eleanor had more to say. She was very serious about this speaking tour: lectures, television and radio. They appeared to be envisioning something really big, bottling whatever it was that John had. Olivia came back to clear, and again Robby helped. While they were out getting dessert, Eleanor excused herself to get a copy of some publicity she wanted to show me.

And it was my chance, John and me alone. I said as softly as I could manage, "You've been smiling all evening like the cat that ate the canary."

"I like being with people I love," he said.

"Oh please. Listen, I want to say, before they come back. I'm assuming that what happened between us last week, well, forget assume, I'm telling you, it was a one time-thing. It was very nice, it was lovely, but it was a mistake. Not a disaster, but I want it to stay where it happened, in the past. I don't want to have sex with you again. Do we agree on this?"

"You're very direct," he said, almost as if to himself. "You have a quality of directness that has a lot of impact. I don't think you recognize it in yourself. You try to speak to everyone as if the kingdom had come and we all knew each other face-to-face."

"Bullshit, John," I whispered. "You never answer questions directly. I want you to answer me on this one."

"What is the question, Martha? I'm hearing you ask that we keep that between us because it would harm people. I agree to that. "

"You agree that it's all over and we don't mention it?"

"I absolutely agree. You're thinking of marrying Robby, aren't you?"

"No! I'm not! It's impossible! That's not the point, I just don't want him hurt–"

To my utter amazement, with Robby and Olivia clattering a few feet away in the kitchen and Eleanor coming back at any moment, he picked up my hand, in plain sight on the table, between both of his, and began to chafe at it, lifted it to his lips. When he had said grace and held my hand, it had been cool, as if he wasn't quite there, but now my whole boozy body tingled.

Footsteps, I snatched my hand away, Eleanor back. She did the tiniest stutter step, as if she smelled something between us, then came in. Smiling but with a little nick of anxiety in her forehead.

"Come over here, Eleanor," he said. "Before Robby comes back. We have a pact to make. Give me your hand."

She sat down, laid her papers aside, offered her hand, and he reached his other toward me, without looking, and I gave it to him. "Now you two," he said, and her long slim fingers came for me too.

"Here it is," he said. "That we three should be thinking of Robby first, what is best for him."

"Oh yes," said Eleanor.

He nodded. "Martha, Robby is a very special person."

"I know that."

"You'll do what's best, Martha," said John. "We'll support you whatever you choose to do."

It was Eleanor's face shining up into his that struck me most, aside from his weird impudence, which I already knew about, I was struck by how Eleanor was all about John.

Oh my god, I thought. She's in love with him too.

Robby came in with plates. "What's going on?" he asked, seeing us all linked up again. "A conspiracy," said Eleanor with a high-pitched cry.

Robby put his plates down and sat beside me quickly, put an arm around my waist, his head on my shoulder. "Conspire me," he said. "I want to be conspired too."

John released our hands. "Namaste," he said. "Do you know 'Namaste?' It's a Hindi word that the Buddhists use too. It captures so much of what Jesus was trying to tell us. 'The Spirit in me meets the Spirit in you.'"

"That's beautiful," said Robby.

"I didn't know you were a scholar," I said.

"Can you do it as a lecture?" asked Eleanor.

At that point, Olivia brought us an almond raspberry torte. As soon as the coffee was served, Robby leaped up and made Olivia sit down, on the banquette with him and me. She ate a piece of the torte and we talked about Robby's childhood and my childhood, and by the time dinner was over, I felt that, like Olivia, I could be part of the family, sort of.

14

Warren Peterson' secretary called me on Monday to arrange lunch for Friday. I wondered if I could push it off till next week, or the week after. Maybe till the fall. But of course I said Friday was fine, and then I bore down on Love Palace and tried to think about nothing but work. John wasn't around, and Robby was sleeping with me in the apartment, which was much easier than celibacy, and of course my sex life gave me and Madame something to talk about.

I started on the next newsletter, and I listened to a couple more lectures from Ace. The Good News Crew came to the Tenants' Council meeting, and everyone got excited about a block party, which immediately started to grow into a Water Street Community Festival. Ace said it would be a good opportunity for building solidarity. Robby was sure the church in Pinnacle would lay out the money for it, and the idea was that maybe we could actually make back the money with donations and food sales. Music provided by the Good News Crew, of course, which got Gil interested in it.

Then, after the meeting, which went very well, I saw Kristen take a call on her cell phone, and when I noticed her next, the Good News Crew was gathered around her. Kristen was crying. "What's up?" I said to Gil, who was standing to the side with his arms crossed over his chest, making a face. Robby and Cara were kneeling beside the couch hugging Kristen. "They told her they're coming to take her away."

"Take you away where, Kristen? When?"

Kristen turned her face up to me. The tears poured down in a beautiful simulacrum of ravaged emotion. "They want to take me to Europe," she said, and then went into another paroxysm of sobbing.

Was she an idiot?

"Europe?" I said.

"Italy!" she wailed.

Robby picked up on the incredulity in my tone. "The idea is to buy her off and get her away from Love Palace and back to school. They want to give her the grand tour and take her away from us."

Cara said, "She says they'll probably just show up here one day with a bodyguard or something and kidnap her, you know?"

"They would, too," said Kristen. "They did it once when I was in prep school and I had a boyfriend they didn't like. They just came and grabbed me and like de-programmed me and sent me to another school."

"They aren't even supposed to even be calling," said Cara. "That was the agreement, wasn't it? To leave her alone. They don't play fair."

"And you don't want to go to Europe?" I said.

"No!" she wailed. "I want to be here for the Water Street Community Festival!"

"Where's John?" said Cara. "We need him to negotiate for her."

Robby looked up at me. "You have to talk to them, Martha."

I said, "I wasn't a party to the original agreement, but we could try for three weeks, till the Festival."

"And then three weeks after that," said Robby. "That's good. One bit at a time."

I did a good job on Kristen's parents, if I do say so myself. I put on my best functionary voice and told them about this festival, which would be an excellent learning experience for the young people, an integration of many skills (I said that this kind of organizing was like running a business). It wasn't as if they'd bought the tickets to Italy yet. They could afford to pay top dollar and go first class at the last minute, of course. You don't even have to make plans far ahead if you're rich. The problem, aside from college, seemed to have more to do with her mother not realizing there was a structured program at Love Palace. Oh yes, I said, creating one on the spot: we begin with the students organizing small groups of children and move on to these larger events, festivals, reporting for the local media (Kristen could do an article for the newsletter). Her father said they really wanted her in college by the fall or spring semester at the latest. I was sympathetic. Kristen's mother complained that Kristen had never explained any of the business about the structured side of the program, and I said Oh well, teenagers, and Kristen's dad seemed to remember that John had said something like this the last time they talked.

Cara and Kristen jumped up and down at my success and hugged me, and Robby looked proud, and Gil looked bored and wanted to rehearse some new songs.

I figured, with that success under my belt, that I could handle Warren Peterson too. Even so, when the secretary called on Friday morning to say "the car" would come for me around 12:30, I wanted to cancel. I didn't, though. I spent a long time obsessing over what to wear. Then, just before the car was supposed to arrive, John called.

I said, "I knew you were back because my sister went to hear you preach on Sunday."

"Yes, she came up and spoke to me on Sunday. She was very kind."

"She may have been kind to you, but to me she went on and on about how the sermon seemed to be aimed right at her. It appears that the Namaste talk is a big success."

"How are things at Love Palace?"

"Things at Love Palace are fine. Nothing that twelve hours a day of organizing and crisis management can't take care of. Oh, and Kristen is going round the bend because her parents called again and they're ready to kidnap her and take her to Europe."

"Her parents have always known where she is. We called the parents of each of the kids to let them know."

"Well, they're harassing her and she's threatening to run again, but we worked out a deal."

"Excellent. You're amazing, Martha."

"I put them off for a couple of weeks. They would rather talk to you. But that's okay, it's under control for the moment. And meanwhile I can get the appliances repaired and organize a street festival and give the nutty kids all the support they need and finish the newsletter and have lunch with Warren Peterson–"

"Your voice has a lot of tension in it, Martha."

"Everyone around here thinks they're a therapist. Well, no time for a session. I'm going to lunch with Warren. I'm tense because there's a conspiracy to get me to marry Robby."

He said, "You shouldn't be nervous about meeting Warren. He's a pretty simple, straightforward man."

I said, "If Mr. Peterson starts pressuring me to get married, I'm going to demand an intervention from Reverend John."

"You'd better leave me out of it. Warren isn't my biggest fan."

Now that was interesting. I waited for details, but John was like Mari and Madame and probably even Robby: much better at waiting than I was.

It was going to be hot, the weatherman said, so I put my hair in a sort of French twist thing to get it off my neck. I went downstairs and stood around waiting for The Car to pick me up. When Ace had heard I was having lunch with Robby's dad, he had given me a lot of instructions on what information we needed. He thought maybe PE Corporation stood for Pinnacle Enterprises or Peterson

Empire or something. He was sure Robby's dad knew all about who owned the buildings on the street, the apartments as well as Love Palace. I told him I wasn't a spy. He told me I was about to join the Peterson family, so it was hardly spying to want to know about them. I said why does everyone think I'm going to marry Robby?

I still kept my toiletry bag packed with toothbrush and spare underwear for a quick getaway. On irritating days, I pictured myself just hopping in the Guzzler and driving west. Or getting a call from Rachman and going to a hotel with him for a weekend. I kept various escape plans floating through my brain just to prove I didn't have to stay here with the bums and teeny-boppers.

A silver gray car arrived, more discrete than a limo, but plenty big, and the driver, whose name was Martinez, wore a blazer and slacks, no cap, no insignia. I had somehow expected Warren would be there too, but he wasn't. Martinez helped me in–back seat, natch– but chatted about how he enjoyed working for Mr. Peterson.

It occurred to me that I hadn't been in a real luxury car since my high school prom, when my little bunch of freak friends rented the biggest oldest most beat-up black stretch limo we could find. We had really wanted the limo place's hearse, but some other people had already rented it. Still, we had a great time with our nose rings, antique slips for evening gowns, and rented orange pimp suits.

I settled back to enjoy the ride, but it turned out we were only going to Riversedge, the high rise at the end of the block, walking distance, if you weren't wearing heels. People from Love Palace never crossed the invisible border into the Renewed Neighborhood, but we were always in the shadow of Riversedge, towering into the sky, reflecting blue and clouds or bright shocks of sunlight.

We pulled up into the half-circle driveway landscaped with small flowering bushes, and Martinez opened my door and handed me over to a good-looking doorman who could have been his cousin, and the doorman led me into a tall atrium with glass-sided elevators dedicated to whisking folks to the very top where the restaurant was. The elevator man looked like another cousin of Martinez and the doorman. We rose with a grand view of the river's breadth and the city beyond.

The elevator man handed me off to the headwaiter, who was even better-looking than the others, and he led me to a table in a glass alcove where a man had risen, light behind him, coming toward me. I was giddy with what I decided later was the rank odor of money: something in Warren's thick grip and aura of self-confidence reminded me of Rachman, who always made me feel delightfully like a material girl. I had that feeling here, too, that I was about to be bought, or bought off, or at the very least offered an attractive bribe.

Warren had silver hair that matched his car, and he was wearing a creamy open-throat sports shirt and a jacket. "Martha," he said, "I hope you believe me when I say I've been looking forward to meeting you for quite a long time."

"Can't be much more than two months," I said. "Nobody in your family heard of me before that."

He turned me slightly to look out over warehouse roofs, the low rises of our street, including the blue front of Love Palace, Bishop Stebbins apartments looming next and the cityscape across the river beyond that. He lowered me into an upholstered chair. "Not as high as the Windows on the World was," said Warren, "but the view is superior. Ninety nine per cent of the people in the world would rather look at New York than be in it. Especially now, after the terrorists."

I said, "It's certainly a great view, Mr. Peterson."

And of course he said, Call me Warren, and of course I said okay.

And then I said, "Do you own it?"

"This place? I'd never own a restaurant. Hardest business in the world."

"I mean the building."

"No, I'm a deal maker. I helped put together Riversedge Renaissance, and I've been involved in a lot of the Warehouse district renewal, but I don't generally own things."

"My sister lives in the Warehouse District," I said. "She bought a condo, and sometimes we sit out on her terrace and look at this building."

"Yes, I met your sister," he said. "At church last Sunday."

"Oh, that's right, she went over to hear John King preach." I confess I was hoping to see a reaction to John, but he only nodded. The waiter delivered ice water and I was suddenly very thirsty: Warren watched me drink. I said, "I've been avoiding the water down at Love Palace. It's got this rusty flavor."

Warren was older than Eleanor, much bigger and thicker than Robby, though not taller. He said, "I'm eager to hear your take on the operation down there."

"I'm just beginning to get the hang of it. There's a lot going on."

"A lot of monkey business from what I hear. Sex drugs and rock and roll."

"Christian rock and roll."

"We've been pouring money into it, the church, Eleanor."

A basket of exquisitely crusty rolls arrived. Spending time with the Petersons was clearly going to include some excellent meals. Warren ordered a martini, and would I like one too? I figured it was only fair, since I'd drunk one with Eleanor. Besides, I'd eat too many rolls to absorb the gin. But I added, "Are you sure you want me drinking martinis on my lunch hour? I mean, speaking as your employee?"

He grinned at me. "What makes you think you're my employee? And even if you were, then your time would be mine, wouldn't it?"

Such nice rolls. I had a sudden clarity about what I wanted, for this moment at least (which is why I've always been good at sex: I can be terminally murky about past and future and decision making, but for any given fifteen minutes I can have a perfect understanding of what I want.) "Okay Warrren," I said, "let's pretend for the sake of argument that I really am at your disposal. You order, I've always been a good eater. I'll eat anything higher on the food chain than beetles. You choose."

He seemed to think this was eminently reasonable, and as soon as the waiter came back with the martinis, he ordered a double bruschetta, also reminiscent of his wife's menu. He called the waiter, a black man of mature years, Winston. "For the main course—the duck salad of course," he said, and to me, "I always have the duck salad. It's very unique."

Incorrect grammar, I thought: Got you there, Warren. Where did you go to college? Did you go to college?

"And a bottle of the good Zinfandel," he said. "Zinfandel is for lunch, don't you think? I'm really a cocktail man, but I like their Zinfandel."

Not a wine man, then. More evidence. Of something.

Warren rubbed his hands together. "They get their ducks from Chinatown. They do everything themselves here, bread, desserts, but they bring in cooked ducks on the ferry every morning from a particular merchant in Chinatown."

Three sips of martini, a power-view of the city, and here I was, flying high. I was Roller Coaster girl looking at the riches of the world, but I had not forgotten that I had a mission. The cloud balloon over my comic book shoulder had Nana and Ace in it, twin consciences.

"So Warren," I said, "what is the relation of the people you make deals for and Love Palace?"

"Ah, Love Palace," he said. "You kids call it Love Palace."

"I'm not a kid, Warren, although I somehow suspect you know exactly how old I am."

"We are very interested in you, because of Robby, of course. And it's the church's money backing your Love Palace. But Love Palace is largely on its own now. The woman who worked there before you, she got it incorporated, and she had begun working on getting grants. It's no longer directly connected to the church, except that the church is still underwriting a lot of it. Eleanor knows more about it than I do. Her family has been in real estate forever. Me, I like my investments to be more liquid. I don't own buildings. No restaurants or real estate."

I pulled off a piece of bread. "So tell me again what it is that do you do?"

"I put people and propositions together. I like big ideas."

"Like redeveloping waterfronts."

"Yes. Redevelopment is good for everyone. It was good for your sister and the others who bought into Warehouse district. People like your sister made a gamble, and their gamble, and the gamble of the investors, is what is going to bring this whole section back. I'm the one making sure that happens."

The bruschetta tomatoes tasted like they'd been warmed on a window sill. Martinis and bruschetta and a fine-looking man just about old enough to be my father. I could get into this kind of life, I realized.

What was it that Ace and Nana wanted me to do?

I remembered. "You say the development is good for everybody, but what about the people who lived in the Warehouse district when the houses came down? What about the ones who live on Water Street now? I mean, people need homes."

"Displacement?" He tossed off his martini and lifted the empty glass in the air. Winston was there in an instant. "Yes, I read your article in the little newsletter. That's a concern of Robby's too, and that Black Panther fellow who hangs around Love Palace. It's never totally clean– there will always be someone who loses, or at least complains that they're losing. The developers offer services to help people find other homes."

"Are you speaking in general, or do you mean they're developing Water Street and putting the people out of 317 Water Street?"

"The whole area is being developed."

"You mean Love Palace and 317 Water Street already belong to the developers?"

He shrugged. "If they don't, they will soon."

"It's a big problem," I said. "I mean, this is a great view, and the bruschetta is great."

"Wait till you taste the duck salad."

"But I know the actual individuals who are going to get thrown out if 317 gets torn down to make another Riversedge Renaissance. I mean, I know people with kids–"

Warren rested his cheek in his left hand. "I told you, I read your articles. Rats. It's always easier to picture the face of one suffering person than to see the whole picture. That's what the politicians do, you know? Get everyone to see this little victim, who always demonstrates the point of view the politician is selling."

He talked about the whole picture, the big picture. About the long run, and prosperity, and collateral improvement over time. That's the way Freedom works. I think he said Freedom, maybe he said Free Market, he used the phrases pretty much interchangeably. Winston brought me another martini too.

I like the Big Picture, or at least, I like being told about the Big Picture, whether it is Ace talking about the rottenness of capitalism, or Warren saying how the tides of prosperity lift all the boats. I tried to make the case for Ace and Nana. "So the people who live in those apartments are just so many eggs that are going to get cracked for the big omelette?"

But I was interrupted by the arrival of the duck salads. And a third martini for Warren. And big-bellied goblets of Zinfandel.

There was a sprinkling of crushed pecans over slivers of duck on some kind of red frisée. A scoop of wild rice pilaf with grapes.

Warren said, "Well, Martha, I'm not much of one for political philosophy and ideology. I'm a pragmatist. There might have been another way, but this is the way it is."

"Delicious, " I said.

"It's all about winners," Warren went on. "I read history. I only wish Robby would read history. In history, there have been much worse winners than the U.S. of A. I know Robby thinks we should all go barefoot like Jesus and give everything we have to the poor, and I know he also listens to your commie Black Panther who wants to socialize everything. What they're both ignorant of, or at least Robby, is how much better it is than it could be."

The duck salad was incredibly rich, and it made it even harder to remember what I was supposed to find out. Maybe I had already found out. Development was happening. An absolutely terrific blend of sweetness and firm poultry and fruity dressing. Robby and I could take care of each other. After praising the salad and the wine and the new loaves of bread, I did manage to say, "You know, my grandmother was an actually card-carrying member of the Communist Party USA. On the other side, my people are West Virginia hillbillies."

Warren seemed more interested in the hillbillies, as if old time Jewish commies were a dime a dozen (and dying off fast) but hillbillies were exotic.

"Well," I explained, "my mom's family is from the industrial north of the Appalachians. That is, they were plenty poor, but not like living up in the hollows. Well, that's not quite true, because everything down there is up a hollow, but their hollow was more or less in a town." I was enjoying the sound of my voice and I thought maybe I had done my part for Ace and the poor people of Water Street, especially with my clever remark about the eggs and omelettes. I talked much too much, recalling vaguely my mom's crappy line about letting the man do the talking, which I had never noticed her doing either. Her present husband always let her talk, but it's possible he just can't get enough breath with his emphysema.

At some point, I must have stopped talking for a while to eat, because I heard Warren say, as if from a great distance, "Martha, I want you to know how much Eleanor and I support you marrying Robby."

I panicked. "Oh no! I've only known him for two months. Why does everyone think–"

"Please," Warren raised a large, exquisitely groomed hand. "I know he's young. I know you may not take him seriously."

"Listen, I know you know how old I am, but–"

"He's a wonderful boy, kind-hearted, but way too sensitive, stopped eating meat when he was a tiny boy, as soon as he realized that it was lambs and calves on his plate–"

I lifted a forkful of lunch: "Make way for ducklings!" I was much drunker than I'd realized.

"Eleanor was always trying to keep up with each new tragedy

that broke his heart: the dead butterfly, the scraped knee, the poor children in Africa, whatever. I was clueless about the whole parenting thing. Eleanor wanted a kid, I was happy to give her one. He was cute. I wouldn't say I've been an absentee father, but he has been more her project than mine. I could see from the beginning he was going to be an oddball, but I didn't care much, because he was going to be a comfortably-off oddball." He leaned toward me. "He's a lovable boy, Martha."

"Everyone's crazy about Robby."

"Sometimes a difficult boy."

"The Jesus stuff?"

"He also has had–sexual identity issues."

Aha, I thought: the disclosure phase. "Yes, he told me about that. Actually, he told me that the first time we met."

Warren grimaced. "He also spent three periods of time institutionalized for being suicidal."

"He told me about two."

"The first one, he was so young, it was three quarters prep school, he may not even know it was psychiatric."

"That sounds right. I don't think he would lie about it."

"But the bottom line, Martha, is that any happiness you can give him–any self-confidence– for any period of time however brief– we would be deeply grateful."

For any period of time however brief. Warren was trying to cut a deal. For some reason, the directness of it appealed to me. Of course, Robby appealed to me, too, but this was the first time I'd actually thought of marriage as a deal. I mean, my break-up with my husband had had financial aspects, but not the original coming-togethers.

I said, "You have some pretty low expectations, don't you?"

Warren gave me a huge smile. "It's one day at a time, you know?" For most people a smile makes their face younger, but Warren gave me this big ingratiating one that sort of popped his girdle, so to speak, and made him seem older and fatter and jollier. "And what I want to say is, if there's anything we can do—if you—if you and Robby get together, we'll offer any support we can—we made extra-sure early on that there would always be the wherewithal for him to be comfortable. He has his own totally separate trust fund, all securities, municipals, blue chip stuff solid as the rock of Gibraltar, not a single venture in the whole portfolio. The capital is tied up, but there's plenty to use. And we always said, that when he married, we would make a totally separate settlement for his wife, so she would be independent of him–"

I'd had two supersize martinis and half a bottle of Zinfandel by this time. I wasn't totally wasted, but I was on the way. Warren was prepared with a lot of details about where what was invested and how he intended to provide for Robby's wife. The whole blue glory of New York Harbor on a summer afternoon was swimming around behind him. Warren was making me an offer.

I said, "What do I have to contribute? Grandchildren?"

"That would be nice, but it isn't a bargain we're working on here–"

"No?"

"We're looking for what's good for Robby. Period. And I don't know that children would be good for him."

The dessert menus were almost as big as the entree menu, and this was only lunch. Warren, in the same rich firm voice he'd used to talk about securities, ordered a banana and chocolate cream tart glazed with honey. This course I decided to choose for myself, and I chose crème brulée. It's something that makes me sick more times than not at the end of a rich meal, but tasting that stuff— and the one at Riversedge was indubitably the best I ever had— is like sucking your mother's milk, or, in my case, how I imagine that might have been, as my mom never fell for the pro-breast milk propaganda.

I said, "All this about money, Warren, I don't really care. I don't think that way, or at any rate, it's not what I think of first. I admit, I've thought of medical insurance. I haven't had insurance in a long time, and that would feel good, to have medical insurance."

Warren gave a deep chest laugh. It made me think I wasn't driving much of a bargain; I certainly hadn't advanced the Tenants' Council cause. "I'll send you papers tomorrow."

"What papers?"

"Medical insurance."

I stared at him. I think he was laughing at me. I had figured out somewhere along the line that Robby had money, and I'd a few times thought, What's wrong with letting someone take care of me for a change? But it had been genuinely peripheral to all my talk with Madame about who I was, where I was going. I said, "Warren, if I do decide to marry Robby, and you want to give me a wedding gift, I'll take information about the building."

He blinked. "Building?"

"317 Water Street. The one someone is going to tear down to

build another Riversedge. I want a fighting chance for the people to keep their apartments. All they want to do is keep living there."

"It's too late. It's going down. It's public information anyhow."

"The name of the holding company is public, I think it's PE Corporation or something like that. But we want to find the guy. We want to go talk to who owns the building. Personally."

He frowned. "For what purpose?"

"So the tenants can apply pressure on a person not to throw them out on the street."

He started the chest laugh again, and this time it came rolling right up his throat and out his mouth and actually made one of the distant power lunchers look up. "Do you really think it would make a difference? Do you think it would make a ratsass of a difference if you and your friends made a demonstration or whatever you have in mind?"

I was drunk enough to feel no humiliation. "That's my offer, Warren. If I marry Robby, I want to that one thing. Information. I really like Robby a lot. He's a darling. I might marry him. I might even make a deal to marry him, but my price, or at least the wedding present, has to be who owns 317 Water Street."

Warren's laugh died down to a rather affectionate or maybe condescending smile. "Let me think it over."

I had a feeling that I was probably going to marry Robby whether Warren got me my facts or not. I thought maybe I was ready to settle down, that the famous drive to California was seeming less and less like something I wanted to do. Warren had a point, anyhow. Not that Capitalism was the Best of all Possible Worlds– Nana raised me too well for that– but rather that it might be possible for me to do a little bit of the right thing, and still have crème brulée and martinis and duck salad for lunch.

15

I dreamed of a strange ritual where everyone wore contraptions on their heads, a perfect dream to tell Madame. In the dream, Robby was an Egyptian god with the head of an Afghan hound.

She said it meant I was getting serious about the idea of getting married.

"You too?" I said. "You're pushing me to get married too?"

"Not at all. I am giving an interpretation of the dream."

"Marriage isn't serious for me," I said. "I've been there done that."

My mother, I told her. There was a woman who made a big deal about marriage. She had had three husbands, including her present consort, old Jimbo. She had begun life as a kind of hillbilly flower child hanging around West Virginia University, although not as a student, and that was where she met and married the Rotter, Nana's wayward son and our father. He was a student, but dropped out post-haste. Her second husband is best not mentioned, and Jimbo seems to be the real thing. She believes women should be married, and in this, both her daughters have failed her.

I said, "I wouldn't mind being married again so much, but I cringe at the idea of how excited my mother would get over the wedding."

"You associate your marriage with your mother."

"I'm too promiscuous to get married, Madame, remember? And besides, I don't want to talk about marriages, I want to talk about they're going to tear down the first place I ever felt like I might belong."

"Ah," she said. "This little community. To belong. This is what you really want then? This marriage is a way of belonging for you?"

"If it was just me and Robby agreeing to exactly what we want."

"Marriage is for other people as well as yourselves."

"Well, I'm not going to do it. I like him a lot. I'm easy with him, he's a pleasure to be with in all ways. But don't you think marrying him would be acting out and impulsive?"

I propped myself up on an elbow so I could turn around and look at her: she was resting her fine big head on her hand and smiling broadly.

She said, "This is indeed fast, but it is not always the worst thing to follow the impulses."

"You! You're saying that?"

"I have a good feeling about your Robby. Will you have him come for a session with you before you decide?"

"Absolutely not! No chance."

"Then you will perhaps invite me to the wedding?"

This may have been the moment when I went from maybe to almost likely. Madame wanted to come to my wedding. Madame approved. "To the wedding? You would want to come?"

"But of course," said Madame. "I always go to my patients' weddings. And for you, this instinct of mine says that for you, perhaps, this is the great step. A step forward. Like your religious leader says, to step into the–"

"Limina."

"Yes," she said, stretching her legs to indicate that the session was over. "The Limina."

She walked me to the door and gave me a big hug that nearly choked me.

It seemed so absurd to me, that I would get married again, that I would marry Robby. That I would marry Robby with John still on the scene if not exactly in the picture. But Robby was telling people, and they kept making hints at me, everyone, even Madame, going soft in the head over the idea of a bride.

My big mistake was mentioning to Robby that I'd talked it over with Madame. "I knew it! I knew it!" Robby said, opening his arms and smiling beatifically into the ether.

We were standing in the main lounge with no one in sight except White Frank napping on the couch. Robby grabbed both my hands, and I was suddenly aware that he was not always young, that sometimes you had a glimpse of a serious, sensitive man there. "Martha, will you marry me?" he asked.

I didn't pull away, but looked straight at him. "I haven't decided. I won't decide, either, especially if you start thanking Jesus. I don't want any supernatural pressure."

He nodded, still the calmer, mature version of himself. "I want this more than anything, Martha," he said. And then the kid was back, touching his finger to his lips, shh, shh, and loping off in a sort of victory lap around the perimeter of the Love Palace Lounge.

I said, "I haven't decided yet!"

But I knew, and he knew, that I was on the homestretch from maybe to almost possible to possible to probable to okay already.

I had more dreams, once me dressed as a bride carrying Robby up to an altar like a sacrifice, once me riding on his back like he was my steed. Meanwhile, Robby made cardboard valentines that he taped around Love Palace. They said, "Pretty please" and "Robby & Martha." He bought me more paperweights, one Venetian glass and one a nicely detailed pewter collie.

I felt like I was at the center in a way I never had before. People whispering about the latest turns in the love drama, but also I was at the heart of the daily operations of Love Palace. They all needed me, Robby more than anyone.

Typical of me, I can never remember exactly when I decided to let it happen. I remember the dreams and sessions and the conversation when Robby suddenly seemed mature to me– possible, as it were. And I remember we were all having a wonderful time putting together the Water Street Block Party. John was mostly away, and I kept myself clear of physical proximity when he was there. My sister came over for the fair and helped at the Love Palace food booth. The Crew organized games for the children, Gil did music, and some aspiring rappers from the Bishop Stebbins houses took the stage between Good News Crew sets.

Robby ran up and said, "Listen, come with me to the fortune telling both and we'll pick a good day for a wedding."

And I couldn't remember when we'd begun talking about dates.

Chickie had tied a scarf on her head and was wearing huge hoop earrings and palming a crystal ball. I decided it was as good as anything. "Hey Chickie," I said.

Robby broke in. "Madame La Futura," he said.

"Hey, Madame La Futura," I said. "We need a good date for a happy event."

"Ah!" she said around her cigarette. She liked the street fair because she could smoke at will. "Weekend or weekday?"

"A Saturday," said Robby. "This month."

"There are only two left," she pointed out.

"Before Labor Day," I said, surprising myself. But once I decide on something, I want it to happen and be done.

She half-closed her eyes, lifted her crystal ball to her forehead, to one cheek and then the other. "It's coming to me," she said. "Not next Saturday because it's too soon. But you could do it the Saturday after that."

"I don't think that's enough time," I said. "To give a couple of people notice that I'd like to have come. Like my mother. She works Saturdays."

Chickie did the forehead cheek cheek thing again. "The last Saturday of August," she said. "It will be the last Saturday of

August." She put down the crystal ball. "Now put some money in the cup for the Tenants' Council."

We did, and to my surprise, Robby didn't start running around. He pressed my hand and we walked the entire length of the block party, nodding to people and smiling and speaking, and then the entire length back, shoulder-to-shoulder, not facing one another. And I realized I liked it. And finally, at the far end, past Love Palace and 317 almost to the rubble lots and Riversedge Renaissance, he turned to face me.

"This is the right thing, Martha," he said. "The very right thing."

He's half a foot taller than I am, Robby is. "It will do," I said, not to be too sappy. "It's our step into unknowing and hoping."

He smiled, and the smile turned into a laugh, and a kiss.

In the movie version, everyone on the street would have turned to us and clapped and cheered, but they didn't notice, which was even better. Mari did, however, squeal most satisfactorily when I told her; as did Cara. Kristen called her parents immediately, and was very strong; she was staying till the wedding, she said. Even if it meant missing the trip to Europe, and she didn't intend to start college in the fall under any circumstances, spring at the earliest. Even if they made her go home, she was going to work in a McDonald's. Danny Boy gave me a private performance. The ladies of the Tenants' Council wanted to know what I was going to wear and informed me that they had better be invited or else. The only person who didn't seem carried away was Ace. He said, "What about your agreement with the paterfamilias?"

I said he'd come through, give us the name for a wedding gift.

"Don't count on it," said Ace.

Being a bride, I discovered, is like sinking into something rich and heavy, like lying down in the late afternoon with menstrual cramps after you've already taken the medicine. You suffer, colors are intense, but you can feel the pain lifting. This didn't hurt much, of course, but it had that deep dark quality.

At work, if I tried to be serious, people grinned at me because I was a Bride. When John stopped by the Good News Crew meeting, I sat close to Robby and reminded John of the missing money. He reached as if to touch me, but I crossed my arms on my chest and he stopped. He said. "Let it go for now, Martha. When you come back from your honeymoon, we'll work on the money."

"Sounds good to me," said Robby.

"I'm not going anywhere!" I said. "Nothing is going to be different!" They smiled at me like I was a cute but irrational toddler.

Eleanor called. For a second I thought the tiny femme Barbie voice was my mother. "This is the happiest day of my life," she said. "You are doing something for my son that no one else could."

"Eleanor?" I said, "is that you?"

"He called me," she said. "The lines of communication have been a little difficult lately. You are making him so happy, Martha, and his happiness is all I have ever asked for in the world."

It was so emotional and so tiny that I had nothing to say. I was glad she was happy, but it seemed overdone.

And then, as unexpectedly as it had come, the little-girl-lost voice was replaced by powerful Eleanor. She offered to handle a few details for the wedding party– food, for example. Also, had Robby and I decided where to do it yet, she'd love to have us at the church in Pinnacle. I made myself firm in return: not Pinnacle, Love Palace. All the people associated with Love Palace. Eleanor didn't miss a beat, she understood, all she wanted was permission to take care of the food, and maybe flowers. Little odds and ends.

We don't need flowers, I said. Much too expensive. And no red meat. Half vegetarian main courses, something chicken for the non-veggies. Eleanor suggested poached salmon, and I realized that she was doing the food. Okay, fine, I wouldn't have to think about the food.

After that, she called me at the office every day, never more than two calls, never less than one. She had ordered a big air-conditioner for the main room, it was something she had wanted to do anyhow. She had an idea for white and pale peach flowers in rustic woven baskets, and of course she would rent tables, flowers on the window sills, more flowers on stands scattered around the room.

Too expensive, I said to each thing.

And she, sometimes using the little girl voice for a pleading moment or two, would tell me she had a friend who would do flowers for cost, and how about big loops of parachute cloth to hide the ceiling with its missing tiles and old fluorescent lights.

I said No, no, maybe, okay. I was this fat empress in the shiny clothes lying in a hammock with pillows and iced beverages, and the rest of them were coming by to fan me and offer gifts.

John stopped by the office and said he wanted to discuss the service. When I saw him in the doorway, I got up and made him back out onto the mezzanine where we could be seen by everyone in the lounge where Cara and Kristen were doing macaroni art with the little kids.

"We'll make up our vows," I said, "You do one of your little meditations, you can do the Limina or Namaste. My therapist is coming, and I think she'd especially enjoy the Limina."

John moved as if to put his arm around my shoulder, and I dodged.

"You keep moving away from me," he said softly.

"I've chosen a life with Robby." I sounded really pretentious. "I don't want you touching me."

"It's good luck to touch a bride."

I had the strange feeling that he was no more or less likely to make a move on me now than before I decided to marry Robby. I said, "Listen. Please listen. I'm marrying Robby. I intend to do it right."

"Of course."

"You're not the Lord of the Manor. You've got no rights in this marriage."

"We are all part of each other," he said.

"I mean it!"

He laughed softly. "I understand, Martha. I admire your courage."

I didn't know what he meant by that, but realized that to ask was to continue the conversation, to give him too much. I said, "Just keep the sermon short. People are going to want to eat."

Later, Eleanor called with more things she wanted to buy. It was her money, I thought, let her go for it. I did recognized the game, that Eleanor was insisting on her subordinate role but making most of the plans. But it was just so damn flattering to have WASP Queen of the West hanging on my every Jew-billy word.

I had take-out Thai at Mari's. She picked it up at a little kiosk at the train station and we met at her condo. I told her that having Eleanor plan your wedding was like having your hair washed in a beauty parlor: it isn't that you can't wash your own hair, it's just that it feels so good. I said, "And besides, don't you think for most people, it's their mothers really making the decisions? Picture our mom doing it. If she had the money, she'd install a fountain that gushes Cold Duck. With rainbow spotlights."

Mari made a face. "Rhinestones vests for the ushers."

"Rhinestones on the invitations and champagne glasses. Not that we're having champagne."

"You mean Eleanor hasn't mentioned the case of Dom Perignon she picked up? But watch out she doesn't try to run you and Robby. I had this boyfriend once, I don't think you ever met him, but his mother got very into us as a couple, and I couldn't handle it. She was a widow, and she wanted to go out on dates with us! And he let her. What a creep. Both of them."

I wanted to get back to my wedding. "I guess I have to start inviting people soon. Like Mom and Jimbo."

"You haven't sent Mom her invitation yet?"

"I haven't sent anyone an invitation. Mostly I'm just telling people."

"Oh, Martha! Don't be mean. Surprise her– make up something on the computer with wedding bells and pink ribbons." Mari sipped the Japanese beer that she insisted goes best with Thai. "Did I tell you I had her and Jimbo over for dinner last month?"

"Did you tell her I was getting married?"

"You hadn't decided yet."

"Oh. Yeah, right. So why didn't you invite me to dinner too?"

"I like to concentrate on one thing at a time. If it makes you feel any better, she talked about you the whole time. She didn't even ask me how work was going. Does she talk about me when she's with you?"

"I never see her," I said, "so I wouldn't know. How is work?"

She made a face. "I'm getting bored with it. I need something new in my life."

"How about tenant law for poor people?"

"You go back to law school and do tenant law for poor people."

"Seriously, would you help out if we needed you?"

"I told you before, yes, if it was something specific, concrete, and short-term."

I enjoyed looking at my sister. I always had, to tell the truth. I wasn't a very good big sister, but I had been fascinated in my own way by her little fingers and toes and her fringey baby hair and smooth skin. Tonight, she was relaxed, charming, her mouth not tight, and I thought, My little sister is lovely.

She still had great skin, too. Actually, we both do. One of the things she and I share is good skin; even though we look mostly like our mother, we got the smooth olive skin from the Rotter, and everyone agrees— especially Mom— that this is a good thing. You'll be damn thankful for that oily skin someday, says Mom,

139

whose neck started to crêpe when she was thirty-five. I'd say ninety per cent due to smoking, but she thinks it's the curse of the Scotch-Irish.

I said. "Do you think if I invite her, she and Jimbo would pick up Nana?"

"Nana was pretty grogged out the last time I saw her."

"I've got to go visit," I said. "I've been really bad about it. I haven't seen her since before I went into that awful funk right before I met Robby. She looked bad then too. I wonder if there's a connection."

"What does your therapist say?"

"I don't know. I never talked to her about it. Isn't that interesting? I talk about Nana back when we were kids, but I don't talk about Nana now." It seemed enormously interesting to me. I was having one of those highs when everything seems interesting. I was having supper at Mari's with the view of Riversedge rising like a knife blade against the softer purple edges of the city on the other side of the river. Everything looking sharp and well formed. The cityscape for the moment seemed improved to me without the Towers, less arrogant, more of a piece. I was overlooking the world from a high floor, and I was going to get my hot-shot lawyer sister to save Water Street for mixed housing. I was going to do something that pleased my mother and my therapist. This is the life, I thought.

Something had to go wrong soon.

16

But nothing did until after the wedding.

I finally called my mother, choosing a morning hour because she works evenings as a hostess at a restaurant. Jimbo is fairly solvent, we think with a pension from his longtime service as a grounds keeper at a fancy country club golf course, but she still works. He's ten years older than Mom, who's pretty close to being able to collect social security herself now. She and I are both baby boomers, which is creepy, if you think of it: she's in the absolute oldest class of boomers, and I just made the cutoff.

Anyhow, she has always patched together a living, and a few years ago, I realized with distaste that I was doing pretty much the same thing: no serious career, getting older– eck settera, as Jimbo would say.

Let's not go there, I thought. Let's go to wedding plans. I'm doing the husband thing, and Robby is very solvent. Mom is going to be thrilled.

I took a deep breath before calling and surveyed my little domain: the computer had reams of paper neatly stacked underneath. I'd got Robby and Gil to assemble a shelf for the supplies (a simple project that took the two of them three quarters of a day). I'd dusted the Prison Pietà (and also moved it to the far wall so that you saw it as you walked in, but that was even worse because you saw it immediately, and also it had left a light patch on the wall, so I'd put it back over the couch). I'd also washed my hair and put in calls in to some government offices following leads on who might own the buildings. I felt really good, thinking maybe I actually have a métier. I'm a generalist, but that's good for administering.

I punched in her number.

Mom answered the phone in a thin soprano meant, I believe, to be an indication of refinement. She has three phone answering voices: one rich and curvaceous, as if Marilyn had picked up an extension from the grave; one flat and nasal, her natural Northern Appalachian hello with the emphasis on hell; and finally there was this little refined voice, like an imitation Eleanor Peterson.

I said it was me.

"Martha! Honey! I know who it is!"

I started slowly. "How's work?"

"Oh," she said, "I cut back on hours, but I still worry about my legs. Right now, I've got them propped up, to make sure the fluid drains out." I could heard her sucking up smoke, and I pressed my lips together not to say anything about cigarettes. So many of my memories of her were puffs: perfume and smoke. I would come in from school, smell her presence, harden my heart against getting excited. I picture her coming in with a suitcase and me and Mari on the couch, pretending to be deep in homework. Isn't anybody going to say hello to their mother? Oh, hi, I say coolly. Mari tries not to speak, but she is still little, so her face scrunches and twists and finally she stretches out her arms and Mom grabs and hugs. So I end up feeling jealous of the hug, betrayed by Mari as well as Mom. And so it goes.

"How are they doing?" I asked, "the legs?"

To hear her talk, you'd think she had dropsy, or at least serious varicosities, but it's really mostly a matter of pride: we're proud of our legs, Mom and Mari and I. Nana has little stumps with fat ankles and we are thankful for Mom and her rangy Scotch-Irish ancestors for thin, longish legs.

"I banged my shin last week," she said, "so I had this awful-looking bruise, but I guess it'll get better. It may leave a scar."

She is an excellent waitress/dining room hostess, and has been complaining that she ought to go into a different line of work as long as I've known her, based almost entirely on concerns about her legs. She wears support panty hose, she lies around the house with her legs gracefully raised on pillows. She exercises the legs languidly raising one after the other and making imaginary ballet feet.

I said, "Mom, you know your legs look great."

"Well, Jimbo tells me I have the legs of a young girl, and I always say You should feel them, and fresh old thing he reaches over and pinches my knee!"

I hear a little squawking and rustling as Jimbo picks up on his cue: Jimbo's main job, aside from his pension and mixing cocktails, is making Mom feel sexy.

"Well, I'm glad you're sitting down, Mom, because I've got some big news. An invitation. I want you and Jimbo to come to a wedding. My wedding."

She said something that combined Goddam and Hallelujah, and I think she may have pounded her heels on the pillows. Squealed and pounded and called it out to Jimbo. I didn't hear his reaction, if he had one. Jimbo is the strong silent type, probably cute at one time, maybe even vaguely dangerous, but now he wades through his borrowed time with impressive, low-key dignity, not counting pinching mom, ignoring his bad ticker and wheezing lungs.

"Martha baby! Oh honey! You're getting married! Jimbo, Jimbo! My baby's getting married! Well praise the Lord and pass the ammunition! Tell me about him, Martha! Tell me everything."

I started in on the whens and wheres of the wedding.

She said, "We'll be there with bells on But Martha honey, tell me how you love him."

It stopped me. "You want me to count the ways, Mom?"

She said, "I just want to hear in your own words what he means to you."

"I'm not good at mushy stuff."

"You just don't want to tell me," she said sadly. "You were always standoffish. You and Mari both were always mad at me for going off to earn a living. Tell me about him. Tell me his name."

"Robby Peterson. He's sweet and handsome–"

"A hunk? You have to watch out for hunks, honey, like Jimbo." (Noises again of Mom fending off lustful Jimbo.)

I tried to get an image of Robby that would please her. "He's a little bit younger than I am–"

"That's all right these days. You got that nice olive skin of Selma's."

"You mean oily."

"You don't wrinkle," she said. "You know what I mean. Now tell me about Robby."

I had an image of his face resting on my breast. I suspected this was more maternal than it should be. I said, "When I look into his eyes–I feel something I never felt before."

She sighed. "Keep going."

I told her it was a fairly last-minute decision, and it was going to be untraditional.

"That's fine with me, honey, I was a flower child before there were flower children."

"Robby's mom is doing the caterer and flowers, but we're keeping it simple. Just people and food."

She was quiet for a beat, doing her private computations. "So his family can afford to do the party?"

"Well," I said, "Yes. They live in Pinnacle."

"Then they're loaded," she said. "That's okay, then, I don't mind them paying, but tell me what Jimbo and I can do. We have to do something."

"It's going to be pretty simple, Mom. We're using the big room here at Love Palace, and Eleanor has insisted on her caterer and stuff. Just come and enjoy."

"I'll bring mints. You have to have cream mints. I know a place that makes their own old-fashioned wedding mints, you know, the pastel-colored butter cream mints."

I said, "It's not like I'm some virgin bride. In fact, if you remember, I've been married before."

"You didn't have a wedding that time, honey, so you're automatically a virgin."

I reminded myself– I could hear Dr. L. in my head– Mar-ta, she too, your mother, was once a deprived child.

"I've always known you'd find security, honey," she was saying. "That's one thing money can buy."

"It isn't why I'm marrying Robby–"

"Of course not!"

"But it is why I'm letting them do the details. Except for an expensive caterer, it's really going to be unconventional. We're inviting the people we work with, I mean the clients. But I want everyone here. Actually, there's one thing I would ask you to do, if you could. Do you think you could pick up Nana?"

"Poor Selma," she said, "Sure, we'll pick her up. I mean, if she's up to it. She hasn't wanted to go out much lately. Have you seen her this summer?"

No, of course I hadn't. Floods of guilt. I said, "It's just that I want everyone at my wedding, all the people in my life. So if she can come, it would mean a lot to me."

I told her more. I got into telling her. I told her about lunch with Warren, about Robby's Miata, the way the family had more or less set up the Love Palace for Robby. I emphasized and edited, generally making Robby sound maybe ten years older than he was, leaving out the time in the looney bin. Mom appreciated the story and was looking forward to giving her version to Jimbo and her friends.

Her version wouldn't be much different from mine, either. One of her talents is to see the world as the other person sees it, at least for short periods of time. This held her in good stead for attracting men, because she always believes their little myths of self. Jimbo, for example, she had described to us as a man of mystery with a light in his eyes that suggested he might do anything, and she kept asking me and Mari if she should marry him. Mom used to do it periodically for us, too, hear what we wanted and be it. She would be a cookie-baking mom for a while.

She was an assistant Girl Scout leader for six weeks when I was in fifth grade.

"So honey," she said, "what can I do, besides Nana and the mints?"

I thought of saying, Get Jimbo a jacket that isn't plaid, but I said, "Just come, Mom. Pick up Nana and come."

Mari and I went shopping for my wedding dress. We warmed up by discussing what Mom would wear. We predicted big hair and shoulder pads as if it she were an eighties country and western star. A short skirt and décolletage, of course, but she would manage those whatever decade she dressed in. After Mom, we moved on to my dress. It was the closest Mari and I had been in years, maybe ever. I told Madame about it later, and she beamed, "But this is why weddings are so wonderful!"

Actually, she was right, at least about Mari and me. We would talk on the phone, or we would eat and talk at Mari's apartment, and she would drive me to the mall to shop. I had suggested shopping in the city, but she said, Absolutely not, the city has distractions— museums, galleries, street life, but at the mall, even if the clothes were less creative, the shopping experience was pure. Like a meditation, she said. Zen Shopping.

Mari kept pulling out expensive little suits with short sleeves, but I said they looked more like something she should wear, so we spent some time trying them on her.

I said, "I want a flowing garment. I want, as I go to meet my betrothed, to Gather Up my Skirts."

Mari said, "Oh God, Martha, just not peasant chic. You'd look like a fool."

"You mean fat."

"No, you're not fat, but you're boob-heavy. You have to dress carefully when you have boobs. I read an article about Queen Elizabeth of England who apparently actually had this great figure when she was young, but since she was the queen, she couldn't emphasize her chest, so she has always looked dowdy."

Most of the time Mari's face is intense and small and focused, something between concentration and a pout— a perfect match for the suits with short sleeves, but then this little wacky grin pops out, just for a second, and you know she's not always what she appears to be.

I found the dress I wanted in Lord & Taylor's expensive-but-not-designer section, smashed into a sales rack. It was lavender with cap sleeves, a fitted bodice, and a long gored skirt. I had an armload of things in the dressing room with me, and Mari had gone out to scout for more, but when I put the lavender dress on, before I ever looked in the mirror, it felt right. I gathered up my skirts like Cinderella on the palace steps and turned to look at myself in the three-way. I sucked in my stomach, of course, but it wasn't necessary because the dress flattered me. It fit at the waist, and it showed off my firm if old-fashionedly full shoulders and arms.

"That's cute," said Mari, coming back in with something silky. "What is it, a prom gown left over from spring?"

"Not cute," I said. "This is it. This is the one I'm getting married in."

"It's a prom dress."

"For me," I said, "it's the sweet sixteen debutante ball coming out party prom and wedding dress. I want this one."

Mari pointed out some threads that might come loose around the zipper if I gained weight, but she heard my enthusiasm, and I could tell from how she looked at me, that she approved.

She said, "It looks good. At least it isn't a dirndl and weskit."

Once we knew what I was wearing and what color, she bought a silvery-violet cocktail dress that would look good in attendance on mine. And then we went off for shoes, and since the dress was long enough to hide whatever I wore anyhow, I chose flat purple ballet flats. And then we went out to lunch at a nouveau French place on the mall premises where the food was supposed to be an adventure but didn't make you feel fat. It was the best shopping trip I ever had.

"I got something new," I said, "but it satisfies something old. I get to wear cheap-o shoes, which satisfies the Nana in me, as does the fact that your outfit cost more than mine."

Mari crunched on a bread stick. "You need to work on your self-esteem."

After I had invited Mom and bought the dress, I had faith that everything else would fall into place. The Tenants' Council loved the dress. Chickie offered me a purple stretch belt just a shade darker than my dress with a big gold-colored catch that made my waist look small. Eleanor gave me her gift early– a necklace and earrings, real gold, with a look of molten, but not too big.

I said yes to Mari's offer of a facial and manicure, but my hair was at a length I liked, so I refused her super special hair cut.

The morning of the wedding was warm, and we would definitely need the new air conditioner. Flowers arrived, couches and chairs were draped in pinkish orange parachute cloth and pushed back to line the walls and make room for the tables with white cloths and the baskets of flowers. Eleanor's people looped more parachute cloth from the ceiling, and they had draped some over Cara's Jesus mural. Everyone came in costume: Gil with a freshly shaved head and an extra earring. Danny Boy and the Franks had been taken by Warren's driver Martinez to a hotel room where they were fitted with tuxedos and showered, shaved and trimmed. Everything was festooned: Eleanor in flowing silk, Mari in her cocktail dress, the ceiling of Love Palace.

Ace wore a dashiki, but took me aside to explain it was for Malika, he didn't want me to think he'd gone Black Nationalist. Malika's kente cloth turban and robe had a different pattern from Ace's but the same oranges and greens. Esta Brown and her kids wore church clothes, the little boys in three piece suits. Olivia came in a magnificent peach suit and a matching hat with tucks and rosettes and veils.

My dress swirled. I swirled into the kitchen to see the plates of curried chicken, the poached salmon with dill sauce, the red skin potato salad, roasted pepper antipasto, lemon squares, the wedding cake, the carved-out watermelon basket spilling melon balls. Danny Boy wasn't happy about strangers in the kitchen, and I had insisted he would do his biscuits. He was incensed that I would come in the kitchen, in my wedding dress no less.

I swirled out of the kitchen, and Warren caught my arm and gave me a big wet kiss in the middle of the blush and powder on my cheek. He held me close and murmured. "I'm still thinking about it."

I must have looked blank.

"Your wedding gift."

"Oh!" I cried. "Of course!" Swimming and swirling in fabrics and love, it took an effort for me to remember words like Redevelopment and Affordable housing. I meant to go pass this on to Ace, but Robby approached and didn't drape an arm around my shoulder the way he usually did, but rather picked up my elbow, held it and my wrist as if he had something very valuable and smiled at his father, showing me off. Robby in a Byronic poet's shirt.

John arrived in a shirt just like Robby's, and I wondered if this was Eleanor's idea, to dress them alike. John exuded power like one of Shakespeare's benign dukes. Esta stopped him, and he held her hand, and then spoke to Malika and Ace, and finally Mari. Mari walked around with him after that, her eyes big and shiny.

I almost missed Madame Doctor Landowska's arrival. This was probably the high point of my survey of the wedding scene: the arrival of Madame, out of context, perfectly self-possessed, hands folded at her waist as if she were about to sing, hair freshly colored ash blonde, head back, smiling over her cheekbones.

Robby said, "Is that your mother?"

"Lord have mercy. My therapist. Do you want to meet her?"

"Very much," said Robby. He was surprising me with his ease in social situations, shaking hands, giving semi-formal little half-bows, elegant turns of phrase.

Dr. Landowska used both hands to hold my cheeks and kiss one then the other. "You are not reserving yourself from the guests," she said. "How very like my generous Martha. And this is the young man?"

She and Robby gazed into one another's faces smiling.

I said, "I didn't think you'd really come."

Madame made a tsk tsk sound. "I adore weddings," she said. "They represent hope for the future. And this is a wonderful place, I can feel it. I am looking forward to meeting this religious man of whom Martha speaks so often."

Robby laughed. "Everyone here talks about John."

But Eleanor had billowed up to us, grabbed Robby's arm.

"And this is your mother?" she asked me.

"Nope," I said, "my therapist. Madame, this is Robby's mother."

Madame smiled. "I'm happy to meet you. It is much easier to be a good therapist than a good mother."

The perfect moment for my real mother to appear. Robby had draped his arm over Eleanor the way he did with me on ordinary days, and then here came Mom and Jimbo. I excused myself, left Robby and Eleanor and Madame together. I hurried toward the door, only slightly anxious, nothing a glass of champagne wouldn't smooth out. Jimbo's sports jacket a relatively staid black and white plaid, and Mom wearing a white suit nearly identical to Madame's, only she wore it with female-impersonator spike heels and blonde bombshell wig.

"Hey gorgeous," said Jimbo, grabbing for a hug, the same style big wet kiss as Warren.

"Don't crush her clothes!" cried Mom. "Look out for her make-up. Oh, honey, I never saw you look so beautiful! But you're supposed to be out of sight!"

I could hear a rise in my voice, closing in on a whine. "Why would I want to be out of sight at my party? Where's Nana?"

"She wasn't up to it. Jimbo and I were going to drive up there, but they said she really couldn't come out. Isn't that right, Jimbo?"

He winked at me. He might have been letting me know Mom was lying or more likely he simply hadn't heard. Oh Nana, I thought, and then her picture dissipated from my mind as had most of the other thoughts that were swirling away as I kept swirling.

Mari found us, got a kiss from Mom, one from Jimbo. Mom said, "Look, girls, what I brought!" And she extended a white cardboard box. "It's the mints! It's real old fashioned wedding mints!"

I had to introduce all these people, Robby for Mom's approval, Mom for Eleanor's approval, all of them to Madame, then John. I was doing a good job of seeing John as an artifact, a monument separated from me by a little brass fence. Mom kissed Robby, Mari introduced John, Mom handed over the mints to Eleanor who smiled sweetly and said, "I'm going to take these right over to the dessert buffet." And as hard as I listened, I couldn't make out any condescension: very classy, I thought.

Everything was picking up speed. I was about to be married, everyone I cared for except Nana here in one place, where one terrorist bomb could blow them to smithereens. Madame's well-modulated tones saying to John: "Martha speaks highly of you. I am eager to hear your message about the constancy of change."

John leaned over and kissed her fricking hand! "Today the only message is how happy we are that these two people are joining their lives together."

Madame answered gracefully, and Jimbo edged over toward the Franks, who had commandeered a tray of fluted champagne glasses. I kept glancing at the loops of parachute cloth, vaguely reassuring myself there were no snipers, that the dangerous looking person approaching Robby was just Gil with his head shaved to say that Cara wanted to sing her song, and they needed Robby to do keyboard. Cara's ballad , which I'd heard her practicing, was far from the worse song the Good News Crew performed.

"This one is dedicated to Robby and Martha," she said:

"You find love wherever you find it
You find love–

or maybe it finds you–
You find love wherever you find it
All around
and then
inside of you."

Oo oo oo, repeat the last line a few times. Nobody ever wrote a love song for me before.

John moved over beside me around the third verse. He put a hand on my shoulder and leaned in close to whisper, "You are a splendid woman, Martha." I let his hand go deep and hot into my shoulder and was yet able to believe he was on the other side of the fence. That it was Robby I wanted.

Cara finished, and then Mom and Mari were hustling me upstairs. Adding lipstick, re-powdering my cheeks. Eleanor coming up to give me the circlet of flowers for my hair. They centered the buckle on my belt and set me on the mezzanine like a doll while they hurried back downstairs.

I had this moment of panic that I wouldn't know when to start down the stairs, but then Robby came out of the crowd in his mature smoothness, waiting for me with a garland around his neck. The bride song started, and I thought, Oh! Of course, that's how you know when to start.

Both numb and burning I came down, and Robby grabbed my hand, or else I grabbed his, in any case we found each other.

The guests opened a path for us, and at the end of the path, in front of a ficus tree (where did that come from?) was John wearing a kente cloth like a stole over the poet's shirt, his hands at waist level, not quite a prayer.

I had a general impression of odd behaviors, especially my mother and Eleanor and Esta Brown all sobbing. Then the music stopped, there was a silence, and I heard Robby sigh, and John was picking up our clutched hands between the two of his and filling the room with his voice.

"Oh this is a glad day!" cried John. "This is the day the Lord hath made!"

"Yes, Jesus!" cried Esta.

That was about the end of theology, with John talking about what people want and what they need, and how all we really need is Love, and that marriage however flawed an institution is Belief in Love, we're on the threshold (did he use the world Limina?). It's the best we can ever have.

He freed our hands but then put a hand on each of our shoulders.

"Oh bless you children," he said, and Robby shuddered, and I realized he was crying. Everyone was crying but me.

The role of religion is to bind us together in hope, said John.

Blest be the tie. Hear O Israel. Namaste.

He released us and lifted his arms in the air the way Moses had to do to keep the Jews winning one of their battles in the wilderness, and Robby read his vows, and I read mine, but our voices were small and our vows seemed pretty unmemorable compared to John finishing it off by calling out, "And may this congregation of friends and loved ones join me in this binding together and call out with me, 'Blest Be!'"

And oh they did, and then John said again "Namaste," and we kissed, and we were all bound together, us and them and everyone.

There had been no explosion and no inappropriate behavior, and now it was done, the documents signed, and Robby and I were officially married, and we could have a party. It was a big relief, to tell the truth. That I hadn't backed out or blacked out. I had done it, for better or worse, so to speak. People hugged us and kissed us and started serving themselves at the buffet, went to the little tables in compatible groups. The Pinnacle people together, Mari with Mom and Jimbo and Ace and Malika. Chickie and Esta and Esta's kids were at a table, with the Franks of all people. Danny Boy wearing a stiff pressed dress shirt never sat down, but kept going around with plates of biscuits to the tables. Madame couldn't stay. She took a little paper cup of pastel cream mints to go and kissed Robby and kissed me. "It was a most true speech," she said. "I am so glad I came."

Robby and I walked around holding hands and talking to people. Gil had put together a mix of recorded dance music, and we all danced. Mom and Jimbo did a convincing if brief Lindy, and John danced with Mari and Chickie and a slow dance with Eleanor. Warren danced the same one with me. "You look good enough to eat," he said.

Robby cut in, and then John cut in, not damp and intrusive like Warren, but I made sure we kept our chests apart. "My therapist liked your remarks," I said.

He brought up his right hand, which was supposed to be on my shoulder blades, and laid it on my left cheek, then kissed the cheek where he had touched.

A chaste kiss that left me tingling, but not much more than everything else did. Then Robby cut back in, and John stepped aside, and everything was all right.

Robby said, "I want to show you your gift."

"I didn't get you a gift!"

"No, it's just something I found. It's out in the car. Your car."

"In my car?"

And we slipped out, across the street, steamy out there, hazy late afternoon, some kids from Bishop Stebbins hanging out in front of the abandoned house, staring at us in our wedding clothes. I waited to feel brought back to earth away from the magic, but instead, the magic carried out here: late afternoon splendor, the old Guzzler looking massive instead of extinct. Inside on the bench seat, between Robby at the wheel and me in the passenger seat, was a stack of boxes about the size and shape of French toast slices, wrapped individually in silver paper with blue and lavender wedding bells, all roped together with a ribbon.

Robby cranked open the window on his side, and I started opening the presents, one at a time: eight-track cassettes, the only thing my car played: Frank Sinatra, Moody Blues, The Sound of Music, Nat King Cole singing Dear Lonely Hearts, Loretta Lynn, Engelbert Humperdinck.

I said, "Oh, Robby, where on earth did you find them?"

"At a tag sale in Pinnacle," he said. "They all work, too. Look–here's a replacement for your Jim Nabors! I sneaked out your car keys and tried them out, and they all work. They've been in somebody's garage for eons." His face was full of such an eagerness to please that I almost cried.

"Oh honey," I said, and that's a word I never use.

"Do you want to listen to them?"

Of course I did.

He turned on the car and we kissed as the Guzzler gently spewed hydrocarbons onto Water Street and the crooners warbled love songs.

Part II

17

When I think back to why I married Robby, I have concluded that it was largely for the fresh start, mine but his too. I was the first woman he ever slept with, and he desperately wanted to keep sleeping with women. I understood that he wanted to get married for doubtful reasons: to have a religiously sanctioned outlet for sex; to avoid another mental breakdown; maybe to avoid the Love That Has No Name – or anyhow used to have no name but is really pretty normal now, at least in the New York and San Francisco Bay areas.

I talked a lot to Madame Landowska about why I wanted to get married. Robby was an angel, Robby made me feel competent; marrying Robby meant I would have medical benefits; I was flattered to have handsome young Robby choose me. Never underestimate the power of flattery, I said to Madame.

Also, and this was maybe the fresh start, Robby made me feel clean. I wanted to feel clean and good forever. I wanted to forget old complications, and new ones like John King as well. I ignored the possibility that Robby might change. I had had occasional glimpses of other Robbies, the socially adept Robby who moved through the world with confidence, the privileged Robby who always assumed he would get what he wanted.

Something else I had ignored was how attractive he was to other people. It struck me early in the honeymoon that eyes turned to him when he walked through a lobby. Sky Caps sought him out to offer their services and seemed grateful for unexceptional tips. Waitresses with tired circles under their eyes chatted him up and brought coffee to our table more often than necessary. I supposed this was stuff provided gratis by his genes– hotel employees glad to see him and strangers staring with approval. I kept an eye on those strangers: women of all kinds and the most fashionably dressed men. I couldn't tell if Robby was aware of it. I thought not, or maybe he was aware but thought it was the same for everyone.

I had never, of course, spent this much time with him before our honeymoon in Aruba. He seemed fuller in the face, less haunted. More intelligent too, but that was probably just because he wasn't making religious proclamations. I wondered if he had been unconsciously up till now showing me only his boyish side, and now he was relaxing into who he really was. I was a little off balance, and once or twice caught myself thinking, Well, we'll be home in ten days and everything will go back to normal.

For the first few days, we did tourist activities in the morning and then lay around on the beach. We looked at the old Dutch buildings, and we went into the caves to see the bats and the pre-Columbian art. We rented motor scooters, snorkeled, and rode horses. I loved the idea of horses and their big mild eyes, but Robby actually knew how to ride. I collected brochures about the things we did to show my mother and Jimbo, who didn't do digital. My main non-brochure memories are of pink buildings and white sand and lying around with Robby.

Looking at his feet. For some reason, especially as I got drowsy on the beach, I found myself taking great pleasure in Robby's feet. He seemed to have fewer scars than other men I'd known, and no calluses. Longish feet, golden brown with a dusting of golden hairs over the high arch, then thicker light brown hair beginning just above the pale skin over his ankle bone. He didn't seem to exercise, either, but had great muscle tone. His forehead as smooth as his feet, and his hands beautiful except for that pale pattern of Asking For Help scars on the underside of his wrists.

I especially liked the pink bottoms of his feet, the long, relaxed curve of his toes at rest and the single flat nevus on the inside of his right arch.

"How do you keep them so clean?" I asked him. "How do you keep your skin so soft? Where did you get such aristocratic feet?"

"You," he said, stroking my arm.

"Not Jesus? Don't you think Jesus made your feet pretty?"

He wriggled closer.

Such a sweet-smelling man. Sweet earlobes, sweet cheeks. This lovely one they all lusted after, and he was mine, for now.

We had a conversation about religion on our second full day. Our hotel had a dining room with one side open to the beach. Dusk had fallen, and there was a melodramatically brooding dark ocean for a backdrop. Between the salad and the sea bass, Robby said, "What does Judaism say about the New Testament?"

I said, "Judaism? Robby, I don't know from Judaism. I told you, my Jewish connection is Nana the Bolshevik."

"She didn't practice Judaism?"

"She was a Red. That was her religion."

"Would you say she worshiped Marx?"

"No, I wouldn't say she worshiped Marx, I would say her political beliefs filled the space some people fill with religion, which is to say that's where she got her world view. Judaism as best I understand it is mostly about how to live in this world anyhow. It's a practice. So in a way, it's probably easier to switch to politics from Judaism than from one of your more supernatural religions."

I was making this up since I knew just about zero religious Jews, but on the other hand, I was confident that no one in that entire hotel was likely to challenge me. I don't mean no Jews, just nobody interested in discussing. All our conversations with other people so far had been about tropical drinks.

Robby said, "Political convictions and religion aren't the same thing."

Actually, I was feeling pretty much into tropical drinks myself, and sarongs. I was building up to buying a lavender sarong with a pattern of big white blossoms in the hotel shop. "I would never say they're the same thing, only that they fill the same space. The 'What I believe' space. A person's world view, most important values. That space. I hope you realize, Robby, that even a lot of Christians would find your religion pretty quirky. You seem to get Jesus and John mixed up, and you never mention God or the whatsit, the ghost."

He templed his fingertips, just like John, and said, "My faith is still in flux, and just because I'm a believer doesn't mean that I never understood darkly. Some of the ways I've seen things in the past were– unfinished at best."

"You mean what you believed ten years ago or what you believed last month?"

He let that pass. "I was too rigid. I wanted it all pre-fabricated, all the questions answered all at once. I realize now that that's the sign of an immature belief system. I'm moving toward something more open-ended. I want to be more accepting. I want to listen to other people and not just try to convince them. I'd like to meet your grandmother."

"Unfortunately, it's probably too late to hear her spiel, but I'd love to have you with me when I finally get up courage to go back to the nursing home."

The sea bass arrived, nicely presented with lots of decorative curls of vegetables and a drizzle of red pepper sauce. And after we ate, the people at the next table invited us for a drink on the terrace after dinner, which led us into a whole new phase of the honeymoon.

We'd been soaking up sun and sand, eating well and having

sex, but it had been, how do I say, undifferentiated. The pink buildings were like sex, and sex was like the rolling surf, the breeze was in my brain, my brain trailed out into the dark waters of the evening.

The new phase centered on the Material People. There were two couples, Bo and Crys (she made us memorize the spelling), and Russ and Suze. They were all four a little overweight, not unusually so for Americans, and very present in their bodies. Bo had big hands that he liked to pat people with, also big shoulders and a big gut. Crys was busty and wore push-up bras to make sure nobody missed the point. She seemed to operate on the theory that sexy clothes made you sexy, whether or not they flattered your figure. The longer I watched her, the more I thought she was probably right: her short legs between tiny stretch skirts and high heeled sandals made you think of long legs, whatever you were seeing. She seemed to believe she was terrific looking, and Bo called her Baby and was always rubbing her shoulder or cupping her rear with his big hand. They all kissed you every time you ran into them even if you'd been together half an hour before.

And they all wore gold. A lot of gold. In private I referred to them as the gold-chain gang. Bo reminded me in his thick splendor of my fancy man Rachman. I liked it that Bo liked fleshy women, and I liked the way his lazy eyelids didn't bother to hide the fact that he liked me too. He liked Suze of the other couple, and all the other women in the hotel. He was that kind of guy.

Crys and Suze, of course, thought Robby was a doll baby. They were fascinated by the age gap between Robby and me. The six of us did a fair amount of drinking together over two and a half days: that night after dinner, the next day at lunch, then cocktails, and at dinner and after. I drank margaritas and let myself laugh at jokes I would ordinarily find offensive. Robby seemed to be practicing openness. I danced with Bo even though he kept laying his hand a little too low on my back when he twirled me around.

The gold-chain gang did most of the talking– Robby smiled and listened, I made the odd outrageous remark to remind them I was there. They talked about where to buy gold (I was under the mistaken impression for a while that Bo was an importer of jewelry) and which islands had the best gambling scene (they were disappointed in Aruba). The women didn't think much of the hotel shop and wished the floor shows had bigger stars. The guys talked about comedy clubs back home, and which comedian had been dirtiest. Crys and Suze offered me make-up tips. I kept trying to get their businesses straight, and never did, although I think Russ maybe owned a music store.

Throughout, Bo kept hitting on me. Whenever Crys went to the ladies' room, he would press his face at me. He loved my skin, he whispered, great shoulders, and my god what a rack! Then aloud, to Robby, he said, "You are one lucky guy! Let me tell you. I wouldn't let her out of the bedroom."

Crude? You bet. They intimated in a general sort of way that they were into the old switcheroo, and if we had any interest, they would be happy to accommodate. I wasn't sure Robby got it, and I allowed myself about ten seconds of including that in my general loose and sensual mood and then said No, Robby and I were much too early on in our relationship. Right Robby? I said, and Robby leaned over and gave me a big wet kiss in the mouth, right over the Smoking Volcano after-dinner brandies, and I realized he did get it.

I asked him the next morning if he wanted to avoid these people. He said no. I said they probably had organized crime connections. I had absolutely no reason to believe that except that the men boasted about sleazy business deals. No, said Robby, no, they were leaving before us anyhow.

The night before they left, Crys and Suze got into a competition over who could dance the most times with Robby. Sometimes Suze and Crys both danced with him. Russ didn't dance, but did drink himself into a stupor, so this left me with Bo. Talk kept turning to my shoulders and my rack, so I finally said Let's dance.

Bo gave a big sigh when the music went slow, and pulled me close. Waves of surprisingly flowery cologne came at me from the pelt over his clavicle. I was dizzy, I was feeling hands on my arms, hands on my butt. I kept pulling my head back, and Bo grunted down in his throat and called me Baby.

It gave me a shudder down in my groin. Unexpectedly, being called baby. Nothing spiritual, nothing combining surf and wind with sexuality, you understand, just a sex itch.

Bo groaned in my ear: Uh-uh-uh and kneaded deep into the small of my back, and I could feel the skirt of the only little cocktail dress I ever owned, creeping up.

I finally said, "Watch your hands, buster."

He pressed his flowery hairy sexually irritating cheek against my temple. "You're the best, Baby," he said. "You're driving me crazy. This is my last night, Baby. I want you."

I said, "Well, yeah, I want a lot of things. But I'm not fucking around on my honeymoon. Have some respect for marriage for godsake."

The song ended, and it was cool on my front, where Bo had been. As he walked me back to the table, he said, "You're not really married to that kid, are you?"

He said it cooly, as if it were part of a business discussion. I looked at him, I looked at the broad expanse of room with palms and rubber plants and chandeliers, and Robby in a little tableau with Crys and Suze, and it hit me: what Bo had just said. These people didn't believe Robby and I were married. We didn't fit into any world they could imagine.

And one insight set me flashing off to another: Bo, thick, dark, smelling of flowers and booze, with enough money to fly down here for a couple of days with someone– no reason to think Crys was his wife, either– Bo was the man my dad had wanted to be.

Or maybe it was the man the Rotter actually had become. What did I know, maybe he'd made a killing somehow and never came back to share it with us. Maybe the next plane in would bring the old Rotter himself to Aruba, silver-haired, double-breasted blazer, pinky rings and loud laugh. He would have a bosomy blonde with him, an older version of Crys, maybe his wife and maybe not. They would have gone places where they could gamble, to the comedy clubs, to the islands. He would make public passes at other women to show off his masculinity and because it was fun. I had a sense that all of them, Rotter and the gold-chain gang, had a kind of stupid innocence: that the most you could get out of life was what you could eat and fuck and buy. I said, "Bo, you remind me of my dad."

He burst out laughing,

"No, I mean it. You're just like him. And yes, I am married to Robby, and this really is our honeymoon, and no, I'd never sleep with someone who reminds me of my dad."

We were right in front of our table, and Bo gave me a big good-humored bear hug and kiss (but managed to squeeze my behind too). Crys said, "Well!" and leaned on Robby, because she'd seen Bo kiss me, but it was late and they were leaving, and nobody was looking for trouble. Least of all Robby, who smiled around the table as if these people were some kind of dolphin show.

That night, Robby and I were awake late burning off alcohol calories. We had sex, we sneaked down the hall wearing towels for ice and sodas. Robby paced the room, knocked back a cola, and when I was finally beginning to get sleepy, started a conversation. "I'm glad that's over! I'm glad they're leaving. What assholes!"

"I thought you wanted to spend time with them–"

"I did. I'm glad. It was important to me, to see what that is like."

"How the other half lives."

He flipped on the television with this intensity in his face and shoulders. Flipped channels, flipped it off. "No wonder people become monks."

He dropped into the chair, leaned over his knees and stared at me. Uh-oh, I thought. This is when the age gap kicks in. Robby is just getting started on a serious conversation, and I want to sleep.

I said, "The guy Bo–"

"Who couldn't keep his hands off you."

"Yeah. He reminded me of my father. I imagine that's how my father is, if he's still alive."

Robby settled back in the chair, sank down, neck against the back, rested his soda can on his belly. "Interesting," he said. Then, "I don't think I want to be a father. I wouldn't know how."

This was new. We'd never discussed children, although I had assumed Robby himself was going to be our child. I said, "When I was growing up, Nana was our mother and father, mostly. She loved us, she did what we needed– not always to our satisfaction, of course. But she also had her own life. We had our lives, she had hers. She wasn't sentimental about kids. The big mystery was how Nana had a child like my father."

I was sinking back in the pillows, thinking of Nana shuffling around the kitchen frying some kind of cheap meat: chicken livers, or sometimes even chicken hearts, while Irv sat at one end of the kitchen table fixing the toaster or the radio. And the two of them, always talking politics.

Robby said something I was supposed to respond to. He was looking at me, waiting.

"Sorry. I didn't hear you."

"I've never believed Warren is my biological father."

"You're kidding."

"My mom had another husband first. She doesn't talk about him. They were two young college kids. It didn't last long. I think he was maybe gay, although she doesn't say so. They got it annulled or something. Then, later, she married Warren."

"You think that first husband was your father?"

"No. It was much too long before I was born."

"So I don't get it. Why isn't Warren your dad? Does she like–have affairs?"

"I wouldn't know. I don't have any evidence, I just don't feel any connection to him."

"He feels connected to you."

Robby said, "When I was crazy, it was one of my fixed ideas. I kept yelling at him he wasn't my father and insulting her. But even when I'm not crazy, there is this emptiness between me and him."

"Well, he seems to care a lot about you. Both of them do."

"I'm their project. I'm their experiment in normal humanity."

"Robby!"

"Oh, I suppose he is my biological father. It just comes over me sometimes, I begin to get– it's like paranoid, but it's different. Everything is suffused with doubt. When I was really crazy, I would start obsessing over whether there was a trap door under the rug I was standing on, sometimes I'd only walk on bare floors. I don't mean I'm like that now, it's just the direction I go when I get crazy. And even when I'm sane, I have times when everything seems uncertain. That's why I freaked out when John first started talking about the Limina."

I sat up. "Seriously, Robby. You should ask Eleanor, you know. You ought to at least get the facts straight."

"But whatever she said, she could be lying, right?"

I said, "I've got an idea. Let's make a pact, just you and me. Let's pledge to be honest with each other, okay? So we always know where we stand– so there's always one person we can trust. Bad or good. I don't mean we have to confess everything we ever did in the past, but from here on in. Okay?"

"That would be really nice," said Robby, sincerely. "I would like that a lot."

We talked about religion again on our last afternoon. The gold-chain gang was gone, and we went back to smelling and touching. We lay in the sand most of the day, letting the surf come up under us. We took long showers before lunch and had drinks with lunch, and then lounged around some more, two slabs of lox under a blue sky.

Later, taking the shade for a change, we lay on lounge chairs under an umbrella. Robby went for more drinks, and I was drowsy. I started flashing on the only other time I had ever been out of the

United States, all the way to England. I put together my college graduation gifts and forgot about the college loans that would be coming due and went to London for a summer. I think I was also running from the specter of gainful employment, but I had an idea of immersing myself in Shakespeare productions and putting my butt where Virginia Woof and Karl Marx had sat in the British Museum. I arranged to stay in a cheap room in University of London housing, and I set out to see London, but in the end, instead of culture, I picked up guys. Usually I don't think of it, or I speak lightly of the summer I slept with two dozen foreign students. Actually, I was there only a month, and I didn't start my sexual adventures till the second week, and it was only two of them: a skinny silent boy from Thailand and then Rachman, who turned out to be an actual relationship of a sort.

It was the boy from Thailand, though, who came back to me. The excitement had been the realization that someone was trailing me through the National Gallery, a slim boy in a sports jacket that hung unevenly on his narrow shoulders. I made sudden switch backs, I feinted, he followed. Eyes meeting. He asked if I wanted tea. Silent tea, more eyes, then his grim room, even smaller than mine. We never exchanged names or phone numbers, but met the second day in the same museum, in the same gallery, and once again he followed me. We did that three days, until, excited by my own power, I decided to disappoint the boy and went to the Tate instead of the National Gallery and ran into Rachman. Rachman was cheerful and talkative and said he wanted to practice his English, although he seemed to speak it perfectly adequately. Part of me always felt that I had abandoned that first boy, ripped the fabric of our strange delicate courtship.

When I got home from England, I went into one of my celibate periods and made an appointment with the doctor to make sure I hadn't caught anything from the far or near east. I got my first low-level job for a publishing company, and then, when I finally got a man in my life again (that would have been Rotter Two, who I married), I stuck to him like a barnacle for much too long.

When Robby came back with our drinks, I was going to tell him about England, but I thought better of it: we'd pledged openness about the future only. That meant I was safe on John, too. So there, under the purpling sky, we two the last on the beach, a heavy damp wind coming up, Robby squeezed into my lounge chair with me and pulled a disposable lighter and a joint of marijuana out of his bathing suit.

"Where on earth did you get that?" I asked.

He held the joint in front of him, the lighter flame a foot away, not touching yet. "One of the bar boys."

"What Would Jesus Do?" I said, a little annoyed that he was changing so fast.

"Jesus is about love, not prohibition. What's the difference with this and a glass of wine?"

"Only that this is illegal in most places. And we're in a foreign country. They do painful things to the body parts of foreigners who get arrested on drug charges. Also you have no idea what's in it. What if it's poison?"

"The chain gang guy told me about the guy I bought it from. He bought some too. Your admirer. He would know."

"Oh yes, he would know."

Robby lit it, sucked in the smoke, and passed it to me, pressed tight against my side.

I said, "I didn't know you ever did this stuff."

I waited to make sure Robby didn't go into convulsions before I took a drag. He smiled over his stopped breath. It had been a while since I smoked grass. It went right through my whole system, made the purple more purple, gave Robby's jaw a dark outline, like a comic book hero.

"You really amaze me," I said, when we had both let out smoke, taken a couple of more relaxed drags. "You keep changing. You surprise me."

He said, "You surprise me for being surprised. I thought nothing would shock you."

"Aha! There's your mistake, Robby. People think I have no neuroses because I have a big mouth. It's like Nana. You should have heard her– she and Irv asserted that they favored nudity as a way of being natural with children–"

He laughed and choked on his smoke.

"– but they would have kissed pictures of John D. Rockefeller before they undressed in front of me and Mari. Nana used to put her nightgown over her head and undress under it like a tent. She'd wiggle a little bit, and then this big boulder holder would appear down around her ankles, followed by slip, underpants. It was an amazing production."

He laughed, and we smoked, and when the thing was all the way to its roach, we threw it and the disposable lighter as far into the waves as we could. I fell asleep.

After a while, I woke to the sound of Robby, who seemed to

have been talking for a while. "Everyone worships something, don't they?" he said to the purple clouds, to the small surf. "Everyone worships something. I think I would have finally killed myself if I hadn't found Jesus. I mean, I'm so much better now, I think I'm healed, and I think about a lot of other things, I feel like I'm broadening out, but people do need something big, something so big it can answer all their needs forever, right? Something you can believe that won't let you end in nothingness."

"The thing about Nana and her boyfriend Irv was that they knew what they should be doing every day of the world: fighting for human rights, better working conditions."

"She wouldn't have approved of all this sitting on a beach getting high."

"I don't know. She had no problem with enjoying yourself. She never had the money to do much of it, but she'd take us to the city to the museum and then we'd sit in the park and eat hot dogs from the street vendors. I just mean that whatever happened at her job, in the world, she always knew which side she was on. It gave her this quality, like she was marching through life with stirring music in her background." I tried to sing, but ended up reciting: "'Tis the final conflict/Let each stand in his place/The International Working Class/shall be the human race. '"

Some time passed. Robby sighed.

I said, "You're questioning it all, aren't you Robby?" and I curled around him, it was getting chilly anyhow.

He said, "What do you believe?"

"My age cohort got cynicism instead of a world view."

"I need to know what to believe."

"I thought you knew."

"Tell me what you believe."

"Okay, I believe in Not Ever Being Sure. As much as I make fun of what John says, the Limina makes sense to me. Maybe that's what I believe in."

He was still not moving. "Maybe Jesus is inside us," he said. "I've been feeling this space around my shoulders, like this gap, like Jesus isn't hovering over me anymore the way he did when I first stopped being crazy. I'm thinking maybe I've internalized Jesus. I don't need to talk about it so much anymore."

"That's good." I was definitely getting chilly. "Internalizing is fine by me, especially if it means you stop making speeches on street corners to strangers."

"It's like maybe I trust now that other people will find their way too. There are different ways. Sometimes I look at those guys in the bar or the gold-chain gang, and it's like I'm looking down from a million miles away. Like Jesus must look at things. It's all one thing."

The high was passing. "You're going to end up a Buddhist. I can see you as a Buddhist. You're already mostly vegetarian."

He said, "I liked the idea about believing in each other. Telling the truth to each other."

"Yes, that's something we could both use. If you decide to go out on me or whatever, just let me know what's going on, okay?"

He seemed to tighten for a moment. "I'm not sure I've told you absolutely everything–"

"No, we're skipping the past, okay? There are tons of dumb things in my past that I haven't told you. But starting now, truthfulness to each other. Nothing to fuck up the other person's perception of reality? Even secrets are okay, but don't pretend there's no secret when there is."

He put his hand on the side of my face. My whole body sighed: I was getting used to regular touches. He nodded yes, then mouthed the word, and finally verbalized it. "Yes," he said. "I agree."

I thought I could live a long time like this. He was less titillating than the chain gang guy or the student in London whose name I never learned. But this was better for the long run. Robby would be my calm and refreshing pool, a safe place to soak between whatever was happening to me in the world. I thought I could live with Robby forever: he was relaxing; he was lovely to look at; there was a kind of dignity about being married to him.

I had a little fantasy that we would both go back to school and become lawyers. We'd have a firm with my sister, we'd do nothing but pro bono work, tenant law, civil rights. It's true that I tended to picture us in very nice clothes, but when we were old and looked back on our useful but pleasure-filled lives, we'd say, Do you remember our honeymoon in Aruba?

18

The cab dropped us in front of Love Palace at two a.m. I was drowsy, but happy to be home. We struggled upstairs, banging our bags on the walls, Robby in front. The short hall to the apartment had a new smell I couldn't place, and then Robby had trouble with the key. I put my things down and moved up beside him. There was a manila envelope on the floor, half under the door, and he picked it up. It had our names on it, with exclamation points: Robby! & Martha! It contained two leather key cases, and Robby handed me one monogrammed with initials that I finally recognized as what would have been my married name had I chosen to use it.

Nothing was making a lot of sense to me. "What happened?" Someone had changed the lock. The door had a new brass lock and doorknob. I said. "Do you suppose there was a break-in or something?"

"No," said Robby, "I think it was Eleanor."

"Eleanor?" I pushed ahead of him and opened the door with my key, very smooth action, the tumbler needed no jiggling. I stepped in, found the switch, and almost walked into a professionally lettered banner that said !!!Welcome Home Robby!!! and Martha!!!

"Eleanor," murmured Robby.

I ducked under the banner, and was brought to a full stop: a huge brown leather couch and ottoman in the living room. White blinds, fresh paint.

I said, "Where's my furniture?"

On the ottoman was a bamboo tray with a note on a cream-colored card. Eleanor said she hoped we wouldn't mind: Just one more wedding gift!! As a sometime copy editor, I was getting pretty tee'd off by the exclamation points. But when my brain finally focused, I realized that one more wedding gift meant that my apartment had been ransacked and redecorated.

Fresh white paint and refinished floors. An Oriental area rug in browns and pinks under the ottoman, track lighting and pillows, real oil paintings, abstracted flowers and vaguely southwestern landscapes also in the carpet colors.

I stood in the middle of the room and made a complete turn.

Robby said, "You're pissed, aren't you? I can tell you're really pissed."

I started walking through the apartment. There were more

enthusiastic notes: Enjoy! More to Come!! She hadn't had time to do much with the fixtures, but the kitchen but did have layers of fresh paint and fresh resilient on the floor and a country style table, oak on top and legs painted green, ditto the chairs. The table was set with placemats and new green stoneware. New coffee maker, cabinets cleaned, lined, and filled with more of the green stoneware.

"You're pissed," said Robby. "You're really really pissed. I can tell because you're not talking."

"Where are my jelly glasses?" I said. "What did she do with my stuff, Robby? Did you know about this? No? Well, it's a good thing, because you're right, I am very pissed and getting more pissed by the second. What did she do with my stuff?"

I pushed past him into the bedroom where there was a new queen-sized bed with a golden oak headboard and golden oak bureaus. I opened a drawer: my panty hose and socks had been neatly folded. That was when everything around me really went red, just the way they say it does: I was seeing a vertiginous whirlpool of red. "Oh my God. Oh my God. She went in my private drawers and folded my socks! That is too much, Robby, that is really too goddam much."

"I doubt it was Eleanor. It was probably Olivia."

"Do you think it makes it better Robby if your mother's longtime family retainer went through my underwear and folded it? Do you really think that is better?" I wasn't totally crazed; I knew I was lashing out at him when he hadn't done anything, but dammit, it was his mother! "It doesn't matter if she did it or the maid did it! They now know how many of my bras are losing their elastic– and of course I took my good ones with me to Aruba, so all the ones here have bad elastic."

"She'll change everything back," said Robby. "All we have to do is ask–"

"She can do anything, right, Robby? Omigod she played me, she played me– I don't give a damn what she can do, she has no right to redo my drawers!"

Bathroom, like the kitchen still had its old fixtures, pink on pink, with cracked tiles and the orange chemical stains, but there were fresh cloth shower curtains and throw rugs and stainless steel toilet paper holder, stacks of new towels.

"What about my sister's housewarming gift? Mari got me a brand-new rug and toilet seat cover! And a soap dish and toothbrush holder– Those were Mari's gifts to me, Robby!"

Robby looked stricken. "What the fuck did she think she was doing?" He rubbed his wrists. I didn't care. I didn't have words to say how wrong-headed it was. "Incredible," I said. "High handed control freak! I mean, How dare she! What if I was allergic to golden oak? What if I don't believe in making furniture out of leather?"

"She'd replace it–"

"You're missing the point, Robby! She's trying to do something to us– Look at those paintings, especially the paintings. I hate the paintings. How could you ever choose something as personal as paintings for someone else? How could you consider walking into someone else's apartment and redecorating it?"

I guess I was being pretty high-handed myself by this time, and my confident golden Robby had gone all neurasthenic and nail-biting, touching those wrist scars.

Another sheet of Eaton's creamiest was stuck to a picture frame. It said the paintings were temporary, from a gallery. If we wanted different ones, we should replace these and get others. She would pay of course. There were notes on everything: on a rolling cabinet apologizing for no TV; it would be delivered tomorrow. There was a small tear in the back of the easy chair; the replacement was on the way.

I started taking down the paintings. "I don't want this stuff," I said. "I'm throwing it out. She said it's ours, I choose to throw it out. Do you want to help? Take down that ugly mirror."

"It belonged to my grandmother."

"Okay, keep the mirror. I'm going to put the rest of the stuff in the hall–except for grandma's mirror–and I'm calling everyone to come and take what they want. Tomorrow. My own personal Free Market!"

We put the paintings in the outside hall. I gathered up pillows and put them out with the paintings. I was beginning to think I might keep the rug. I could feel myself slipping from the height of what my mom calls a hissy fit. I sank down on the couch, and it was mighty comfortable.

Robby said, "Are you okay?"

"I am fucking outraged."

"I never heard you curse so much."

"Fuck your mother, Robby. And the horse she rode in on. I feel totally violated, manipulated–" But his expression was so sad that I began to feel bad for him. "I know you didn't do it."

"It's the way she is. She goes overboard."

"I'm not having it, Robby. I'm really not having it."

We finally went to bed, but I almost got set off again when I opened the closet and found that Eleanor had chosen sides for us, my things toward the window, his toward the interior of the apartment. "I'm calling her first thing in the morning, Robby. Don't try to stop me. I have half a mind to call her tonight–"

"No," he said quickly in his Aruba voice. "Save it till morning."

"Okay, okay. You're right. I'll give myself till morning. She really did go too far. You agree, don't you?"

"Yes. Absolutely."

"And I'm not crazy? You agree she had no right to go in my space– our space– and moved personal possessions? You're her kid, that's bad enough, but there's no excuse with me."

"They're like that," said Robby. "My parents. I was hoping, I was thinking, with us getting married–"

"You were hoping I would protect you from them. That's what you were hoping. Well, don't count on it. It may take too much energy. I may just dump her stuff and wait for her to apologize. Do you think she's going to call us?"

"She'll probably wait for us to call. She won't want to wake us in the morning."

"I'll call her. I want her to know exactly where we stand on this." I had a strong mental image of Eleanor with her tennis bracelet and champagne-colored hair, wringing her hands and rubbing her wrists like Robby and asking for forgiveness. "I think I'm going to tell her that if she pulls another one like this, I'm going to move to the West Coast and take you with me. That will give her something to think about."

Robby smiled in the dim light from the street lamp that filtered through the new Roman blinds. His face on the pillow, his eyes closed, but he was awake if I wanted him. I decided that he had at least partly liked the hissy fit.

I let him drift off to sleep and lay awake awhile. I'd drawn my line in the sand. Take that!, WASP Queen! You showed your hand, made your move a little too soon. I'm on guard now. I lay awake a long time, thinking about what I knew about Eleanor; I couldn't get her face out of my mind: the way she's sneaked up on me with the details of the wedding. How she had had a new copier delivered at the office one day when I had no idea it was coming. I thought of old Rhonda, the previous Office Person: had Rhonda left because she couldn't stand Eleanor running things? And where was John in all this? Above quotidian details like redecorating and new TVs, of course.

I slept badly and woke early. I went down to the Love Palace lounge for coffee, declining to use Eleanor's coffee-tea-espresso robot. I was going to go to the office and call her, but as soon as I came into his line of sight, Danny Boy started yelling about a leak in the kitchen ceiling, and then Cara appeared, whining that the juice boxes for the little kids had disappeared.

I called her, though, before I took care of the Love Palace crises. Olivia answered and said that Mrs. Peterson was out. I certainly didn't intend to yell at Olivia with her operatic contralto that discouraged bad manners. I did almost ask what she thought of my underwear, but I knew if I went down that road I'd end up screaming and then apologizing and explaining how my good bras went to Aruba. Next, I called John.

We all had his cell phone number ("I'll be there for you, I'll always be there for each one of you"), and I realized while I was waiting for him to answer that I didn't have his home phone or, for that matter, the address of his home. Who knew the details of his life? Probably Eleanor.

I was about to give up, thinking, Oh yeah? What about being there when we need you? when he picked up, sounding muffled so that I thought he was maybe still asleep (at eight-thirty in the morning! What was he, a man of leisure?). "How was Aruba?" he murmured.

I got in touch with my indignation and said, "Aruba is in the distant past. And where do you live anyhow, John? You never invited any of us to your place, no one has even seen it! You've seen our places, and for sure your boss has not only seen my place, she redecorated my place, which is what I'm calling about. She broke into my apartment and threw out my stuff and replaced it with shelter magazine shit."

He seemed to be taking a breath, changing the angle of phone to mouth so that he sounded more alert. "You're angry with Eleanor."

"Angry? Angry? You bet I am, John! She redid my private drawers, John! She infantilizes Robby. Well it stops right now, John! It's over!"

He listened, he asked for the bare minimum of details, and after I'd run my course like an enthusiastic little wildfire, he said, "Yes, she was overstepping boundaries."

"Damn straight!"

"I told her it was probably a bad idea."

"Bad idea! Beyond bad! Evil! I'm packing up Robby and taking him to California."

"Martha," he said, "it's only a place."

"No, it's not only a place! It may be Love Palace's apartment, but it was my stuff, and my stuff has disappeared, and it was supposed to be where Robby and I started our life together. It was our place, not her place."

"I'll talk to her," he said. "Are you calling from the apartment?"

"No. I'm in the office. I can't stand being in the apartment. You go ahead and talk to her, but tell her I'm throwing it all out," I said.

"Let me talk to her first," he said.

I said, "I'm having my own private Free Market. Today. Early. I'm getting rid of everything she bought. I'm giving it all away— It's only things, right?"

"I'll come over later," he said.

In spite of everything, when I was off the phone, I felt better knowing that John was on the case. Then I went back to the rest of it: calling the plumber who said the leak sounded like a job for the roofer, so I called the roofer, and while I was calling the roofer, I spotted the missing juice boxes buried under some reams of copy paper, and by the time Cara made it upstairs, Robby was with her, on their way to pick up the kids.

Robby said, "My mother called. I told her how pissed you are."

"She called the apartment?"

"Yes. She said your things are in the basement."

"Great!" I said. "In the basement with six inches of water! Terrific!"

Cara said, "Everyone was wondering how you'd react."

"Listen, tell anybody you see that first thing after lunch, there's a Free Market in the little hall upstairs. I'm putting out the paintings and pillows and all the decorative-shit touches for anyone who wants them."

I called Esta and Chickie, left a message for Malika. Danny Boy and White Frank and Black Frank came up, and Cara and Robby brought the little kids. Everyone came to Martha's Free Market. It was sort of like a post-wedding open house, all these people around in the hall while I brought out more paintings and pillows for them to pick over.

Esta, clutching two pillows with needlepoint birds, rolled her eyes to move me a little farther from the others. She whispered, "Martha, did you hear? While you were away?" She jerked her chin toward Malika, on her way to work in pink scrubs and silver bracelets, looking at one of the pseudo-southwestern paintings. "Malika broke up with Ace. She just threw him out on the street. I don't know how we're going to have our Tenants' meeting without him."

"Ace is gone?" That struck me as almost as bad as the redecorating.

Esta nodded.

"Why did she throw him out? Can't he come back for a meeting?"

"Malika won't talk to him, and she's the president. It turns out he still visits his old wife over in Newark. He has some grown children, too, but Malika knew about them. She didn't know he was still married to his wife. Malika threw his stuff out on the street. He says he broke up with that woman a long time ago, but Malika says that woman has the marriage certificate, and she don't live with married men."

I felt a kind of bleak disappointment: that Ace, too, would get hampered in his work by love, just like my mother and me. And Esta was right about the Tenants' Council, it was a good group, but they depended on Ace.

Esta didn't seem satisfied with my stunned silence. "No, she won't take him back till he gets a divorce. You talk to him, Martha."

"Talk to him? She's the one who threw him out."

Esta hugged her pillows and shook her head. "And now Ace don't have a place to lay his head either."

Then I started feeling guilty because I still hadn't found out who really owned 317. And it hit me that I didn't have the energy to start over on the apartment just to spite Eleanor. Not if I was going to do anything else. Like find out who owned 317. Robby was just coming out with the giant ottoman to give away, and I stopped him and said we'd keep that, and I made him take it back inside and don't give away the coffee pot either, start a pot of coffee for everyone.

Then he and the Franks brought my boxes up from the basement, and I kept thinking I should say something to Malika (Sorry you found out your lover had a wife?). But then the fifty inch HDTV arrived, and we decided to have it set up in the main lounge downstairs, not in the apartment, and brought my old TV upstairs.

Malika went to work, and a few other people showed up and took stuff. John didn't come that day after all, and I didn't hear from Eleanor and didn't try to call her either. Robby and I had take-out Chinese for dinner, and by the next morning, when I started looking around the rooms without the paintings and pillows, I realized I liked the cream, white, brown leather and golden oak. Austere but rich. I had Mari's accessories back in the bathroom, and our dirty clothes had begun to accumulate on the bedroom floor and my posters were parked in the corner waiting to be taped onto the fresh paint. What with Robby's huge sneakers in the middle of the living room and the empty take-out containers on the ottoman, it was feeling like home.

Of course I continued to get a lot of mileage out of complaining. The next morning I called Madame, and she agreed it was high-handed, but seemed more amused than indignant, as did Mari when I talked to her. She wanted to tell me about John's latest sermon at Pinnacle. "You feel so uplifted when it's over," she said. "I don't know how he does it."

We ended by making a date to go visit Nana.

Then the roofer patched the roof and the day after that, the Franks replastered and painted the kitchen ceiling. That day, Cara and Robby took the little kids' group to the museum, and John called to apologize for not coming when he said. Followed by, as soon as I'd gotten off the phone with him, a call from Eleanor herself. She blathered about how she got carried away, always overdid things, had our best wishes at heart, etc.

"Martha?" she said after a while in the irritating little girl voice. "Martha? Are you still there?"

I gave it the old college try, attempted to give her a real taste of my indignation. I said, "You were way out of line, Eleanor. I can't tell you how out of line you were. You put my stuff in that crummy basement: my bed, my posters, the new bathroom stuff my sister gave me for a moving-in gift."

"If there was any damage, we'll have it repaired of course. It was just that I was trying to do it all before you came back. For a surprise."

"I don't like surprises. Maybe you do. How about this one? I gave away all the paintings."

"Those paintings were—" she said, and I could hear her hesitate, decide not to tell me what they were worth. "Keep whatever you want, Martha," she said. "Throw out what you want to throw out. It's yours. It's completely yours. I made a mistake. I know I made a mistake. I know I have to stay out of it. I apologize. It's all yours, do what you want with it. I'll send the movers to bring your things back upstairs."

"It's already done. Robby and the clients did it."

"I'm really sorry, Martha," she said. "You'll never know how I regret this. I'm just so used to doing things for Robby. I've been so absurdly happy about him finding you. He's been– he was my only baby, and he's always been so fragile–"

"I'm not sure that's true," I said. The indignation flames were dying down to little coals. I was interested in the family dynamics, even from her point of view. "Robby seems to be doing very well, actually, at least he is when nobody does things to infantilize him."

"I know I protected him too much. But when it's your child–you are so exposed–you can't imagine the pain you can feel when your child is hurting–"

I bit my tongue. I was not going to empathize, I refused. And I didn't want to remind her or me either that I was forty-something years old and I didn't have a child. And didn't intend to, if that was where she was going.

She adjusted her tone. "Well," she said, "I truly hope you'll accept my apology, Martha. It was–crude of me. To try to do so much, without asking."

"Whatever," I said. "But, Eleanor, listen, you had better stay out of our business. For a long time. I really mean that. If I feel pressure from you, Robby and I will move. We really will. And don't call us, we'll call you. Okay?"

After I had hung up, I sat for a few minutes going over it in my mind: first I liked it that I had said we'd call her, then I decided that sounded ridiculous. Had I been firm enough? Had she been abject enough? I had one passing unpleasant thought: Eleanor had called immediately after John, which made me suspect he had alerted her that this was the best moment to catch me. Martha is busy and distracted, I imagined him saying: This is the moment to call her.

He finally showed up in the late afternoon in the middle of a Tenants' meeting at which the tenants spent the whole time complaining and no one had any ideas about what to do without Ace. They were overjoyed to see John, and I was glad too. He took Malika aside to discuss mediating between her and Ace, and when they came back, she said she was willing to talk to Ace, and John led us all in prayer, and Esta thought it was the best meeting they'd had in a long time.

19

That was a kind of high point that was followed by an end-of-summer malaise. The green of the scrub trees and bushes in the empty lots had taken on that rusty edge. The good stuff was over, the block party and the wedding. Things became routine: school started, so we organized a homework club for the kids. Cara complained that she and Kristen did all the tutoring, and Gil never showed up anymore.

Robby said Gil had found a secular techno-band in the city that he wanted to work with for a while. Gil wasn't the only one missing: John disappeared again, with no sign of his promised intervention between Ace and Malika. Our evening meetings seemed pathetic with just the girls and Robby and me. Danny Boy must have thought we were pathetic too, because he took a nap on the nearest couch and snored while we tried to talk. Kristen said she might as well have let her parents take her to Europe.

"Fine," said Cara, "So go."

Kristen got tears in her eyes: "You guys," she said, "All of this. I couldn't leave, not really."

She and Cara embraced, and Robby put his arms around them and hugged too. They all irritated me too, and I was feeling restless, like maybe I'd made a commitment too fast. Out-of-doors, the heat was shifting and the young trees over by Riversedge Renaissance had crisp leaves. When I sat down to do the bank statement, I was shocked by new withdrawals: two hundred here, three hundred there, over and over, it seemed. For the first time, it affected the daily balance and put us below what was required for no fees. We weren't overdrawn, but close enough. I began to get mad: Gil, I thought. Gil of the flickering energy and sarcastic remarks and no real loyalty to anything but his unpleasant music.

I made one more stab at looking for missing withdrawal slips, for records of who had bank cards. I went way back into the files I had put off organizing, and instead of bank records, ran across magazines and books about nonprofit organizations, some with book marks made of sheets of paper scribbled in the large sloppy handwriting I had come to recognize as Rhonda's. I paused, thinking for a second that she might be the culprit, but the notes were just lists of articles she seemed to want to remember, and then one sheet with some doodles of boxes and ovals and the name Rhonda Phelps, Rhonda J. Phelps. Then she wrote Reverend John King a few times and scratched out something that might have been Rhonda Phelps King.

Oh God, I thought. Her too. A crush on John and probably more. Not me, I said, not anymore. And went through the bank account again, but any way I looked at it, the bank had recorded seven withdrawals I didn't have receipts for.

It had to be Gil. The little fucker was stealing our money. He must have got hold of a bank card somehow. I never trusted him. He used Love Palace when he needed back-up musicians or a place to sleep. Now he had a better band and no doubt some lover of whatever gender who had given him a place to live, and he was still using us as a source of involuntary donations. I sat steaming and thinking that he had probably been making passes at Robby too. The way he inclined his body toward Robby when they talked. How he had set the girls against each other. It was all circumstantial evidence, but I couldn't help myself: a little wanted poster of Gil with the ring ln his ear popped up in my mind.

I was sitting there trying to figure it out when John knocked on the doorjamb, and in spite of myself, I was relieved: it was like, now something will happen.

"You," I said. "Back in town, are you? Everyone just blows town when things get slow. You and that little jerk Gil."

Smiling serenely, he took his usual seat under the Prison Pietà.

I kept going. "Everybody has a crush on you, don't they? My sister is always talking about your sermons. She says you don't preach much about Jesus. You'll lose your fans if you don't do God talk."

He lifted an eyebrow. "What's bothering you, Martha?"

"Nothing's bothering me! Stop analyzing me and listen to what I say!"

He nodded. "All right."

"Did Old Rhonda come to hear you preach too? Rhonda who used to have my job?"

"Ah, Rhonda," he said. "Rhonda left precipitously. I think she lost patience with–"

"Living in the Limina? She wasn't stealing, was she?"

"No, I don't think so."

"Well, someone is stealing from us now. I'm getting sick of the disappearing money from the account. We're almost overdrawn, and I'm the one who has to keep the books and I suppose you're going to expect me to make a report or face the accountant or whatever at the end of the year."

I could feel my voice getting shrill, and I expected him to repeat,

Martha is obsessing, or maybe, Martha, something is troubling you, but he lifted his arms behind his head, barely missing the Prison Pietà. He extended his slim brown leather loafers, legs crossed at the ankles. His hair almost needed to be cut, but not quite. He said, "I've been thinking a lot about– what we're all seeking– what a lot of people call God. I've been thinking about where I want to be in five years, how I can best help other people."

"You'll be head honcho of some big church, won't you? Or running a string of Love Palaces? I know you won't be worrying about petty cash."

"I'm very bad on the details, Martha. Administration is not my strong suit. Do you know that the pastors of the largest churches spend as much as three-quarters of their time on fund-raising and business? It's why you've been such a godsend to us, Martha– you see, I do still use God language– you've whipped us into shape."

"Oh please."

He sighed, resettled himself. "There's also the possibility that the church won't be open to what I'm doing now."

"Which is what, exactly?"

It made him laugh. "I'm sorry, Martha," he said. "I'm not laughing at you, but so often you touch the thing itself. I'm having trouble explaining what I'm doing. I'm having a crisis in what I think of as– the container. I have something real, something powerful, something that I believe totally and profoundly. I feel it, I know it, and I can even communicate it under certain circumstances – but it doesn't have a name yet. Some people will call it Jesus, and that's one way of containing the message. But there are others. What I am looking for is the container that holds the water for those who need to drink."

"It sounds like some kind of stupid universal religion."

"There you go again, putting your finger on the thing itself. You're one of the truth tellers, Martha."

I could feel the sucking. I wanted to tell him not to use my name. I had the feeling that if I had sex with him again, he would be something different, whatever I needed this time.

I said, "Why don't you ever talk about yourself, John? About your past. I know where Robby came from and Cara and Ace and even Danny Boy– but you never talk about yourself. You're not a kid, you've only been at the Pinnacle church for a couple of years. We don't know anything about you!"

He looked mildly surprised. "I grew up in western Pennsylvania and Ohio. Wrong career choices. A marriage that failed. Does that matter?" He had said it so easily (too easily, some part of me complained). "May I tell you something about yourself, Martha? Something I want you just to listen to, to take in, and not respond to."

"All right."

"You are radiant," he said. "Your new status– your marriage, your work here– something– has made you glow. People want to be near you."

"I got a tan in Aruba," I said. "Stay on your side of the room, okay?"

He laughed. "You can't just listen, can you? You have to keep the barriers up. I'm going to tell you something, Martha. About my plans. I'd rather you didn't spread it around because it's still exploratory. I'm thinking of taking steps to make the change. We're hiring a publicist. Eleanor Peterson is working with me on this."

"Of course."

"She thinks I should experiment with more than lectures, try a DVD set, weekend seminars. A book eventually, cable television. I told her I was still feeling my way, that I didn't have the container yet, but she has suggested that the search might be as gripping as whatever we finally name it, and I see the justice of that."

"You mean you're leaving the church?"

"Not at all."

"And Love Palace?"

"Martha, dear Martha, this is an exploration. I've been thinking over Eleanor's offer for a long time, the publicist, testing the waters. To step out and see what happens."

I had this vision of him stepping into a pool of light, a spotlight. "You wade into the Limina and Love Palace falls apart."

"You give me much too much credit, Martha. You are the one. The moment I saw you I knew I was looking at the one who could make Love Palace finally work."

"I bet you told that to Rhonda too."

He shook his head. "Martha, you have become Love Palace!"

"What about Ace and Malika? You were supposed to get them back together."

"I'm not turning away," he said, "just trying something in addition."

"Well, whatever, go, spread the message, whatever it is. Enjoy yourself. But we're going to be in big trouble soon. Eleanor did what are probably illegal renovations to my apartment, Kristen is probably leaving, Cara is thinking about leaving, Gil hasn't been here for two weeks, and this time I'm sure he's the one taking money from the bank machines. That's what you have to do something about immediately. There are more and more withdrawals, and nobody accounting for them, and I'm sure it's Gil."

"That's a serious charge."

"Yes, it's what I think people call stealing. I mean, I don't know it's Gil, I don't even know if he has a bank card. I just know he hasn't been around much, and somebody is making withdrawals."

"And Gil seems the most likely person to you?"

"I need to find out who has the cash cards. Who can take money out from the Love Palace Account? Robby and I share one–"

"Eleanor has one, and I do."

"But nobody seems to know who else."

"Clearly we need to sit down together and straighten this out," he said.

"We were supposed to do this two months ago! And how are we supposed to do it if you're going on tour?"

Instead of answering, John got up and closed the office door and came around the desk. I raised my hands toward him off, but he didn't touch me, only my chair. He leaned close to my ear and said, "You are too burdened, Martha." He rolled me in my chair to the center of the room. "First you need to relax."

"Leave me alone."

"Shh," he whispered and touched me. There was a cool electricity of his palms on either side of my neck. I jumped, but he kept his hands in place. "Let me see where the tension is," he said.

"I don't want a massage," I said, in fact, I did want a massage, or wanted something.

"Here," he said. "The base of your skull. Your shoulders too."

"Don't," I said, but I said it softly because I was overcome by how huge his hands felt on my shoulders. They were immense, large enough to calm the irritations that danced like metal filings in my brain.

"Let me help you with this tension," he said. "You need to loosen up, to practice stillness. Stop talking, shut your brain for a little while."

I tried to talk. "You think I'm over-reacting to this. No one else seems to care about the money, it seems like Queen Eleanor always comes up with more–" More noises, a kind of shushing, a murmur. Working on the back of my neck, my head wanting to droop forward, me blabbing on, trying to stay upright. "You're right about me being burdened, I mean I came back and just plunged into work– it's like nobody here is responsible and then there's the thing with pulling down the houses and who owns 317 so the Tenants' Council can get their buildings fixed–"

"Shh," he said, "shh."

He worked down the back of my neck, out my shoulders. I stopped talking. The sensation was not so much in my muscles as around me, as if this great mink-dark thing were pressing against me, pressing me toward some release.

"Very tight," he murmured. "Very tight. You're carrying so much on your shoulders. Don't hold it off, Martha. This is for you. Let it go. Let your eyes close."

So they closed. After a while, I was aware he had stopped kneading. He cupped his hands over my ears, then slid them forward over my eyes and temples.

"Now, Martha," he whispered. "You think you need information, you think you need facts. And what you really need is to know that we don't know. We don't know about this money that is troubling you, we don't know the answers to the big questions. Sometimes those close to us leave or die. Sometimes we can't balance the check book, but in the case of the check book, the funds will come in." His cool hands slid down to my elbows, and he lifted me to a standing position, rolled the chair away. I felt him incredibly near, along my whole back, his body lined up with mine, as if I were his puppet. I wanted to lie down with him on top of me. He whispered: "You need to let go of your burdens and live where your body is."

And then he kissed me: a dry kiss– the whole thing was dry–on the side of my face, away from my lips. I should have spoken then, but my mouth was dry too, and then his hands were doing a different thing, one stroking down my flank, pressing me back against him, and I was conscious that I had to hold perfectly still if I were to keep more from happening, and all the time the dark relaxation was running down my sides to my thighs and spreading as heat inside my jeans. He began to tug at my jeans, one hand on the back band, one reaching around me to the fly, and I was thinking Of course he won't unzip me. I won't let him unzip me.

He didn't, but he began to move the jeans back and forth, the thick crotch seam rubbing against me, and I gasped and felt myself melting inside my clothes, wanted to lie down, not stand, but he made me stand and only touched my clothes, only touched the outside of my clothes, and whispered in my ear, an entirely different voice, that I had never heard from him, hard like the teeth through lips. "You like this, don't you? You're really here with me now aren't you? You are totally here now."

I went through to a very dark place, felt it as deep gasping breaths, came out suddenly on the other side awake and surprised.

"Stop that!" I said, jumping away, turning to face him, grabbing the chair to put between me and him.

He smiled. "You were there for a moment , weren't you, Martha? You were completely there."

"Don't ever do that again." I could feel tears rising in my eyes, but I wasn't going to let them brim over.

He saw them too: "Cry," he said. "Let yourself go fully, Martha, that's what you need. You found a moment without your burdens, Martha," he said. "You came fully into the present."

"Go away," I said. "I will not fuck you ever again."

"This was a good thing, Martha."

But it wasn't good, because I had a flash of Robby's face and realized that I would not be telling this to Robby. I shoved the chair away and left John under his picture. I ran upstairs to the apartment. I locked myself in, paced around the living room, looked out the window, and his car was still parked out front. Then I went in the bedroom and locked myself in there and lay on the bed until the light changed and I was sure he was gone.

I got through the day by thinking about how I would work it all out at my next session with Madame, but when I got to Madame's the next day, I lay down on her couch and crossed my arms over my chest like some greenhorn immigrant determined that a good doctor should be able to figure out what was wrong with no hints from the patient herself.

She seemed mildly surprised by my silence, and said, after a while, "You have still the tan."

"It's not like that's a good thing. Ultraviolet rays give you cancer."

"Sunning, a glass of wine, a nice omelette with cheese–Americans make all the pleasant things in life immoral. Don't you think you may enjoy in moderation, Martha?"

"Thanks once again for your European superiority."

There was another silence, long enough for her to shush her

stockings. "Yes? And how is it going, Martha?"

"It's all going to hell, thanks." I started in on my list of what was wrong at Love Palace.

When I had wound down, she said, "These are indeed difficulties," she said, "but you said they will make up the money in the account again, and there will be an investigation. You have rearranged your apartment to suit you, you have spoken directly to your mother-in-law–you seem to be dealing with the problems as they arise. You are a capable and competent woman, Martha. What you are describing seems to me like life not tragedy."

She'd spread a sheet over her couch since the last time I was there. My feet in yellow socks were tugging it out of place, so I sat up, straightened it, then dropped back again. There was a curtain dropping in my brain, alarms and confusion, distracting her and me from something important.

"I don't know why you insist on treating patients in your living room."

"Again my living room?"

The little impressionist tidal scene with its giant gold baroque frame, the ceiling moldings; the green and cream Oriental rug on top of beige carpeting. I had spent one entire session talking about the way she had rugs on top of rugs. The worst thing, of course, was the goddam bust of her sitting on a pillar next to her curly-legged desk.

I said, "Nana would plotz if she knew I took seriously the advice of someone who has rugs on their rugs."

"I'm not so sure you do take my advice. I like your Nana, though. Why would she do this plotz?

"Because it is so totally bourgeois."

"Go on."

"About what? About how bourgeois you are?"

"Go on about what you would like to go on about. You have begun to flop and kick my furniture with your feet. We should discover what your feet are saying."

I waited, still hoping and fearing that she would guess.

"Yes," said Madame after a while. "I am a bad therapist. I do not please you. Your mother-in-law fills your apartment with beautiful furniture and this does not please you–"

"I knew you were on her side about the furniture!"

"On the contrary. I am not on her side. She is clearly interfering where she should not. But I am thinking, is it possible you can't believe your good luck? A fine husband, a nicely decorated apartment– I am afraid you begin to take measures to undermine how things are going well."

"You're going to tell me these are nothing compared to when you crawled under the Iron Curtain back when there was a real Iron Curtain." Maybe it was nothing, anyhow, I thought. All I had to do was steer clear of John King for a while. I said, "And of course nothing compares to your patient who lost everything in the stock market and came home to find his wife had killed herself with his sleeping pills. I'm nothing, my problems are nothing! I'll have to come up with something better to catch your attention! I don't know why you fool with such a worthless patient anyhow. Maybe I should just quit therapy."

"You are upset, Martha," said Madame.

"And I didn't tell you, John is acting totally awful."

"Ah. Tell me about your religious mentor."

"He's not my mentor. I'm sick of him. He manipulates us all and he's going to go off and be a famous guru." I gave her a chance to pick up on something in my voice, and when she didn't, I said, "He's got a lecture tour, and of course he's leaving me with all the responsibility for Love Palace."

"Ah," said Madame. "People are leaving you. People always fail in their promises to you."

You're missing it, I thought.

"Your young husband?"

"Please stop calling him that."

"Your husband Robby. He has stayed with you. You trust him."

"We've been married three weeks. People ought to manage to be faithful to each other for three weeks."

"This is good," she said, "that you have decided in favor of your husband. And there are others too who have not left you. Your mother came back. And you had always the loving grandmother and sister."

"Mari and I are supposed to go see Nana tomorrow."

"Good," she said.

I had this expanding sense of desolation. She didn't know what had happened. It hadn't been unfaithfulness exactly, except that it was. But she wasn't going to guess, and I felt a heavy impossibility of telling her.

She said, "You have made a conscious choice. You have not been a person who makes a commitment very fast or very often. It is good you will visit your grandmother and that you trust your husband."

"What if he can't trust me?"

"Ah," said Madame, with the rich fruity sound of the final bars of a session ending. "The question is, do you trust you?"

Driving home, keeping the Guzzler to the right because of a suspicious new clunk, I was full of regret. I had kept waiting for the magical Madame to read my mind, and she had failed. I thought making an emergency call to her and confessing. Nonsense, I told myself. Everyone had their clothes on. It had been creepy of John to do it, creepy of me to let him, but nobody got naked. There was a time in my life when my guilt would been totally laughable– a little petting in the desk chair. There had been no skin, so this wasn't a real sex act.

And people keep secrets all the time, don't they? Isn't that actually a sign of maturity, to not have to dump all your business in everyone's face? Didn't I have more serious things to do than waste therapy dollars on than a little masturbatory aberration? Even Nana and Irv had secrets. It was supposed to be a secret that Irv slept over nights. He never went in Nana's room till Mari and I had gone to bed, but it was a tiny apartment and who could not know that they slept together, which I thought was totally disgusting, they both had gray hair for Godsake and Nana had fat ankles and wrinkles and Irv was bald.

Nana's other secret, far more serious, was that she read Harlequin romances. And hid them, also not so easy in an apartment. She kept them in a paper bag on top of the bathroom cabinet. I added this to the fuel for my fire of cynicism and always meant to throw it in her face some day.

I'd give myself a pass on this one, I decided. Ease up on yourself, Martha. Judge this one by how you did next time. And the next time, I promised myself, no sex and no dry humping either. I didn't have to confess, if it was really over now. Next time I'd say no and really mean it.

20

Parked in front of Love Palace was an enormous silver block of an SUV with one of those aggressive names like Colossus or Incursion. I thought it might be Eleanor or Warren, neither of whom I'd seen since the debacle over the redecoration. I slowed down. In fact, I was about to turn around and go to Mari's or up the hill to Jo-Jo's Caribbean for a plate of greasy eggs, but Chickie came out the door, lighting a cigarette. I asked her who was inside.

"Kristen's parents came for her," she said. "Everyone's saying good-bye."

For half a second I felt relief, but then indignation: "I talked to them again two weeks ago! They were supposed to be letting her stay for the fall semester!"

"Yeah, well," said Chickie, crossing the street. "They come and they go, don't they."

Riding my wave of indignation, I went in. There seemed to be a lot of people, clients standing around the periphery watching the show, which centered on a mound of suitcases and bags, Kristen dressed in one of her tiny skirts and lots of jewelry, sitting on the largest suitcase, sobbing, with Robby and Cara kneeling beside her. The grown-ups hovered just behind, the man tall and slim, the woman an upscale version of Crys the Aruba bimbo.

Gil was back too. He was standing with an elbow on the balustrade of the stairs, dressed in black, hair a new pink hair color that matched the amoeba-shaped logo on his tee shirt.

"Oh you guys!" wailed Kristen, and the mother made a move toward her and the father stopped her.

"It'll be okay," said Cara. "It'll be okay."

It registered with me that the packing was neatly done, maybe even planned in advance.

"I have to say good bye to the little kids–" she sobbed. "I have to say good-bye–where's Danny Boy?"

He came out of the kitchen as if he'd been listening, wearing a tablecloth around his middle, and Kristen got up and kissed him, and circled the room kissing the Franks, everyone in sight. I introduced myself to her parents.

"She called us," the father told me, a little defensively. "She said she was ready."

"It was time," said the mother with her chin high and defiant. "It's been a long time."

Kristen saw me and cried, "Oh Martha! Martha, how can I

leave! I'm coming back! I've already decided! It's only a vacation! I'll be back. I know I'll be back."

It was Kristen's big number. She was having a wonderful time.

She turned to Gil, opened her arms and embraced him, and he had this strange crooked smile, and her parents still hovering, as if expecting someone to attack their baby.

I said to Robby and Cara, "So she called them?"

Cara nodded. "I mean, she's sad to be going, and she definitely has mixed feelings, but she was ready. She'd been giving her stuff away for two weeks."

"Like a suicide," said Robby. "I don't mean she was suicidal, but just that that's a sign that a person is planning to go away."

The Kristen-Gil embrace was continuing. "Did she call him too?"

They nodded.

I was indignant now at Kristen: she gets bored and she calls Mommy and Daddy and then it's off to Paris or Rome or wherever rich people go for fresh air. When I was a kid, we were lucky to get a day at the fricking Jersey Shore.

Gil and the clients helped carry her bags out. Robby hung back said, "I'm going to the city tonight to hear Gil."

"I thought you and Mari and I were going to visit Nana tomorrow. You said you wanted to go."

"I'll be back," he said. "I'll be late, but I'll be back. This is a big deal for Gil. He should have stayed to rehearse today, but he came back for Kristen, and Cara and I are going to go support him tonight. It's his new band's first gig."

"Is he financing his new band with Love Palace funds?"

Robby moved away from me. "That's not funny."

"Who said it was funny? The money is missing and Gil has been missing too."

He went down two more. "He hasn't been missing. We've been talking to him every other day."

"Who has?"

"Me, Cara. We were never out of touch with Gil. I knew you were going to react this way. Why don't you come too?"

"No thanks."

"Gil hasn't quit Love Palace, he's just doing some music with this group in the city for a while."

"Why didn't anyone tell me about it, then, and what about the money?"

"You make such a big deal about money, Martha."

I was losing it, and I really didn't care. "This might just possibly be because I didn't grow up in a situation where you can lose three hundred dollars a week and no one cares. I grew up where you actually have to be careful what you spend."

Robby started down the steps. "He wouldn't steal."

"Exactly how do you know that? How do you know he wouldn't? What makes you so sure? Why didn't you tell me you've been talking to him?"

"He's my friend, and he isn't a thief!"

I thought I had my voice under control, but it came out very loud: "Then who the hell is stealing from us, Robby?"

"I have no idea. And this is the wrong time to talk about it." He dropped his hands. "You know what? I don't need this. I'm going with my friends to the city to hear some music, to support my friend. I don't need this from you. I'm out of here. You never did like Gil. You've had a thing against him. I don't know why. My friends are important to me." His face was so cool and still that it took my breath away, and I had a flash of him in ten years, perhaps even more handsome, perfectly self-possessed and very intimidating.

It was our first fight.

21

Love Palace was so empty that night that Danny Boy declared he was going out on a bender because there was nobody to cook for. I felt mildly hurt that I didn't count, but I said Fine with me, I've been looking forward to a quiet evening.

But it was too quiet, and I got jumpy in the apartment and came out and checked through the whole place, sure that I was going to be robbed and raped and burnt to a crisp by arsonists, as if every bad actor in the Waterfront Section had passed the word to all the other bad actors, and they were approaching in a murmuring mob. It was as if I had never before noticed that we were in a sketchy neighborhood. That razing it and starting fresh might not be such a bad idea.

I called Mari and talked to her for a while about our plans for visiting Nana tomorrow, and I kept waiting for her to invite me over or out for dinner, but why would she since we were seeing each other in twelve hours?

I barricaded myself in the apartment finally and listened to the radio and made myself some oil and garlic pasta and drank the rest of a bottle of wine, feeling a vague irony about how this was what I was doing when I met Robby not even a year ago: living on garlic and oil pasta. Only back then I'd been out of wine and using the grocery store brand mixed oil and garlic powder and now I had fresh garlic and expensive extra-virgin olive oil.

I went to bed early, and seemed to wake every hour, thinking someone was coming in the door, hearing sounds from inside the building, and sometimes shouts and music from outside. Toward morning I had a dream about Nana, in which her face was a big close-up like in an old-time movie theater. In the dream, she banged her tea mug on the kitchen table and shouted, "I am not a Secretarian!" I knew that was a made-up word, but I yelled back at her anyhow: "Oh yes you are– you're the thesis, and I am the anti-thesis!" To which she shouted back, "You think you know Hegel, you little shit? What about Sin-thesis?"

Not that Nana would ever have called someone a little shit, nor would she have made a pun with Sin in it. And I don't even think I ever heard her mention Hegel.

I woke twisted in my sheets, with a sense that something was wrong.

Robby was sitting on the floor with his back to the closet, knees pulled up, staring at me.

"Oh my God, Robby," I said. "What time is it? I was having a nightmare. About Nana. She was mad at me. Did you just get home?"

"I've been back awhile," he said. "I can't sleep."

The clock said 5:57 a.m. "How was Gil's band?"

"Good."

I started to drift toward sleep, and Robby was still sitting there. "Robby? Don't you want to come to bed?"

He said, "We hung around the club for a while. They had another set to do, but I came home." His eyes seemed too wide, as if he'd seen something he didn't want to. "Cara stayed."

"Oh God," I said. "She stayed with Gil? Kristen leaves and Cara stays with Gil?"

Robby shrugged. "They're not having sex. She might want to, but Gil doesn't. I talked to him about the money. He thought I was crazy. None of the Crew ever had those bank cards. He's going to come over and get it straightened out."

There was something wrong with his eyes. The shade was up and a shaft of first sun was coming through, and there was a strange look in his eyes, too much pupil. I said, "You're high, aren't you, Robby? No wonder you can't sleep." I reached out, and he pulled away, but not very fast. I touched his shoulder. "Get in bed."

He got up and sat on the side of the bed. He started rubbing my shoulder, down my arm, pressing his face into mine. It felt urgent, almost rough. Repetitively, anxiously, he rubbed my arms, rubbed my forehead with his. There was an odor to his skin or clothes too, late hours at a club, smoke, sweat, and this urgency. He smothered my mouth with his, and he began that repetitive rubbing again, all over me, my pelvis now, pressing at my bones.

It surprised me, how suddenly I was excited, out of sleep, out of the fight with him and the dream fight with Nana. We did a really fast kind of Slam Bam thing. I came like fireworks, and a little voice from the dream in the back of my head said, Well there's your Sin-thesis!

I almost fell asleep again, but looked at the clock. "I've got to shower. Mari will be here in half an hour. You go to sleep."

"I came back early so I could go with you to meet Nana."

I was touched. Robby had been thinking about Nana while he was smoking dope and listening to Gil's music.

While I showered, Robby changed shirts and made coffee. I watched out the window as I drank some coffee and ate half a two-day-old bagel, and then Mari's yellow Volkswagen came down the street right on time. She waited for us, and I had to bang on the bathroom door to tell Robby to hurry. Mari likes a schedule.

I took my coffee down and sat in the car with her. She had a cardboard container of Starbucks, and I had my mug. She looked glum and annoyed. "You didn't tell me he was coming," she said.

"Do you care?"

"No. I just thought we'd have a chance to talk. It doesn't matter."

"Talk about what?" But he was coming out, wet-haired, shirt sticking to his poorly dried chest. She shrugged.

Robby promptly fell asleep in the back seat.

I stared out the window as we drove off. We went by the Bishop Stebbins Houses and up the hill past Jo-Jo's toward the highway and the suburbs.

I thought Robby was asleep, but he said, "John was on TV this morning. At 5:30."

"5:30 a.m. ?" I said.

"I saw him too," said Mari. "I always watch public access stuff when I do my work out."

That's how she stays size 2. "Why didn't anyone tell me? What was John doing on TV?"

Robby said, "My mom called me on the cell last right. It was just a local show, but it's a start."

Mari said, "They announced it at church on Sunday. The interviewer was an ass, but John was good, although I think he's better in person. I don't think he's figured out how to present himself on TV yet."

"He's too old to look good on TV," I said, not very pleasantly, but I was feeling like I was being left out of things. Mari cast me a disapproving look, and her cheeks had turned a little pink. Of course: I forgot, she had a crush on him too. I barreled ahead: "The main thing on TV, the sine qua non, is youthful skin, no wrinkles. John isn't a spring chicken, whatever a spring chicken is. What did he talk about?"

"The spiritual ramifications of true self-enhancement," said Mari.

"And why it isn't selfish," added Robby.

"Lord have mercy," I said, which was, I think, an imitation of my mother's mother, who I'd only seen about once when I was five years old, and I don't think Mari ever met at all. "This is the message he's taking to the world?"

"You're just pissed at him," said Mari.

"No she isn't," said Robby. "You can't be mad at John. It would be like being mad at God."

"Oh Lord have mercy," I repeated, liking the sound of it. "John has been promoted from the Son to the Father."

Robby was half-lying down in the back seat now, sounding dreamy: "I would have thought I was being blasphemous to say that back when I was trying to be– absolute. When I thought there was one answer to every question."

"John is not like God," I said. "For one thing, John exists."

"He's just a man," said Mari, but in a remarkably different tone from mine.

"He's a man," said Robby, "but he's gone farther than the rest of us. He's gone, like, beyond good and evil."

I made a gagging sound and Mari glanced at me sideways. "Are you okay?"

"I'm fine. John is not beyond good and evil. I think sometimes he's confused about good and evil."

"No," murmured Robby. "He's gone beyond the rest of us." When I glanced back to argue, I saw that he had dozed off with a little smile on.

We shut up for a while. Mari concentrated on the ramp that took us off the highway onto utilitarian suburban streets and then the increasingly green environs of the Miriam Sisters. The big sign, the long driveway, beautiful lawns, shade trees, lots of glass, spacious views of suburban sprawl. It was less than forty-five minutes from Love Palace. I had been living with this sense that it was infinitely far, beyond my ability to get here.

You shouldn't have to visit your family in nursing homes until you're at least fifty-five or sixty.

When the car stopped, Robby muttered groggily.

I said, "Just stay in the car and sleep, Robby. You don't have to come in this time."

He had had his eyes closed, was curled up. He muttered "I'll catch up, go on ahead."

So it was only Mari and me going through the big plate glass doors, past a guard to the elevator. Mari said, "I wasn't expecting Robby. You never mentioned it when talked last night."

"I thought he wasn't coming. He was out nearly all night. Do you care?"

"No, of course not. Why should I care?"

"Because you've mentioned it twice, that's why."

The elevator opened at the intersection of three long halls.

There seemed to be a traffic jam of wheel chairs and slow-moving walkers. It was probably two wheelchairs and one walker, but I was feeling like I was in some cheap horror movie where they all come at you waving their canes and prosthetic devices. Any way you sliced it, no matter how many soft abstracted landscape paintings on the walls or views of suburban New Jersey out the windows–it smelled of Endgame and Too Many Old Lunches.

But I smiled at the nurses and at the ranks of ladies in quilted pink robes and said to Mari, "Now I know why I never come."

At the nurses' station they directed us to Nana, who was in a wheel chair all the way at the end of the hall in a sunny little bump-out lounge with big windows on three sides. She was facing us rather than the windows, and with light behind her, and as we approached, she seemed to have an aura of gold.

Blue robe and matching scuffies, not looking at all like herself, of course. Her head was tilted to one side with decidedly un-Nanalike cuteness. The nurse who came down with us adjusted her wheelchair and straightened her posture while we cried Nana Nana! I kissed without breathing so I wouldn't smell anything. Nana made some little smacking noises that may have been response kisses or may have been mucous bubbles.

It was a great relief to me that it wasn't the real Nana. The real Nana either gave you a big buss on the forehead or let you alone. This Nana seemed likely to squash if you pressed too hard. My Nana, the real Nana, had worn her hair chopped off and utilitarian. This woman had little beauty shop curls. The real Nana smelled not of baby powder but of fried onions and white fish.

It appeared that the nurse was staying. She stepped to one side, and Mari and I pulled up chairs. Mari took a little ballotin of Godiva chocolates out of her bag and laid it on the false Nana's lap. Of course Mari would bring chocolates. The other lady in the little lounge had her hair up in a French twist with a lot of pieces gone wild, and she had a book on her lap. She looked like a real person.

The nurse, tall, broad, and emphatically blonde, said that our grandmother hadn't been eating well lately. She was a very good girl, but she needed to eat.

Mari and I were co-conspirators for one instant, eyes meeting over the Very Good Girl. Mari started jabbering to Nana about her job and my wedding and the pretty robe and the nice view.

The candy box was slipping off Nana's lap. I put it back. I looked at Mari's tense little features and her full cheeks. I looked away. The French twist old lady appeared surprised by something, maybe by waking up and finding herself ninety years old and in the nursing home. I felt a dull terror that the same thing was going to happen to me. The second half of your life goes much faster, they say.

Nana (the real Nana) had objected to Miriam Sisters because it was a Jewish facility. She had shouted, barely comprehensible out the side of her stroked-out mouth: Internationalist not Zionist!

The nurse seemed to have decided that things were going smoothly enough, no leakage from Nana's diaper, no contraband from us, so she told us it was lovely to see us again, and she rolled the lady with the French twist down the hall. The French twist lady leaned toward Mari as she passed and said, "She isn't all there, darling. She hasn't been for some time."

The nurse did a tsk tsk as they retreated down the hall.

"That's the one I'll be," I said. "When they drag me into this place, it will only be kicking and screaming. Although they probably wouldn't take me anyhow since Mom's not Jewish."

Mari asked Nana if she should open the chocolates.

I said, "She's not here. You know that, don't you?"

Mari ignored me and told Nana an excessively boring story about the special store at the mall that had nothing but Godiva chocolates.

"She's not here," I repeated. "Why are you trying so hard?"

Mari kept chattering.

I decided to take a stroll around the sun space, which took about fifteen seconds. I knew I was handling this badly. I was being a brat. The anger wasn't at anyone in particular, certainly not at Mari. I should have made Robby come up, I thought, looking out the window, almost able to make out where we were parked, but the building was at the wrong angle.

Mari used to say so little, at home. I was the talker then, her nose always in a book. Now I wanted to say, Mari, stop wasting your breath, just shut the fuck up. But Mari cooed and murmured. She's actually good at this care-taking thing, I thought, in a kind of shock: Mari who used to try to dissociate herself from all family activities.

I made myself sit down again. I said, "She was mad about something the last time I was here, only I can't remember if we ever figured out what it was. It was something in the news, I was pretty sure."

"Let's not talk in front of her like she isn't here," said Mari.

"But I keep telling you, she isn't! What does she care? I know I've been bad about not coming, I mean, I've been awful about not coming, and I really am sorry."

Mari got back into her chair and crossed her arms over her chest. At least she had stopped inflicting that terrible jabber on the old dried leaf in the overstuffed robe.

There was a silence, then Mari said in a tiny tight voice, "I've been here since you have."

"Oh yes, you're the good granddaughter, everyone knows that. You come every week."

"No, I don't, once a month, usually."

To the blank face with no resemblance to Nana I said, "You were mad the last time, but I don't think you give a flying fuck now." Mari looked around to see if anyone had heard me. I pushed the chocolates up a little on her lap where they were sliding off again. She didn't blink, and she didn't grasp the box. She didn't lift her head or tip it more. "Shit," I said. "She's like an egg shell with the egg blown out."

"Shh! Shh!" Mari was getting frantic over my bad behavior.

But I wasn't out of control, just contrary. I was the bad granddaughter. I felt the old familiar high of being bad, of proving something to somebody.

"Nana," I said, "Nana, honey, if you're in there, forgive me. But this is why parents should raise their own children. I'm not ready for this. Maybe Mari is, but I'm not. I'm still at the stage where I'd kill myself before I'd be where you are."

Mari was twisting her hands together, turning her head from side to side, scanning the hall for people who might hear or maybe help. "Shut up!" she whispered, "I mean it Martha, shut up shut up shut up!"

"You're freaking out, Mari," I said. "I'm very very calm." I waved down the row of ladies in wheelchairs. They smiled and waved back.

"I'm leaving," said Mari. "You're ruining this." She got up and put her bag on her shoulder. I could tell she was about to cry.

"I'm being bad, Nana," I said. "I'm making a scene. Or Mari thinks so. If you're in there, you should know, you'd be proud of me. I've got a job as a community organizer, like Saul Alinsky in Chicago."

"Oh fine!" cried Mari. "That's just great! As we're leaving you manage to tell her the one thing she'd like best. You're a community organizer! That's so typical of you!" She took off, all but running down the hall.

"I'm a selfish jerk, Nana," I said. "See what I did to Mari? We're going to get her to use her law degree to help the working class, though. But just so you know, on the off chance you can hear me, if I ever do anything in my life, it will be because of you."

And then tears started down my cheeks. I took off after Mari's tiny receding butt.

The nurse looked up from her desk. "Leaving already?"

"You bet," I said, and managed not to add, And you won't see me again until I'm a hundred and three and peeing on the floor.

I caught up to Mari just as the elevator door opened– and we almost collided with Robby. Mari cast him a look as if he were the problem and threw herself backward against the wall of the elevator. For Mari, this was the height of melodrama.

Robby stepped back into the elevator, and I stepped in too, and we let the door slide closed. "Thanks for coming up, Robby, but don't waste your time. She's gone."

Mari said, "Oh shut up Martha! She didn't die."

"There's nothing for Robby to meet. There's an old eggshell with a curly wig and frankly I'd rather he didn't see it."

He looked from one of us to the other.

Mari said, "All I know is I'm not going to end up like that. I'm not going to go out that way I swear it!"

"Well, I'm with you there, Mari."

"You!" she said, as we got to the first floor. "You with the Saul Alinsky the community organizer. And you have a husband." She flounced out ahead of us.

Robby still looked pretty groggy. "The way it works," I explained to him, "is when I'm upset, she's calm, and vice versa. Like I was in a crisis all through adolescence, and she was making straight A's."

Indian Summer outside. We got in the car, and Mari gripped the wheel and stared ahead, but didn't start the engine. I said, "Listen, Mari, I know. I was totally self-indulgent, but I was right. Nana is way gone."

Mari's forehead sank down, down, pressed against the steering wheel, and she started to sob. Big boo-hoos, her forehead sliding down when she let her breath out, sliding up when she took breath in.

It made me feel awful. My baby sister was sobbing. I sat with my hands feeling swollen and useless. "Mari? I'm sorry. I mean I was upset too. I'm sorry."

Robby leaned up over the seat and put his hands on her shoulders and patted and made a soft noise.

"Nobody gives a damn," she sobbed. "I never even had breakfast!"

I said, "There was a diner at the bottom of the hill. Let's go get something to eat. Do you want me to drive? Can you drive while you're crying?"

She sniffed and started the engine. She would show me.

The diner was New Jersey-style, like the grille of an antique Buick. In the parking lot, she paused to sob some more, and while I was rooting around in my bag for a Kleenex I never found, Robby got out of the car, opened her door, and helped her out. He held her elbow, and then put his arm around her, and she let him.

She looked up at Robby and said, "I want ice cream. And mashed potatoes. I want a whole plate full of white food."

Robby chose a booth for us, and he took the side with Mari, keeping his arm around her. I put my elbows on the pink and gray Formica with the little boomerang pattern. The waitress brought metal bowls of pickled tomatoes, garden slaw, and a basket of dinner rolls.

Mari ordered a banana split.

"That's not all white."

She glared at me: I wasn't out of the doghouse yet. She had long mascara exclamation points running down her cheeks, but she was perfectly clear in her instructions to the waitress: two scoops of vanilla, one of strawberry, no chocolate of any kind, pineapple sauce on the strawberry ice cream, butterscotch on both vanillas.

Robby wanted rice pudding.

I ordered rice pudding too, but then I called the waitress back and asked for a bowl of Manhattan clam chowder, then called her back again to switch it to New England clam chowder. Bring the chowder first, then the rice pudding and no whipped cream.

Robby said, "You know what? I think I want to change too."

The waitress leaned her hip on the booth near me. "Okay," she said. "I'll wait." She was a little younger than Mom, but a similar physical type, rangy and big bosomed.

Robby didn't want rice pudding any more. He wanted a burger. I had never seen him order meat. He picked pepperoni off his pizza, and ate around the meat in Danny Boy's stew. In Aruba he ate fish.

"A rare burger with onion," said Robby. "And ketchup."

Mari was still crying, a quiet, sad little crying with the anger gone, her chin smooth. Just tears pouring down her cheeks.

I said, "This is why I stopped visiting Nana. It always makes me feel like you look."

Mari got into her bag and found a mirror and a packet of tissues and also took napkins from the dispenser. She wiped off all the mascara, leaving hardly any gray under her eyes at all.

Robby moved over to my side and said, "Poor Martha." Then laid his head on my shoulder and I'm pretty sure went to sleep again. Mari worked on redoing her face until the food arrived. The banana split came first, and Mari ran her spoon along the rim and tried the caramel. She tasted it and wrinkled up her nose.

"Not good?"

"It's good. I'm just checking it out."

Then came my rice pudding with whipped cream. The waitress said she'd be right back with the burger and chowder.

Mari said, "You told her no whipped cream, and you told her soup first, then rice pudding."

"I don't care," I said. "When it comes to food, it's all good."

"You shouldn't just take what they give you. How can they improve their service if you don't give them feedback? And the white food was my idea."

"God, Mari! Yes, I admit it. I got the idea for New England clam chowder from you and rice pudding from Robby. Okay? And the way I look at it, Fate has decreed that I eat whipped cream, so I have no choice."

She shook her head.

"I don't always know what I want," I said. "Sometimes the waitress knows best."

Mari started to cry again. "Do you see what I mean?" she said. "People take care of you! No one takes care of me!" Drowsily, Robby started to move to her side of the table again, but she said, "Oh stay with her, she's your wife!"

I said, "Eat your beautiful banana split, Mari."

So she did. Cherry first, then right down through the middle scoop of strawberry with pineapple sauce.

The burger and clam chowder came together. Robby stared at his burger. He bit in. I heard the onion crunch. There was a little red juice, a.k.a. blood, on the corner of his mouth.

Mari finished the entire middle ice cream ball with its syrup and its section of banana before going on to the next one. She asked me, "Are you going to eat all those crackers?"

She ate my crackers plus Robby's cole slaw and a pickled tomato and then went back to the banana split. She said, "It's so unfair, you know. That Nana lived her life, and that's what's she got at the end."

I said, "The way I look at it is, it's no different from if she'd just died."

"I visited her every week for a while. Then it felt like there was no point at all."

"Well, I admit that's it: the less there was of Nana, the less I could visit. I'm not saying I don't feel guilty about it. But whatever is left, in there, if anything is left, I don't think it has any sense of time. And I don't think it's suffering."

"You're rationalizing."

"I have this image of a tiny Nana all the way inside, reviewing her life. She's like sitting on this little pouffe that turns slowly, and all around her are cityscapes and the events of her life–"

"And us?" said Mari.

"Yes, and of course the people she loved are there too, including the Rotter when he was a little boy, not when he was disappointing everyone, and of course us. And she's circling slowly, and saying, I should have done that differently with the boy, but those little girls came out all right, even if they don't visit their old Nana–"

"You're making this up," said Mari.

"Of course I'm making it up! But it makes sense, don't you think? She's going to die very soon, or she's already dead, the part that matters, but I'm imagining that there is this little part of her that has been given time to see it all, and maybe edit out the bad parts–"

"That's beautiful," said Robby.

I went on. "She didn't look unhappy. She just looked absent. That's why I'm saying that if she's there at all, she's far far inside. This is hard on us, not her."

Mari started to cry again, but it turned into a burp and she giggled instead. The waitress wanted to know if we wanted anything else, and I said coffee and so did Mari. Robby ordered hot chocolate.

Mari sniffed a deep snot-clearer. She said, "People love you, Martha, and you were always better at everything than I am."

"Mari! I am such a loser compared to you!"

"No, you're good at things. Like figuring out what's happening to Nana."

"Yeah," said Robby. "That was pretty good."

"That was a story I made up!"

"You always had a better imagination than I did," said Mari. "You made up that story about Nana, on the spot, it just came to you. You invented a whole myth to explain what happens when a person is dying, and it made me feel better."

I was touched. Had I been trying to make her feel better?

"Do you know," said Robby, "I always prayed for a sister."

Mari said, "Not a brother?"

He smiled a charming, gentle naive Robby smile. "A sister. I think I wanted someone to take care of. I couldn't have a dog because of allergies."

I remembered when I got my little sister, who I had not prayed for. She would look at me big-eyed and I would make a face or do a dance step, and whatever I did, she ate it up like I was candy on a stick.

She said, "Your best story was the one where we were these mice or voles or some kind of fuzzy animals that flew."

"Bats?"

"No, I'm pretty sure you called them voles. And the big sister vole put its arm around the little sister vole, and they would fly over the countryside and have adventures." She started to cry again.

Robby moved over to her side and stayed there, put his arm around her. I said, "You're having too much fun crying, Mari."

"I have to work six times as hard as you, and I get nothing."

"You were valedictorian of your class!"

"There were four valedictorians! Everyone got to be valedictorian! Oh, I know you had your problems too, but Nana loved you best."

"No she didn't. She just knew me longest."

Mari snorted. "It amounts to the same thing. Do you know what she said to me once? I called, not long before she went to the Miriams, and she said 'How's my favorite granddaughter?' and she thought it was you."

"How do you know she thought it was me?"

"Because she said, 'Martha, how's my favorite granddaughter.'"

I couldn't help it: I had a warm glow. It had been true, Nana and I had had a nice time before this baby arrived whining and peeing. "How did she manage to get out of it?"

"You have to hand it to Nana, honest to the end. When I said, 'It's Mari, Nana, not Martha,' she just said, "So how's my second favorite granddaughter?'"

"Are you sure she didn't say 'favorite second granddaughter?'"

"Whatever. I'm the one who visited her in the nursing home, and I'm the one who did the dishes and ran the vacuum on Friday afternoons while you were out with your pot head punk rocker boyfriends–"

"Not true! I cleaned the toilet and emptied the garbage. Nana had a real lack of insight, you know, making us do all that stuff on Friday afternoon insisting it had nothing to do with Shabbos, she didn't believe in that stuff. She was a hypocrite in her own way. And besides, Mom loved you best. She actually wanted you. I was a mistake, but she chased down the Rotter so she could get pregnant with you."

"Yeah, well, it didn't work. I mean, it didn't keep him with her."

"But me, the main thing she remembers about my birth is not having her make-up with her. The kit was misplaced, and Rotter got excited and insisted on rushing her to the hospital before she could find it, and anyhow, she was totally infuriated when she arrived at the hospital without her make-up, and nothing happened. I didn't show for twenty-four hours. Of course she sent the Rotter home for it, but he stopped off at a bar, and she was still cursing him out and screaming for the make-up kit when they wheeled her down to the delivery room."

"That's so Mom," said Mari affectionately.

"Right. Labor was just an annoyance. I was just an annoyance. You were the little cute blond she dressed up and took around to show off. At one point she was going to put you in some Little Miss Beauty Contests, like Jon-Benet Ramsey." Actually, even as an adult her features were small, too small, except for a reasonably emphatic nose courtesy of the Semitic side. She hated the nose, of course, but it was the only thing that gave people a way to remember her face.

Robby had his cheek on his fist. "Everyone wants to be loved best."

I said, "We have to dig out Nana's address book so we can invite all her old Commie friends when she dies."

To my surprise, Mari said," We should use Love Palace for a memorial service. I think people would be more comfortable there than in, say, my condo or a restaurant."

Robby went to the rest room, and I said, "What did you want to talk to me about, Mari?"

She shrugged. "Nothing. Nana I guess. I've decided I'm not

going to end up alone. That's all. I've decided, one way or another, I'm not going to be alone anymore."

22

I like to staple. It's my favorite part of doing the newsletter for Love Palace. Actually, I think I like most repetitive actions: they keep my mind off unsolved problems, like what's going to happen to Nana, like where the money goes. Like my mistakes with men. Like John. Stapling is also probably part of my blue collar genes. Nana had an ideological commitment to the industrial and working classes, and Mom believes work is just what your hands do in life. You take out your garbage, you wash your own dishes. You clean if someone's coming over. Mom's only caveat about work is that some jobs suck because they break your nails and make your feet hurt.

I was stapling contentedly when Gil appeared. He filled the doorway to the office suddenly– that threshold my own private Limina where people appeared and disappeared. Black tee shirt, black jeans, silver in his ears and nose, messenger bag. Ready for fight or flight.

"Well, well," I said. It had been more than a week since Kristen's good-bye kidnapping party. "Back again, are you?" He didn't put down the bag. I stapled two more newsletters. "Robby tells me your new band is good."

He shrugged. "Maybe someday."

His hair color was deteriorating from pink to mustard and it made him look unhealthy. Or maybe this was the club life he'd been living.

"Are you coming back to work? Because I've got some things that need doing."

"I don't know. Robby says you think I'm stealing."

"There's money missing. It's been going on as long as I've been here. It gets withdrawn from the bank machines." The best thing about the Good News Crew was that I had always felt free to say anything to them. They were like little brothers and sisters, not requiring politeness. "Did you make the withdrawals?"

"No," he said. "I'd lift something from a WalMart, but I wouldn't steal from Love Palace. You can believe me or not, but I wouldn't."

I believed him. Just like that. It was no more rational than my weeks and weeks of accusing him. I've discovered this about myself: my deepest convictions come on impulse. I said, "The problem is that nobody seems to know who has bank cards."

"I never had a Love Palace card. I didn't even know Love

Palace had a bank card. I was never like one of the Inner Circle."

"And who in your opinion is the Inner Circle?"

"You and Warren's parents and John. The Older Generation." He grinned suddenly, showing white, nicely straightened teeth. "Maybe one of the Older Generation is stealing it." He clearly liked that phrase. "The way this place is run, nobody pays any attention to money. I don't know why you care. It's not going to last. Everyone here is a loser or a user."

"You too?"

"Sure. I'm a user. I'm just working here until the band is doing well enough for me to do that full-time."

"So you are here to work?"

"Whatever. Play with the kiddies, hold Cara's hand while she decompensates. If you let me."

"I can't fire anyone," I said, but of course that wasn't true, and he was right that I was one of the Older Generation. The trouble with me, if you haven't figured this out, is that in spite of energy, wit, inspiration, impulsive convictions, and a rich imagination, I lurch through life like a drunk in a fog.

He put down his bag. "So what do you want me to do?" I handed over the stapling to him and started stacking the finished newsletters in groups of ten. There in the close quarters of the little office, I could smell the faintest cigarette smoke clinging to his clothes.

After we'd worked a little while, he said, "I don't know what you're complaining about anyhow. Robby chose you."

"What do you mean, chose me?"

"I mean, you're the one he married. What do you think I mean?" He showed his teeth again. "Gender identification? Sexual orientation? Duh? But, no problem. Don't worry about it. He chose you."

I had this furious urge to shout Damn right he chose me! In fact, Robby and I fucked twice last night in spite of having had a fight last week, so put that in your pipe and smoke it, you little turd. But I'm one of the Older Generation, so I pulled myself up to my full extra twenty years. "How about if you staple a little more and talk a little less, Gil."

"Touchy, touchy. But, like I said, Robby is very clear on the subject of sexuality."

I was wondering what went on when Robby and Gil were alone together. What had happened the night Robby stayed out in the city with Gil and his band? What crisis had come–and, I hoped, gone?

I said, "What kind of music do you play anyhow?"

"Oh don't fucking condescend, Martha. You could care less about my music."

"I care about music. Everyone has some kind of music. Me, I liked Pink Floyd and even Michael Jackson a little bit. For a while I was into Willie Nelson."

"Oh my God."

"And the Grateful Dead. I always liked the Grateful Dead."

He shook his head.

I said, "Now who's condescending?"

We worked in silence a little longer, Gil beginning to do a rhythm thing with his fingers between staples: Ka-thump on the stapler, cha-cha-cha.

I said, "Listen, Gil, did you and Robby ever–No, never mind."

"You want to know if Jesus-Is-My-Master ever strayed to the dark side? Or is it John-Is-My-Master? Robby is a bona fide tightass, Martha. He is giving the straight and narrow his best shot, so to speak, and he insists it's the best thing that ever happened, and he recommends it to everyone."

That was nice. Still, there had been a discussion, a reason to talk about this.

"Don't get the idea that I'm broken-hearted," said Gil. "I'm a committed bi-sexual, so I have no problem with Robby going any which way he wants. I just think it's dumb to repress a whole aspect of yourself because you're scared."

"Maybe we should go for three-way housekeeping."

"I'd try it," said Gil.

"I didn't mean it. My mouth gets ahead of my good sense. You two morons would probably expect me to do your laundry and cook your meals. No thanks."

Gil grinned for probably the third time this morning, probably some kind of record for him. "Sounds good to me."

They called me downstairs to take a delivery, and then Gil went shopping for supplies with Cara, who loved to shop for anything including for crayons and toilet tissue. Later in the day I thought maybe it was Cara stealing the money. On the other hand, there hadn't been any withdrawals for a while, so maybe it really was over. For all I knew, Eleanor had been short of cash while she was organizing the wedding and redoing my apartment. In fact, given the speed with which the amounts had been made up, it might be the most likely explanation.

Too bad I wasn't speaking to Eleanor. Not officially not speaking, but I hadn't seen her. There hadn't been a Free Market since long before our wedding.

Now I started wondering if I'd decided to blame Gil because subconsciously I thought he was my enemy, my rival with Robby? I could hardly wait to get to Madame to do a reality check on this. She would want to know how I felt about it. I had a sudden thirst to be lying on her couch getting in touch with my feelings. Maybe everything was going to be fine. Maybe my thing with John was just another aspect of my crush on him, and all I had to do was what Robby had done, which was choose. Just choose Robby, the way Robby had chosen me.

There were some smooth days then, as we approached the end. I had my session with Madame who agreed that there was probably something between Robby and Gil, most likely never acted on. That I should talk with Robby about it, but not in a confrontational way. I was even circling around mentioning Oh by the way this sexual thing happened between me and John. But I chose to talk about the money instead, and then it was Time's Up.

Meanwhile, at Love Palace, Cara was happy and busy because she had Gil to herself. The Franks came in to read the papers. Danny Boy tried cheese in his biscuits. There was a Good News Crew meeting when we discussed beverages for the little kids. Jo-Jo had given them free sodas, which Cara thought was okay occasionally, but she insisted we ought to be serving fruit juice at Love Palace instead of the Pink Additives drink that Esta Brown always bought when it was her turn to do snack. Then the issue turned into whether it was more important to let the Community, i.e., Esta, take the initiative, or should we step in and insist on healthy drinks and thus get in the way of Esta's self-empowerment? I found the discussion mildly interesting for about five minutes, but the Crew kept going for the better part of an hour and then tabled it.

The morning after that meeting, before the Crew got up, I gave Esta money and told her to buy juice this week, not Pink Additive. I figured this would eventually result in another long meeting about whether or not I was disempowering the Good News crew as well as Esta, but there was always a chance they would be distracted by something more interesting and never get back to it.

Which is what happened.

It was time to get the Guzzler's oil changed, and also, there had been the new clunk for awhile. Mari told me about a great mechanic three and half towns away, so I called up and drove over and waited for the car, reading *Road and Track* in their shabby waiting room that smelled of oil or oily workmen. From time-to-time, I took a break to look over the displays of key chains and car deodorizers. When the car was ready, I drove home slowly, making an excursion of it, stopping for bread at a bakery Mari had also recommended. This bakery claimed to have been in the basement of its old frame house for fifty years. As I drove, I ripped off a piece of bread, which was all the crusty chewy things good bread should be, happy that the Guzzler was still running, listening to Nat King Cole on the eight track.

I drove past Riversedge Renaissance and the warehouses, and just where the street name changed to Water Street, I had to brake for a police barrier. The barrier and an attending police officer obscured my view of Water Street. I stopped, slow-brained in the way you get when some very habitual action is interrupted. The cop drew a big U-turn in the air. I cranked down the Guzzler's window and said, "I live about five houses down."

He was short and buff, with pink cheeks and a shaving cut. "You have to go around by the projects."

"But I live on this end, in the blue building."

"Just turn around, go up the hill, take a right at Jo-Jo's—"

"I know how to get there, but I always come this way. What's going on?"

"They're taking down a building."

"What building? Not the blue one?"

He shrugged. "I don't know which one. They're just setting up their equipment. For tomorrow, I think."

I did as I was told, drove the long way round, past Jo-Jo's, down the hill past the projects, right onto Water Street, past the Blue Lagoon, the really crummy tenements, the secondhand store. To my relief, I could see Love Palace almost immediately, still standing, but beyond it, in the middle of the street, a yellow earth mover.

As I parked, I saw Ace on the street in front of Love Palace. I slammed the car door shut and shouted, "Ace! Hey Ace! We missed you! What's going on?"

He waved toward the earth mover. "The shit's hitting the fan," he said with a big smile.

I almost knocked him over with a hug, so glad to have him back. He felt skinny to me, as if he hadn't been eating well.

He embraced me in return. "We've finally got something going, Martha," he said. *"Luche por el communismo,* baby! One working class, one party, one world!"

"But what is it? I've been away three hours–and there are bulldozers. What is it?"

"It's the ruling class cashing in its chips," he said, "but it plays into our hand. This is going to be the best thing they could have done to us. Councilman Bishop Stebbins coming out with his flunkies and the press. The kids are staging a sit-in. "

"What kids?"

He walked backward away from me, toward the earth mover. "They started bringing in this equipment to knock down 315–"

"They can't knock down 315! 317 would collapse!"

"– and our job is to make sure they don't do it! This is what we've been waiting for– they're endangering the lives of the people! We say people live in those houses, and the demolition boss says they're supposed to knock down 315 tomorrow, and we started making phone calls. Robby calls his parents, and I call the Councilman's office–"

"I thought Councilman Stebbins was a corrupt lackey of capitalism!"

Ace was beginning to grin now, walking backward, raising his voice as he went. "He'd be a corrupt lackey of whatever system, but he likes to get his picture taken. So we've got people in 315 putting their bodies in the way of the demolition crews. It's going to be all over the papers and the TV now!"

"Somebody's in 315? Like waiting to get bulldozed?"

"That's the sit-in. Robby, Gil, Cara, Frank and Frank, Malika–"

"Oh my God!"

He was laughing at me. "You're not their mama, Martha. No danger. Believe me, would Robby's dad and mom knock one shingle off a house with their baby in it? Robby's our best protection."

I had my big bag on my shoulder with three loaves of bread sticking out of it. "What about John?" I shouted after Ace. "Did someone call John?"

"Damned if I know." Ace strode off toward the action.

I hurried after Ace. I saw the women first. They were on the stoop of 315, Malika with her arms crossed over her chest. I realized she had been watching the exchange between me and Ace. She stepped over and gave him a big lip kiss, with one eye on me. I felt a surge of optimism. Ace and Malika were back together!

I waved at Esta. In the empty lot directly across the street sat a second yellow bulldozer, and, on a big flatbed truck, a crane with wrecking ball tied close to its shaft. A couple of workers were sitting on some steps to nowhere left over from a demolition before I came to Love Palace. They were sharing a pizza with the cops. Chickie was crossing the street toward them, and she put one hand on her hip and simply stared defiantly at cops and workers both, smoking her cigarette. Two of Esta's kids followed Chickie and started creeping up on a police officer, staring at the gun lashed to his belt with *muy-macho* black leather. Esta ran over and retrieved the kids. "Pray for justice, Martha!" she called to me, holding hands with a boy on each side. The kids were pulling back, toward the cop. "And Martha, Councilman Stebbins is coming!"

315 had police barriers around it, but everyone was ignoring them. Cara was in the second-floor window with some of the teenagers from the block. Black Frank was looking out the bay window at stoop level with his arms crossed over his chest and a scowl. In the other bay window were Robby and Gil in identical black tee shirts. Robby was waving at me.

A kid with dreadlocks and a camera had come up and started interviewing Ace and Malika. "This is harassment," said Ace. "They're taking down the empty houses here to get people to move out faster."

Malika said, "I live in 317, and it's going to collapse if they mess with 315. And even if it stays up? it's going to be more rats and roaches!"

Robby was leaning way out the bay window toward the stoop and waving his cell phone at me. "Warren wants you to call him."

I gave him the bread and took the phone.

"Why? What does he want?"

"I don't know. He called me. He's pretty pissed. I left messages for Mom and John. I told Dad he had to do something."

"John ought to be here," I said.

Robby said, "It's his speaking tour."

"He still should be here."

"Well, Warren wants to talk to you."

I'm always glad to be part of the show, even when I miss the first act. A flavored ice salesman had shown up, and a line was forming at his cart. The kid reporter was taking pictures of Esta and her children in front of the ices cart.

Warren's secretary answered, and Robby gestured for more

bread. I passed it up, and said, "It's Martha. Warren told Robby he wanted to talk to me."

"I'll put you right through, Mrs. Peterson," she said. Even on the honeymoon, as far as I knew, I'd never been called Mrs. Peterson.

There was no wait. Warren said, "Okay, what's going on? What did you let those kids do over there?"

"I have no idea what's going on, Warren," I said. "I just got here, and I didn't let the kids do anything. I was out all morning getting my oil changed, and I came back to cops, bull-dozers, an ice guy, people in the street."

Ace had gone over to the lone African-American police officer to convince him to change sides while Chickie lit up a new cigarette and blew smoke toward the white officer and the demolition guys.

"How many people?"

"Let's see, from my vantage point, and I'm on the front steps of 315 Water Street, which I understand is the one your people are trying to pull down–"

"Not my people."

"Somebody's people. Robby is in the window of the parlor floor of the building. And lots of other people are in the building. Directly ahead of me is a police barrier and then people lined up for ices– It's essentially a circus, Warren. They're expecting lots of publicity. They've got Councilman Stebbins and the TV crews coming momentarily."

"Stebbins won't come."

"They said he's on his way, but with or without him, it's a circus. They've got some kind of reporter here snapping pictures–"

He said, "I need to sit down with you."

"I'm flattered. Why don't you call off the demolition derby, then we'll talk?"

"I don't have anything to do with them. The company that bought the empty houses must have decided–"

"Oh come on, Warren. You know what's going on. And people still living in the house next door to the one they're trying to take down. It'll collapse! They're supposed to have six months to get out!"

"They aren't taking down inhabited buildings, are they?"

"If they take down this empty one, the next one over, which is totally occupied, will collapse. The vibration of these big machines may bring down the Love Palace too."

Gil leaned around Robby and shouted, "Tell him it's illegal harassment!"

"Robby and Gil say it's harassment to get the people out sooner. So you and your buddies can make a buck."

"It's a mistake," said Warren. "They weren't supposed to take it down yet."

"You mean somebody like wrote down the wrong date on the work order? Then call somebody. Pull a string, make a deal."

"Are they knocking down the building now?"

"No, because Robby and Gil are sitting in the building and Councilman Stebbins is coming."

"Stebbins isn't coming," said Warren.

But to my delight, at that very moment, from the end of Water Street near the projects came a big black car followed by a white van with transmitter equipment on top.

"Bad news for your side, Warren, but I see what looks like a TV crew arriving as we speak. I don't know if Councilman Stebbins is in the Lincoln Town Car in front of it, but the TV people are definitely arriving."

"Which channel?"

"Not sure. But it's early yet. Plenty of time to make the evening news."

There was a brief silence while he weighed something. "Let me make a few more calls. But I want to speak to you directly. Can you meet me at Riversedge Renaissance in, say, forty-five minutes? You can tell me what goes down with Stebbins, if he's really there."

I said, "You still haven't told me who owns the buildings, Warren."

He hesitated. "I'll tell you."

"Now that the Councilman is getting involved? I'll tell you what, I'll meet you, but make it at Jo-Jo's."

"What the hell is Jo-Jo's?"

"It's the bar and grill and newsstand up the hill from Bishop Stebbins Houses. Two blocks from here."

I gave Robby back his phone. "He wants to talk to me in person. We're going to meet up at Jo-Jo's."

"Warren will stop them," said Robby.

"Are you all right in there?" I asked. "Do you need supplies? Blankets?"

Gil grinned at me and put an arm around Robby's shoulder. "We've got each other," he said. Robby shrugged him off.

I passed them my last loaf.

Meanwhile, it was indeed Councilman Bishop Stebbins himself in a beautifully cut dark suit that made him look much more handsome than he probably was. "Here he comes!" cried Esta, pressing her baby to her cheek and running toward him. Ace thrust a fist in the air, and the photographer kid snapped the gesture: the Black Panthers rising like a phoenix from the ashes. The crowd moved toward the councilman, except for some of some of the little kids who preferred the TV crew unpacking their equipment.

Gil said, "This is so cool," and climbed out the window to join the crowd.

I said to Robby, "Well, I'm going to walk up the hill and meet Warren."

Robby's eyes were following Gil. I had the urge to ask him now, Madame said we needed to talk: Listen, Robby, if you and Gil. If you have feelings toward Gil. And I have to tell you about what John did to me.

But of course even Madame wouldn't say to do it in the middle of a street demonstration.

23

I walked up the hill to Jo-Jo's past a block of brick row houses and more empty lots and a lot of heaved and uneven sidewalk. I had worn slip-on clogs that morning that were meant for waiting for your car to be fixed, not for hiking uphill on bad sidewalks. I kept switching shoulders with my bag. It was unpleasantly humid for the season. I was going to be sweating and maybe have a blister if not a twisted ankle by the time I made it to Jo-Jo's.

Jerk, I said to myself. Stop whining. Warren will have Martinez drive you down the hill.

I glanced back once, and could see Riversedge Renaissance overlooking Water Street, and behind it, the sky scrapers across the river. A subdued skyline now, more moderate without the twins.

I made it up to Hudson Boulevard where the street was busy with traffic. Jo-Jo's was a newsstand as well as a Grill, and in the early morning and late afternoon, bums from the Blue Lagoon came up to peddle newspapers to drivers at the stoplight. I saw Warren's car parked in front of Jo-Jo's, and Martinez leaning on the fender smoking. "He's already here," he told me, disapproving of my lateness.

Still, he opened the door for me, and Warren got up and came to meet me. He was sitting in the empty table section with plastic tropical print covers on the tables. Jo-Jo and his daughter and the people at the counter were following his every move, of course, pretending to watch sports on the TV Warren already had a mug of coffee.

"I'm sorry I'm late. I decided to walk."

"I would have sent Martinez down."

"I wanted to walk."

"It doesn't matter," he said. "Sit down. They told me it's not table service, so I'll go over to the counter and order. Do you want lunch? What's good here?"

I hadn't eaten anything all day but half a loaf of Italian bread. "He makes Jamaican meat patties, that kind of thing, but the only thing I've ever had is breakfast. I'll take eggs and toast. Scrambled, coffee, and I need a glass of water."

He went up to the counter, which was having a little surge of business, some people hurrying in before their bus arrived. Jo-Jo was wearing an apron that looked like he'd been making meat patties in the back. He made Warren wait a while, but Warren played it cool, just filling space with his suit until Jo-Jo took his order and refilled his mug and sent one back for me.

I slipped out of the clogs. If Fate had blown Warren a different way, would he have ended up like the purple-faced newspaper-sellers?

"You're smiling," said Warren.

"I was imagining you as one of our clients," I said. "Sorry. It's nothing personal. I like to imagine who people would be if they'd gone in an entirely different direction."

"If things hadn't worked out for me," he said, "I'd be back home in Indiana, where they still remember my football career. I was a good high school player. We had a championship team in our division."

There was a little silence as I revised my mental image of Warren back home where people pointed him out as a football star from forty-five years ago.

"The counter man said he'd bring over the plates."

"That's Jo-Jo. He's the owner and cook too. He must like you, if he offered to bring the plates over. So, do you want the report? Just as I left, Councilman Stebbins was making a speech."

Warren did a thing with his face that you would have called, if he were a teenage girl instead of a captain of industry, wrinkling his nose. He said, "I want you to know–actually, I thought you did know– that the demolition was planned months ago. Water Street's been slated for renewal for years. This kind of thing doesn't just pop up. Until a few days ago, no one cared. Everyone thought the tenants down there were going to be glad to be relocated and get on with their lives."

"Did anybody ask them?"

"Not my department."

"But it wouldn't have made a difference, would it? If anyone did know what the people down there wanted? Well, let me be the first to tell you. A little community, weird but devoted, has formed around Love Palace. After all, you guys are who set up Love Palace with nonprofit status and everything–"

"Eleanor," said Warren. "Eleanor and the Most Reverend John King. I never thought much of the idea, frankly, especially when Robby started taking it so seriously."

"Well, you're right about that. Robby takes it seriously. He and the others think they're doing community organizing for a community that is going to be there for a while. They thought– we think– that something important is happening down there. A year ago, I would probably have agreed with you, Warren. Of course you should develop old broken-down streets with second-hand stores and cheap liquor outlets and Single Room Occupancy hotels. Of course it would be better to have some nice high rises with a view of the city." I took a breath. I hadn't put this into words before. I was surprising myself. I said, "But something has been going on. What used to be just some temporary cheap housing for people on their way elsewhere, plus the ones who didn't have anywhere else to go, has formed into a community."

"Fine," said Warren. "But now the community has to get realistic and move on." He leaned forward a little. His skin up close had blotches. "Whatever you've got cooking down there has to cool off. You need to explain it to Robby and the others. They'll get what they need to relocate, or get services. We'll help Robby find another place for his—"

"Hobby?"

"For his energy. Water Street is being developed. It's part of the same development plan as Riversedge, and it will be developed."

"We just want to know who owns the houses. You promised to find out for me. It was supposed to be my wedding gift, and you never found out."

He made a sour face. "We gave you plenty. And, yes, I know who owns the houses. Whose name is on the deed. But it doesn't matter, once there's a general order condemning the buildings—"

I felt my hands grab one another as if they needed support. "Condemning the buildings!"

"It's how you make sure you can buy all the property for a big redevelopment. You get it condemned."

Jo-Jo brought our eggs. "Hot plates," he said.

"Excellent," said Warren. "This looks wonderful. Could I trouble you for the ketchup, though? I always eat scrambled eggs with ketchup."

Jo-Jo's lifted his head and gazed down over his nose. "Is there anything else your heart desires?"

"Just ketchup," said Warren, "and refills on the coffee."

Jo-Jo nodded, as if something very serious had been proved beyond a shadow of a doubt to him. Jo-Jo's daughter came over with ketchup and the coffee pot. Warren praised the eggs and home fries, which had a nice greasy red crust and some spice I didn't recognize.

We both shoveled in some eggs and toast and home fries.

I said, "Are you going to tell me?"

"Yes, but I also have something I want you to tell Robby."

"You know, don't you, that Love Palace is important to Robby's life? He believes it's part of God's plan for him."

"Robby is a fanatic. He won't listen to me. I'm hoping he'll listen to you. He needs to get a new interest. Religion is personal. That's my opinion. It's something a man should keep inside his clothes, like his underwear. It's nobody's business if I wear jockeys or boxers, and I think there's something wrong when you start putting religion in every sentence." Warren dipped a piece of bacon in his little pile of ketchup. He crunched the bacon and stared at me. "I need you to explain this to Robby."

"To explain what? And I'm not on your side," I said. "You're not doing the right thing by those people in the apartments."

"They're coming down," said Warren. "Get used to it. It's not my fault anyhow, it's goddam Eleanor and John. They set up those kids, and then the kids went ahead and set up the rest of them. I say Goddam John King for leading on those poor bastards. Including you, believing you could create this little slum paradise—you're all delusional. I got you a stay on the demolition—"

"Are you sure?"

"I'm sure."

"You made the calls yourself, didn't you?"

"Yes, although your councilman Stebbins will probably claim he did it which is fine by me. The demolition will wait till the whole block is empty, which is what they should have goddam done in the first place. I know you think it is some kind of big plot, but the demolition crew is over there today because of human error. It wasn't supposed to happen till all the buildings were empty—"

"The eviction notices gave us another six months."

"That's when it's supposed to happen. All the buildings were slated to come down together, when the deals were all complete. So meanwhile, two years ago, here were these half empty buildings, and Robby saying he needed meaning in his life, and Eleanor wanting what Robby wanted, and meanwhile the Reverend John King saw another opportunity to run a scam—"

"Why do I get the feeling you don't like John?"

He made a tooth-sucking noise. "Your reverend is a con man," he said. "A sleazy piece of shit excuse my French. The whole thing got out of hand. Goddam Eleanor and goddam Reverend John cooked this up, to occupy Robby and make Reverend John look good. I wasn't privy to the details, I got it in bits and pieces. Eleanor has always been interested in strays, especially the kind of strays that she can use for a project. There was some kid in the loony bin with Robby that she brought home and kept around for a while because he was an artist, until he set the drapes on fire. I'm not sure what rock she found John under, but he's her favorite. She has big plans for John."

"Lectures and TV and self-help tapes."

"Oh, it's so much more than that. Get her to explain it to you. They're founding a self-actualization movement that will have all the emotional uplift of a religion without any of the petty details like believing in God or acting morally. She wants to follow up on this by running John for Senator. Only it isn't going to work out. Eleanor is going to get a surprise about John."

John, I thought. John, John, John.

"I'm going to tell you the whole thing. I want you to have the whole picture. They have poured money into that place. Into that street! And it has always been clear that the street was going to be flattened, you understand? Love Palace stands in the central atrium of Riversedge Renaissance II."

That gave me a shudder. "You could still stop it, couldn't you? It's your company isn't it? You can' t just run these people out into the street."

"You refuse to believe me. It isn't my property. I'm not the owner, I'm a deal maker. One or two of the properties haven't officially changed hands yet, but it's only waiting for the paper work and for the people to leave in six months."

"Which ones haven't changed hands yet? Is it 317?"

Warren leaned forward and made me look into his red-rimmed watery blue eyes. "Martha, the whole area has been condemned."

"The occupied houses are structurally fine!"

"It's a legal term. It doesn't mean the buildings are falling down, it means that the city can seize the property and sell it for market value. Give it a rest. Love Palace was supposed to relocate the people who lived on Water Street. That was the original mission."

"I never heard that."

"You never heard it because everyone ignored the original mission. But the original idea, when Eleanor decided to fix up the goddam blue whorehouse was that the kids were supposed to work with the city housing authority to get the people apartments and services, but instead, they've been running this giant soup kitchen and sleepover party. John gets publicity, John and the idealistic teenagers, John and the poor minorities. John photographs well. John King– which I happen to know is not his real name– has been misleading a lot of poor pathetic losers, including my son. He ought to be shot for that if not for everything else."

I ate the rest of my toast. This is why I will never be skinny. My reaction to stress is to pack in extra calories, just in case.

"Let me put it to you this way, Martha. John is fucking you over. All of you." There was one last piece of butter drenched toast on Warren's plate. I pressed the heel of my hand against the table so I wouldn't take it. "She wants to run him for Senator, but it won't work because Eleanor doesn't do her research."

"And you have? You've been doing research on John? Like, detectives?"

"Absolutely. In business, information is all that matters. I now know that your Reverend John is using the whole Love Palace scheme as a way of socking away a little for his future. I don't mean that Eleanor doesn't know, I'm sure she's given him free rein, she has given him cash, securities, buildings–"

"Does he use money from Love Palace?"

"He has total access. Not that I care. This is a heads-up Martha, to you and the kids. Especially to Robby. I want you to explain this to Robby."

"Are you saying John is like dipping into the till? There's been money missing at Love Palace. I mean, it isn't missing long, but I never know who's using it."

"John is a professional thief. But in this case, I doubt it's actually theft. Eleanor gave it to him. It's all his, Martha."

I said, "What you're saying is, even if John is withdrawing money from the Love Palace account– you're saying he has permission to do that, right?"

Warren used the last quarter of toast to wipe his plate clean of egg residue, no more potatoes, no more toast. "I could use more coffee," he said, looking around, catching Jo-Jo's eye and waving his mug at him. Jo-Jo didn't move a muscle or an blink an eye, but his daughter came toward us with the coffee pot.

"Thank you," said Warren. "It's excellent coffee. And the eggs– top notch, and I would make a return trip for the home fries alone." When she was gone, he leaned forward again. "John is the owner. John is the name you've been begging me for. He owns the houses."

"What houses?"

"As of two days ago, unless they've signed on the dotted line,

John owned the house with the tenants in it and your Love Palace. The property used to be Eleanor's. The whole damn street was Eleanor's. Eleanor is the only heir of a very rich old grandfather who left her property in more places than she knows herself. I am nothing. I'm a lawyer she fell in love with for a little while back when her project was to have a baby. Now she uses me to make her deals. Which is fine, I have no complaints about my part in it, as long as Robby doesn't get hurt. But she owns it all, or rather, she did own it, before she started giving things to him."

My stomach was pressing up on me. My voice came out little and whiny. "She owns Love Palace?"

"She gave it to him. John owns Love Palace and the building across the street and probably more. Eleanor gave all this to John so he could be independent from her, to prove her commitment. Or some shit like that. Frankly, I don't care about the property or the money or their new fake religion. The only thing I'm interested in at this point is for my son to come out of this psychologically intact. I don't mind if John slips away unpunished, which seems to be, by the way, his *modus operandi*, to do things that aren't quite illegal, or where the embarrassment factor mitigates against indictment. What I want is for him to get away from my son. And I want her to have as little as possible to do with Robby, as long as she's with John."

I said, "They're sleeping together?"

"Of course. Sex is always part of her projects."

Our charismatic leader was shtupping my mother-in-law. Why didn't I find this amusing?

"This is what I need you to tell Robby."

"That his mom and John are sleeping together?"

"That his mentor is a scum bag. That all of you have been duped by the scum bag."

"What if I don't believe you? Why didn't you tell me this stuff sooner? Why are you telling me now? And if it is true– I mean, Robby thinks John is Jesus. Robby is going to be devastated."

Warren waved his hands in impatience and irritation. "I didn't do it. Eleanor did it. Help Robby get through this and get on his way. Take him on a vacation."

"We just got back from a vacation. You have a theory but no proof."

"Oh, I have proof all right. You can also ask John about the picture. The famous one."

"Prison Pietà?"

"Yes, ask him what he was doing at the prison was when he got his picture taken. Ask him about that."

"He was the chaplain, wasn't he?"

"No, he wasn't the chaplain. He was doing time for passing bad checks."

I thought: That's too much. I thought that what I would have liked most in the world right then was to be in the Guzzler driving west to somewhere orange and pink. Maybe the Grand Canyon. If the Guzzler died, I'd just get out and keep walking west. I said, "I think I have to leave now."

"We'll drive you down the hill–"

"No, I want to walk."

"Fine. Think it over. You're going to tell Robby, aren't you? Soon?"

"I don't even know if I'm going to tell myself," I said. "Oh, okay, I'll tell Robby something."

"When?"

"Soon."

"By tomorrow at the latest."

"Listen, Warren, you can tell him yourself if you're in a hurry."

"I'll call you tomorrow. I need to know this is taken care of."

Martinez came to attention as I walked out, but I passed him, started across the Boulevard with this feeling that I could stop traffic with the enormity of my burden. But the light was in my favor; the traffic had already stopped. My blisters were getting worse, so I kicked off my clogs and walked down the hill barefoot like some kind of ridiculous penitent, avoiding broken bottles, stepping out on asphalt grayed with spit and transmission fluid. In no hurry at all to talk to Robby.

24

By the time I got back, Councilman Stebbins, the TV truck, and the demolition crew had all departed. There were still a few people on the street, including Robby and Gil and the kid reporter. I slipped inside Love Palace without anyone seeing me, even though there were a lot of people milling around. In the apartment, I threw myself on the bed and stared at the ceiling for a while, meaning to think this through in a disciplined way, what I would say to Robby, how I would say it, but I fell asleep and had one of those deep naps where you wake not knowing where you are or when.

This happened to me once the semester I lived at college– I woke thinking it was morning, and went to the dining hall, but the dining hall smelled wrong, cheap meat instead of burnt pancakes. I remember the strange sensation of gradually realizing it wasn't morning, and how long it took me to get oriented, how the wrongness of everything horrified me, and it seemed essential to keep it all a secret.

That was how I felt when I woke that night, into an aura of nightmare. Why was I dressed? Why did my feet hurt? Where were Nana and Mari? It didn't last long, of course, the confusion: I put on flip flops and hobbled out into the hall, heard noise downstairs, and went to the mezzanine– and saw a party. I was pretty sure by now that it was evening, and I remembered the day and my meeting with Warren. All kinds of people down below: the boy reporter and the clients and Ace and Chickie and Malika and Esta and her kids and the Good News Crew and the kids from the other end of Water Street. Gil and Robby were setting up amps, and Danny Boy was coming out of the kitchen with jam tarts. I don't know who I felt sorrier for, Ace and his misguided tenant troops or Robby with his traitorous spiritual advisor and mother.

Or me. I definitely felt most sorry for me.

I was beginning to think I was invisible. Or that my dark aura made them not want to notice me. White Frank was fooling around the TV, and Robby was carrying some cables to Gil, and I said to myself, I have to tell him, but Chickie started yelling that the news was on, and everyone gathered around.

"I was never on TV," said Malika.

I finally went downstairs. The TV was a false alarm: they had sixty seconds of international news first. If Warren hadn't dumped so much on me, I would be as thrilled as the rest of them. I wanted to be as thrilled as the rest of them.

Ah, said Madame-in-my mind: this then is what Martha wants: to be a part of it. Robby waved, and I winced.

"What's wrong, Martha?" he said, coming to me.

"Your dad said the houses are going to be demolished whatever we do."

"Don't let Warren bring you down. He loves to bring people down, telling them about the Real World."

"He said the developers have made the decision and the whole street is coming down, sooner or later."

"But we're not going to let that happen."

He was radiant. He was both the Robby who was too simple and young for his age and also the Robby who knew how to move competently through the world. After all, maybe Warren was wrong. Why believe Warren? Why not believe Robby? Even if it wasn't true? Can you believe what you know isn't true? I said, "Robby, I have to tell you something about John—"

He tipped his head toward me, so innocent.

But suddenly everyone was shushing each other. Drawing closer to the television. The interruption stopped my momentum. I could have gone on, but I chose not to.

Another false alarm: a report on a big fire two towns up.

Robby even prompted me: "John?" he said.

"John should be here," I said.

"They had something in Texas," he said. "Mom called, though, they're coming back tonight."

I made one more try: "Warren told me that all the property on this street once belonged—"

"Oh God, I know! To my grandfather."

I had a little bubble of righteous indignation: "You mean you've known that all along? Why didn't you ever mention this, Robby?"

"But Eleanor says it was sold off a long time ago."

Again, I could have gone on and chose not to. I chose not to say Your mother lied. She is sleeping with John. His is the name on the deeds. John is a thief. John made me come with my jeans on. But I didn't.

"We're going to stop this, Martha. You have to believe in it. We'll talk to John. John and Ace together. You'll see, we're going to turn this around."

This time it really was our part of the news coming on.

I decided I'd tell Warren to talk to his own son. Better yet, let Eleanor and John tell Robby. Why should I be the bad guy? John was the bad guy.

The TV segment opened with a brief longshot glimpse of Esta and Malika, Malika with an attitude, jabbing her pointer finger. We all cheered, and the real Malika and Esta hugged each other in excitement. Then there was a clip of Councilman Stebbins vowing to save Water Street. Then the camera zoomed in on Black Frank and Ace, especially Ace's Afro and Frank's scowl. The live Frank slapped his knee and laughed. He was on the couch with the other Frank and Chickie, and he and Ace gave each other an old-fashioned high five, and then came more of Malika, speaking this time. Malika with her elaborate hair and perfect complexion and terrifically defined jawline. She said her words strongly, with emphatic enunciation and just enough street attitude. We cheered, and Malika jumped up and down like a little girl.

We were all deliriously happy. We had made the evening news, how could they take down the buildings now? There was another tray of tarts from Danny Boy, and the Good News Crew doing sound checks, people moving couches so we could dance. I danced a little with Robby while Gil played a mix of disco and soul and a little current stuff. No Christian rock, I noticed. Then Robby deejay'd, and I danced with Gil. After a while, my feet hurting again, I stepped outside into the dusk, to get away from the noise.

Chickie was out there smoking, wearing her too-high heels, too-tight jeans, and a tee shirt with décolletage.

"Whew," I said. "What a day."

She sucked in her smoke, looking blue in the street light. She'd had her hair cut in the last day or two, and there was nothing scraggly.

"Where's your mom?" I said.

"I'm on my way to check on her. That would be ironical, wouldn't it, if she burned the building down after all this? Frank checked her a while ago."

"Frank?" I said, surprised.

"They take turns with me watching her, Frank and Franklin. My guys." I must have looked blank, but she seemed to expect it. "A lot of people don't know," she said. "Frank's my brother. He's one of the reasons we're still here– Ma still recognizes him, sometimes."

"White Frank? He lives with you?"

"Sometimes. Sometimes he lives over the Blue Lagoon with the rest of them. With Franklin. You call him Black Frank, but his name's Franklin. You didn't know that either, did you?

Franklin's my ex. Yeah. I used to be married to him. He was always a sweet man. People think they're bums, but they're both the best, when they're sober. And when they're drunk, they never get mean, neither one of them. I get tired of people calling them bums. I know you and the kids try to talk about the clients, but you mean bums."

I said. "Everybody likes them—"

She snorted. "They used to play baseball. Back when this was a nice family block. Our family went to St. Rocco's and Franklin went to public school, but everyone hung out in the evenings. You can't imagine how nice it was then around here. Not rich, but families. A butcher, a candy store, a little hardware store, movie theaters up on the Boulevard. Everything right here, and if you needed a special dress, you went uptown. And even though it was unusual back then, me and Franklin going together, people never even said a thing. I suppose some did, but not to our faces. My brother Frank would have broken their noses."

Chickie seemed to get younger and softer as I watched. Black Frank and White Frank, and Danny Boy too and all the others by extension, extras in my little private drama. And all the while, they were Chickie's ex-husband and her brother, athletes who had lived on Water Street their whole lives. I was finding this out, when it was all ending.

"Did you and—Franklin—have children?"

"Twin girls, they live in Pennsylvania. Three grandkids. We went to the oldest grandkid's graduation in June. Frank stayed here with Ma, and Franklin cleaned up, and we rented a car and drove all the way. You should have seen us!" She choked out her smoke. "Shit. I read that nicotine will kill you sooner than booze. This was a nice street, you know, but it isn't anymore. We've been here too long. My ma's people have been here for a hundred years. They came over on some boat and worked on the wharfs and in the factories. One of them was a whore who got respectable and ended up owning a tavern, at least that's what my uncles used to tell me, but since they were also liars and drunks, I've never been too sure."

"If you have to move—if they tear down the houses—will you go to your daughters'?"

"Probably. I don't know."

"What about—them? Frank and Franklin?"

"They'll follow along." She started coughing again, and when she'd caught her breath, said, "You know what's the strangest thing? My grandkids think they're black. They know I'm their grandmother, and the they love me, and Franklin has some really good people on his side, so I don't mean there's anything wrong with it, but they chose that side, not mine. It always seemed strange to me."

"Maybe they think they didn't have a choice." Chickie shrugged again. "Oh Chickie, I think it's a dirty shame. They're going to tear down your past. I think we may have slowed them down, but not stopped them."

"It isn't worth saving anymore," she said. We were silent for a few seconds, then she added, "My girls are good girls, and they married good men, but I wish they'd gone to college."

I started to say something inane about college not always getting you so far, but her posture changed: she was looking at something behind me. I turned, and it was John. I hadn't heard a car. I hadn't heard anything, and now John himself was filling my field of vision. I waited for him to turn ugly in my eyes with all I knew about him, but instead, he was as handsome as ever. Open and smiling, reaching out to embrace us. I stepped out of reach and let Chickie have the hug.

"We caught an earlier flight," he said. "I came straight here."

I asked, "Where's Eleanor?"

He looked at me, picking up something. "She went straight home," he said, and meanwhile Chickie was dragging him toward the door, pulling him inside where all the people started to welcome him: the usual shift as of iron filings toward the magnet. They stopped dancing, they turned off the TV and the music, everyone trying to give him their version of what had happened. They had taped the news show, of course, did he want to see it now, no, he wanted to Be With Them, that was what he called it. He just wanted to Be With Them for a while first. Didn't anybody know anything, except me? Was I crazy?

Robby peeled off from the crowd, grinning at John. "You see?" he told me. "He came back. You see?"

He joined the starstruck others around John, who had seated himself on the arm of an easy chair high enough to be seen by everyone. Something about the pyramidal shape of the little scene struck me as familiar, and then I remembered a bad painting from one of the churches I used to visit: Suffer the Little children to Come Unto Me was the text being illustrated: Jesus with an emptied cornucopia of kids at his feet, in his lap, tumbling around.

Tell me, tell me, said John to his little children. Tell me more.

Tell me all of it.

The only person other than me outside the charmed mound was Ace. He was sitting on the stairs, shaking his head. I joined him.

"Do you believe this?" I said. "He comes in at the last minute and acts like it's his show."

"Since when is he on your shit list?"

"Ace," I said, finally able to say it. "I found out something today. I met with Warren Peterson, and he told me that John is the one we've been looking for. John's name is on the deeds."

Ace went perfectly still, his whole face focused on John and the crowd so that he was in silhouette to me, but I could feel his intense listening. He waited for the rest of it, the evidence, the whole thing. It was the first time I had felt really good in hours.

"Robby's mom signed over the buildings to John. The buildings are in John's name." Ace still waited. I said, "Her family owned most of Water Street from way back, and she gave a lot of it, maybe everything still standing, to John: Love Palace and 315 and 317. That's what Warren told me. Robby knew her family owned it, but he thinks it was all sold off years ago."

Ace's head ducked down, and he started to grin, and then the grin turned into a big laugh that went through his whole body.

"What? What's funny? Don't you believe me?"

"I believe you! Of course I believe you! I'm thinking Good God Almighty why didn't we figure it out sooner? Why didn't Mr. Robby think to give us his clue? Why didn't you and I figure it out? Totally stupid to miss it! Look at your Preacher! He goddam thinks he's the Man!"

John's hands were open on his lap, not quite blessing the crowd, but something very close to it. This is the last time, I thought, full of an energetic revenge that surprised me. Enjoy it, you sonofabitch, because this is the end. I said, "It's a terrible betrayal, not a joke."

"Naw, baby," said Ace. "Not a joke, and not a betrayal. Not at all. But damn we should have figured it out. He's just doing what his kind do, this is good news, baby."

"Exactly how is it good news?"

"It's good news because he's here! I expect he still thinks he's doing good among the poor minorities. We've been looking for the man with his name on the deeds so we could shame him, and he's here. Are you sure his name is still on the buildings? He hasn't sold them yet?"

"Warren says they're still his, but he's supposed to sell to the developers any moment. It was actually a mistake, the demolition guys coming in today."

"You and me, Martha, we're going to go get him!"

I shook my head. "Not tonight. You can go get him, but not me. Not tonight."

"Why not tonight?"

"Because I don't think it's such terrific news, that's why. I don't understand what he's doing. Why would he not tell us?"

"Damned if I know," said Ace. "And damned if I care. You can psychoanalyze him, I'll leave that to you. First, let's plan a strategy. My idea is, we get him to sign the buildings over to us."

"To whom?"

"To the Tenants' Council, maybe. I'd say the Love Palace Corporation, but that's Robby's parents. Even one building. Get him to give 317 to the tenants, and then we have something to fight with."

"Fine," I said. "But not tonight."

"It has to be tonight. He'll take off for wherever again in the morning."

"Then you talk to him tonight. However you want to do it. I'm not up to it."

"I need you—"

"No you don't. You go ahead and deal with him. But talk to him where Robby can't hear. I'm going to tell Robby myself."

John's voice was filling the hall now, speaking to his little children. Ace looked positively lovingly toward John. "This is so good," he said. "Just look at him. Oh my."

I said, "Ace, will you? If you talk to him, will you do it in private? I mean it about keeping it from Robby. Let me tell Robby."

He shrugged. "Whatever. I just don't want him to slip away. He's the best kind of ally, the kind you got by the *cojones*."

"This is a fine thing," John was saying to his little children. "A far far better thing than you've ever done." Dickens, I thought to myself. *A Tale of Two Cities*. "And we shall be a beacon to all peoples," he said. "We will be like a City on a Hill. " That's what's his name, I thought. The Pilgrims. Plymouth Plantation. At least a degree in English is good for recognizing who's stealing material.

25

Sometime after midnight, I was awakened by voices, Robby and Gil and Cara. This troubled me in my sleep, and then Nana was in my dream again, dressed like Chickie's mother in a pink sleeveless house dress with snaps. She popped open the house dress, so her naked front was exposed, and then she was standing there naked, smoking a cigarette. She was smoking with one hand, with the other one on her hip, shaking her head. I became anxious and said, "Don't Smoke, Nana!" She passed the cigarette to me, and I took a deep drag and realized it wasn't the kind of cigarette that gives you lung cancer, but a life-giving cigarette.

I woke at six a.m. wondering if everything was taken care of, after all, if Ace had done it all last night. I was going to talk to Robby, get it all straightened out. Robby wasn't in bed, but sometimes the kids curled up on the couches where they were talking or listening to music. They weren't in the living room, though, so I put on my sweats and went out. Cara's bedroom was open and empty, and Robby's too. Gil's door was shut, which gave me a bad feeling: who was in there with Gil?

I was going down to check the lounge, but there was a light under the closed office door.

I stood at the door and listened, heard a creak and shuffle inside, waited, and it stopped. Standing back, ready to run, I pushed open the door– after all, it was my office– and saw John sitting on the couch with papers on his lap, a wastebasket in front of him, and an old leather briefcase next to the wastebasket. The Prison Pietà was off the wall, propped beside him on the couch like a companion. He smiled at me with that perfect welcome that in spite of everything still gave me a feeling of being special.

"I'm so glad to see you, Martha," said John. "I was hoping to talk to you."

I held the door knob, ready to run. "What are you doing here so early?"

He made a gesture with the papers, slightly twitched his lips. "I never went to bed. I had to go through some papers."

He was preparing to leave. "Ace talked to you last night and you're running away, right?"

"Ace and I had a long talk," he said. "Come and sit down beside me."

I shook my head.

He said, "Ace and I came up with a strategy."

"A strategy! Is that what you call it?"

"Will you sit down with me, Martha?"

"Not a chance, you have no idea how much there's not a chance."

He touched the papers, he picked up the photo in its frame and added it to the pile on his lap, making room for me if I changed my mind. "I should have taken these things out of the office a long time ago."

I moved toward the desk, staying close to the wall, and I sat down with the desk between him and me.

He said, "I'm withdrawing from active participation at the Love Palace, although I will always be available for consultations."

I said, "What about the houses? I want to hear you say it. It's true, isn't it, that all along, while the Tenants' Council has been scrambling to find out who owned the houses, it was you? All along? What kind of bullshit was that, John?"

He looked back at me sadly. How could he keep his face so calm? "You have a right to be angry–"

"You're not the therapist. Warren says you own the houses. Warren says you're fucking Eleanor and making a fortune selling Love Palace and the houses to the developers."

He said, "Eleanor and Warren–their marriage has been over for a long time."

"I don't really care so much who sleeps with who–Robby is going to care big-time, but I don't care. What about the houses?"

"Technically, Warren was correct when he told you."

"What does that mean? You've already sold them? You sold them out from under us? Esta Brown is on public assistance and I don't know where she's going to go. Chickie is disabled and her mom has Alzheimer's–"

"Wait, Martha. First of all, they were always supposed to get relocated. That was what the whole Water Street Project was supposed to be about in the beginning. And I take responsibility, Martha, full responsibility for failing to make the young people focus on helping people find homes–"

"This is going to be so devastating for Robby."

"– but it began to take on a life of its own. All these people with their beautiful idea–"

"Oh my God. And you just admired the beautiful idea so much that you forgot to find homes for the people? And did you forget you owned the houses, too? And meanwhile you were fucking everything that moved– what about old Rhonda? Did you fuck old Rhonda too? How about Esta? Do you pay back-door visits to Esta too? How about the teeny-boppers?"

Again his nod, his famous understanding nod that makes you feel that whatever else is going on– whoever else was hurting you or doing you dirty– at least there was this one person hearing you. He said, "You're way off base, Martha. Eleanor fired Rhonda."

"Eleanor was jealous? Right? Eleanor was jealous?"

John closed his eyes, then opened them. "Let me tell you my story, Martha. Let me tell you where I come from, and where I'm going."

"No."

"You'll be interested. It sheds light on the plan Ace and I came up with." He took a deep breath. sucking in air, church-steepling his fingers. "I always have plans, ideas, goals. They come to me like free gifts from the universe. More ideas than I will ever be able to realize."

"You mean have the money for."

"I've never been good with money. Frankly, I don't think much about money, but in this world– in this real world–" an unsteepling of his hands, a pulling something out of the air with his right hand. "In this world, to do large things, you need large resources. And I have always wanted passionately, even desperately, to do large things. I have ideas like mountain ranges and spreading shade trees—and money like tiny dirt yards in front of row houses. I had to work my way through college–"

"You're breaking my heart."

"I'm stating the facts. I went to Yale–"

"You didn't go to Yale. Nobody works their way through Yale."

"I didn't graduate from Yale. I'm being totally honest here. I had only myself, my intelligence, my vision. I was in school with people who are famous now, people who had all the resources in the world, so easy with their wealth, with their position in life, the sons of rich men. I was never bitter, not after a certain point, because I saw what they didn't see."

"Which was exactly what? Do I have to hear this? I'm feeling extremely unsympathetic."

"Yes, you have to hear this. Think of it as my confession. I have long had a vision, a sort of visual representation of hope like a great wall. The embodiment of that idea included Love Palace. The Pinnacle church would never have set up Love Palace without me."

"And Eleanor's money."

"Of course. She and I have been working as a team for several years now. My objective has always been to make an impact in the world."

"So you became a preacher to accumulate wealth and power and have an impact?"

"Pinnacle was my first job in the Christian ministry," he said.

"You weren't the chaplain, then?" I pointed at the Prison Pietà.

"Informally," he said.

"Warren said you were doing time for bad checks."

He opened his hands on his knees, palms up. "I've never had much of my own. That's what I'm trying to explain to you. I'm not trying to excuse or avoid, especially because I know that you are capable of understanding. Nothing was given to me. My mother left, and my father became more punitive, even abusive."

"So what, John? My father disappeared, and my mother was gone half the time too and my grandma was a Communist. Everybody's got a story, John."

"The point is that I was determined to go forward, and whenever an opportunity arose, I seized it."

His professionally manicured nails, the gold chain on his wrist. Those softly draped clothes. He was slim, he was broad-shouldered. He looked far wealthier than Warren Peterson.

He said, "I wish you'd sit beside me. You look so tight."

"Fuck you, John. You steal You're a thief."

"When the opportunity arises, I do what seems most effective in reaching my goals."

"How long were you in prison for passing the bad checks?"

Let me give him credit. He didn't look away. He met my eyes, full frontal face. On the other hand, I honestly don't think he felt remorse. "Two to five," he said. "I got an early release for my role in the riot. I helped save the lives of two prison guards. I learned a lot there. I never should have been sent to jail for it. Someone with more resources would have gotten out of it."

"And poor Robby still gets you confused with Jesus."

"I could make a case for Jesus as a rule breaker, but what's more important, what I really learned there, was that I had the ability to inspire people, the prisoners, even across racial and cultural lines. Again, I'm not boasting, I want you to know the facts. I learned what I could do. That young man really did die in my arms, and I wanted so much to make things better. I wanted to do something big– for him, for that lost young man. And I knew I was capable of it, given the resources. I wanted to help people actualize their inchoate yearnings. To live the lives that young man never got to live. To embody all the potential. Eleanor understood immediately; I have the ability to convince people to be happier. It's like a little switch, you don't have to change anything except how you see things– and that changes everything."

"So you sell their homes out from under them, but they still feel great, is that what you're saying?"

"Eleanor gave me the property so I would never be beholden to her. So we would always be a partnership. The redevelopment plan was already in the planning stages. I understand that the properties have been condemned anyhow, or will be momentarily. But as I told you, I have a plan."

"You mean Ace has a plan."

"There is a plan, which I am about to share with you."

I had this little sizzle of expectation, of something good coming, but I held it off. "But what about our money? You took out all that cash on the ATM card, didn't you? Didn't you steal our money?"

He looked confused for the first time.

"I told you about that months ago! I said someone was using our money, and you pretended you didn't know."

"I use the card," he said, "but Eleanor always covers it when there's a shortfall. It's such little sums."

"It was two hundred dollars three times and three hundred dollars six times!"

"We'll pay you back."

"It's already been paid back! Don't you get it, John? It's how you use people! To further your, whatever it is. Your grand fucking vision. You play us, I don't know why. You don't even seem to know it! This is going to tear Robby up."

"Does he have to know?"

"Yes! He has to know!"

He shrugged, as if he' d rather Robby didn't get hurt, but, whatever. He said, "I never hurt anyone intentionally."

"Oh please." My hands waved in the air; they wanted to get rid of his face. "Your intentions are going to mean mouse doody to Esta Brown when she gets thrown on the street."

He leaned forward over his lap full of papers and the picture frame. "But she won't be, Martha. She doesn't have to be. I'm signing the houses over."

"To the Tenants' Council?"

"No, to you, Martha. It seemed to be the simplest and quickest way."

"To me? The houses? I don't want them! What do you mean? You're signing them over to me?"

He leaned back. "I already did it. I called your sister, last night, from here. I went over to her apartment. I signed documents."

"You went to my sister's in the middle of the night? Oh my God, are you fucking my sister too, John?" Doors were opening. He was, I knew he was.

"She's filing the papers today."

"Are you fucking her?"

"They're your houses now, Martha. The same parcels that Eleanor signed over to me, they're yours. It will be most interesting to see what you do with them."

"This is bullshit. I can't own houses! You can't give something to someone who doesn't want it! What about taxes? What about repairs and the rats?"

"It will be a challenge, Martha. This is your opportunity to make your idea of community concrete."

"I don't have an idea of community! I came here to get a job! I married Robby for the health insurance!"

"Martha, Martha," he said, as if he knew me better than I knew myself. "You have an enormous opportunity. You can do whatever you want with the houses. Build wealth for a planned community, build your own wealth. Give the houses to the tenants. The possibilities are astounding."

"You're doing it to goddam get out of a tight spot the slickest way possible. I don't want the houses and I don't want you fooling around with my sister!"

"When you think this over, you're going to see it is a good thing, the best thing. You have never taken real responsibility, never maximized your real talents."

I was so appalled, finally, that I couldn't say anything.

"I've never claimed not to make mistakes, Martha. Think of this– I told them in Texas, I told a thousand people in St. Louis, that I had stolen money. I told them so they'd understand the hunger, the ambition. I hid it from Eleanor at first, and she was making plans for politics, she thought we could run for office, think of how she felt when she found out I was a convicted felon, but we've moved on, we've changed our plans. You may have to change your plans too, your community building may have to take place somewhere else, or perhaps it will happen here but not in the way you imagine. I'm giving an opportunity to you to do great good."

"What about Robby?"

He put his papers in his briefcase, snapped it shut. Stood up. He put the framed photo on top of a box of more papers and lifted the box in his free arm. "Robby will grow from this. Robby has to give up his idols. It will be better if you're the one who tells him. He needs to hear it from someone who loves him, Martha."

"While you make your escape. You're a con man and a coward both."

"Martha," he said, standing, really looking at me, looking all the way in me. "Make a good thing of what I'm giving you. Believe," he said, "and it will be so."

I didn't recognize that quotation and wondered if this one might actually be John's own words. I held very still as he inclined his head in a short bow, resettled the box, tightened his grip on the briefcase, smiled one more brilliant smile, and left.

I listened to his steps going down, I waited for him to come back with a final word. I imagined myself running after him: Wait, wait, can't we try again.

Try what again?

I started in on a long list of his sins, but there was a kind of sobbing in back of my eyeballs because he was gone and in spite of everything, part of me really wanted him to stay and make it all right.

And because I certainly had no idea what to do. What was I going to tell Robby? What was I going to tell Madame Landowska? And did I really own the buildings now?

26

I decided to run away. I went back to the apartment to grab some things. I didn't call Mari, I didn't look for Robby. Sorry, Robby, I thought, as I got my toiletry bag and stuffed underpants in its pouches. I'll find a computer in a library somewhere and send you an email. I went back to the underwear drawer for cash. I hurried through the empty lounge, saw no one. No one saw me. It wasn't even six forty-five.

Sorry Water Street, I said, out in the pinkish gray morning, damp and shivery. The Guzzler was sluggish, but turned over after only three tries. I made a U-turn, drove up around the projects, got to the highway ramp quickly and headed out, long shadows of the overpasses pointing the way west.

After about five miles, my resolve, or my neurotic episode, or maybe just my adrenalin, began to peter out, and I took the exit for Miriam Sisters. I told myself I ought to say good-bye to Nana properly, if I was going to start my life over.

It took me a while to find a parking space. Why were there so many cars here? It was too early for visitors, and if it was the staff, why were they parking where visitors ought to be? I sat awhile, then got a lipstick out of my toiletry case, started to color my lips, but tossed it back in the case and went in. I was stared at but not stopped by the old guy at the guard desk. On Nana's floor, to my chagrin, the large blonde nurse who had been working the last time we were there recognized me. "Well, well," she said. "It's one of Mrs. Miller's granddaughters."

"Hi," I said, "I know I'm early, but I'm going out of town, I hope it's okay–" I kept moving. "I can find her on my own." I hurried toward the sunroom where I'd seen her last, but there was no one there at all, so I had to go back to the desk to ask for her room number. I said, "We met her in the little sun room place last time. I don't really know her room number."

"You don't know her room number?" she said. "I'll let you see her, but sometimes, this early, we haven't finished breakfast clean-up. It happens that we have, today. I ought to tell you that she hasn't been so alert the last few days."

"Yes, well, she didn't seem so alert the last time I was here either," I said.

Nana's room had two beds, one neatly made up with its occupant in a wheel chair beside it, wearing a flowery pink wrapper, pink flowers in a vase on her table. I knew that wasn't

Nana.

I said, "Sorry to bother you–"

"No bother," she smiled.

"But is that– Mrs. Miller? On the other bed?"

"Oh yes," said the flowery one. "She hasn't been up in days." She leaned toward me conspiratorially. "I think she's giving up. Some of them do that, you know. She used to be one of the biggest talkers on the floor."

"Now, now," said a voice behind me: the nurse had followed me down the hall. She swooped in behind the flowery lady and said, "Let's give Mrs. Miller and her granddaughter some privacy," and rolled her away.

I was left in the middle of their room half decorated like a nineteen fifties teenager's and half spare and plain. Nana had always collected stuff, folded grocery bags and stacks of second-hand books on history and politics. This room had no stuff. Nothing in her room, nothing in her head. Not even teeth.

I approached the heap on the bed. It was on its side, right cheek on the pillow. If I hadn't been so intimidated by the nurse, I might have checked the room number again, to be absolutely sure it was Nana. I pulled up the chair and sat on the edge of the seat. I whispered, "I wanted to tell you, I'm leaving."

There was yellowish gunk in the corners of her mouth. I got up and found tissues on the other woman's bedside table and dabbed at it. It seemed stuck, so I sat back down.

I said, "Actually, it's more like, I'm running away."

I had run away once when I was small. I made it to the bottom of the stairs and sat on the stoop next to the florist shop and realized I didn't have any clean underwear. I cried for a while and then went back upstairs. This time, at least I had panties.

I said, "I've had it with–all these people. The ones I've been living with. Everyone. So I decided to leave." It sounded incredibly stupid. "There's nothing to hold me. You know? I was careful not to get too entangled. All I have is the job, and there's Mari and you and Mom. And of course I married Robby, but he's just a kid, he'll move on. And now they've given me the houses, and the people who live there are going to get thrown out on the street."

It was sounding less and less like I had nothing to hold me.

"I've been dreaming about you, Nana," I said.

When had she had her first stroke, anyhow? I'd already left home, so the first one would have been in the mid nineties. She had smoked since she was fourteen and was overweight nine-tenths of her life with high blood pressure and chronic fury at the state of the world. Oh the fights we used to have. I would accuse her of being a Stalinist, and she would smack the table with her fist. Stalin was a thug, she would cry, but the answer is not Slavophile religious Fascism and certainly not Capitalist Imperialist thugs!

The Slavophile Fascist part would have come up because I was *reading One Day in the Life of Ivan Denisovich,* and she didn't like Solzhenitsyn.

She shouted, "At least nobody was homeless over there! No one was starving in the streets over there! And have you ever been in a subway in Moscow? Well I have, a long time ago, I went ! I was there! And you should know their subways are for the working people– every subway station a work of art!"

The question was, I realized, staring at the closed eyes and flaccid cheek, did I really want to start over again? Wasn't starting over in California or even a calm place like Oregon just a new opportunity to make mistakes and form complications?

I stared at her big lobed ear, long and soft. Some tears leaked out of my eyes. "Actually, I don't have any idea what I'm going to do next." My nose was already stopped up from crying so at least I didn't have to worry about smells. But you have to give that to Miriam Sisters, they keep their old ladies clean.

I cried a little, over the good old gone days, over my confusion, over not being able to measure things by Nana anymore. I had always been so good at setting her off. I would tell her she was a narrow-minded sectarian, and she would shake her tea cup at me and shout, "Better a sectarian than some kind of *meshugenah* nihilist!"

"It's dialectical, Nana," I would say, "you know what I'm saying? The Republicans are your antithesis, and Nihilism is the synthesis."

"You argue for the sake of argument!" she screamed. "You have never worked with your hands!"

I would point out that I had just washed the dishes, and she would make one of her imaginary expectorations: Pfui! She meant factories and grocery stores. She was the union rep. She knew from working with your hands.

I would have given a lot to have one more shouting match with Nana.

Finally, I said, "And if I don't run away, Nana? Then what?

I'm thinking that nothing is simple anywhere. It's like I've already lived too long for things to be simple." I waited, still hoping for some kind of response, I guess. But there was no movement at all.

What would she have thought of Love Palace? What would she have said to me?

Of course she would have told me to stay.

"You have to stand up to them," she would have said. "Those people and you too, you have to stand up to the bosses! But the first thing is to make sure they have a place to live. You have to start somewhere."

27

When I got back to Love Palace, I went upstairs to shower, went into the bedroom– and found Robby sitting on the bed in a tee shirt and sweats, holding his jeans as if he'd started to change clothes and become paralyzed halfway through.

"Where were you?" I said.

"Where were you?"

"I've been visiting Nana. You never came to bed."

"I've been walking."

"All night?"

"Most of it." He lowered his head and for a second, with the illusion of a lower, thicker brow, he looked like his father. He said, "Why didn't you tell me?

I thought: he knows about me and John.

But he went on, "Last night late, Gil heard Ace and John arguing. He said– he heard part of it, but I want to know the whole thing. I want to know what's going on, and I want to know from you."

"I tried to tell you last night."

"If my dad said something about John, it isn't true. My dad hates John."

"He said John owns the houses. Or did."

He blinked. "Warren hates John. He would say anything."

"He has evidence that John is the owner."

Robby shook his head.

"Robby, listen to me. I talked to John myself, really early this morning, and he admitted it. He's the owner, and now he's leaving. With your mother."

His face was still.

I said, "Robby, I should have told you all this yesterday but I was afraid. Your mother gave the buildings to John and they sleep together. He's gone and he's not coming back because Ace confronted him. Ace got John to sign the buildings over to me, and now he's leaving with your mother. Is that clear enough?"

Robby's face went cold. "My dad hates John and he's jealous of him."

"You're really not listening. I talked to John."

"The houses used to be in my family. But that was a long time ago."

I was beginning to get pissed. "Get over it Robby! He's been using us all–"

He shook his head.

"And your mother, Robby, don't you hear what I'm saying about John and your mother?"

He closed his eyes and shook his head. "John has always saved me. John saved me when I was at my worst. He was– I never told you this– I touched John and he forgave me."

"Oh shit. What did he do to you?"

"I did it. He stopped me. John would never–"

"Oh don't be too sure. I don't think there are many things John wouldn't do."

"I touched him. He stopped me–it was my fault. It was just before I met you. I was suicidal, and John pulled me away from the brink. He had his arm around me, comforting me, you know. And I got–aroused. It was my fault."

"Oh, bullshit, Robby, if you got aroused, believe me, John was fully aware and liked it. Sex is just one more way of getting hold of people for John." I was ready to dump everything, I was ready to tell him about me and John too, but I held back, I don't know why, it felt like it would be for me not for him if I told. I said, "This is his *modus operandi*. He totally gets off on this stuff. Saving people, having sex with people, surprising people. That's what John does."

He kept his eyes closed, and spoke a little more softly. "No, Martha, I'm the problem. John told me I was strong enough to redirect my sexuality, if that was what I wanted to do, and that was when I started going out to bars and met you."

"Well, fine, that's just fine. He encouraged you to use me and he used all of us. Now I feel really great. Do you fantasize about John when we have sex? Don't answer that. I've really decided there's a limit, there really are some things better left unsaid."

He finally opened his eyes. "I'm telling you the truth about John–"

"And I'm telling you the truth about John! I admit I should have told you yesterday but everyone was just so damn happy with the news coverage. Did you hear me say that John sleeps with your mother? Do you hear me?"

"No," said Robby.

"Yes. Listen to me. John sleeps with everyone. John would have sex with Danny Boy if it got him something he wanted. He has wonderful qualities, Robby. He's enormously attractive. But he lies. They never meant for the Love Palace thing to go on so long. They meant for Love Palace to be like a summer activity for you, and John's name was on the property, it was a gift from her to him, so he could be independent of her."

"My dad and my mother never did get along."

"Totally beside the point. Oh, and John is the one who's been using Love Palace money whenever he felt like it."

"How long?"

"How long what?"

"How long have they been, you know, together?"

"John and your mother? How should I know? Since he came to Pinnacle? Not sure. Oh, there's still more, Robby. This goes on and on. John wasn't a chaplain when the Prison Pietà was taken, he was doing time for embezzlement. No, for passing bad checks. For something. He's been fucking us all. Robby. He's a bad man."

And yet I felt like a hypocrite saying it, because I didn't really believe that part, the bad man part. And I was still holding back part of it.

Robby got up, pulled off his sweats and pulled on his jeans. "I want to hear it from him."

"He signed over the buildings to me. We have to figure out how to save Love Palace."

He said, "I'm going to find them. Don't try to stop me. If they're not at Pinnacle, I'll go where they are."

An image came to my mind, a freeze frame from a movie, them in bed with a sheet over their chests, horrified. Cut to Robby and a sawed off shot gun. Blam! Blam!

"Let them go, there's nothing you can do."

He stood there with his pants on and his feet bare and his face balled up like a little kid, and I wanted to say, Don't do anything crazy, don't drive the wrong way in traffic, don't drive off the overpass, don't buy a gun and shoot them. He made a fist and banged it on my bureau, hard, but deflected at the last instant so he didn't smash anything. Then he smashed his fist into his own hand and pressed his high-arched feet into sneakers that he didn't tie. He left without even a jacket.

I sat on the couch for a while, trying to think things over, but I was only heavy limbed with indecision and dread. I thought I should call the cops, or somehow warn Eleanor and John. But all I could think to do was call Warren on his cell phone. I told him Robby was on his way to Pinnacle, looking for John and Eleanor. Warren sounded inappropriately cheerful. "Thank you, Martha," he said. "I'll take over from here."

28

After I talked to Warren, I continued to sit. My cell phone rang, and I turned it off. The house phone rang twice, and I didn't answer. This is stupid, I thought. Don't you want to know what happens? I heated a can of tomato soup and made a toasted cheese sandwich. Halfway through eating, I turned on the radio. If there was a murder or a fatal car accident, it would make the news, wouldn't it?

There was something important I had to do. I remembered: call Mari about the houses.

She answered with a low hello, not like herself.

"Mari?" I said. "You were up, weren't you?"

"Where have you been? You're not answering your phones!"

"I'm having a bad morning," I said.

"Mom tried you first."

"Mom?" My first thought was Jimbo had a heart attack.

She was silent again. It was like she and I were at a great distance from one another. "It was about Nana," she said at last.

"I visited her this morning. How did you know?"

There was another odd chunk of silence. "She died."

"I was just there," I said.

Mari started to cry. "It would be you! I can't believe you were the last one to see her alive. That is so perfect, I go to see her every week of the world, but you're the one who sees her last. They called Mom. They told her Nana had a visitor, and then she just seemed to let go." Mari sobbed harder. "They said that Nana just let go, and of course it would be you not me. She died because she loved you best, and you came to say good-bye and she had been waiting for you, and you came and she just died and it's so unfair, Martha!"

She was boo-hooing, and I was thinking about how she could talk and cry and what a marvel that was. "I don't think she even knew I was there–"

"Why didn't you tell me you were going? I could have said good-bye too."

"I didn't know I was going. I didn't know– listen, Mari, for all the response I got, she was dead when I was there. She was like a lump. And I didn't plan to go, I just went. Is she really dead?"

"You always do the right thing in the end, don't you? You don't even have to plan it, you just do it, it's just natural to you, everything I have to work at. You're the one she waited for.

You're the one he gave the houses to–"

"Mari, I'm not even sure she was breathing. And I don't want the houses, I was calling to tell you I don't want the houses."

"How can you even talk about the houses?"

"You mentioned them–"

"Well, it's done. John dropped everything in the FedEx box last night. He's leaving, you know. He's leaving and Nana died and it's just too much."

"You say it's just too much? What about me? I don't want the damn houses. You should never have done the thing with the houses without telling me."

"I don't want to talk about the houses! I want to talk about Nana! We have to go deal with the body. We're supposed to meet Mom and Jimbo at the funeral parlor."

"She just wanted to be cremated."

"We still have to go to the funeral parlor! You have to make arrangements for a cremation, too!" She started to sob harder. "My grandmother is dead! Everyone is leaving!"

She means John, I thought. "Which funeral parlor? Where are we supposed to meet Mom and Jimbo?"

She kept sobbing.

I said, "And why didn't you ask me first about the houses, Mari?"

"Give it a rest, okay? Just give it a rest and think about Nana. John told me you'd come up with something good, a nonprofit or something."

"Whatever John said I don't want to do. Do you have any idea what he has been doing?"

"I don't care. He's gone. He's–" a little hiccup of a sob here, a soften of his voice: "He's over."

"He slept with you, too, didn't he, Mari?"

She hesitated, and I thought she was going to ask what did I mean "too"? But she missed that, or let it go. "He told me he was leaving, but I didn't think it was going to be this soon. It's got nothing to do with him. I decided to have a baby on my own."

"Oh my God."

She finally seemed to have stopped sobbing. "Don't misunderstand for one second, Martha, it was not a mistake. It's a plan. I knew about him and Eleanor, I know more than you do. I had decided before I met him that I wanted to have a baby. Everyone else has someone. Mom has Jimbo. You married Robby. John and Eleanor, I don't know if they have a good relationship, but they have something. And I wanted a baby, and I'm having a baby, and it's just that it's still hard to say good-bye to someone and I'm queasy this morning and then Mom called about Nana and it's too much, but it's not a mistake!" And then she started to sob again.

"You're having a baby with John?"

"No, I'm having a baby on my own."

"Does he know? Does Eleanor know? Does Mom know?"

"Nobody else knows yet."

"That is so–do you know how screwed over I feel by him? Do you have any idea? Do you have any idea how he's treated–all of us. And now he's been fucking my baby sister–"

"I'm in complete control."

"That's why you're sobbing like your heart will break?"

"Nana died!"

"Mari–"

"He inspired me. I know you're mad at him. I know he's half a con man–"

"Nine-tenths."

"I know he made a pass at you. He just– he needs intimacy with everyone."

I actually agreed with her, but I said, "He's a bullshitter." That was true too.

"He told me about the houses and how bad he feels about Robby–"

"Yeah, right. And I got to tell Robby about him and his mom and the buildings, by the way, and Robby freaked out and took off and he's probably going to track them down and shoot them."

That got her to quiet down. "Robby has a gun?"

"No, of course not. But I'm mad enough to shoot John myself."

"He has a lot of confidence in you, Martha."

"Let me get this straight. He sleeps with Robby's mother and Robby doesn't know. He is the secret owner of the properties we've been trying to find for a year or so. He's dumping us all to go out on a lecture tour and tell the world that the Limina is the place to be, and oh by the way he got my sister pregnant–"

"I got pregnant. He's just a donor."

"But he was having sex with you, right? He noticed that, didn't he? Oh, and you may not know this, but Robby is in love with him not to mention my predecessor Rhonda–"

She said, "Martha, don't tell me all this right now, okay? Tell me another time?"

"Fine. Whatever you say. But surely you know he's a convicted felon–"

"Yes. He told me. The Prison Pietà. I know everything."

I said, "Maybe not. He's been stealing money from Love Palace, admittedly the money gets put back in the till–"

"I said I don't want to hear it now."

"Are you really planning to keep his baby?"

"My baby. It's mine. And it isn't a matter of keeping, it's a matter of having consciously chosen to have a baby. I have the money, I'll hire a nanny, I'll do what I have to do. I'll work as hard as ever, it will take a lot of support, but that's what the money is for."

"I can't picture you being– you know, a mother–"

"You think I won't be good at it? Is that what you're saying?"

"No, I'm just saying– I'm saying it's going to be hard."

"I was thinking, Mom would come up sometimes. I was thinking you'd be around, at least to talk to. Sometimes."

There were still highways to the west, I thought. The Guzzler still had a few miles left in it. "Maybe I'll have a baby too. Only not at the same time as you. You'd just think I was being competitive."

"It would be nice, to do it together."

"Let's do your baby first."

"Let's do Nana's funeral first."

Again, one of our nurturing silences. I said, "Will you help me with Love Palace? Since you did the paper work that got me into it?"

And she said, "Will you be my birthing coach?"

29

The past is gloriously innocent. I don't mean blameless, I mean simply that we never know what's coming next, so we feel tender toward our earlier selves. The woman who got raped and beaten to a bloody pulp in Central Park– how perfectly complete and hopeful and unbeaten and unraped she was as she tied on her running shoes that day. And the boys who did hard time for raping and beating her and were finally exonerated– how innocent they were as they went out with their friends that day. It's not that everything is bad, but that once the bad things happen, there's no rewind.

I didn't see Robby again until the memorial service for Nana. I stayed in touch with Warren, so I knew Robby had gone to Pinnacle and stayed there. Eleanor called me the day before the service. It was a low, strained voice, not a whisper, but with some of the tension you get with a whisper. She said, "I know you don't want to talk to me, but I have to know about Robby."

I was in the middle of planning food. "He's in Pinnacle with Warren and Olivia. They're watching James Bond movies."

"I can't call them," she said.

I thought I had a lot of things to say to her, but then I realized I really didn't. "My grandmother died."

She said, "I heard," and made a choking sound and hung up.

So much for upper-class courtesy.

The memorial service was a big success. When we met to plan at the funeral parlor, Mom had a little notebook with puppies printed on the cover with her. Inside it were Nana's hand-written instructions. Nana wanted to be cremated, as we knew. She wanted her ashes, or at least a pinch of her ashes, scattered at the site of the Triangle Shirtwaist fire in New York City, and if that wasn't allowed (take a guess as to New York City's regulations about spreading human remains on the streets), then maybe someone could sneak a little pinch there, and dump the rest in some lovely natural spot, like Coney Island or the Jersey Shore.

She wanted no gravestone and no funeral, but she would appreciate a catered memorial service, and had set aside some money for it. She wanted the Solidarity Singers Labor Chorus, who had once sung with Pete Seeger, and no trees in Israel, because she was an internationalist, not a Zionist. If anyone wanted to honor her name, she provided a list of civil rights and free speech groups for donations.

Mari had started crying in the funeral parlor when we talked about scattering the remains. She tightened herself up into a little ball, and I wondered how she expected to mother a child if she was going to fall apart all the time, but of course, being Mari, she never lost a beat in discussing the arrangements. Jimbo and I were the distracted ones. He kept fingering the wrapped cigar in the pocket of his sports jacket, and I kept having this puzzled awareness of Mom's jiggly but assertive bosom showing between the lapels of her black jacket. I realized I felt the same kind of admiration for her that I felt for Ace and Nana and all the people who stay true to their principles.

Nana had never been to Love Palace, but we all agreed she would have fit right in. A place for renters and workers, or, in the case of the Franks and their friends, former workers. After a while, Jimbo got up to stretch his legs, and beckoned to me over Mom and Mari's heads. I went into the foyer with him and accepted a little toot from his flask.

Nana's memorial was the last event at the old Love Palace. After the memorial things got complicated–not necessarily bad, but complicated, and they're still complicated. The memorial service had some guitar ballads courtesy of Gil and Cara and jam tarts courtesy of Danny Boy. The Tenants' Council all came, and the Solidarity singers sent a quintet. All of Water Street seemed to turn out in respect for our good intentions and of course for the free food.

There weren't that many of Nana's old comrades left, but a couple did make it, impressively halting members of the very old Left including one elderly man on two canes who had fought the Fascists in the Spanish Civil War as a very young teenager. We had rousing renditions of "Solidarity Forever" and "The Ballad of Joe Hill" and "This Land is Your Land" with the original, anti-landlord lyrics. Jimbo turned out to be a more-than-adequate master of ceremonies, and a couple of the Old Comrades spoke.

That parade from the past at once moved and emptied me. She had been grouchy old Nana who disapproved of high heels and raw vegetables. I had seen her Struggle for Justice as a personal quirk, and now I regretted I had never told her that I was able to see it too: that great tide of people fighting the good fight stretching back to the first guy who sat down and took an unscheduled break at the pyramids. It seems harder to find them now, but maybe it always looks that way. I may even be one of them, although I'm getting a late start.

Madame Landowska dropped by on her way to her beach house. She couldn't stay, but she gave me a hug and asked where was my young husband. I looked her in the eye and lied and said he was on his way. I promised myself I'd tell her everything later

Then, she left, and it turned out not to be a lie: Robby showed up. He was wearing super-dark sunglasses and a sports jacket. I had only spoken to him once, by phone, in the preceding week. "She chose him over me," he had said. "Not that I'm surprised– I would have chosen him over her."

Now he came and stood beside me, and we watched everyone eating from the deli platters and trays of ziti and salad. Robby and I went upstairs to the office and sat on the leather couch under the light spot on the wall where Prison Pietà used to be.

He took off his sunglasses, and his eyes looked sunken and bruised. "I'm sorry about your Nana," he said. "I'm sorry I haven't been here for you."

"Nana's been gone a long time, Robby, but I'm really glad you came today. How are you doing?"

He looked off into the distance somewhere. "The one thing I know is that I'll never speak to them again."

"Cutting off communication is probably a sin. I mean a real sin, like hurting children."

"Maybe. And I suppose Never is more than I can handle anyhow."

I laid a hand on his thigh, just a pat, because he and I really do care for each other, whether or not getting married was a good idea.

He said, "I've been self-indulgent. I was so sure I was wronged by everyone. I think it's a kind of spiritual arrogance," he said. "When I found out– about–" his mouth twisted. He had trouble saying it. "John–and my mother–when I found out, it was like the floor went out from under me." He lowered his head, and for just an instant, touched his forehead to the side of my face. He said, "Martha. I want you to be in my family forever."

He said Ace had told him about a special program at the community college for people to get their high school diplomas at the same time they took college courses, and Gil was thinking of staying around and taking classes at the community college too.

Then I told him about Mari being pregnant, and that seemed to please him. Then we just sat for a while. I was contemplating how much we don't know. Which way Robby would ultimately go sexually, for example. If he and his mother would ever be reconciled, if there was still time for me to have a baby or even if I wanted one and if I did, with whom. If the new Love Palace arrangement had a chance of working.

We went back downstairs, and the whole Good News Crew sang Cara's song "You Take Love Wherever You Find It," and Danny Boy sang his song, and I cried over Nana and her swollen ankles and her scuffies. I had a feeling John would walk through the door. He didn't, but it seemed to me that he should have stuck around and tried to do something concrete with his life.

The day after the memorial service, Ace invited me for coffee at Jo-Jo's and told me that if I really didn't want to be the owner of the buildings, we would need a separate organization to run them. I said I wanted it to be a collective of him and Malika and Chickie and Esta and me and Robby and the whole crowd, and he told me I'd be crazy to try and depend on good intentions and the expectation that other people would be as committed as I was. I said he sounded like he'd lost faith in the Masses, and he said sometimes you have to fight capitalism using its own tools.

Robby moved back into Love Palace, but so far he's back in his little bedroom instead of living with me, and that's good because I finally had my tell-all session with Madame and laid out all the things I had skipped, and we decided for me to go celibate again for a while, to make no big revelations to anyone for a while.

I miss the soapy young smell of Robby.

Meanwhile, Mari is doing the legal work to set up the Water Street Community Corporation. We'll have a big shot board of directors with professors Ace knows and Councilman Bishop Stebbins, but Ace and I insisted that we also have a community board. At this point, I'd say we have an even chance of making some kind of a stand against the developers. But if we lose, we still have the Community Corporation with mixed income housing in its charter and the potential for some money to fund it. Of course, the big guys are very big, and way ahead of us on the curve. But we haven't lost yet. We're starting lawsuits, and we'll fix up the houses. Also, Robby turns out to have a knack for raising funds from his preppie friends, particularly the ones from the upscale looney bin where he stayed for a year. And that's how it stands at this moment, all of us innocent of what's coming next, but not totally unprepared.

Often, I think of John, who wanted his hungers to be our

hungers. Who wanted to feel the electricity of my being through my shoulders and the weight of my breasts in his hands and my breath in his lungs and your breath, and to resuscitate us or else suck us empty. To be inside us and around us and everywhere at once.

That's all he wanted.

The End

About the Author

Meredith Sue Willis's fiction has been published by Charles Scribner's Sons, HarperCollins, West Virginia University Press, Mercury House, Ohio University Press and many small presses. Her book of literary short stories, *In the Mountains of America*, was praised in the *New York Times Book Review* as an "important lesson on the nature and function of literature itself."

Recent books include a collection of short stories, *Out of the Mountains*, and the novels *Their Houses* and *Soledad in the Desert* as well as a novella, *Saving Tyler Hake* and a book abut writing called *Ten Strategies to Write Your Novel.*

She lives in New Jersey, a short train ride from New York City, where she is an Adjunct Assistant Professor of Creative Writing at New York University's School of Professional Studies. She is active in local racial integration politics, and chairs the Social Action Committee of the Ethical Culture Society of Essex County. She is married to Andy Weinberger, a rheumatologist, and their son Joel and his wife Sarah are the parents of Shira, Eli, and Lev.

To learn more about her and her books, see her web page at www.meredithsuewillis.com